MANHATTAN
TRANSFER

john e. stith

A Tom Doherty Associates Book
New York

This is a work of fiction. All the characters and events portrayed in this book are fictitious, and any resemblance to real people or events is purely coincidental.

MANHATTAN TRANSFER

This book is printed on acid-free paper.

A Tor Book
Published by Tom Doherty Associates, Inc.
175 Fifth Avenue
New York, N.Y. 10010

Tor® is a registered trademark of Tom Doherty Associates, Inc.

Design by Lynn Newmark

ISBN 0-312-85285-1

Printed in the United States of America

For the forces of change:
Russell Galen, Patrick Nielsen Hayden,
and Claire Eddy.

And for volunteers who have suffered through early
drafts with no reward:
Joe Costanza, Lou Grinzo, Heather Pierce,
James K. Sabshin, Bob Taylor, and Robert Woodhead.

1

GOING UP

MANHATTAN NEVER SLEEPS. It doesn't even blink. By three in the morning, it was as close to lethargy as it ever gets, but that was still busier than a nursery full of hyperactive kids with mega-doses of sugar and caffeine.

As something quite out of the ordinary began, Manhattan lay awake in the dark.

Slightly past the orbit of Saturn, over forty degrees above the plane of the ecliptic, ionized particles of the solar wind encountered a disruption where none had existed before.

Space twisted. An artificial rotating singularity deformed the fabric of space, bending it in on itself until a black hole formed. Charged particles that would normally have sped directly through the region, instead began to move in arcs, most of which ended at the singularity. They accelerated as their paths curved tighter toward the gravitational lens, speeding faster and faster as they approached, and, during their final nanoseconds of existence outside the event horizon, spewing X rays like tiny distress calls.

The event horizon bloomed to a diameter of several hundred kilometers before it stabilized. While the solar wind funneled into the region, an enormous black starship emerged from inside the event horizon. The starship, almost as black as the region of space it slid out of, absorbed radiation across the entire spectrum as it spun sedately. As the nearby singularity was switched off, the event horizon shrank until it vanished, and the only obstruction to the solar wind was the ship itself.

The huge squat disk-shaped ship sported octagonal rather

than circular endplates. The disk was over 100 kilometers in diameter, as big as a small moon flattened into shape. The ship's spin slowed until it hung motionless in the dim starlight. The black ship then began to pivot into the solar wind. It kept adjusting its orientation until one octagonal surface pointed generally at the distant yellow G-type star. The precise alignment was at the small blue planet, third from the sun. Moments later, the enormous ship began to accelerate smoothly toward Earth.

The *whup-whup-whup* from the chopper's blades rose in pitch and volume as the pilot pulled back on the collective, and the chopper rose a meter off the concrete at the edge of Manhattan. The six passengers were all secured, and the sounds in the pilot's headphones were positive, reassuring. He let the craft hover a moment on the ground-effect cushion as he readjusted his shoulder strap. As soon as he felt in control, he let the chopper continue its rise. Below him the circular markings of Manhattan's East 60th Street heliport began to shrink. As he rose, he let the chopper turn slowly, and he scanned the space over nearby building tops. When the chopper faced the East River and JFK International beyond, the pilot pushed on the cyclic stick and tilted the chopper slightly forward, still rising as the craft began to move toward the airport.

The pilot enjoyed the runs between Manhattan and JFK, particularly at times like now—the morning rush hour. This was one of the few jobs in flying where you could "drive" over the roads below in Queens. He took a lot of pleasure in passing slow-moving traffic on the Long Island Expressway, BQE, and Van Wyck, cruising right over the stalls and backed up sections, ignoring pileups and emergacharge trucks.

He reached cruising height just before the East River. Below was the Queensboro Bridge, doing its best to jam more people into Manhattan.

A sudden shadow was the first indication of trouble. Reflexes took over and he lost a little altitude just in case. If the passengers complained, he couldn't tell, because the headphones and the rotor roar would block anything up to a scream.

The helicopter pilot had just convinced himself there was no problem when a faint pencil of red light cut the grimy sky vertically in front of the windshell bubble. He jammed the stick and tried to veer away, but he had no time. The whine of the rotors suddenly changed pitch as the rotor blades hit the shaft of laser light. The chopper became a machine gun, firing severed pieces of rotor off to his left. In milliseconds, the slicing light had whittled every rotor down to half its original length, and then the chopper itself hit the beam. A band saw moving at the speed of light, the laser sliced the chopper right down the middle. The engine overhead exploded as the casing surrounding the whirling components split into pieces.

Shrapnel from the exploding engine perforated bodies of the pilot and passengers as the two halves of the chopper began their plunge to the East River. The pilot hadn't even had time to utter the one word traditionally heard as black box recordings terminate.

Matt Sheehan had heard little more than the roar of the A-train subway since it sped away from the Jay Street station in Brooklyn and lurched under the East River. He'd taken a small detour through Brooklyn after landing at JFK and taking the subway through Queens.

As he stared out the window into the dark, he saw nothing except an occasional utility lamp as the car rocked on its rails. He was aware of snippets of conversation, but paid no attention. The morning rush hour crowd was so dense, Matt held his small flight bag in the same hand that gripped the overhead bar. The woman in front of him faced the door, pretending as he did that it was comfortable to be as close as lovers. The mass of bodies rocked with the motion of the car. Through the front of the car, Matt could see the lead car making small zigzag motions.

The woman suddenly turned and looked around angrily. She scanned nearby faces, returning to Matt's. Her eyes were green. Her skin looked tanned, but the smooth texture said her complexion came from parents rather than the sun. She said, "I really don't appreciate that." Matt got a glimpse of even white teeth.

It took Matt a moment to realize someone in the crowd must have pinched her or touched her in a way even more intimate than the close contact necessitated. He almost said, "You sound like my wife," but instead he hunched up one shoulder and extricated his free arm from the mass of bodies. He held his hand palm out. "I didn't touch you," he said calmly. "At least not anywhere except here." His gaze flicked down to where her shoulder touched his chest.

The woman, whose hair was shiny black, held his gaze a moment before she said, "I'm sorry," and started scanning other faces again.

Me, too, he thought as the subway continued to jostle the riders, a giant hand rocking the crib too energetically. Matt felt tired. He hadn't slept well on the flight from Mexico City to JFK, and wished he had more energy for his stop in Manhattan.

He let his eyelids droop closed, then popped them open a second later, when the car lurched violently. The overhead light went out. In the same instant, a shower of sparks splattered from somewhere behind him, and the screaming and shouting started.

A rumbling series of loud explosions sounded, so many of them separated by so little time that the noise was more a high-speed *rat-a-tat-tat* than distinct booms. Matt felt his body pushed forward into the woman ahead of him as emergency brakes decelerated the car, and he felt a sudden breeze behind him. The floor of the car lurched again, and by the time the car jerked to a stop, the floor seemed to tilt toward the rear.

As the screams and shouts finally gave way to angry and panicked loud questions like "What the hell's going on?" directed to no one in particular, the car jerked several times and came to a halt in blackness. A woman's voice split the dark, yelling, "Get your goddamn hand off me!"

The echoes from behind him had changed texture and lengthened, as if they no longer came from an enclosed car. People began spreading out, and suddenly a man cried, "Hey—" His voice trailed off until an impact forced more air out of his lungs. A few matches and cigarette lighters pierced the darkness. At first all they revealed were the forward half of the car and a confused throng of people. And Matt drew in a breath as he realized what *didn't* show—the rear half of the car. He pushed his way toward the back as more cries came from that direction: "Oh, my God." "Harry, Harry! What happened?"

As he got closer, Matt realized that the back half of the car was gone. He swallowed hard. People cowered at the sides of the vehicle, hanging on tightly and looking into the blackness behind the car. A man who apparently was the one who had just fallen got to his feet on the floor of the tunnel and looked up in surprise. Matt reached the severed edge of the car, and the temperature from packed bodies dropped noticeably. He took a deep breath and tried to control his fear.

The subway car had been sheared in half. The metal edges of the floor, walls, and ceiling still glowed a dull red from the heat of whatever had done this. Matt had once seen the edges of a hole created by an armor-piercing missile smashing through a tank wall. That hole reminded him of these edges, but here were no curling can-opener edges, just the shaved nubs, looking like plastic cut with a very hot knife, a hardware-store 3-D model of how walls were made. On the floor of the car and on the clothing of a couple of people apparently in shock were splatters of what could only be blood. In the air were musty smells of machine oil, ozone . . . and fear.

In the tunnel behind the car, Matt could at first see only faint reflections from the rails. He took a tiny penlight from his bag. With help from the light, he jumped to the track bed, careful to stay clear of the extra rail on the outside, even though the power was almost certainly off. A couple of meters from the severed edge of the car he found a man lying on the tracks, moaning. Careful not to make body contact, Matt grabbed a hunk of fabric and pulled until the man's leg no longer touched the rail. His heart pounded, but finally it began to slow as the initial adrenaline rush faded.

The man's right hand was gone, cut cleanly at the wrist. He heard gasps from behind him. The wound seemed to be partially cauterized already, but blood oozed and pulsed into the cinders. Matt took the man's belt, looped it a few times around the bare wrist, and fastened it tightly enough to bar further blood loss. Quietly, in what he hoped was a reassuring tone, he said to the injured man, who probably couldn't hear him anyway, "Okay, fellow, I'm here. We're going to get medical help for you. You'll be fine."

Matt played his penlight over the nearby ground, but he saw no sign of the man's missing hand. Behind him a couple of people jumped to the cinder track bed. He called toward them, "A man here needs medical attention if there's a doctor around."

He moved farther down the tracks. The next couple of meters could have been the aftermath of combat. There would be no helping the people here. What was left of a man had been cleaved vertically just to the right of his head. The rest could only be described as large and mostly recognizable pieces of human bodies.

Matt had seen casualties this horrible before, but he had always known *why.* Here he was totally confused. Was this the result of some terrible accident? Earthquake? The work of terrorists? Nothing made any sense. Somewhere behind him, a nervous laugh got out of control and turned to a repetitive wail before it ended with the sound of a slap.

He walked past the remains and stopped. Instead of the rear half of the severed car, or even empty rails extending under the river, here was nothing. The rails themselves were severed, butting up flat against a dark wall that completely blocked the tunnel mouth. As Matt came closer, he could feel the heat radiating from the dull-black surface barring the way. Water pooled on the tunnel floor. *Where the hell was the rear half of the train?*

As he played his light on the mottled surface, voices behind him said, "What the hell is that?" and "Mother of God."

Matt glanced behind him and saw an array of tiny flames piercing the black. A man in a business suit stumbled forward. "Agatha. Agatha! Can you hear me?"

Matt walked back to the man, passing a couple of onlookers with lighter flames flickering. "I'm sorry, but unless Agatha is in the car you just came from, she probably can't hear you. Come on. We've got to get out of here fast. We're probably still under the river, and something's cut the tunnel. We could be flooded at any time."

The suited man shook, his gaze directed toward the blocked

end of the tunnel. The man who had lost his hand still lay on the ground, surrounded by three people who looked at him with horrified expressions, but weren't helping. Matt moved closer.

"Help me carry him out," he said to the onlookers. He forced his voice to be calm despite his urge to run. "It's risky to move him because he might have a concussion or broken bones from the fall, but he's got to get medical attention, and it's going to be a while before any help gets down here."

"What happened?" asked one of the three, a woman with dazed eyes.

"I don't have any idea at all. Maybe a bridge above us collapsed. I hope we'll find out when we get above ground." He hoped the prospect of finding out more when they got moving would appeal to them, but he didn't give the bridge theory any real credence. This was something worse. How much worse, he had no idea.

"Take off your coat so we can use it as a litter," Matt said quickly to the taller man, who wore a raincoat.

The man didn't respond.

"Come *on.*" Matt grabbed the man's arm.

The man took the coat off as though in a trance. Matt laid out the coat next to the injured man.

"Come on," he said as he knelt beside the man. "Help me move him."

Like obedient automatons the three each gripped a shoulder or a leg and helped shift the injured man onto the coat. Matt took the edge of the coat next to the man's damaged arm so he could make sure nothing bumped against it. Together the four of them lifted the man to waist height and started up the tunnel. "If anyone gets tired, say so *before* you lose your grip. We're taking a big enough risk already."

As they reached the severed car, Matt stopped to retrieve his bag, and he found some passengers were still inside the car. "Something is blocking the tunnel back there. Everyone who can walk had better get started. No help is going to be here anytime soon from the way things look. Walk forward to the next stop. Anyone who's in good enough shape to run should do it and call nine-one-one. And stay away from the extra rail. Move fast, but stay calm."

Someone in the dark said, "My buddy says you can call for help from phones on the tunnel walls."

"If you see one, try it. Otherwise just keep going. But help anyone who needs it. Who can pass the word to the people in the lead car?" As soon as he heard a voice say, "I can," he and the others moved forward with the victim. Seconds later Matt realized that a blinking minivid "active" light was tracking them as they walked. Whoever it was even had a pinhead lamp shedding dim light on the tunnel walls. Irritated that someone was photographing them, he said, "Take your home movies somewhere else, why don't you? We need to get out of here."

A feminine voice sounded from behind the light. "This is for WNBC. What's your name, please?"

The voice seemed familiar. As a man with a lighter moved closer to the person with the minivid, Matt saw that it was the black-haired woman whose shoulder had bumped against his chest since the last stop. Matt made no reply.

They maneuvered past the walkway beside the severed car and past the lead car. Matt made sure no one was left aboard as they passed. Flickering light illuminated a scattering of possessions left behind. A headphone lay near a dark spill of blood on a bench. Someone must be in one shoe, because a lone sneaker with its laces still tied rested in a corner. An expensive video player had been left behind, along with a few coin-sized disks that by now would have footprints on them. A half-eaten sandwich wrapped in a deli bag lay flattened on the dirty floor. As they passed the lead car, Matt understood why the motorman had been no help. He was dead, smashed against the glass by the sudden stop.

Matt and the others were able to walk without jarring the injured man too badly, and they began to head up the moderate slope as quickly as they could without risking further injury to the victim. Steam rose slowly from a grate somewhere ahead. A couple of other people stayed close to them, holding cigarette lighters and matches in turns so the group could see a little of their surroundings. The woman carrying one corner of the raincoat got a couple of offers to have someone else take her place, but she turned them down. Ahead of them, the other passengers seemed to be taking it all in stride. Matt supposed living in New York required people to be adaptable.

Matt kept walking, trying to jostle his passenger as little as possible, as he wondered what they would find when they got out of the tunnel.

Rudy Sanchez got a second cup of coffee from the machine in the hall and took it back to his office. The hall was dark. No one else was in yet, and Rudy liked to savor the feeling of being in before the rest of the offices began to fill. He got twice as much done when the building was calm and quiet as he did when office hours began. Beating the morning rush enhanced the feeling.

He glanced out the window at the stream of cars coming across the Brooklyn Bridge and sat down, ready to get back to planning the replacement for the old generator on the Upper East Side. He'd been thinking about how to start the next phase when he realized something about the sound of the city had changed. He went back to the window.

At first everything seemed normal. Traffic was a little slow, but that was hardly surprising. As Rudy watched, his eyes widened as a black shape of some kind came out from behind the Chase Manhattan Bank tower. What the hell? It seemed to be some kind of craft, paralleling the coastline, and as it moved, it directed a dim red pencil of light through the dirty air, toward the ground. Where the pencil touched land or water, destruction followed.

In awe, Rudy put down his coffee cup and stared. What the hell was going on? He put his face nearer the glass and looked to both sides. Another identical black ship was moving along the coast farther to the north.

Both black, windowless craft flew an even course as they slanted what had to be high-power lasers toward the Manhattan shoreline. Rudy looked at the nearer craft. From just aft of the laser's origin, a gun muzzle threw a stream of pellets so fast and so frequently, there seemed to be a brown shaft of light right behind the laser.

A deep rumbling sound reached Rudy, quaking the floor

under his feet and vibrating the windows. He had the impression of thousands of small explosions occurring in the slit opened up by the lasers.

As Rudy moved to turn on the radio on his desk, the lights went out.

Abby Tersa had left Grand Central Terminal and was on her way to the United Nations General Assembly building when the traffic lights went off. Normally she enjoyed the six-block walk, but today she stood on the sidewalk in front of the Chrysler Building and backed against the wall as the crowd roared and the car honking intensified, as if to fill the gap caused by the sudden absence of subway sounds and the hubbub from freight elevators and exhaust fans.

Abby had never seen a power failure since she'd moved to the Bronx three years earlier. It made her nervous.

She edged along the base of the building, feeling the urge to get to work quickly, but knowing that without power for microphones, amplifiers, recorders, and lights, she wouldn't be needed for much translating. She was wondering if the power would return any time soon when she saw the black craft move from behind the tall slab of the U.N. Secretariat building. The craft aimed its laser down toward where the East River met the Manhattan shore.

Fighting down the panic, Abby began sprinting toward the U.N. Fifteen years ago she had been in training for the Olympics. In a timed run during physical education in junior high, she'd been surprised to learn that she was the fastest runner in her class. Encouraged by her parents, who saw running as a good thing to balance out all the hours that she spent in her room studying, she had gone out for the track team. At first she had rationalized the activity partly because it was one more way she could exercise her foreign language skills, but she grew to enjoy the running itself, finding that when she hit her stride she could block all her worries. This time she found herself unable to block the image of that strange ship.

Arsenio Hecher pulled into the right lane fast, finding a spot that wasn't directly behind a delivery truck. His fare, a white couple with a kid, didn't complain. Out-of-towners were quieter than the natives.

Arsenio kept watch in the cab's rear-view mirror as the vehicle moved onto the Brooklyn Bridge, heading northwest into lower Manhattan. The traffic was moving fast for rush hour, but it was never fast enough. Sometimes Arsenio thought about finding someplace less congested so he could really *move,* but when it came right down to it, he liked the way New York itself *moved.* Anyplace else would seem like a sleepy country afternoon, and he could never go back to that.

Faint sunlight hit gray waves cresting in the East River. Arsenio honked a reply to a fellow yellow as the other cab edged past him. Why was the *other* lane always faster?

The cab had just emerged from the shade of the large bridge support near the Manhattan shore when a moving shadow flashed over the roofs of cars and trucks ahead. Someone must be on a hell of a low path to La Guardia. Arsenio craned his neck to see what kind of plane it was.

The woman in the back seat asked, "Does this sort of thing happen a lot here?"

He didn't know what she was talking about until he looked forward again. A field of red taillights glared at him, and horns began to honk even faster. As he watched, a sparkling red light flashed across a truck ahead of the car in front of him.

Arsenio slammed on the brakes as the truck exploded. The car behind him smashed into his rear bumper, and the man in the back seat yelled, "What the hell!" as in the rear-view mirror Arsenio saw a truck plow into the guy behind him. The kid began to cry.

From the corner of his eye, Arsenio saw steam explode from the water at the edge of the river, as though a long thin heater lay just below the surface. As the cab finally showed signs of stopping successfully, the road surface began to tilt forward. The bridge was coming apart! "Crap!"

The goddamn bridge was turning into a drawbridge, but backwards. The section Arsenio's cab was on tilted down. As his panic rose, and he jammed his foot on the brakes hard enough to force the antilock on, he could see cars on the other side of the break burning rubber as they tried to gun it up the slope.

Electric motors whined, climbing to the top end of the scale as the wheels spun, and cars slid backward, smoke rising from their tires. His heart raced even faster than the time he'd been mugged.

For just an instant, Arsenio thought the cab was stopped precariously on the slope, but the bridge lurched again, and the car behind him hit his bumper one last time.

The cab slid off the end of the broken bridge. The screams from the back seat blended into one loud roar.

Arsenio cursed uncontrollably, his hands locked on the steering wheel and his foot still pistoned into the brake pedal for the entire time it took before the cab smashed into the water.

From his darkened office, Rudy Sanchez looked out at the destruction along the Manhattan shore. The Brooklyn Bridge had been severed, two trucks sliced in the process, and cars had spilled like toys into the river. Boats docked along the piers had been cut in two as steam roiled into the morning air. Rudy stood in shock, the dead telephone still gripped in one hand.

He had been tempted to run to help someone, anyone, but now he just stood, temporarily locked by indecision and fear. It seemed to him that anything he did now would be bailing a tidal wave with a teaspoon. A couple of fires had started where natural gas lines ran under the East River to Brooklyn, but cutoff mechanisms that didn't depend on power would limit the amount of gas available to burn.

The black craft closest to him switched off the red light, undoubtedly some unbelievably high-power laser. The craft rose swiftly with no vapor trail until Rudy lost sight of it.

The city sounded sick. The occasional rumble of a passing subway hadn't been audible for several minutes. The increased frantic honking from cabs and trucks gridlocked without working traffic lights more than made up for the lack in volume, but provided no comfort.

A flicker of black caught Rudy's eye. The craft were returning. He leaned forward and could see two more of them flying in formation but spreading the pattern as they fell. And what they were doing was even stranger than before. There seemed to be some filmy transparent material stretched between the craft. They looked as if they held some enormous soap bubble. *What in God's name was happening?*

The nearest black craft settled slowly toward the shoreline, stretching its corner of the bubble as it fell. Moments later the craft hovered over a severed dock. The corner of the soap bubble widened, and the edge of the bubble began to pull itself down toward the shoreline, apparently sealing itself to the ground or to some material the ship had deposited in the groove it had cut earlier. Within minutes, the filmy bubble had settled into a smooth seal for as far as Rudy could see. It seemed big enough to be covering the entire island of Manhattan.

The black craft rose, moving away from Manhattan as it did. Another one entered Rudy's field of view. Seconds later they both stopped, and stayed where they were, hovering.

Rudy had no warning. In one moment the ships just hovered. In the next moment a giant flashbulb went off. Rudy could see nothing but sparkles surrounding a large red spot for the next minute, but slowly his vision returned. When it did, he could see the bubble was still in place, but now it seemed more tangible. It was still transparent, but the reflections seemed brighter and they no longer wavered.

The hovering craft were gone. As Rudy tried to see where they might be, an enormous shadow crept over lower Manhattan.

Julie Kravine took a last few shots with her minivid, then shut off the sand-grain light. The image of the stalled subway cars faded from her retinas, and she turned to follow the stragglers up the tunnel.

Ahead of her were the four people carrying the man who had lost his hand. Julie cringed, just thinking about it again. And she remembered the severed bodies they were leaving behind. She had taken shots of them, too, more so that people would believe her report than because they'd be used on the news. She hadn't felt this ambivalent since she left Tom.

Julie felt uneasy. The ground rumbled with some unidentifiable tremble, and things just felt wrong. If the tunnel collapse were some localized catastrophe, she'd be hearing the rumble from other subways as they traveled nearby. Instead, the only vibration was that constant faraway tremor.

The rumble stopped. Suddenly the underground felt completely quiet, unnatural. Something was definitely very wrong. Julie hurried ahead, following the flickering lights. She stumbled, then got back to her feet and started picking cinders out of her palms. The tunnel smelled oily.

She caught up with the foursome. A couple of men walked with them, holding cigarette lighters, obviously ready to take over for anyone who got tired. She turned on her tiny light and minivid, capturing ten seconds before turning them off. She felt pride in how well New Yorkers were responding to the trouble. Her sister in Columbus complained about the crime rate and the apparent unfriendliness, but when things got tough, New Yorkers found ways to cope.

Julie moved to catch up again. She was tired from covering a late-night hostage crisis in South Brooklyn, but the good part was that it had left her with all her recording gear and a moderate battery charge at just the right time.

She caught up with the others and turned on her minivid, set to voice-only to save the charge. The tall man who had been next to her in the subway when it all started was gripping one corner of the raincoat holding the injured man. He was the same one who had calmed the crowd with sensible directions and a take-charge attitude that didn't smack of dictatorship. And he was the same one who had declined comment earlier. Was he a cop?

The man was going to be the focus of this piece, whether he liked it or not, Julie decided. She moved deliberately to one of the other three people carrying the injured man.

"I'm Julie Kravine with WNBC," she said to the woman who carried one corner of the raincoat. "What's your name?"

"Bette Waylon." The woman wore a dark jacket with the bracelet cuffs made popular in *Way Down and Way Over.*

"Can you tell me what you thought when the lights went out?"

"Nothin' I guess. That I'd be late for business."

"Any ideas about what might have caused this?"

"Naw. But we can find out on TV when we get back up."

"Anyone else here with a theory?" Julie watched the tall man. He opened his mouth but he didn't say anything.

Julie moved around until she was next to the tall man. He glanced at her, then looked ahead.

"And your name is, sir?"

The man replied without looking at her. "Matt Sheehan."

As she formulated her next question, Matt added, "And I apologize for being rude back there. I thought you were just another idiot with a camera. I guess I was a little edgy."

"I think we're all a little edgy," Julie said, thinking that he seemed the least edgy of anyone down here. "You a cop?"

"A cop? No."

"You seemed to adapt pretty quickly to the situation. What's your background?"

"I've spent some time in the service."

"Ah. So, do you have any theories about what happened back there?"

The man was silent for a moment, and several pairs of feet crunched gravel on the dark tunnel floor. "Not really."

"Nothing at all?"

"No. Just that I'm betting the problem isn't just down here."

"What makes you say that?"

"Just because this section of tunnel goes under the river. It's got to be going through bedrock. Anything generating enough force to do damage like what's back there isn't going to be confined to one tunnel."

Julie had been so intent on getting pictures and reactions that she hadn't thought much about anything else, but a sudden lurch in her stomach told her the man was probably right. An instant later she wasn't so sure the reaction had been nerves.

The ground shook. People carrying the injured man stumbled as they passed through a plume of rising steam.

Julie crouched in the dark tunnel, feeling the same sensation she felt in an elevator as it accelerated upward.

In the Columbia University computer science department building, Dr. Bobby Joe Brewster awoke with a start.

For an instant, he felt he was at sea. The desk his head rested on didn't seem solid, and neither did the chair he sat in. He jerked his head upright.

"Piss!" Bobby Joe looked at the dark computer screen in front of him. The atmospheric simulation run had been almost complete when he must have finally fallen asleep. And now he'd have to start over. The power had gone off, and it had stayed off long enough for his uninterruptible power supply to use up its charge.

The floor lurched, and a stylus on Bobby Joe's desk rolled a few centimeters and stopped. "What—"

Either some of the students in his computer modeling class were playing one hell of a trick on him, or something was really screwy. He rose and moved to the window.

Yup, something was really screwy, Bobby Joe decided.

He rubbed the sleep out of his eyes and took another look over nearby building tops and watched New Jersey sink.

"All right, you guys," he said loudly. "It's a convincing display."

He listened for laughter or some other response. Nothing. He looked out the window again, first as far to the left as he could see, and then as far to the right. He'd spent enough time in VirtReal simulations to know what was real and what wasn't. This was real. But it was unreal.

Traffic had come to a complete standstill on every road he could see. In the distance a huge mall vaguely resembled an aircraft carrier from this high up. Boats left their trails in scummy water. Slowly moving out into the Hudson was a line of turbulence.

He looked up as best he could with his cheek flattened against the glass. Overhead was a solid black cloud. Or was it? The edge looked awfully straight.

Bobby Joe looked back at New Jersey. He could see roads he'd never seen before, and the shoreline was beginning to disappear from view as it fell below nearby rooftops.

Fear forced him into nervous humor. This was not going to be a good day.

* * *

Annie Muntz was eating breakfast and watching the morning news in Queens when the lights flickered and the TV picture froze on the last frame. Motion out the window caught her eye.

On the table next to the couch was a thick tumbler with an inch of Scotch in it. She rose and moved closer to the window for a better look, taking her drink with her.

At first, Annie thought somehow her apartment building was sinking into the ground, because the Manhattan skyline was slowly but undeniably rising into the air. And the skyline was under a huge transparent arc, as if all the buildings had been put under a giant cake cover.

As she watched, her knees felt weak. The entire bubble-covered island of Manhattan was slowly rising into the air. As it continued to rise, she saw what was underneath the island. Below street level was a huge cone that extended even deeper than the Empire State Building was tall.

A dozen dark lines led from points all around the island up into the air. Annie's gaze followed the cables, and she saw an enormous black ship even bigger than the captured borough, hovering above it. A puzzled expression wrinkled her forehead. The alcohol level in her blood was high enough that for a long moment she considered the possibility that she was witnessing the advertising stunt to end them all.

Finally Annie yelled to her husband in the next room, "Hey, Herb, come here. You really should see this."

The rear half of the A-train subway had sustained far more damage than the front half. The rear half had crashed into something very hard.

Groans filled her ears as Shirley Hamilburg regained consciousness. Her first thought was that she'd had a super-realistic dream about going to work, and then she worried that she'd overslept. Finally she opened her eyes and managed to convince herself she really was awake despite the fact that she couldn't see. Where was Frankie, and what was wrong with her eyes?

Light flickered somewhere to her left. She turned her head to see where it was coming from, and she finally realized that she really had been on a subway car. So where was she now? The light flickered again. It was someone with a cigarette lighter or a match. Suddenly she realized how hot she was. The air was stifling. She was still in the car.

Shirley lifted her head, feeling the pull of pain from her shoulder as she shifted position. Lights flickered from somewhere outside of the car. She was in a mass of bodies like some nightmarish orgy.

Shirley tried to extricate herself from them. When a nearer flame lit the darkness, she saw that the man ahead of her must have hit the handrail support pole very hard. From near the front of the car came the sound of someone throwing up, and Shirley winced. She'd almost rather be dead than be throwing up.

Shirley finally managed to free herself. She moved over a few still bodies by supporting most of her weight from the overhead bar. The door had already been forced open. Outside, to the right, near the front of the train, lights flickered. She edged between the car and the side of the tunnel. The car itself was obviously not sitting evenly on the rails, and it leaned toward the opposite side of the tunnel. She passed the end of the car and walked beside the car ahead, which had jackknifed.

Shirley caught up with a small group of people holding flickering matches and lighters.

By the wavering light she could see that the first car in line had somehow been cut off as though God possessed a giant meat cleaver. The crumpled half-car rested against a solid obstruction blocking the entire tunnel. Two lifeless faces gaped and stared unseeing through the blood-smeared window.

Shirley stared at the blocked end of the subway tunnel. A man beside her said, "I don't understand. What's going on?"

Shirley shrugged. She had no answers.

A sudden rumbling and creaking began. Someone in the small crowd said, "It's moving!"

Sure enough, the black barrier at the end of the tunnel was sliding upward. And outward. Light filtered into the tunnel, and Shirley squinted as her eyes adjusted.

The gap between the tunnel mouth and the upward-moving plate widened. The gap kept on widening. Instead of revealing the other side of the tunnel, though, a chasm opened just past the mouth of the tunnel. Someone in the group murmured, "Holy crap."

The others in the crowd seemed as speechless as Shirley was until the bottom of the moving shape reached eye level. More and more light filtered down until daylight finally reached the bottom of an immense cavity like a strip mine. And above the void, an incredibly large dark shape floated higher and higher.

Water began to spill past the tunnel mouth, but not before Shirley had gotten a view of gaping tunnel mouths on the sides of the elongated chasm. The pair of holes more or less in line with the direction the severed subway tunnel pointed had to be the Holland Tunnel, and just to the right was a PATH rail line tube. To the north were another pair of severed tunnels that would be the Amtrak rail lines. God almighty.

Even farther north was a trio of tubes, the Lincoln Tunnel. Grimy black smoke poured from the rightmost circle. Water began to slosh past the other tunnel mouths as Shirley's mind finally began to come to terms with what was fairly obvious but very difficult to accept: all of Manhattan was rising into the air, leaving a huge long hole in the ground in the same shape as the island.

The waterfall grew louder and louder, but for the moment, the water was moving past the tunnel mouth fast enough that little water entered. By that time, the entire perimeter of the lip looked like Niagara Falls.

A man in a sweater and a vest said slowly, "Oh, God. Do you realize what will happen when the water fills the hole and reaches this height?"

Suddenly Shirley knew exactly what would happen. At about the same time someone else said, "We'd better schlep our butts out of here!"

A kid in a black jacket said, "We'll never get all the way back before the water runs down the tunnel and reaches us. We'd be better off jumping in." By now the falling water made a thunderous noise.

"Yeah, sure," said the man in the sweater. "Be my guest. Go ahead and jump. It's like a goddamn blender out there. And if we wait for the water to reach here, we'll just get caught and sucked back down here as the water drains into the tunnel."

"Well, we gotta to do *something,*" the kid said.

"Right. I'm running." The man ran back into the dim tunnel. Most of the others followed, and Shirley went, too.

They ran through the nightmare blackness until Shirley's lungs threatened to explode. They hadn't even managed to reach the lowest section of the tunnel before the water began flooding in. The *whooshing* made her heart race even faster. Wind started rushing out of the tunnel, and two cigarette lighters went out. Cold water swept past Shirley's ankles, and seconds later she was sloshing through calf-deep water.

The water suddenly seemed to move faster, and it swept Shirley off her feet. The current carried her in total darkness. Her feet dragged against one wall. Her body tumbled in the turbulent current. She couldn't tell which way was up, but she had to breathe.

Shirley had held her breath as long as she possibly could by the time the current smashed her head against a maintenance panel.

Rudy Sanchez stood transfixed at the window as the Municipal Building creaked around him as though in a high wind. Some enormous ship above the city was obviously lifting the entire bubbled island into the air. A disturbance spread into the water in the Upper Bay as though a drain had opened in a giant bathtub. The Staten Island ferry had been moving toward Manhattan, but by now it had turned 180 degrees and was trying desperately and in vain to move south before it was dragged backward into the depression. Rudy could see a mass of people at the back rail of the ferry as the crest of turbulent water began to shake the ferry apart. Rudy had to shut his eyes.

When he opened his eyes again, Rudy could no longer see the ferry, but as he craned his head and looked southwest he was just in time to see the Statue of Liberty disappear below the horizon, looking for all the world as if she were waving good-bye.

In less than a minute Brooklyn dropped from sight, and within minutes Rudy could no longer see the Atlantic Ocean. The atmosphere slowly shifted from blue toward black. The image of the Statue of Liberty still burned in his memory.

Rudy glanced at people on the ground. Hardly anyone was

moving, and almost everyone seemed to be staring at the dome.

The sky outside the dome now looked almost black. Rudy could see stars around the edges of the huge black shape overhead, and on the ground shadows seemed sharper than normal. The sun was brighter than he'd ever seen it.

As Rudy watched, the dark shape overhead suddenly grew wider, blotting out more and more stars until the only stars Rudy could see were almost level with him, visible through the side of the dome. His stomach twisted as he decided the ship towing the city hadn't come closer, but instead they were now underneath a ship that dwarfed the one that had picked up Manhattan. Rudy swallowed hard.

The black shape started to blot out more and more stars, as though a huge black cylinder was being lowered around the island. Rudy watched helplessly as they were pulled upward into the giant ship.

The light from the sun was cut off, and Manhattan moved into darkness.

2

FREE UTILITIES

AS UNNATURAL DARKNESS spread over the Manhattan morning, Dorine Underwood, the mayor of New York City, watched in shock from her west-wing office window in City Hall. Her job demanded her to expect the unexpected, but this was absurd.

Dorine had also been at her desk before the regular start of the business day. Getting in early was the only way she could keep up with the steady stream of daily visitors and still manage to keep the city mechanisms operating smoothly. Long ago she had learned the importance of delegating, but she still had to make sure all the tentacles of city government waved in a consistent manner. Her predecessor had served but a single term, thanks in part to snafus like having scheduled tours of area medical research labs on Animal Rights Day.

The changed city sounds had brought her to the window, where her body momentarily seized up. She couldn't breathe, couldn't swallow. She just stood there petrified, on the verge of panic, as Manhattan rose through the atmosphere.

The darkness was not total. The few buses, cabs, trucks, and cars stopped on the streets below and not yet abandoned by their drivers showed twin sets of lamps cutting through the artificial night.

Dorine would have felt more comfortable in the dark. The dark could let her pretend nothing had changed. None of the headlights below penetrated the bubble she had seen placed around the edge of the shoreline. Instead, the lights reflected off the bubble, creating a fun-house mirror image of the panicked city and making the recent changes impossible to disbelieve. She shivered uncontrollably in the warm room.

For a moment she closed her eyes in another futile attempt to pretend everything was normal. In the self-imposed blindness, Dorine Underwood realized that even in darkness the events of the last half-hour could not be ignored. She felt lighter.

She opened her eyes again and this time focused on herself instead of on the panic outside. She lifted her arm. Her wrist seemed to have strings attached, pulling gently upward. She knew what that meant—that the island of Manhattan was now in a weaker gravity field than Earth's—but she still had trouble accepting it.

As a test, she jumped. Fortunately her office ceiling was so high that she didn't hit her head hard enough to hurt. She fell back to the floor in slow motion, and the time it took her to fall was so long that she tipped on the way down and landed awkwardly on one ankle before falling to the floor with far less dignity than proper for a mayor of the Big Apple.

Unhurt but astonished, she regained her footing and looked out the window again. Her breath came in short bursts. Nothing in the mayor's manual had been adequate preparation for *this.*

Julie Kravine had felt the tremors as she hurried along with the others in the subway tunnel, and now she, too, realized that somehow she was much lighter than before. Walking was no longer an instinctive act; she had to concentrate on keeping her balance between steps, and the ground seemed slick. The foursome carrying the wounded man had all stumbled, twice almost dropping the victim.

One of the men said, "What's going on? This feels like one of those low-gravity rides at Epcot."

Flickering lights from the cigarette lighters seemed slightly taller and thinner than before. The tall man who had more or less assumed command, Matt, said, "I can't think of any explanation. Let's just get this guy to safety, and we'll all find out."

Julie found herself wanting to participate in the discussion rather than just acting as an observer. She said, "This isn't just some tunnel cave-in, though, don't you think? I'm nervous."

Matt said, "I'm nervous, too. But there's not much we can do about it, is there?"

Julie shook her head. Probably no one saw the gesture in the dim light.

After a few more steps, the woman in the foursome suddenly said, "Look! Up there! There's a light."

A train. Julie was suddenly nervous. Was there enough room for the train to pass without grinding them against the tunnel walls? Would it crash into their stopped train, killing even more people? The worried thoughts all flickered through her brain so fast that it was not until a second later that she realized the idea of a running train no longer made sense.

She was right. Far ahead was the first working emergency light Julie had seen since they left the stalled cars behind. They must be close to the station. Finally they'd find out what was going on.

Matt and the three helpers maneuvered the man who'd lost his hand up onto the subway platform. The man rested on his back while they climbed up to the platform easily in the lighter gravity.

As Matt picked up his corner of the raincoat again, the injured man's eyelids fluttered, then opened. "What?" he said groggily. His eyes focused somewhere behind Matt, and his forehead wrinkled in puzzlement. Matt glanced where the man was looking and saw a subway poster from the Ultimate Savior Church, showing in huge black letters, REPENT!

Matt looked back at the man and said, "We're here. You've got help. Don't worry about anything."

Pain flickered across the man's face, and Matt wished they had some anesthetic for him. The man looked to be in his forties, with thin lips, black eyes, and lopsided eyebrows. His eyes closed, then opened slightly and closed again, like the eyes of a child who wanted to stay up late but just couldn't last any longer.

Even as they made their way up the dark stairs from the subway tunnel, Matt saw additional confirmation that whatever had happened was something far out of the ordinary. If the problem had been local, they would have found help at the station, or even before. On their way up, they encountered no one, and the city sounds seemed strange even to him.

Car horns filtering down the stairwell didn't sound like the normal jumbled mess of short blasts. Instead, maybe a dozen horns of various pitch and volume blared steadily, as though a dozen accidents had left drivers slumped over their steering wheels.

Matt and the others reached the final stairs to the street without finding any lighting other than the occasional emergency lamps. From the distance came the sounds of crying and a mass of mumbling people. The reporter moved ahead of them up the stairs. Matt watched his footing carefully and kept checking on the injured man. When they reached ground level, they moved past some people cowering near the wall, and Matt found the reporter standing there motionless, looking up.

Instead of the daylight Matt had expected, he found night. Suspended over Manhattan was a reflected image of a darkened city lit only by the headlights of buses, cabs, trucks, and cars stalled and abandoned in the gridlocked streets. The sidewalks were lined with people in clumps staring up at the distorted reflections. Here and there a person lay flat on the ground. Someone maybe a half-block away wailed steadily. Matt's stomach lurched. He could understand the people lying down; the image suspended over the city, coupled with the low gravity, gave him a sharp twinge of acrophobia.

One of the men in the foursome wobbled a bit, then recovered. Luckily the victim's weight was much less of a burden than before. Matt glanced around. Down the block was an ambulance caught in the traffic snarl.

"Let's get this guy down there," Matt said, and pointed.

They threaded their way through the people on the sidewalk and street. When they reached an open area and walked faster, Matt almost lost his footing. The pavement seemed too smooth, no doubt thanks to the low gravity allowing less friction.

The ambulance attendants stood on the pavement next to their open doors, both looking up at the sky.

"We've got someone who needs your attention," Matt said to the driver.

It took a moment for the driver to focus on Matt and start to react to what he was saying, but after a few seconds his training must have taken over, and he and the other attendant started to put the man with no hand onto a stretcher. Matt explained that they hadn't been able to locate the man's hand.

The reporter came up beside Matt as the paramedics started puffing medication into the man's arm. The man's eyes fluttered open again, and the reporter asked, "Do you remember anything about what happened to you?"

The man glanced toward the arm without a hand. He licked his lips and said softly, "I think God's trying to tell me something." His voice was mellow, resonant, despite the softness.

"What do you mean by that?" she asked, but the man's eyes closed and his features relaxed, no doubt thanks to the medication taking over.

Matt got back to the curb just as a bright light came on in the sky to the west of the city. A round spot the size of the sun penetrated the reflected images above the skyline and began to grow brighter. A hush fell over the people on the sidewalks and in the street.

The "sun" grew brighter and brighter until it hurt to look at it, and the city streets lightened until they were as bright as day.

When the "sun" reached what seemed to be its maximum intensity, the dome started losing its reflectivity, and in stages began to grow transparent. Matt moved a few steps so he could see better to the east. The first thing he realized was that although his memory told him the Brooklyn Bridge should be in view, it wasn't. Rather, all that showed was a stub of the bridge.

The dome continued to increase in transparency, and Matt felt his mouth go dry. He could see through the dome, and what he saw didn't bear any resemblance at all to Brooklyn.

Instead, the island of Manhattan rested on a vast gray plain. In the distance was another dome sitting on the plain, and to its left another. Slightly farther away than the pair was yet another dome. Matt shifted position again as the crowd came to life with screams and loud voices. He could see two more domes in the distance.

Beneath the other domes were what seemed to be other cities, one a jumble of prismatic arches, another that looked like one enormous building, another a mass of needle-thin spires with halos near the top—and even someone much less well-traveled than Matt would have instantly known these cities had never existed on Earth.

Julie kept her minivid active and tried as hard as she could to focus her thoughts on the mechanics of her job. Thank God the recorder still had a moderate charge. The minivid optics were attached to her headband, feeding what they saw into her glasses and to the recorder that hung lightly at her waist.

She had made several deliberate pans of the dome overhead and recorded the stalled traffic with drivers milling about on Fulton and Broadway before the artificial sun came on and the dome cleared. Now she used her telephoto on the cities inside the domes out there on the plain. In one of the nearest bubbles, which contained maybe a hundred very large pyramid-shaped blue buildings with irregular windows, she could make out the motion of what looked to be people.

Light glinted from the dome over the blue city, and in the short time she recorded the scene, the brightest reflection moved just a hair to the right. The "sky" was brighter over that side of the dome, as though it had its own "sun" pointed at it but was shielded from view in this direction. She waited a few moments and the reflection was again slightly to the right of where it had been before. In her telephoto image, she could see a couple of distant domes that looked dark. Some domes were simple portions of spheres; others were distorted to accommodate tall structures, the way the tent-shaped dome over Manhattan was.

Julie looked back up at the dome above Manhattan. The bubble came close to touching the tip of the southernmost of the twin towers of the World Trade Center. She moved past a small crowd of people on the sidewalk and took some more shots. The honking seemed to have died down a little since she and the others had gotten up to the street, but people clogged the road, walking between stopped trucks and buses, or standing rigid and looking up. A couple of people near the intersection were shouting unintelligibly.

Julie noticed more eye contact than normal among people

in the crowd, as though many of them were silently asking, "Do you see this, too?" In the street she recognized another journalist but couldn't tell if he was wearing a minivid.

"Are you going to be all right?" asked a voice behind her shoulder.

She turned and found Matt Sheehan standing there, his small flight bag held in one hand. "It's a little too early to tell right now, don't you think?"

"I meant as far as getting around the city."

"Sure. I'll be fine. Do you realize that there seem to be people living under those other domes?"

"No, but I'm glad to hear it. That probably means they intend to keep *us* alive."

Motion in the direction of what was left of the Brooklyn Bridge made them turn in unison. What seemed to be an enormous transparent hose was extending down from somewhere above, the top end invisible. Julie turned and saw another hose to the "south." She turned full circle and could see four different hoses dropping around the island. Presumably more hoses were dropping near the north end of the dome, near Harlem and Washington Heights.

The end of the nearby hose almost reached the flat plain outside the dome. Julie started her minivid again and watched through the telephoto viewfinder. "That hose, or whatever it is, is starting to curve," she said for Matt's benefit.

The hose continued to curve until it completed a ninety-degree turn, facing the dome. "It's coming closer to the dome," Julie said.

As the large transparent tube came closer, the end grew in diameter. Finally it stuck itself against the side of the dome, maybe fifty meters in the air, about as high as the Brooklyn Bridge support.

"So are the rest of the tubes," Matt said as he turned back to face the closest one.

Where the lip of the hose touched the dome, a bright ring formed. The dome material in the circle and just outside the circle shimmered, and then the clear dome material within the circle melted away from the center until it looked as if some huge glass blower had just perfectly formed the spout on a glass teapot.

Julie was aware of several distant sirens as she stood watching the dome material near the hose lose its shimmer. Within seconds the dome and hose were back to their normal transparency, as though they had been connected forever.

"What do you suppose those things are for?" she asked.

Matt glanced at the ring of tubes. "If they want to keep us alive, we're going to need air pretty soon. I'd vote for ventilation."

Another set of hoses began to drop from the sky. As Julie and Matt watched, she realized she could feel a breeze when before there hadn't been one.

"You must be right about the air," she said, then looked around. "Tell me something. Does it look to you like the light has moved since it came on?"

Matt glanced toward the "sun." "Maybe a little. To the right?"

"That was my guess, too."

"I always wondered what it would be like to live in an ant farm."

"You're kiddin' me."

Matt looked at her. "Yeah, I'm kidding."

One of the second set of hoses had melted through the dome. This hose was smaller and lower to the ground, and whatever was happening to the dome itself was different. Instead of a simple hole in the dome, part of the dome, or part of the hose, was extruding a shape into the interior of the dome. They watched in awe for several seconds before Matt suddenly laughed.

"What?" Julie asked.

"It's a bird-feeder. That cup is going to fill with water, I bet you—" He hesitated. "I don't know that betting your money makes any sense anymore."

Julie looked back at the junction and the interior shape as it stopped mutating. He was right. A bird-feeder was just what it looked like. "I've seen a lot of things, but I'm having a tough time believing this is all real."

"Me, too."

Julie heard cries from somewhere in the crowd behind her. She turned and saw several people looking and pointing upward. She looked to where they pointed, and she saw shapes appearing on the top of the tent-shaped bubble.

She and Matt watched in silence as what looked to be lettering of some kind formed on the dome. Through her telephoto, the large black shapes split into a few smaller shapes, as though the aliens' paragraphs themselves formed two-dimensional shapes. The characters were completely foreign to her. Most of the marks had such ill-defined shapes, they looked more like a child's doodling than actual writing, possibly alien pictographs rather than characters.

"Any guesses as to what that says?" she asked.

Matt took a long look. "I suppose it must be a message to us rather than some label for themselves, but if it were for their own use, I'd be afraid it said something like 'Manhattan Zoo,' or worse."

"Worse?"

"Yeah, it could say 'Laboratory Animals.' "

Minutes after the artificial night began, Dorine Underwood saw the "sunrise" from her office, and it gave her new hope. If their captors were providing light, they wouldn't be preparing to kill everyone right away. She hoped.

Given that the city was still alive, she had an organization to run. Her thoughts still flicked from topic to topic in her typical stress reaction, and she willed herself to calm down. She *must* be calm. Dorine took a couple of deep breaths and forced herself to look for something good in the situation. It took her several minutes. Finally she decided that the only slightly good news was that she wouldn't have her day constantly interrupted by out-of-towners.

She paused for a few seconds and picked up a picture of Rafael. He was off designing a new theater in Cleveland, however far away that was now. She gripped the picture tightly enough that the glass popped as it pressed more tightly against the photo of her husband. "Dear God," she said softly. "Give me strength to do what must be done. And give Rafael the strength to handle . . . whatever it is that's happened."

She dabbed at her eyes briefly, then strode into the hall. No one was going to say Sherilyn Underwood's little girl wasn't up to *anything* the Lord threw her way. And she'd be damned if anyone got an opportunity to say a white mayor would be handling things better. She hadn't gotten to be mayor of New York City by caving in whenever the unexpected happened.

She found Freddy, the night guard, still near his post. He stared out the hallway window completely entranced.

"Freddy," she said softly, and touched his arm.

Freddy jumped. "God *damn.* Don't *do—*" Freddy regained control. "Oh, it's you, Ms. Mayor. I'm sorry. You just scared the—"

"It's all right. I understand completely. Something very strange has happened out there."

"You're damn—er, you ain't wrong there, ma'am."

"Look, I've got a job for you. Are you ready?" Seeing the man's hesitation, she added, "We've got a city to run. Something bad has happened out there, and the people of Manhattan need us more than ever."

"Yes, ma'am. You're right. I'm ready."

"That's good. What I want you to do is walk over to Barnaby Jolliet's office. Tell him I said for him to use his best judgment about getting the police out there to reassure people. And ask him for three of his walkie-talkies so we can talk until the phones are on again. You got that?"

"I got it, ma'am. And bring you all three walkie-talkies?"

"Right. Unless you see Ken Randall. Give him one. And when you get back, tell everyone you can find in the building there'll be a meeting in the planning room in twenty minutes—at nine-thirty. Tell that to Mr. Jolliet, too, and Ms. Phillipe in the Municipal Building."

"You got it, Ms. Mayor." Freddy seemed visibly relieved to see that someone was reacting as though this were something that could be handled. Dorine hoped the rest of Manhattan would react the same way.

Dorine went back to her office and looked out the window. On the street, a pair of men jumped straight into the air. Their heads must have cleared the second floor before they fell gently back to the ground.

She looked over the skyline. One more good thing about this. The air looked cleaner than it had in decades.

Julie turned off her minivid after training the lens on the message on the dome. "I hope you're wrong about what it says," she said. "I hope it says, 'We'll have you back in twenty-four hours.' "

Matt looked at one of the domes outside their own. "Doesn't seem too likely, though, does it?"

"No," Julie said. "Damn, I hate to admit this, but I'm scared."

"Me, too," said Matt. "Me, too."

Some of the buses and cars in the street were abandoned. By now, many drivers had just parked as far from the center of the road as they could, and left their vehicles there.

Matt hesitated. "I was on my way to visit a friend who works in the Municipal Building. You're not going to have any trouble getting home or wherever you need to go?"

"I'll be fine. Who's your friend, if I need to get hold of you?"

"Rudy Sanchez."

Julie reached into a pocket. "Here's my card in case you need to reach me."

"Thanks. You take care of yourself."

"You, too." Julie turned, and within seconds she was lost in the crowd.

Matt walked over to Park Row, past City Hall Park, which was packed with onlookers staring up at the reflections from the interior of the dome. People on the street were slipping and sliding with the lower friction and the unfamiliarity with low gravity. A few people adapting more quickly ran with long, high bounding steps or jumped straight up as far as they could. A cab surged through a gap in traffic and tried to make a hard turn, but wound up sliding sideways until it mashed the fender on a stalled truck. A couple of street people slumping on the sidewalk next to the building pulled their coats more tightly around themselves.

Matt found the Municipal Building straddling Chambers

Street. No one questioned him as he checked an office directory that said Rudy's office was on the nineteenth floor, then started up the stairs.

The nineteenth floor was a long dim corridor lit only by a few emergency lamps and light filtering through office windows. Matt reached the southern end of the hallway and found the name tag he'd been looking for. As he hesitated in the hall, a man he didn't recognize hurried out of the office.

Matt rapped on the door frame. "Hello. Anybody home?"

From behind a tall file cabinet, Rudy Sanchez appeared. Rudy had grown up in East L.A., then gotten his degree in mechanical engineering before entering the military, where Matt had met him. He'd shaved his mustache since Matt had seen him last, and added maybe ten pounds, but in the light from the window, he looked fit. "Matt? You're a day early. God, it's good to see you."

"Same here." Matt shook hands, and he smiled despite the tension. Rudy's grip had lost none of its strength. It felt good to see a familiar face in the middle of all this.

Rudy sighed. "If you had just been a day late, you might have been spared all this."

"Well, I *am* here." Matt moved to the window, and Rudy joined him. From this height, he could see a few more domes that, from ground level, had been hidden behind the closest domes.

Matt said, "God damn. I still can't believe this is really happening." His face felt hot.

"I know what you mean. I feel like I'm dreaming." Rudy hesitated. "I don't mind telling you this whole business scares me."

Matt stared at one of the distant domes. "Me, too. A person would be pretty damn stupid not to be scared right now."

"What the hell do you figure's happening?"

"You mean other than the fact that we've been captured by some pretty advanced aliens?" Matt said with a forced chuckle.

"Yeah, other than that little detail." Rudy's face showed the tension running through his body.

"You got me. That they want us alive. Those big hoses out there seem to be supplying air at a comfortable temperature.

Those slightly smaller hoses seem to be bird-feeder water supplies."

"Makes sense to me, too, but for God's sake *why*?" Rudy asked.

"I've got no better idea than you do."

Rudy shook his head. "I've got to go to an emergency planning meeting in five minutes. Your skills could come in mighty handy right now. Want to come along?"

"Fine by me. I'd like to be doing *something*. I feel terminally edgy."

Rudy turned his head. "Is Nadine all right? I thought you said she'd be meeting you here."

Matt stared out the window. For a brief moment, he was looking out the window of a chalet in the Swiss Alps, and Nadine was beside him. "Nadine had a change of plans. She's still in Cairo. I talked to her a couple of nights ago. She wants a divorce."

For a moment Rudy stared out the window toward the domes in silence. "Well, I guess you could say she got it, huh?"

In spite of himself, Matt laughed.

Dorine cut short the premeeting nervous conversation and convened the emergency session promptly on time. Fortunately the room had a large window, so they didn't need artificial lighting. The group was smaller than she had expected. No doubt that meant some people were walking to work from stalled subways, or had gone home to deal with emergencies there, or had been outside the borough when it was pulled loose. Perhaps a fair number of people simply couldn't cope with the strange circumstances.

She scanned faces in the group. Good. The police commissioner, Barnaby Jolliet, was here. She saw people from the city council and the office of emergency management. "Where's Michelle Phillipe?" she asked. "Anybody know?"

"No one has seen her this morning," said a man in his late thirties or early forties. "I don't think anyone senior to me in the city manager's office is in right now. I'm Rudy Sanchez."

"All right. Let's start with quick department summaries and then go to planning. I suppose we all know equally little about what's really happening, so all we can do is get this borough functioning as best we can. There may be a couple of million people in Manhattan right now, and they're going to need protection, food, water, electricity, waste disposal, medical help." Dorine scanned faces.

"Barnaby, how do things stand with the police?"

Barnaby Jolliet, a man with a ruddy complexion, shifted in his chair. Despite his slightly blustering manner, and an occasional unwillingness to admit he didn't know an answer, Barnaby was competent and hard-working. "We've made a good start. All the precincts except for the sixteenth and the thirty-fourth are in communication with walkie-talkie relays. We've got officers with bullhorns going up all the avenues, restoring order and telling people we're getting things under control. We've stopped looting in several spots, but so far most people don't seem to be trying to take advantage of the situation. It's more like people are still in shock."

Barnaby held up his walkie-talkie. "For those of you with walkie-talkies, stay off channels A through G; those are for police use. Channels H and I are emergency channels. Channel K is the city government party line." He put the walkie-talkie on the table and looked at Dorine. "We need to keep people in check, and we can do that. The tough part is when, not if, we have a big fire. Without water, we're going to be flat out of luck."

"I know. Good summary. What *about* water?"

"Why are we bothering with this?" suddenly asked an older man who Dorine recognized as a long-time city employment worker. "You're treating this like just another emergency, but it's not. It's crazy out there!"

"We *have* to do what we can," Dorine said forcefully. "Without us the chaos will be a damn sight worse. There are some areas, like yours, and like the tourist bureau, that won't be as busy as normal, but other groups will be a lot busier. Anyone without something to do should volunteer in another area. Back to my question about water."

Michelle's stand-in, Rudy, spoke up. "It looks like the aliens are making water available to us. One of my people is getting a battery-operated computer ready so we can find what we need in inventory. With some luck, we can run hoses from the alien supply into the water mains. With pumps we can get it up to near the same pressure we had before. I've sent a team of people out to shut off pipes to sections that were severed.

"I've also got people on their way up to generators that should be working, but they'll only run until reserve tanks of natural gas and oil are empty. Probably we should restrict the use of gasoline to emergency needs."

Dorine nodded. "Good idea. Barnaby?"

Barnaby nodded. "I'll get the word out."

"What if that water they're giving us is drugged?" asked a woman next to Barnaby.

Rudy answered, "Then there's nothing we can do about it. If we don't drink, we don't stay alive. The only significant amount of water we brought with us is in the Central Park reservoir, in the pipes, and in storage tanks in some of the higher buildings. But that and what's in City Tunnel Number One won't last long without recycling, besides which, water may well be leaking from several tunnels. I've got someone checking on the possibility of using local chemical labs to distill water, but I doubt we can find a quick way to keep up with the volume we need."

"Anything else in your area?"

"Steam we won't need, as long as the aliens are providing air at a reasonable temperature. Telephones will be up once we have emergency electricity. Sewage will be a problem pretty soon, but I'll see what we can do. Food's going to be the worst problem. And I can use almost all the help I can get."

"Noted. What haven't we covered?"

The room was silent for a moment, then the sandy-haired man sitting next to Rudy said, "Alien contact?"

"We don't have an office for that," Dorine said lightly. "Don't you figure they'll contact *us*?"

"Perhaps. But we can push the process along. That message on the 'roof'—we should be decoding it. And apparently there's not only one set of aliens."

"Okay, you're in charge, Mr.—"

"Matt Sheehan."

Rudy spoke up. "He's on, ah, the same floor I'm on."

"Just a minute," said the man from employment. "Who is this guy, and what are his qualifications?"

Rudy said, "Well, for one thing, he's *here.*" After a couple of chuckles faded away, he added, "Matt's an army colonel, one of the best organizers and best leaders I ever had the pleasure of serving under when I was still in the Army."

Matt spoke up. "If anyone else wants the job, I certainly won't be offended. My feeling is that whatever experts we have in the city may know how to approach various aspects of the problem, but might be better utilized if they're free to do the actual work. What I can do is listen to expert advice, plan, and get resources available for whoever winds up on the team. I think I can do that well. And if at any time the mayor wants to put someone else into the job, that's fine with me. Would anyone else prefer to do the job?"

Barnaby drummed his fingernails on the hard black walkie-talkie case. "There was a Colonel Sheehan or a Major Sheehan in the news a couple of years ago. Something in Paraguay. Alvoranza somebody led a successful coup against the new democratic government. An Army team went in and took him out. They moved in so fast Alvoranza didn't have time to blink. Are you that Sheehan?"

Rudy opened his mouth before Matt did. "That was him. Order was restored in thirty-six hours. And the only casualties were a half-dozen of Alvoranza's thugs."

Barnaby nodded as he filed away the information.

Dorine let the silence last about five seconds before she said, "All right. What else hasn't been covered?"

The seconds of silence were again broken by Colonel Sheehan. "Someone should coordinate an ambulance patrol around the shoreline, including everything underground, like subways and car and rail tunnels."

Barnaby used his walkie-talkie briefly to pass on instructions. When he was done, he looked at Dorine and said, "I had people on the shore, but we hadn't started on the PATH tubes yet."

Dorine nodded. Again a short silence was broken by Colonel Sheehan. "If a team worked on getting all the buses and cabs back to garages or stations, the streets might be passable for emergency vehicles."

"Good." As Dorine scanned the group for someone in transportation, she found a face and saw an acknowledging nod.

"Anything else, Colonel Sheehan?" Dorine smiled despite the tension.

"While the police pass the word that people are trying to restore city operations, maybe they should be telling people to turn on their TVs and radios to some local station as soon as Rudy has a generator back on-line, in case we need to get information to as many people as possible, or ask for help from specialists."

Barnaby said, "Makes sense," and he used his walkie-talkie again.

Dorine looked at Sheehan again. His dark eyes looked calm, in contrast to more than half of the people at the meeting. He saw her looking at him, and he said, "If there is a supply of cots available, maybe some could be placed in the main city government building lobbies so anyone who anticipates working out of the office for a while can get some occasional rest."

Dorine nodded and scanned the group. A woman Dorine didn't recognize raised her hand and said, "I can arrange that."

Dorine let the next silence last several seconds. "Okay, then. Let's get busy. And, Barnaby, can you get Colonel Sheehan a walkie-talkie?"

Barnaby agreed. As people started to rise, a woman wearing a high-neck collar asked, "But what's *happening* to us? Don't you want to know?"

Dorine said, "Of course we want to know. But we can't waste time right now speculating. Once we know the support systems are in place, we can devote more effort to the next steps."

The woman was clearly unsatisfied by the answer, but she didn't press the issue.

On the way out of the room, Dorine instinctively brushed her hand against the wall to turn off the light switch. She wondered briefly how many other habits she'd have to break.

Rudy Sanchez was waiting impatiently as the cherry-picker slowed to a stop and the driver stepped down from the cab. Rudy could have assigned this duty to someone else, but he had to be doing *something*, and he had always enjoyed hands-on work more than management.

"Sorry it took me so long," the driver said. "The streets are a little crazy still."

"I don't doubt it," Rudy said. "Okay, here's the deal. I want to get up close to that." He pointed at the bird-feeder embedded in the dome over the severed concrete of Pier 17, right in front of where the Pier 17 Pavilion had been left behind when Manhattan made its move. Pieces of wreckage from severed boats floated in isolated pockets of water caught near the bubble.

While waiting for the truck, Rudy had suddenly thought about the people left on the pavilion. They would have been stranded on their own little rectangular island until help arrived. If their telephone lines hadn't gone through Manhattan, he could imagine the disbelief on the other end when someone called to explain that they needed a boat to pick them up because Manhattan had gone away.

As soon as the driver had maneuvered the truck into position, Rudy grabbed the end of a large hose and tied it to the cherry-picker cage, then stepped into the cage and thumbed the controls. He glanced at the "sun," which had moved maybe thirty degrees to the right in the last two hours.

As the cherry-picker cage started lifting him up toward the large interior cup that held what he was convinced was water, two more police cars arrived, escorting a truck with more piping and the large pumps he would need. People from his department, assisted by volunteers, started unloading the material.

The cherry-picker cage moved to where Rudy wanted to be, and he stopped about fifteen meters over the ground. The cage bounced more slowly than normal as it came to rest. From his pocket he took a pair of vials, and carefully dipped each into the liquid. Moments later he was reasonably convinced he was dealing with normal water. He filled another set of vials to send out for chemical analysis. They wouldn't pump this into the city until the verification was complete, but Rudy's gut told him the water would pass all the lab tests, particularly when using it was the only choice.

The bird-feeder tray was shaped a little like an oversized bathtub stuck on the inside of the dome, constantly filled by the hose coming from somewhere above. Rudy couldn't see any mechanism that told a valve somewhere to pass more water or to shut off, but there had to be one.

He touched the side of the tray. The material felt cool to the touch. He rapped his knuckles on it, and the sound it produced felt more like he had knocked on the side of a huge cube of material instead of on an extruded piece no thicker than his thumb. He got no sense of vibration at all; just a sensation like tapping on bedrock. He got out a sharp pocketknife and purely out of curiosity tried to cut a sliver of the material off the edge. He could as easily have scraped a sliver of glass off a crystal goblet by using a sharp piece of cardboard. Finally he remembered the people on the ground.

He called to the volunteer near a portable generator connected to a self-priming pump, "Let her rip."

The man yanked the cord, and the noisy generator sprang to life, the large stand vibrating on the pavement. Rudy swung the end of the hose over the lip of the bird-feeder, and it started to make noisy snorkeling sounds as water displaced the air in the hose. The surface of the water in the bird feeder grew turbulent, and Rudy pushed the hose deeper. Water started spewing out the hose on the other side of the pump. Rudy let it run for several seconds, and the water level in the bird-feeder didn't diminish.

"Okay," he yelled, "now push that red lever toward the white mark."

The man did so, and the roar from the pump increased in pitch and volume. The pump vibrated so strongly that it started creeping along the pavement and had to be restrained. The surface of the water in the bird-feeder grew more and more choppy, but the water level stayed where it was. Water shot out the pump hose into an arc that spanned fifty feet. Rudy was about to make an educated guess about the velocity that implied before he remembered that the reduced gravity spoiled his rules of thumb. Still, his gut told him that with enough pumps and hoses leading from the bird-feeders down to nearby fire hydrants, water was not going to be a problem.

About the same time he reached that conclusion, another set of tubes started coming down from the "sky" outside the dome.

* * *

Matt Sheehan walked north on First Avenue, past the Bellevue Medical Center, its white glazed brick reflecting the artificial sunlight. He had thought about getting a ride, but the low gravity made walking a fairly efficient way to get around. His knees twinged a bit due to the lunar-walk motion, but otherwise his body felt fine. From his belt hung a small walkie-talkie.

He had come north through Chinatown. At Chatham Square the statue of Confucius had been surrounded by people who apparently felt that would be as good as anyplace to find answers to the obvious questions. No one had been using the pagoda-shaped phone booths, but the exotic-vegetable vendors had been swamped as they tried to pack up their products.

Matt suddenly checked his watch to make sure it really was still morning, assuming "morning" meant anything anymore. The "sun's" position made it feel like afternoon, but it wasn't.

He had passed Bellevue Hospital minutes earlier. The frequency of passing ambulances wailing like huge mechanical babies made it obvious they were busily dealing with people who'd been on the perimeter when the city was cut loose. What wouldn't be as audible was the process of dealing with all the people who must be suffering psychological problems that would be just as damaging, if not as immediately life threatening.

All along his walk, he had seen glimpses of crowds to the east, pressed against the base of the dome, peering out at the other domed cities. From a distance the throngs looked like spectators merely curious about a construction project. He'd be willing to bet that almost every one of them would pay a year's salary to be able to get a glimpse of the dirty East River. Once in a while someone in the back ranks would jump straight up. Matt wasn't sure whether the jumping was to get a better view or simple experimentation.

A couple of kids rode their bicycles past Matt very carefully. The low gravity reduced the tire friction enough that turning and stopping looked difficult, and the kids seemed nervous. Perhaps they just didn't want to leave their bikes wherever they had been. Walking seemed a much better way of getting around now.

Once Matt adjusted to the new walking motion, he began to function almost on automatic, wondering what the hell had happened and why. But despite trying to concentrate on what should have been by far the biggest issue, his thoughts kept going back to Nadine.

Matt should have worried more, he supposed, when she hadn't objected to being transferred to Cairo, when the assignment to Argentina would have left open the possibility that they could get together if there was a break in the war. At the time, he'd just assumed she was as fed up as he was with the no-win drug wars that few people here seemed to appreciate.

He'd felt numb since that call a few days ago. Today, he felt a stronger sense of purpose than he had in quite a while, but even that wasn't enough to keep his mind totally occupied. He continued north, passing more war-zone streets of stalled traffic and confused pedestrians. Sirens near the entrance to the Queen-Midtown Tunnel brought his thoughts back to the city.

At the intersection of First Avenue and 40th Street, a red Terra sports car almost ran him down as it careened up First, zigzagged around stopped buses and trucks, and swung onto 40th, its tires skittering across the pavement, rather than screeching. The car almost flipped over in the lighter gravity. The driver gave Matt a rude gesture as though Matt should have known the car was coming and should, therefore, have waited inside.

When Matt reached the enormous lobby of the U.N. General Assembly Building, it was nearly empty. A baffled-looking guard watched warily as Matt approached. Matt was still surprised to see so many people functioning on automatic. Apparently New York had less than its share of people who folded up completely under emergencies.

"Yeah?" said the guard.

"I've just come up from the mayor's office. I need to locate several translators."

"Yeah?" said the guard. A couple of his shirt buttons looked close to popping. The man's eyes looked glazed.

Matt decided maybe this guy wasn't functioning quite as well as he had thought at first. "Yeah. Can you tell me where I'd be likely to find them?"

"Kinda slow day here."

"Yeah." Matt hesitated. He was convinced now that the man was shell-shocked. The man's eyes were virtually motionless except for an occasional blink, and his features were fixed in a permanent state of confusion. He was reacting to stimuli, but taking no action on his own.

Matt said, "Okay, I'm going to look around, see if I can find some translators. This is official city business. You got a problem—" Matt caught himself and quickly rephrased the question. "Ah, that should be okay, don't you think?"

The guard said, "Yeah."

Matt was about to give up when a blond woman in a windbreaker and carrying a collapsible umbrella pushed open a door to Hammarskjold Library.

"Are you perhaps a translator?" he asked.

The woman glanced up toward the dome. "Well, yes. But I don't have any experience in translating for aliens."

"Well, then, I'm afraid you won't do us any good. We need people with at least five years' experience."

The woman was silent for a moment. "You don't know me well enough to tease me." Her voice held a hint of British English.

Matt blinked, then smiled. "You're perfectly right. I have no idea why I did that."

The woman smiled back, revealing even white teeth. Her gray eyes gave her expression a questioning look containing more ease than anyone Matt had seen that day. She hesitated, then said, "I might be able to help."

"You really *are* a translator, then?"

"Is twelve languages enough? I'm really only qualified in five of them, but I can at least read the others."

"You're teasing me now."

"No, I am not."

Matt smiled. "My name is Matt Sheehan."

"Mine is Abby Tersa. And I don't think you actually want translators if you want to talk to the aliens. You want linguists or cultural anthropologists. Translators just use what they've been taught. You want someone who can figure out a *new* language, I assume."

"Oh. But you—"

"You're in luck. I love the nature of languages, and my primary background is cultural anthropology. I had to take a fair number of linguistics courses on the way. Actually, I was just doing a little moonlighting as a translator."

"Well, good. You're hired." He paused. "I don't mean to be rude, but we need as many people as possible."

"No offense taken. I can put up a notice in the translators' conference room where people are more likely to see it when they calm down."

"Terrific."

Abby disappeared inside and was back in a couple of minutes. "What now?"

"I'm on foot. Can you handle the walk to the Municipal Building?"

With a smile Abby said, "I think so."

Matt and Abby had almost reached Houston Street on their way south when someone threw a large empty packing box into their path.

The slow-motion, long-stride gait they had assumed gave Matt time to see what was coming, but no way to react. His feet hit the box, which promptly spun underfoot, and he went down, skidding in the low gravity. From a recessed doorway emerged four grubby young men in their late teens or early twenties. Two of the four had knives in their hands.

Matt tumbled slowly, his inertia complicating recovery. It took him less than a second to realize that any money in his wallet was virtually worthless. These guys must have a different target: Abby. They'd try to put him out of commission, then move in on her.

"Keep running!" he yelled to Abby. He tucked his body as he approached the sidewalk and rolled on one shoulder, then onto his back. He came to a kneeling position a moment later, by which time the men were moving toward him as fast as they could in the underwater mode forced by the low gravity. Matt stood up, and just as quickly sat down again. All four men were moving quickly enough and awkwardly enough that they windmilled right by him. Matt managed to hit one man's calf as he sped past, and the man went into a slow spin that made him hit the sidewalk face first.

Matt cursed himself. He should have figured that part of the population would be the kind to take advantage of a situation like this rather than going home and waiting for word about what was going on. With four of them, he needed a smaller playing field. He turned, took a couple of steps, and leaped high, hoping his instincts would be good enough. His body arced into the air, carrying him an easy couple of meters higher than the top of the stalled bus he had aimed for. He tilted forward, windmilling wildly to keep from going over face forward, and just in time his feet landed on the roof of the bus. He bounced and skidded and came to a stop centimeters from the edge of the slick roof.

The thugs weren't very smart; the first one came alone. The guy in the dirty brown sweatshirt jumped up as awkwardly as Matt had. Matt feinted and punched the guy in the nose, and the guy started a slow-motion spin back to the ground. Matt tipped backward for a couple of seconds before he regained his balance.

Two of the thugs, one with a knife, jumped up simultaneously. They started to approach warily, and behind him Matt heard another pair of feet dimple the bus roof as they landed.

3

SIGNALS AND NOISE

THE ROOF OF the bus had about the same area as a boxing ring, but here the edges of combat territory bordered on a steep drop to hard pavement.

At the sound of the feet behind him on the bus roof, Matt turned, wanting to deal first with the single attacker. But the person behind him wasn't the other thug; it was Abby Tersa. She held her collapsed umbrella ready to use as a weapon. Her blond hair slowly settled beside her face in the light gravity, and anger had reached those cool gray eyes.

Matt turned back to the two approaching men. Both of them looked as if they had last shaved four days ago without help from a mirror. One of them held a knife. Another good sign that Matt was dealing with amateurs—the knife was on the inside. The man wouldn't be able to take a wide swing without damaging his partner beside him. That handicap would be wasted if Matt took his partner out first, so Matt concentrated on the knife.

The man with the knife moved ahead of his companion, possibly figuring that he'd use his weapon to soften up Matt first so his buddy wouldn't have to work up much of a sweat. He moved toward Matt, but his companion moved to catch up, holding almost even with him.

Matt moved suddenly and directly for the knife-wielder. Surprise flashed across the man's dark eyes, and he made a feint with the knife. Matt took a calculated risk, and the second time the man lunged, Matt crouched sideways and kicked one foot hard toward the man's kneecap.

The kick connected. In the low gravity, Matt's recoil tipped him over, but the man he'd kicked was no immediate threat.

Matt had heard no grinding crunch when his kick connected, so the man probably wasn't going to suffer any permanent damage, but he was off-balance and definitely in pain. He lurched in a small circle, like a bear with one foot in a trap, until he fell off the bus, his knife flying away in a graceful arc. Matt got back to his feet while the remaining man was still watching his partner's slow-motion spill.

The man's unarmed companion looked so shocked, Matt decided the time was right for some psychology. Simultaneously Matt grinned with the intensity of someone absolutely certain of a favorable outcome, moved toward the man confidently, and slowly reached inside his jacket. That was enough for the remaining man. He turned and took a running leap from the roof of the bus to the roof of a stopped car and kept going.

Matt turned toward Abby, relieved that they were unhurt. As she took a step toward him, the fourth thug sprang into view. He had also jumped too high, and his arc carried him and his knife in a trajectory toward Abby. The man was tilting forward a little, obviously no more experienced in low-gravity jumping than they were.

Matt started to move closer to where the man was going to land, but Abby beat him to it. Just as the man approached the edge of the bus roof, Abby sent a strong high kick directly into the man's stomach. The air whooshed from his lungs, and the knife went flying harmlessly away.

The man hit the corner of the bus roof. If he'd been able to draw a breath already, the impact would have left him breathless all over again. He grimaced in pain as he slid off the roof.

When Abby had kicked, she had lost her balance. She hopped on one leg, tilting into a backward series of hops that merely postponed her eventual fall. "Oh, no!" she cried.

Matt caught her just before she hopped backward off the roof of the bus. Abby wrapped her arms around him tightly and shuddered.

Abby's hair smelled fresh. Matt pushed a loose strand back into place. A long moment later, Abby let go. "Ah, sorry," she said.

"My pleasure." Matt smiled. "You do that sort of thing a lot?"

Abby shook her head, and her blond hair swirled slowly.

Together they moved to the edge of the roof where the man had fallen. He lay on the ground, groaning loudly. From his position, it was obvious that his fall had been interrupted by a fire hydrant. In normal gravity, he might well have suffered a broken back. Probably now he just felt as though he had one.

A small crowd gathered on the sidewalk as Matt used his walkie-talkie to tell the police they were needed. When he finished, Matt glanced at Abby and said, "Going down?"

Abby nodded and together they leaped. As they floated back to the ground, Matt recalled a slow-motion jumping image from the remake of *The Six Million Dollar Man.*

Stuart Lund awoke in a hospital bed and realized almost instantly that his right hand was gone. Severed at about a thirty-degree angle at the wrist, the stump was covered with something that looked like a thin layer of gauze. He stared at the stump for a long moment, then out of curiosity imagined the hand was still there and tried to make a fist. The action sent pain into his wrist. He felt a muscle tighten in his forearm and then relax.

With his arm still in the air, he looked around. The long room was filled with the constant commotion of a too-busy staff trying to deal with all the problems of patients occupying two long rows of beds, but Stuart paid almost no attention to his present surroundings.

A series of images raced unbidden through his brain. On the subway, he had been taking advantage of the crush of people to rest his right hand against the derriere of an attractive woman farther back in the car. He could still feel the pain where the hand had been cleaved from his wrist.

He had regained consciousness while resting on the subway platform and the first thing he saw when he opened his eyes was the REPENT! sign in the row of advertisements.

Stuart had never been a strongly religious man. In fact, he hated the times when his aunt used to force him to attend services at the Church of Modern Christian Discipline.

The sign right next to the REPENT sign had been a ballet advertisement proclaiming, DANCE ALL YOU CAN BE, but Stuart felt certain God hadn't been trying to tell him to become a dancer.

But there was no denying what had happened to him. God had intervened in an unmistakable way. God had cut off his hand to say, "Sin no more," but God had left Stuart alive and had shown him the REPENT! sign for some reason. Stuart didn't feel he knew a lot about God, but he did know from Albert Einstein that God didn't play dice. God must have a definite purpose for Stuart.

But what was it?

Rudy Sanchez looked over the Pier 17 pumping installation with satisfaction. A hose ran from the bird-feeder into a generator-driven pump, which sent a steady flow into a nearby fire hydrant. The hose vibrated with the rush of liquid. The "sun" had traveled about 180 degrees around the city since it had come on, and about six hours had passed. Unlike the real sun, this one provided no radiant warmth. Moving from shade to "sunlight" made no change in the temperature, which was a steady twenty-five degrees Celsius everywhere air moved freely.

"That's good," Rudy said to Victor Krunkale, a waterworks supervisor, a big man with hands so large that Rudy imagined he had a hard time buttoning his shirt. "Can you get your team to install at least another ten setups like this? Then we'll make some measurements and see if we've got enough capacity. And I want constant monitoring. The samples tested fine, but we may need to worry about purification if anything changes."

"It will take me three shifts," Victor said. "We had lots of no-shows today."

"Whatever it takes. Maybe the fire threat will be lower since no one's using natural gas, but if we get a bad fire, people are going to need water even more than they already do." Rudy turned to Nicholas Dunte, who had been waiting for the last few minutes. "Okay, let's go see this thing you're talking about."

Nicholas gestured toward the cherry-picker. They got in and the driver took them southwest past a few severed piers. Before they reached the place Nicholas had told him about, Rudy suddenly asked the driver to stop. He got out and approached a discolored spot at the base of the bubble. "Just a sec."

Rudy knelt in front of the patch that had caught his eye. For a moment he just looked through the clear bubble at the flat plain beyond. From here he used to be able to see Squibb Park in Brooklyn. Outside the enclosed city, the featureless gray surface was unbroken except by other domes. Rudy couldn't see signs of motion in the nearest dome, one with scores of multicolored spires. The plain itself had the texture of matte-finish paint. It showed no reflections, just a uniform gray surface that could have been diamond hard or bubble-gum soft. The surface of the plain was roughly even with ground level, so the subterranean portion of Manhattan had to be embedded in the gray stuff.

Rudy looked more closely at the base of the bubble itself. In most places the clear surface extended straight into the slit between the city and the flat gray plain. Here, however, the bubble gradually blackened as it approached the ground. Level with the concrete Rudy knelt on, the bubble was black. Between there and the clear section seemed to be a boundary layer, where what looked to be two kinds of materials flowed together, establishing a strong bond.

The seam reminded Rudy of tinted sunglasses, the kind that were clear at the bottom and dark at the top, but when he ran his fingers over the surface he could tell the texture change was more significant than mere tinting. Above the boundary layer, the dome felt perfectly smooth and slick, like clean glass. Just above ground level, the black surface was slightly rough, and it felt like wrought iron.

Next to him, Rudy saw that Nicholas had found a loose piece of packing material to kneel on. Nicholas was one of the most capable city workers under Rudy, and he was also probably the most fastidious.

Rudy got his knife from his pocket and applied the blade to the black surface. He pushed hard on the knife and drew the blade along the surface. When he looked closely, he could see no sign that the blade had made any impression.

"Got any theories?" Rudy asked.

Nicholas ran his fingers over the clear part and then over the black section. He pulled a handkerchief from a pocket and cleaned off his fingers as he thought. Finally he said, "Two possibilities occur to me. One, this section of the bubble has been damaged somehow. Two, the bubble doesn't go all the way down to bedrock. They must have supported the section of earth they excavated to ensure the island wouldn't fall apart when they lifted us. Perhaps the black material is what was used below ground, and what we see here is the region where it was fused into the bubble material."

Rudy stood up and realized they had attracted a small crowd of curious onlookers. "Okay," he said to Nicholas. "How much farther is this other tube?"

Nicholas got back up and looked southwest. "Not far. We're halfway there already."

They traveled a minute or two in the cherry-picker, then the driver stopped, and they got out. Nicholas pointed up at a large silvery circle where a smaller opaque hose met the side of the dome.

Rudy and Nicholas rode the cherry-picker cage upward to the spot. The cage hung in the air, vibrating slightly as Rudy took a closer look. Inside the large silvery circle were four more circles, two medium ones side-by-side on top, each with a small circle directly below it. The large circles were a somewhat darker shade of silver.

The two smaller circles seemed to be controls. Around the perimeter of each of the smaller circles was a series of dots, a little like minute marks on an analog watch. In the "clock" on the right, the dot at two o'clock glowed. In the "clock" on the left, a dot near three o'clock blinked on and off.

After examining the array of circles, Rudy finally said to Nicholas, "Are you thinking what I'm thinking?"

"Probably. If you're thinking about electricity."

As Rudy nodded, Nicholas took a multimeter from a pocket in his overalls. He wiped some lint off the display face and handed it to Rudy. "You want to do the honors?"

"How about if we each take one lead?"

Nicholas took the red lead and Rudy took the black. Rudy set the multimeter to "volts" and they each extended their probes to the large circles above the "clocks."

"You feel that?" Rudy asked. He pulled the probe away from the silver circle and let it snap back again.

"Yeah, it feels like a magnet. But I really don't believe these probes are ferromagnetic."

Both men let their probes just hang from the silver circles.

"Forty-two volts at eleven Hertz," Rudy said a moment later even though Nicholas could easily read the display. A small green light on the multimeter stayed on steadily, indicating a clean sine wave. "You want to try the adjustment on your side? Here, this pen is pretty well insulated."

"Thanks anyway." Nicholas took a long plastic adjusting tool from his pocket. Carefully he reached forward and pressed the plastic tip against the dot next to the one that glowed. The glowing dot went out, and the one Nicholas touched came on, glowing slightly brighter.

The display said a little over fifty volts. "All right!" Rudy said. "Do it again."

The next step up was about sixty volts. Nicholas poked one dot after another until they got 104 volts, then 125 and 150. Rudy set the meter on the lip of the cherry-picker cage, and Nicholas kept going as each successive light got brighter and brighter until the voltage rose to the point where the two men didn't trust the meter leads to insulate safely, so Nicholas set the voltage back to 125.

"Can I use that?" Rudy asked.

Nicholas handed him the insulated tool, and Rudy pushed the dot next to the blinking dot. The blinking one went out, and the one Rudy pushed started blinking faster than the previous one. The meter said the new frequency was 13.2 Hertz. In a series of steps, Rudy took the frequency up to about fifty-seven Hertz and then a little over sixty-eight Hertz as the lights flashed faster. As a final test, he made sure he could get up to 440 Hertz.

"I think we're in business," Rudy said. "We should be able to do anything from wall-socket to substation. We'll probably have a little extra work dealing with two-phase instead of three, but I think we can get from here to there." He reached to pull the meter leads loose, but they stayed where they were. "I'll be damned," he said, and looked closer. The leads seemed to have been pushed into the surface of the silvery circle. By pulling with steady pressure for several seconds, he was able to get the leads back out. The silvery surface looked totally smooth and unblemished.

Nicholas looked closely, too, then raised his eyebrows.

Rudy pushed the controls to lower the cage to the ground, not far from still more onlookers. When the cage reached the pavement, Nicholas let Rudy swing the gate open, no doubt to keep his hands from getting dirty.

Abby Tersa was looking out the window of Rudy's office when he returned. Matt was sitting at Rudy's desk with the Manhattan yellow directory on the portable computer's screen.

"Hello," Abby said.

Rudy unsnapped an equipment belt and set it on the corner of the desk. "Hi." He wiped sweat from his forehead. "Those stairs are murder. Thank God the gravity is low." He came closer to Abby. "And you are . . . ?"

"Abby Tersa." She shook Rudy's hand as Rudy gave her his name.

"Abby's our first translator—er, make that linguist," Matt said. "How's it going so far for you?"

"So far, so good. I've got several teams working on water and power. We may have water to midtown in six or eight hours, and water in most areas in a day. I just pulled back the team working on the Con Ed generator up north, because we're being provided electricity, too. My guess is, we'll be ready to turn on switches during the next day or two. The biggest problem is recycling high-voltage cable—taking sections from where they're no longer needed to where we need them."

Matt said, "There are some other problems. You know of any way to make food from nothing but water and electricity? Every place I saw selling food had a line long enough to buy them out. And I suppose stuff in freezers is spoiling all over the city."

Abby spoke up. "What are people using for money?"

Matt shook his head. "I think it's a variety of things. Drugs, cigarettes, sex. Some people are apparently using actual money. I guess I'm not as optimistic as they are that we'll get back to a place where money will be any good, but who knows?"

Abby said, "If they're supplying water and electricity, don't you think they'll supply everything?"

Matt and Rudy looked at each other as though deciding who got to answer. Matt said, "My guess is you're right. I just hate not knowing. And if people get too hungry, there's going to be even worse panic."

Rudy said, "I agree. And I'm hungry, too."

Matt looked at his watch. "Okay, so what do you say to Windows on the World? With a hundred stories to climb, we shouldn't have much competition."

Rudy nodded. "Sounds good to me. What about you, Abby? Hungry?"

Abby scrutinized the two men. Both looked quite serious. "No, why don't you go without me?"

Matt said, "We can't have that. How about if we eat in, instead?"

"Well, all right," Rudy said, as though he were making a huge sacrifice. He walked to a vertical two-door cabinet and flung the doors open. "So, what's your pleasure? Breakfast cereal, pop-morsels, cookies, a banana or an orange?"

Abby approached the cabinet with amazement. Every shelf was fully loaded with food, including several choices of tea, crackers, Tangy-Treats, and a huge supply of microwaveable EverLast snacks. "Did you get some warning that this was going to happen?"

Rudy shook his head. "I'm here a lot of hours. I just decided I might as well be comfortable."

Matt said, "He's a workaholic."

"And you're not?" Rudy grabbed a banana and started to peel it.

Suddenly hungry, Abby took an orange. "You two are old friends?"

"What is it now?" Matt said. "Fifteen years?"

"Something like that." Rudy took a bite of his banana. "So, what were you doing when I came in?"

Matt glanced at the screen. "We're making a shopping list. Most of it won't do much good until we get power. Oh, that reminds me. Can you put in a request with the mayor to give us a floor on one of the World Trade Center towers, near the top?"

"A whole floor?"

"As much as we can get of one, anyway. I'm sure a fair amount of the towers will be used for transient housing, but it's not like a whole lot of world trade is going to be happening, right?"

"True. What for?"

Matt pointed at the window and the domes beyond. "I'm feeling a little voyeuristic."

The walkie-talkie on Dorine Underwood's desk crackled, and Barnaby Jolliet's voice came over the speaker virtually interference free, thanks to the inactivity of most local sources of electrical noise. "Mayor?"

Dorine picked up her unit and pressed *talk.* "I'm here." She turned off the portable computer she was using to compile to-do lists and turned to face the window as she talked. The "sun" had traveled almost 360 degrees since it had come on twelve hours ago.

"The megaphone team has reached the north end again, and they're ready for the next sweep. They were delayed by some more looting on 47th Street, but things seem under control for now. Any changed information you want to be in the new broadcast?"

Dorine didn't need to look at her notes. "Yes. The water pressure in midtown, including Bellevue, is reported to be adequate for moderate use. Anyone concerned about dehydration can get help there, but tell them to stay where they are if they can. Water should be available almost everywhere by noon tomorrow.

"Power will probably be restored to the Civic Center area and to midtown by sometime late tonight. Other areas will follow over a period of about two days. Anyone with industrial power experience who's willing to volunteer to be on a work crew so we can get more power up faster should meet at Times Square at midnight or six A.M. Nothing else right now."

"Got it. Thanks."

Without taking her eyes off the window, Dorine reached behind her and set the walkie-talkie back on her desk. By her watch, the city had managed for about twelve hours, and it was still intact. Of course, they really had no idea yet how many people might have been killed on the perimeter of the city, or had jumped from windows, or were now going quietly out of their minds.

As she sat at her desk, exhausted, the "sun" went out.

The first thing Dorine realized was that one of the two nearest emergency lights had gone dead after this long without a charge. The second thing was that the "sun" hadn't actually gone completely out. It was still where it had been, but now it was much dimmer. As her eyes adjusted, she realized the light's intensity now made it an artificial full moon.

The "sun" had been too bright to look at, so the illusion was adequate as long as she didn't think about its circular path, but the "moon" was an outright fake. No craters, no dark seas, just a uniform dull silver like a distant porthole in a huge ship. Dorine felt her face grow warmer.

Dorine got up and closed her office door and locked it. She went back to her desk, sat down, and put her head down on Rafael's picture. Only a minute later in the big and lonely dark room, beneath the light of a silvery moon, she cried.

Abby Tersa woke in darkness. For an instant, she didn't know where she was or what had wakened her. Then she recognized the dark outlines of a desk, a bookcase, and a couple of file cabinets. She was in an unused office down the hall from Rudy Sanchez, lying on an uncomfortable cot. Then the rest of it came back to her, and she suddenly felt lost, helpless.

Immediately she forced away the feelings, swung her legs over the edge of the cot, and stood up. At the window was the same view of the darkened financial district, lit only by the glimmer of the huge lamp traveling around the city, still on the dim setting. Motion on the ground caught her eye.

On Chambers Street a group of eight or ten people walked through the silent street. Puzzled, Abby watched as they approached one of the cars abandoned near the center of the street. The group surrounded the car, one at each corner, one at each side, and one in the middle of each bumper.

As though on signal, their heads all dipped. An instant later the car moved sideways toward the curb. They were carrying the car. Automobile theft was suddenly much easier than it had been. But what could people do with the cars?

When the car was fairly close to the cabs and trucks already at the side of the road, the group set the car down on the pavement and walked up the street toward the next one in the middle of the street.

At the same instant that Abby understood the group wasn't stealing cars, but was in fact clearing the roads, a deep-throated rumbling noise sounded for a second and then stopped. The fluorescent lights overhead began to glow, but went off again before lighting fully. That was what had wakened her. Now that the air conditioning fans were off again, the building once more seemed artificially quiet.

As she looked back out the window, the rumbling started again, and the overhead lights came on. Lights in City Hall came on, and lights along Chambers and Lafayette and Park Row came on, too. A whole little section of Manhattan had power.

Across the island, the twin towers of the World Trade Center remained black.

Abby checked her watch. Almost five A.M. She moved to the cot and slipped into her shoes, then opened the office door. She started toward Rudy's office, but stopped as she reached the open doorway to the office Matt occupied. From the doorway Abby could see Matt staring through the window into the darkness beyond, as though he were oblivious to the newly restored power.

She wasn't sure if the attraction to him was sexual or maternal. He was an unusual mix of strength and vulnerability. He made decisions easily and quickly, but she knew something was bothering him a lot, something beyond the obvious predicament.

Abby knocked lightly on the door frame. Matt didn't respond. She knocked harder, and this time he turned around.

"Oh, hi," he said.

"Good morning."

"Morning."

"Are you all right?" she asked.

"Sure, fine. Just fine."

Sometimes people can lie convincingly, but Matt didn't seem to have the energy to try. Abby didn't believe him.

"I think I see a tube that wasn't there yesterday," Rudy said. He squinted at the dome wall. He was almost positive that dark hose was new. "I need to go investigate. Can you guard the fort until I get back?" He moved quickly to grab his tool belt.

Abby looked up from the small photo of the message on the dome roof. "Sure. If the phones start ringing or if any other linguists show up, we still need all the help we can get, right?"

"Right. And Matt should be back in an hour or so, I think."

"No problem." Abby hesitated. "Is he all right?"

"Matt? Sure, as much as any of us are. And he's been through some pretty tough stuff and come out fine. Why do you ask?" Rudy buckled the belt.

"No reason." Abby wasn't sure why she lied.

Rudy started for the door. As he was almost through it, Abby asked, "Does he have any family left behind?"

"His wife," he called behind him, thinking more about the new hose than anything else.

The hose *was* new. It met the dome near the East River Park, just south of the severed end of the Williamsburg Bridge.

Rudy drove onto the grass. As he got close enough to see that the hose was equipped with a bird-feeder tub, too, a cherry-picker drove up and Nicholas stepped down from the driver's seat. "You saw it, too, huh?" Nicholas said.

"Yep."

They stepped into the cage and Nicholas hit the controls. Rudy looked at Nicholas's bloodshot eyes and said, "Didn't you get *any* sleep last night?" Rudy had gotten the four hours that he'd recommended to everyone on the crews. The "sun" had come back on at the same time and position it had gone on the first time, so the pattern was obvious: one twelve-hour rotation on "sun" and one twelve-hour rotation on "moon."

"I know what you said," Nicholas said, "but I just can't sleep at all as long as the problems we've got aren't solved. Haven't you ever been so upset you couldn't sleep?"

"Yeah, but these problems are bound to last longer than I can go without sleep."

The cage reached the brown bird-feeder and Nicholas slowed their approach. He stopped a foot from the edge. "Why do they put these things so high?"

"No idea. Unless they think we're much taller. Or they figure the height keeps the masses away so they don't cause any damage or get hurt while experts figure out how to hook up internal systems."

"What internal systems do we have that interface to Rabbit Chow?"

"That's sure what it looks like, isn't it?" The tub must have held a hundred liters of small green stubby cylinders smaller than pencil erasers. Rudy bent over for a closer look. The tiny cylinders had the mottled color of old green linoleum, with mirror-smooth curved sides and flat non-reflecting ends, as though the little pellets were extruded from tiny tubes in the larger hose, and sliced off every centimeter as the material came into the tub.

With one hand, Rudy scooped air in the direction of his nose to try to sense the odor without getting an undiluted dose that could conceivably be dangerous. He smelled nothing.

Rudy took a piece of paper from his pocket. With one end he scooped up five of the pellets. As they rested in the curve of the page, he carefully folded the paper several times.

Nicholas said, "They've taken care of air and water. Don't you suppose this is intended to be food?"

"Yep. But I'm not sticking that in my mouth until I'm sure it's safe."

"But people are running out of food already. You want to wait until the lab checks it before setting up a way to handle distribution?"

"No. I think you're right. I just want to play safe. There's nothing wrong with working both in parallel. But let me make a call and get a cop car to take this up to Bellevue so that's not the critical path."

Nicholas nodded, and Rudy used his walkie-talkie to make the request.

"So," Rudy said when he was finished. "What are the choices?"

"Well, we can't pump this stuff like water. And depending on how concentrated it is, it may take a lot of work to shovel and deliver. We could maybe get some industrial vacuuming equipment and beef it up to get the stuff out of here. I'm not sure about transportation. Too bad there weren't a bunch of tanker trucks in the city."

A police siren in the distance came closer and closer. Rudy gazed north for a moment and said, "You know, we *do* have a lot of cement mixers."

The ringing phone startled Julie Kravine.

When power had been restored to the WNBC offices a few hours earlier, she had immediately tried the phones. Dead. Her next action was to start recharging her minivid batteries.

The sound of the phone ringing in her own cubicle was reassuring, a touchstone that for an instant could let her block out the reality beyond the short, tan walls.

"WNBC, Julie Kravine," she said into the mouthpiece.

"Hi. This is Matt Sheehan. We met on the subway."

"Hello. How are you doing?"

"Fine. I'm assisting in the city manager's office. I want to ask you for two favors. I probably should have talked to the station manager or something, but this seemed easier."

"Shoot."

"One, power's up everywhere but the Heights and Chelsea, and they think they'll get those problems solved in the next few hours. You may have heard already, but a work crew has just finished checking out a link from your studios to an antenna on the World Trade Center. We'd like you to start broadcasting the message that at eight P.M. the mayor will address the city, and we'd like you to get a video link set up so she can talk from her office."

"You got it. I'll need to do some coordinating, but we'll do it. What's your number?"

Matt gave it to her.

"Okay, what's the second thing?"

"I need to borrow a bunch of video cameras with long lenses

and a bunch of other video gear. A cop car with a truck can be there in an hour."

"Gonna be doing some big-time home videos?"

"In a sense."

Dorine Underwood sat at her desk at a few minutes before eight P.M. Behind her a sign listed the audio channels viewers could turn to for the five languages her speech would be translated into. The overhead office lights and the light spilling in from the hallway provided more comfort than she had realized they might, somehow being unmistakable signs that life went on. She hoped her presence on TV screens in the city would be a similar reassurance for the residents. That would be possible only if she was calm and matter-of-fact, so she took a couple of deep breaths and glanced at her notes again.

"Madam Mayor, you're on in ten seconds," said one of the television crew. Six broadcasting organizations were represented tonight. The man counted down on his fingers . . . three, two, one. The red light came on.

"Good evening, my fellow New Yorkers." Dorine looked into the lens and spoke coolly. "I don't have to tell you how strange the situation in which we find ourselves is. In fact we still don't know the true extent of what's happening to us. I'll tell you the official view, just so you don't worry too much about whether you're personally going crazy, as I know I felt for a little while. At seven-ten A.M. Eastern Standard Time on Tuesday, March twentieth, 2012, Manhattan was somehow cut loose from its surroundings and taken, presumably by some very advanced race of aliens, into a huge ship. Whether we're here as part of a zoo exhibit, or these aliens thought they were doing the equivalent of removing a tumor, we don't have the faintest idea. I'm sure we'll find out.

"What I'm here to tell you tonight is that we are coping. As you hear these words, every district in Manhattan now has electricity and water. Natural gas is apparently going to be unavailable for the duration, as is steam. Crews have been out around the clock, rewiring substations, adjusting valves to equalize water pressure, putting out fires, and shutting gas valves to prevent any more accidents with the gas still in the pipes. We have no way of obtaining further supplies of gasoline, so its use is restricted to authorized emergency and police vehicles and occasional official business uses such as transporting equipment needed for utility operations. Anyone using such vehicles is urged to use them *only* if equivalent electric vehicles are truly unavailable.

"Food is probably of primary importance to everyone, and I want to tell you there is food available, and there's enough for everyone. No one will go hungry. What we will be is bored.

"I'm sure you realize we don't have the facilities or the raw material to manufacture enough food for everyone in Manhattan. The supply we do have is being furnished by our captors, as is the electricity and water we are using. We have no alternative. The food the aliens are providing has been run through exhaustive testing by doctors at Bellevue. It contains more calcium than most of us will need, but not so much that it's unsafe.

"Twenty minutes after I stop talking, and that won't be too long now, city cement trucks are going to start an around-the-clock sweep through the city, stopping at every intersection. They're carrying loads of small nutrient pills." Dorine much preferred that designation to "Rabbit Chow."

"The Bellevue doctors have determined that an average adult can subsist on about a half-liter per day. Anyone can take up to a liter every time a truck comes around, and we believe the supply to be unlimited. We'll be working on better delivery methods, but for now, at least we can all eat. I'm sure that you're going to find this whole process irritating, from the food itself to the delivery method. But we *have* to have food, and it has to be distributed quickly. This is our only choice.

"I do have some requests. I know that natural food already in the city is going to be more appetizing than what we're being provided, and I fully expect it will be eaten. What I ask is that you donate any unopened soft food you have to any area hospital so it can be available for the very young and for the sick and injured. In addition, we need to consolidate all extra supplies of medication, to make sure medicine is available for emergencies and so that until it's needed it's carefully stored for longevity."

Dorine put aside a page of paper and looked at the next sheet. "Other needs exist; I know that and you know that. One of those needs is housing for people who don't live in Manhattan. At the end of this broadcast will be a series of phone numbers for people to call. City employees will be standing by, ready to coordinate referrals to area hotels and businesses. If you have space for a visitor in your home or apartment, please let us know.

"Another need is information. I know you want to know what's going on, as do I. I'll have a status update at this same time and channel every night. I'll tell you the key things we've learned. Probably highest on that list is whether we are contacted by our captors, or if we can translate the message on the dome above us. Also following this broadcast will be a series of telephone numbers where you can ask questions you'd like to see me answer. The most-asked questions that we find answers to will be handled every night.

"City employees have been working around the clock to make essential services available to you. I think they've done a tremendous job. And now I need to ask for your help. We need special skills in a variety of areas, and again there will be numbers to call after this telecast. First of all we need to decipher the message from our captors. Any expert linguists or cultural anthropologists, or people with experience in cryptography or mathematics are desperately needed. In addition, we can use any experts in communications systems, video image analysis, and physics, as we try to learn as much as we can about our new environment. If you've got those skills, please call and give us a summary of your abilities. And tell us how to reach you so we can do that when the need arises. We also need more volunteers to help with city utility support, and we need volunteer firefighters.

"Finally, I want to say how much pride I have in you all. We've gone through a terrible misfortune, and although I've seen reports of looting and crimes against persons, by far the majority of you have reacted admirably, by helping people in trouble, by sharing personal property and resources available to you, and by generously aiding strangers. That makes me very proud. And I want you to know that law and order has been restored. The fire department is ready to roll, and all hospital emergency numbers and hot lines are functional.

"You have all done a splendid job of coping, and I'll pass on news of any new developments as they happen.

"Good night, Manhattan."

Dr. Bobby Joe Brewster turned down the sound on his small office TV.

He leaned back in his chair and put his feet on the desk, still amazed at how much quieter the Columbia campus was now. He considered what the mayor had said. It would be an interesting challenge to try to decode alien transmissions, if that was the goal.

He glanced at his computer. Cut off from Earth, he'd be deprived of his constant supply of new programs and upgrades. That had to be the worst aspect of this entire mess. The sooner they established communications, the sooner they could return to Earth, perhaps.

Bobby Joe had grown up doing everything at a younger age than expected, so he had acquired a fair amount of public modesty to reduce the jealousy of people he was overtaking. Now wasn't the time for modesty, though. He was very likely to be one of the best people in the dome for what the mayor had talked about.

He took his feet off the desk and leaned forward to reach the loop recorder on the desktop. He had it perpetually recording so he could always repeat anything from the previous thirty minutes. He touched the *reverse* control and sped the image back until the phone numbers came up on the small screen. When he found the right number, he froze the image.

As he picked up the phone, he felt excited. If they got back to Earth, he could go back to eating real food.

Matt stepped out of the elevator onto the 105th floor, five floors below the observation deck on the southern tower of the World Trade Center, just as thankful as he could be that the power had been restored.

The hallway was quiet as he turned toward the south wall, but the sounds of activity from inside a large office ahead grew louder as he approached. He entered the room. Near the windows was a group of journalists, some with their lenses directed at the scenery outside, some focused on the activity at the center of the room, all of them under strict notice that any disruption to the workers would mean immediate expulsion.

The room reminded him of a combat operations center, with large wall-screens covering most surfaces, but no combat operations center he'd ever been in had a view like that out the south window. For a moment, he ignored the activity in the room and walked to the window. From here, the reflections from the top of the bubble were only a hundred meters away, and Matt knew the bubble almost touched the WTC observation deck not too far over his head.

A dozen bubbles poked out of the gray plain below. Two of them rose even higher than the World Trade Center. In each bubble, the ground was roughly level with the plain. Matt drew in his breath involuntarily even though he had seen these domes before. One dome contained what looked to be a large hill with bluish grass-covered slopes and scattered black spots that Matt assumed to be cave or tunnel openings. No recognizable sign of intelligent life showed on the surface.

The strangest enclosed habitat, to Matt's naked eye, was an impossibly tall and thin bubble surrounding a trio of incredibly high trees with huge, circular, sun-tracking yellow-green leaves. In the middle of the triangle formed by the trees was an alien version of a city. Huge ropes looped around the giant tree branches suspended a series of woven structures rising vertically in a column that seemed to be fifty percent taller than the World Trade Center. Stringlike tubes from the dim recesses overhead stretched down and connected at points all the way up and down the dome, which looked more like an inverted test tube than anything else. Matt wondered if someone in that dome was watching him.

"I still get the shivers looking out there," said a feminine voice next to him.

Matt turned and found Abby standing nearby. "Me, too. Sometimes I just want to refuse to believe it somehow."

Abby stood silently looking out the window until Matt said, "I really appreciate your help in getting things organized up here. You're a hard worker."

"And you're not?"

Matt smiled and ignored the question. "On the observation deck, they told me the new camera seems to be fully functional. What does it look like down here?"

"Take a look." Abby motioned him over to one of the wall screens.

The screen she directed him to displayed a large image of the message on the top of the dome. Abby said, "Bobby Joe set up a frame buffer, so we've got this good image to work from while the cameras are busy looking at other things." In a semicircle before the screen sat four more linguists with their computers, busily trying to make sense of the message. The message itself looked even stranger in closeup. Five large shapes were each composed of several smaller shapes, which in turn were composed of smaller shapes that could have been icons or crude pictures. Matt had no idea if some of the subelements were merely elements of characters like the three straight lines in a capital *A* or if somehow even the small elements contained significance of their own.

"You make anything of it so far?" Matt asked.

Abby shook her head, and her blond hair swayed. "Obviously it's going to be tougher than finding clues based on similarities to a lot of our known languages. What we need first is a conceptual breakthrough, something that will get us a start on figuring out generically what kind of message they're trying to tell us or what basis they have for communication."

"This may be a stupid question, but what if the message is reversed? I mean what if it reads correctly from the *top* of the dome, or what if they write from bottom to top, or some other variation?"

"Right now we're trying to stay open to any possibility. The computer can easily make mirror-image versions and other views, so we can look at it in a number of ways."

"I don't envy you your job. I wouldn't know where to start."

"I'm not sure we do, either. I wish we could see the people who wrote that message. We might be able to get some clues from their appearance."

Motion on a nearby screen caught Matt's eye, and he and Abby moved on. Across one wall was a huge mosaic screen, showing high-resolution views of over a dozen habitats, most apparently in normal color, a couple of them obviously false-color enhancements. At a controlling computer where he could see all the screens was Dr. Bobby Joe Brewster, the electronics and video whiz who had responded to the mayor's calls for expert help. He hadn't even waited for morning, but had come right over after the broadcast and met the crew.

"What do you have going, Bobby Joe?" asked Matt as they approached. Matt had to ask twice to break the man's concentration.

"Oh, hi. God, isn't this terrific? I know people who would have let someone nail them into a coffin for a year just to have a shot at something like this. I mean, just look at all those *cities.*"

Bobby Joe was in his mid-twenties, with blue eyes and a skull shaved bald. He radiated excitement and enthusiasm. Fortunately, from Matt's point of view, he also radiated competence. Matt still felt he should be calling the man "Dr. Brewster" after seeing the article in *Time Multimedia Magazine.* Bobby Joe had used computers to find a solution to a long-standing control-system problem that had baffled more than one genius. He'd been a child prodigy, moving so rapidly through correspondence classes that he'd been called in for a spot quiz that lasted an entire day. After that session, no one had any doubts that Bobby Joe honestly knew everything he claimed to know. He was on the Columbia staff working with experts at least a decade or more older than he was.

Bobby Joe had been a great help in configuring several cameras and the computer systems, and Matt was sure his usefulness was far from ending.

Bobby Joe pointed at a section of the screen in the lower left. As he did, the view changed very slightly. "I've got one of the cameras cycling through a sequence of sixteen cities. On each pass, I grab the latest image and plop it up on the screen. I've got the computer doing some quick comparisons between each successive frame, so it can sound an alarm if something significant changes."

As Matt watched the wall mosaic, one at a time the views of each city flickered as a new image replaced the previous one. One of the views showed an immense perfect cube with the visible surfaces divided into a sixty-four-square chessboard pattern, half of the squares with a brown tint, half with an orange tint. Each of the sixty-four surfaces seemed to be further subdivided into sixty-four smaller squares where every other tiny square on the sides was black. On the top of the gigantic structure, the non-tinted squares were white.

Two other cities were also cubic, one of them with lots of open air. An enormous structure of girders formed the cube itself. Thirty or forty horizontal girders at equal intervals lined each side, and in turn supported sets of horizontal girders that ran through the cube at each level. From that network of girders hung individual boxes like small buildings of varying sizes. The screen had enough resolution for Matt to see creatures that resembled large caterpillars. One was in the process of leaving one building and going to another by first spanning the gap with the front of its body, then shifting most of its body to the destination, and finally pulling its tail end in after it.

The other cubic city was one huge building with large, irregularly spaced round windows. Matt couldn't see anything through the windows.

One of the cities was completely concealed from view. All that showed under a very short dome was a mound of red dirt reminiscent of an anthill. Matt assumed the rest of the city lay under the surface of the ground.

Matt said, "Have you seen any species that looks more like—"

He was interrupted by a chiming sound from the computer.

"Hang on," Bobby Joe said. "We may have something interesting here." He gave several commands with the keyboard, and a blinking box formed around one of the city views. That view grew to occupy half of the large screen. The resolution made the alien city look like it was just on the other side of a large window. In very general terms, the city looked more like Manhattan than did most of the cities. It was generally level, with walkways on the surface of the ground. On the land lay an array of mostly conic structures, like large tepees, some much taller than others. At the top of one of the tallest cones, Matt could see a light that changed colors in a seemingly random pattern, as though he were watching just one square centimeter of a large screen showing a TV broadcast.

Bobby Joe tapped on the keyboard, and he centered a small circle on the light source. "Let's set up a real-time oscillograph."

A square appeared on one side of the image, with a dotted line between the light source and the graph. In the graph box was a vertical spectrum bar, the color ranging from red at the bottom to blue at the top, and a continuously moving trace appeared, showing the color versus time. The moving point drew a sine wave extending higher than blue on the scale, and then began drawing what seemed to be noise. It went back to a sine wave for a couple of seconds, and then back to noise.

Bobby Joe leaned back in his chair. "I do believe someone's trying to talk to us."

4

VIDEO GAMES

RUDY STEPPED UP into the cherry-picker cab with Nicholas. The driver took them south without needing to be asked.

"Where's the closest one of these new tubes?" Rudy asked.

Nicholas took out a handkerchief and patted some sweat on his forehead. "About where the Wall Street helipad used to be."

Once they were on the South Street viaduct, they made good time. The driver stopped the truck in the northbound lane closest to the edge of the dome. Rudy and Nicholas took the cherry-picker cage into space over the edge of the viaduct, moving closer and closer to the connection point between the dome and a blue hose that disappeared into the sky outside the dome. The circular junction looked unlike any of the others Rudy had seen so far. This one seemed to be a transparent membrane, a thin layer of flexible plastic wrapping stretched across the opening.

Rudy looked at it for several seconds before he finally said, "Okay, I see it. Now what did you want to tell me about it?"

Nicholas smiled smugly as he took a few paper clips from his pocket. "Here, take one."

Rudy did.

"Now toss it at that membrane."

Rudy raised his eyebrows, and then did as Nicholas suggested. The paper clip sailed right toward the membrane and it hit. After that nothing happened. The paper clip just wasn't there anymore.

Nicholas sailed another paper clip at the membrane. It, too, reached the thin layer and apparently ceased to exist.

After a moment of considering the waste disposal ramifications, Rudy began to smile, too. "So, what you're telling me is that pretty soon we'll be able to flush our toilets again?"

Abby stared at the recording graph as her spine tingled. A bright dot on the left edge of the trace fluctuated up and down as it spewed a fine line to one side. The trace moved slowly to the right and disappeared as it reached the edge of the box and new data reminiscent of an electrocardiogram constantly replaced it.

"I'll accept your statement that this implies an intelligent message, but it doesn't tell me anything yet," Abby said. She looked back at the screen showing the distant light source as it changed colors. The conical building supporting the light showed a dark line spiraling around it, reaching all the way from the top to the ground. She wondered if it was a spiral staircase.

"Are you recording this?" Matt asked Bobby Joe. Several times earlier, Abby had caught Matt staring off into the distance, obviously sad, no doubt feeling the loss of his wife back on Earth. But now his expression was interested, showing none of the pain she'd seen before, and she was glad for him that he had something to take his mind off the woman he was so obviously in love with.

Bobby Joe didn't turn from his chair in front of the small console, but he said, "You're nuking right."

Matt turned to Abby. "It doesn't mean anything to me, either, but I'm willing to bet Bobby Joe can make some sense of it." He leaned over Bobby Joe's shoulder. "Where's it coming from? I mean, which dome is it? I can see what it looks like, but where is it on the plain in relation to us?"

Bobby Joe used the controls to change the view on a big screen next to the one showing the graph. At first the view included just the conical building the light came from, but then he made the camera zoom back more and more so the cone began to shrink to a dot as the dome containing it came into view, and then several more domes entered the sides of the picture. By the time the view stopped changing, it was obvious that the dome was one of the farthest ones away.

"Just a sec." Bobby Joe hit some more controls, and the screen suddenly showed little green *X*s at the top of each dome. Then the domes vanished and the only thing left was the set of

Xs. One of the *Xs* changed from green to red, the one where the transmitting dome had been. Finally, he tilted the display, so the band of *Xs* spread vertically and the ones near the top spread out horizontally, and Abby could tell Bobby Joe had somehow translated the screen image to a crude top-view map. Even as she realized that, a distance marker came on the screen, showing the length of one kilometer on that scale. The nearest dome was about ten kilometers away. The dome with the light must have been five times that far away. An octagonal outline showed on the screen, marking the boundaries of the huge area they were in. Manhattan was fairly near the center, and the transmitting dome was near one wall.

"You're saying that dome is, what, over fifty kilometers from here?" Matt asked.

"You got it," Bobby Joe said. He sounded pleased with being able to provide the information. Abby hadn't yet heard Bobby Joe sound in the least bit disturbed by recent events; in fact, he seemed positively excited and intrigued.

"So, what are they trying to tell us?"

"You got me. But we can try a few things. Let's convert it to sound, and see what we get." Bobby Joe's fingers played over the controls, and a minute later every head in the room popped up as strange squawks came over speakers next to the screen. A second of noise like a radio receiver tuned to an empty channel was followed by a second of a clear tone a few octaves above middle C. Bobby Joe listened briefly and shook his head. "Let me speed it up."

He traced his finger across a bar on the small screen in his console and the noise increased in pitch to the point that the tone became a repeating click, and the sound in between became high-pitched noise.

"Okay, let's slow it down." Bobby Joe drew his finger across the screen right to left, and the noise dropped back to where it had been and continued getting deeper until the tone was so low that it rattled the tables in the room. The rumbling in between became no more intelligible.

Bobby Joe hit some more keys. "Okay, let's try some video. If we assume the information between the sine waves is a picture built out of frame lines like a TV, then—then this is going to take me some time. Give me a couple of hours, okay?"

Julie Kravine reached the 105th floor in the south tower of the World Trade Center and the elevator doors opened.

Directly in front of the doors was a guard. He took his feet off the table in front of him and stood. "I'll need to see some ID, miss, if you want to get past here."

Surprised, Julie took out her card. "Isn't this a little unusual?"

"It sure is. But the folks on this floor have already had a couple of crazies come up to kvetch about how they shouldn't be talkin' to aliens." The man checked her ID against a list that fit on one sheet of paper. "All right, Miss Kravine. Down that hall as far as you can go, then turn and it's the third door on the right."

Julie hesitated. "And what do you think about talking to aliens in those domes out there?"

"Well, ma'am." The guard scratched the stubble on his chin. "I guess if we can talk to them, maybe they're not all that strange. And if we can't, what's the harm in trying?"

I don't know, Julie thought as she walked toward the room on the south wall. Would they be punished for breaking some unknown rule?

The room was even busier than she had expected it to be. On the perimeter of the room were several journalists, some of whom she recognized. She noticed some of the screens borrowed from the station, but some of the rest of the equipment must have come from a communications company or a school. She slipped on her viewfinder glasses and turned on the minivid resting on her hip. The rectangular viewfinder border came on, and she turned her head so the optics on her headband would catch the center of activity.

Two men and two women worked their computers in front of a large screen showing the symbols on the dome overhead. Matt Sheehan and some people she didn't know stood behind a bald man at a control console. The large screen held a rectangular array of flickering black and white confetti. As the man at the console moved his hands across the touch screen, the rectangle of confetti changed aspect ratio and became a horizontal bar. In a series of steps, it narrowed and grew in height until it was square, and then kept changing until it was a vertical bar. The confetti inside was the only consistent property.

Julie turned her minivid toward the expanded views of other domes. One of them covered what looked to be glass houses. Inside the structures were creatures that looked vaguely like cockroaches that walked upright. In one of the larger structures, behind two or three transparent walls, a group of a dozen or so of the creatures sat in a ring. In a small building, three of the creatures tumbled and gyrated in unison. It was only then that it occurred to Julie that perhaps even though she could see through these walls, perhaps the creatures living there could not.

She turned back to Matt and the group at the largest screen. She caught his eye and he came closer, bringing with him a shorter blond woman.

"Thanks again for the equipment loan," he said. "It's invaluable."

"You're welcome. I'm glad it's being put to good use."

Matt introduced the blond as Abby Tersa, who was in charge of several people working on translating the message overhead. Julie shook her hand. Abby seemed calm but ultra-alert, as though she were really enjoying the job.

Julie said to Matt, "Well, I'm here for the return favor. Is there anything you *don't* want on the news?"

Matt glanced around. "I can't think of anything that needs to be restricted. This screen is a display of a signal we're getting from the dome in that view up there, the one with all the cones. So far it's not making any sense, but—" Matt suddenly stopped and looked at the screen showing the conical buildings. "Just a minute."

Matt went closer to the bald man at the console and tapped his shoulder. "Say, how hard would it be to try to convert that image to a triangular picture?"

"Triangular?" the man said.

Matt pointed at the screen showing the conical buildings. "Like that shape."

The bald man was quiet for a moment. "Why not? I'll give it a shot."

Matt came back to Julie and pointed at the bald guy. "That's Dr. Bobby Joe Brewster. He's from Columbia U, and he's been terrific for getting this set up."

Matt pointed to the upper left dome on the display and started giving her a rundown on what little they knew so far about each view. About the time he finished the last screen, Bobby Joe suddenly cried out, "Yes!"

On the center screen was a triangular screen full of confetti. Besides the shape of the outline, the only thing different from before was that the confetti was changing much more slowly. Julie didn't see that it was much of an improvement, but she moved closer with Matt.

Bobby Joe manipulated the controls as he spoke to Abby. "I think we're getting closer." A second later, the triangle began to shrink and then expand. Abruptly it locked into a fixed size, and the confetti was gone. In its place was a distorted view of something that moved slowly down the screen.

Bobby Joe continued his efforts, and the screen image came closer and closer to an image that made sense. No longer bits of pure black and white, the screen became a gray-scale view that looked like an old photographic negative sliced into horizontal strips. The slices disappeared as Bobby Joe did something with his left hand, then the blacks swapped places with whites, and the image was suddenly a monochrome view of a room, containing two people who looked very much like human beings, one a Latin male.

The male spoke. "Lucy? Lucy, is that you?"

The woman looked nervous. "Oh, no, señor."

As the woman averted her face, the man said, "That *is* you!"

What sounded like an old-fashioned laugh track came from the speakers.

Matt, looking incredulous, turned to Bobby Joe. "*That's* what we're picking up from the dome out there?"

Bobby Joe looked up at Matt and gave him the biggest grin Julie had seen in days. He said, "Oops, sorry, wrong channel."

One of the women behind Julie suddenly started to laugh hysterically, and her laughter cut off just as abruptly.

* * *

Matt tapped Bobby Joe on the shoulder. Bobby Joe looked up.

"Come with me for just a minute," Matt said.

Bobby Joe looked puzzled, but he rose from his chair and followed.

Matt left the operations center and entered an unused room down that hall. Bobby Joe looked nervous. "I'm sorry about the *I Love Lucy* recording. It's from a file of stuff I keep."

"It's all right," Matt said. "I'm not going to hold that little incident against you, and it'll be forgotten the instant we get back in that room. But if you're going to be of any help, you are *not* to waste anyone's time with jokes like that. We've been tasked with an important job. When the pressure's off, I can laugh just like anyone else. Right now we can't afford the luxury of unproductive time."

"I'm sorry. It's just that sometimes I—" Bobby Joe turned away, then seemed to screw up his resolve, and he turned back to Matt. "Sometimes I feel like a geek. I'm not strong and tall and macho. And especially in this company, I'm a little intimidated. I guess humor is what I do to overcome that."

Matt nodded. "I think I understand. But maybe you're underestimating us. No one has to be tall or muscular or articulate to help us save ourselves. What we need from you is your intelligence and your skill. No one is going to be looking down at you because you're not a football player. We don't *want* a football player. We need you. We need your skills."

Bobby Joe seemed to stand a little taller. "I understand. I'll do my best. But just so I understand, is all humor off limits?"

"No. But if it costs us time, or if it unsettles people, or if it irritates people, it hurts us all right now."

"Understood."

Julie watched as Bobby Joe touched the controls again. A new image formed on the screen, this one a view of a planet's surface.

Noise in the room fell to nothing until the only sounds were those of Bobby Joe's hands on the console controls. Colors replaced some of the shades of gray, and the picture took on a false-color look common in satellite photos of resources.

The colors mutated for several minutes, and a true-color

moving image formed on the triangular screen. In the foreground were two conical structures in vivid detail, showing people walking down the stairs. Only these people weren't human. They made Julie think of humans who had been very badly burned. Their skin was brown and leathery, clearly showing a web of white veins everywhere it was visible. The most unusual feature of their faces was the single eye, centered just below the forehead.

The view moved sideways, and a black shape appeared in the air. The sky suddenly changed to a deeper blue, probably because Bobby Joe was still making adjustments. The black craft looked exactly like the ones Julie had seen in amateur recordings made as Manhattan had been lifted. The view swung downward and the horizon came into view. Stretching far into the distance were clusters of cones much like the ones sitting under the dome they could see on the other screen. Running between the clusters was a grid of bridgelike connecting structures. Below the black ship, a line of destruction followed its path. Clouds of vapor steamed off the surface, and a crack opened up, as though an earthquake were ripping apart the surface.

The view moved to the left, following the rift in the ground as it lengthened, and an enormous structure came into view. It was a high, square platform supported by four huge leaning columns, each with a stairway winding around the perimeter. The platform grew in the image, and it became obvious that what had at first seemed to be a mottled surface was instead a huge crowd of people. Julie was trying to guess how many people might be there, certainly many thousands, when the violent slicing reached the platform. In what seemed to be super-slow motion, a swath of destruction cut through the multitudes, and the platform split into two city-sized plates that began to tilt then fall toward the ground as masses of people slid off the edges.

Many seconds passed before the first falling people hit the ground. A cloud of dust began to rise as the structure reached the ground and began to crumble. Julie felt dazed, numb. Thousands upon thousands of people must have died in a period of one minute.

Julie was still in shock as the image showed black ships

putting a filmy bubble in place. The sudden flash of light made her blink. Behind her someone was crying.

The recording continued as the land beyond the edge of the dome lurched and dropped away. Suddenly the image started jumping violently. The recording had been taken from near enough the edge that whoever was on the camera side of the lens ran toward the dome and reached it in time to aim down at the planet's surface.

The planet already seemed as far below as it would probably look like from a commercial airliner. The planet was predominantly gray, with far less surface water than Earth. The view tilted upward and showed a huge black shape blocking out most of the stars. Unfamiliar constellations disappeared as the black shape grew larger.

The view tilted back toward the planet, now far enough below that the thin layer of atmosphere glowed over the curved horizon.

Two things happened concurrently. Starting at the apex of the picture, a black band expanded downward and cut off the view entirely after about ten seconds. During the last three or four seconds, something happened over the planet's horizon. Julie thought of a huge lightning storm as seen from several miles away, but this was on a planetary scale. The air in the thin band still visible flickered with bright light, as though a fireworks display to end them all had started just out of direct sight.

The black band reached the bottom of the screen, and the view of the horizon narrowed to a slit before it was cut off completely and the image went black. In the silent room, Julie could hear her heart beat.

The recording began all over.

Finally Matt swallowed hard, then said to Bobby Joe, "If we provide you with equivalent recordings from the ones made in Manhattan, can you translate them to this format and send them to the people in that dome?"

"Probably. It'll take some doing. The hardest part is the transmitter. Most of our stuff's intended for transmitting in a fairly narrow spectrum, but I can probably cobble something together."

"Okay. Let me know if you need resources you don't have."

Matt turned to Julie. "You've probably got a fair selection of amateur videos at the station. When you get a chance, can you get someone to edit some video equivalent to what they saw, and get it to Bobby Joe?"

Julie nodded. She still wasn't sure if she could speak.

Dorine Underwood faced the camera and worked toward the conclusion of her nightly message. She still had a headache from a long, angry conversation with Oscar Anklehunt, the U.N. Secretary General. Oscar plainly felt the situation was one of Earth dealing with an alien threat, whereas Dorine argued that it was the city that was in the unenviable position of dealing with aliens. As she had most of her normal network of support intact, and Oscar was in charge of a large group of delegates cut off from their home countries, Dorine had never doubted who'd win the argument. It just took some time to convince Oscar.

He kept insisting on getting all the information available to anyone, and he demanded that support be provided him so *he,* as the sole representative of the world's collective governments, could deal with the situation. When Dorine had finally had enough, she asked Oscar how many people reported to him. When he answered, Dorine explained that a thousand times that many people were in place in the city government, all under her direction, all of whom knew their jobs and were getting a steady supply of new guidance as more information became available.

At the end of the conversation she threw him a bone and said she could still use more translators and she'd appreciate his help in sending them her way. Oscar was enough of a statesman to know when the battle was over, and he finally backed down from his original demands and promised to help. He was obviously unhappy to have to be fitting into *her* plans, but he knew when he was outgunned.

Dorine looked back at the camera and tried to keep her tone casual. The audience was bound to include people on the verge of suicide. ". . . so I'm happy to report the restrictions on toilet usage and water consumption have been lifted. Garbage collection will start tomorrow, but I caution you not to throw away anything that might have future use.

"Following this telecast will be a series of numbers to call for medical help for withdrawal symptoms. Area hospitals have already responded very well to those who are suffering from drug withdrawal, and they've got specialists ready to help with the tobacco and alcohol withdrawal that's not very far away. Better get used to it, folks: the supplies have been cut off. Chemical labs and home brew will last just so long. It's only a matter of time until every ounce of controlled substances in Manhattan is used up. The area trauma centers have been extremely busy, and additional operators are standing by on suicide hot-lines. We will do all we can to help. And we *are* going to make it one way or another."

One thing that gave Dorine even more faith was a visit earlier in the day from a senior member of the Italian families, saying they would be doing their part in discouraging gang violence and pitching in for the common good, just the way they had done in World War II. A week ago, Dorine would have been pleased to see the gentleman in jail, but at the moment Manhattan could use all the help it could get. The drug problem was going to get a *lot* worse than it already had, but she didn't want to panic people.

"On the subject of food, I know there's a sizable number of people who are either too proud to eat anything delivered from a cement mixer, or are suspicious of anything provided by our captors. I understand both of those feelings, but we simply don't have any choice. There are too many of us, and too little conventional food left. We eat what we're being provided, or we starve.

"And finally, to answer the most-asked question from yesterday's phone messages, the reason we're trying to contact other races in this giant zoo, or whatever it is, is that we want to learn as much as we possibly can. That's the same reason we're trying to decipher the message on top of the dome. I don't want to hold out any false hopes, but we need to keep learning. For all we know, by finding out more and more about why we were taken, we can possibly negotiate our return. The point is that ignorance leaves us in the worst possible position.

"There are many theories about why we're here, ranging from some grotesque biological or sociological experiment to crackpot ideas such as us being a food supply. We need to find out what the real answer is. We might not like whatever we find out, but perhaps we'll get some answers. I'm assuming that not many people listening to this broadcast would willingly stay here forever. We may not have any choice, but sticking our heads in the sand is the coward's way, and New York isn't known for its cowards.

"Good night, Manhattan."

Stuart Lund switched off the television in his hospital room. This wasn't right.

What could the mayor be thinking? The message on top of the dome was obviously a message from God. What else could this whole business be but the second coming of Noah's Ark?

The only other possibility was the millennium coming a little late; but, one, God could certainly count; and two, if this were the millennium, then God would have saved only those worthy of saving, and while Stuart had high regard for many people he knew in Manhattan, he couldn't possibly accept the monumental coincidence that every single person worthy of saving happened to be in Manhattan at exactly the same time.

He struggled to get out of bed and find his clothes. The task would have been easier with both hands, but Stuart had flatly resisted the idea of a prosthetic hand. God had made him this way. Who was he to try to reverse God's will?

He had to get out. Whoever interpreted the message from God on the dome above should be someone called by God, not some scummy bunch of scientists.

Matt awoke on a cot, high in the World Trade Center, the dream of Nadine still vivid in his mind. Her decision still cut deep, and he found himself recalling danger signs that he'd ignored because he wanted her so much.

Nadine had always been something of a flirt, a woman very conscious of her power over men. Before they were married, they'd had an argument on the way to a picnic with other military personnel assigned to Fort Lewis, south of Tacoma. They reached the picnic grounds, a football-field-sized irregular area partly cleared of trees but surrounded by forest.

Matt had tried to apologize for his share of the sharp words spoken in the car, but when they arrived, Nadine was cool, unforgiving. They drifted in and out of conversations with friends and casual acquaintances, all the while Matt feeling frustrated that they couldn't get closure on the argument and put it behind them. As people were getting ready for the big meal, a male officer whose name Matt couldn't even remember anymore pulled a muscle in his back while carrying a huge bag of ice. With hardly any coaxing at all, Nadine volunteered to give the guy a back rub.

Matt watched for a couple of minutes as Nadine started the back rub and threw in some flirting for good measure. As Matt watched, the pain inside his gut grew and grew, and somehow summoned up that old unrelated feeling from his childhood, the feeling that no matter what he did, it would never be enough to satisfy his parents. After a few minutes he couldn't stand it anymore. He had to get away.

He backed away from the small group, turned, and strode toward the woods. As he did, he was aware that he held the slim hope that Nadine would see the hurt, and that she would follow him, that maybe they could talk and smooth things over. He made a point of not going much farther when he reached the edge of the trees.

He walked maybe ten meters into the trees and came to a small clearing, barely hearing the cries of birds in the trees, amazed at how strong his reaction had been. He waited there twenty or thirty minutes, feeling that if Nadine cared anything at all about him that she would have been there by that time. Finally the feelings built to the point that he cried, and the feeling of loss of control just made him hurt that much more.

When he finally recovered, he went back to the picnic area. The back rub was over, and Nadine was casually chatting with a couple of people from their unit.

That night, sex was more fiery than it had been in several weeks. Matt had lain awake for a long time afterward, wondering if that had been Nadine's goal, and angry at himself that he was so easily manipulated.

Matt took a deep breath, blinked away the recollection, and swung his feet over the edge of the cot. He stretched and walked to the window. The array of domed cities in the distance focused his attention on the present.

Minutes later he was back in the operations room. Bobby Joe had beat him there again and was busily engaged at the control console.

"Any word?" Matt asked.

"None so far. I really think our transmission is getting out there, though."

Matt sat down beside Bobby Joe. "We've been transmitting for"—he looked at his watch—"coming up on forty-eight hours so far. You'd think that would be enough time for them to realize we're answering their signal. Why don't they transmit something else to tell us they understand?"

"I wish I knew."

"Any chance the atmosphere outside the dome absorbs more than we think it does? Maybe our signal is a lot weaker than theirs."

"Don't think so. I can pinpoint the portion of our signal that's reflecting off that dome, and my computer and my gut say they should be getting just as strong a signal as we are."

Matt leaned back and rubbed his forehead. He was still sitting there when Abby came in and sat down.

"Good morning," she said.

"Hi."

"You look tired."

"I shouldn't be," Matt said. "I got plenty of sleep. How are things with your message?"

Abby shook her head. "Still no progress. We all feel quite inept."

"No one said it would be easy. Whoever wrote that message isn't very much like us, I'd bet."

"Still, there's got to be a way."

"You want to cut a hole through the dome?" Dorine Underwood said. "Isn't that a bit drastic?"

The council meeting was slightly larger than normal, since Matt Sheehan had brought some of his team along.

"I know it sounds that way, Ms. Mayor," Matt said. "But we've given it a lot of thought and it seems to make the most sense. Can I outline our reasoning?"

Dorine hesitated. "All right. It can't hurt to hear it."

"First of all, every indication we have says we're going to be here for a long time, if not forever, if we accept the status quo. We've heard nothing from our captors except the sign over our heads, and we've been beaming messages via radio frequencies and broad-spectrum light in every possible direction, and we still haven't heard a peep out of our captors. I understand that they might have trouble decoding what we're sending, and we'll probably have trouble with any message from them, but we've received *nothing*. Either they're unaware of our transmissions or they're ignoring us.

"I believe that getting out of this enclosure is the only thing that might increase our chances of being taken home. If we're enough of a nuisance, maybe they won't want us."

"Possibly. But they might just dump us in space."

"That's a risk. I don't think it's very likely, but that's a risk."

Dorine searched Matt's eyes. She was used to watching people's eyes. Who was it that said something about eyes being the window to the soul? He looked honest. He had readily admitted her fear had some justification, rather than just brushing aside the objection. "Go on, Colonel Sheehan."

"Okay. First some background." Matt gestured at the bald man sitting next to him. "You may recognize Dr. Brewster from a *Time* article last year. Dr. Brewster, with a couple of associates from Columbia University, has made an extensive series of spectroscopic measurements, looking at the atmosphere out there, between the domes, and in addition they've been able to make measurements of the atmospheres inside most of the other domes. Their findings indicate the air outside between the domes is breathable, although at a lower pressure than in here. About eighty percent of the domes contain various mixtures of oxygen and nitrogen with minor amounts of carbon dioxide, water vapor, and trace gases that won't hurt us. There might be circumstances where we'd need oxygen masks, but in general, we'd be perfectly safe."

Barnaby had grown increasingly agitated while Matt spoke. As soon as Matt paused for a breath, Barnaby said, "Sure, maybe we can breathe the air, but what about bugs? Who knows what kind of germs might get in here?"

Matt nodded. "You're right that that's a factor in this decision. And it's not just the microorganisms that could get in here; we could be letting our own germs loose on everyone else. Doctor?" He turned toward an older woman near him. "This is Dr. Rosenthal. She's a molecular biologist, also from Columbia."

The woman cleared her throat. "As Mr. Sheehan says, this question involves several calculated risks. In our own experience, many microorganisms work on fairly specific targets. Many diseases that attack humans, for instance, don't have the slightest effect on most other mammals, let alone reptiles, amphibians, or birds, or creatures even more different from us. The odds suggest that microorganisms from alien worlds are unlikely to be dangerous to us, and vice versa. Mr. Sheehan's plan does involve taking precautions, in case we're wrong, but in any event my feeling is that the risk is smaller than what we have to gain."

"Thank you, Doctor," Matt said. "Again, one of the key aspects of this decision is the basic question: are we willing to live in prison for the rest of our lives?"

Dorine said, "There might well be a significant number of people here who *do* want to live as long as they naturally can."

"I understand that, Ms. Mayor. Again, our plan would strive to isolate the people going outside from the people staying here, so that even if there is a health problem, it will affect only the *volunteers* on the team."

"All right. Go on." Dorine was glad she hadn't had to run against this man in the last election. He was ready for every question, and had convincing arguments for all his statements. Her most recent opponent had been a wealthy man who had gotten his way so often that his debating skills had atrophied.

"I guess the final reason for wanting to go outside is that we hope to learn more from the residents in other domes, but we're having difficulties trying to talk to them from a distance. The linguists feel, and it makes sense to me, that direct two-way contact has the best chances of speedy communication. If I'm in the room with you, and I point at a chair and say 'chair,' and you tell your computer to record what I said and what object I pointed to, then we can swap roles and both sides can begin to build up a vocabulary. Of course, I could have meant 'sit down' or 'wood' or 'cushion,' but with a face-to-face opportunity, we can assemble enough data to start finding out what's really being said. Right now, with only one-way communication established, we're having a tough time doing anything more than verifying that one of the other domes experienced something like what we did. Also, it could turn out that some of the races that we'd find it easiest to talk to might be races with no electronics communications equipment. A team would continue trying to establish radio or light-beam communications, so we wouldn't be abandoning that process."

"You present a compelling argument. But what if we're unable to cut through the dome?"

"Then we haven't lost anything, have we?"

"You don't really expect to cut through it with that, do you?" Matt asked Rudy Sanchez. The two men stood on the grass in Battery Park, looking at a small plastic bubble sealed to the inside of the dome. Inside the sealed volume was a city worker with an oxyacetylene torch ready to go.

"Not really, but we have to try it, right?"

Matt nodded. The first test they'd conducted was to see if they could scratch the surface with an industrial diamond. They hadn't been able to mar the surface. A sledge hammer driven against a tungsten carbide bit didn't do anything except make a lot of noise. A variety of strong acids and bases had done nothing more than make a mess. The only result from an attempt with a strong laser was a discolored spot on the surface of the gray plain outside the dome; the laser light went through the dome material without causing any measurable change.

Rudy responded to a gesture from the city worker, and he raised his thumb.

Matt heard the *whoosh* of the twin gas jet lighting, and bright white light danced on nearby reflecting surfaces. After about five minutes the light died, the gas jet popped as it shut off, and the man inside the bubble lifted his helmet and shook his head at Rudy.

"Damn," Rudy said.

Matt sat in silence with him for a couple of minutes, as they waited for Bobby Joe. Bobby Joe was shaking his head as he approached.

"No good," Bobby Joe said. "I've got temperature readings from about a meter from the flame, ten meters away, and a hundred meters away."

"And they all read the same, right?" Rudy said.

"You got it. They all rose a few hundredths of a degree. Whatever that stuff is, it's one superfine heat conductor. We can't get any one spot hot enough to do any damage because the heat spreads through it so fast."

Rudy raised an eyebrow in Matt's direction. "I don't think we've got anything that'll do the trick."

Matt sighed. "I believe you. I guess it's time we went for a drive."

The caravan of city trucks traveled south in the northbound tube of the Battery Tunnel, moving deeper as they approached the blocked end. The two lanes in the tube bound for Brooklyn still had too many abandoned vehicles clogging them. Two large trucks trailing the procession stopped before the others did. Teams from each truck got out and prepared to build decontamination barriers across the width of the tunnel.

Power was on here, too, although there hadn't been much need for it recently. The existing Battery Tunnel lights reduced the need to bring in additional artificial lighting, and the fans would help to keep the air breathable, at least until, and if, the crew was near to breaching the barrier to the outside. Matt listened to the metallic whine of tires as the noise bounced back from the tunnel walls.

The lead truck pulled to a halt in the right lane, fifty feet from the black seal at the end of the tunnel. Paramedic teams had removed the victims left behind when the tunnel was severed, but the last twenty or thirty feet of roadbed still bore the dark stains of blood and oil.

To Matt the black material blocking the tunnel looked just like the stuff at the end of the subway tunnel. He walked the final meters to the wall and put his fingers against it. It had the feel of wrought iron. The surface tilted away from him, so it was maybe forty-five degrees from vertical. He pulled a fingernail down the surface, and felt the roughness. When he scratched sideways, he could feel a series of tiny ridges.

"Can I borrow a hammer?" he asked Rudy.

Rudy set a small toolbox on the stained concrete and withdrew a ball-peen hammer.

Matt swung the hammer against the black surface. Wrought iron would have absorbed more of the energy. Against this surface, the hammer snapped back as though Matt had hit a cubic meter of stainless steel. "Doesn't sound encouraging, does it?"

"Not really," Rudy said. Six more people from Rudy's organization approached the wall and started their own investigations.

"How did this layer get here?" Matt asked as even more people formed several smaller groups to attack the surface with a variety of techniques.

Rudy shrugged. "We don't know, really. No one reported seeing any material brought down, and I'm sure it isn't a simple layer of melted rock. Quite a few people reported hearing a series of explosions like you heard. One possibility proposed by metallurgists is that the aliens shot a huge number of explosive pellets into the cut formed by the lasers. If the pellets contained material that sprang into its original shape and fused together, what we could have is a huge cone underneath the city."

"Sounds a little strange to me," Matt said.

"This whole business is a little strange. One of the things the metallurgical folks found is that the material is magnetized, and that the direction corresponds to the direction the magnetic flux would have been oriented on Earth. That's one reason they think that for at least a short time, a lot of the barrier material was fluid, so the magnetic dipoles could move freely and align themselves with the strongest magnetic field present."

"So, if that theory's true, even if we can't get through this section, there's a possibility of a gap at the very bottom of the cone. All we'd need to do is tunnel down who knows how far through solid granite."

"Simple, eh?" Rudy grinned. "And we should be able to figure out how deep we'd have to go. We can measure this angle"—he pointed to the black barrier—"and we can measure the angles in other locations. My guess is the hole they cut is at least a kilometer deep in the center."

* * *

Julie Kravine put her ID back in her pocket and walked deeper into the tunnel. Ahead were flashing yellow lights of city maintenance vehicles parked in the right lane. She turned on her minivid and started recording as a matter of habit.

A pinpoint of brilliant light turned on in the distance ahead, and a shower of sparks flew to one side. The sparks fell to the ground so slowly, the display seemed more like faraway fireworks.

Rudy Sanchez sat on the back bumper of a city electrical truck. He looked tired. Julie got within a couple of meters of him before he looked up and smiled as though he were glad to see her. Too many people looked away when reporters arrived.

"Hi," he said.

"Hi, yourself. How's it going?"

"Slow. Very very slow. Or not at all, depending on your point of view."

The sparks were still flying in the air near the barrier ahead. "Don't you think you're gonna be able to cut through it?"

"I just don't know. Isn't that the kind of answer reporters hate?"

"Not when it's honest."

"It's honest. We've tried acid, diamond-tipped blades, torches"—he jerked his thumb toward the sparks—"welding equipment. Nothing."

"Why keep trying if you're sure it's impossible?"

" 'Cause I'm not sure. Different materials have different weaknesses. Maybe we'll find a weak link."

"Sounds like wishful thinking to me."

Rudy was silent for a moment. "Maybe so. But you remember paper newspapers from when you were a kid?"

"Sure."

"You ever try to tear out an article on part of a page? If you did, you probably noticed that tearing the page vertically was easy. But tearing across the page was damn near impossible to do, at least in a straight line."

"Yeah. So?"

"So the paper was stronger in one direction than the other, because of the way the fibers lined up. Other materials are like that, too. Some of them you can pull on the ends really hard and they can support thousands of pounds of tension, but bend them in two and they snap just like a little piece of wood. We need to figure out how to snap this stuff."

"You know you did that very well?" Julie said. Rudy looked puzzled, so she went on. "When I talk to technical people, most of them either don't try to explain very well because they want to feel superior, or they really do try to explain, but they sound like they're reciting their doctoral thesis—they don't know how to explain things to people who don't talk their jargon."

"Well, thanks. You do your job well, too. I've seen reporters who ask all the questions and just absorb the answers like some mechanical person. Or they ask questions to impress the audience. You seem to care about what you're hearing. And you think about what you hear. You've asked some pretty interesting questions in the last few days—questions that should be occurring to the people you're asking, but you beat them to it."

The light sparking against the barrier went off. Julie felt uncomfortable with the compliment, and said, "Yeah, well, thanks."

A guy Julie hadn't seen before approached and said to Rudy, "No luck. That was six cycles of hot and cold, and it still looks exactly the same."

"OK, thanks," Rudy said. He made a mark on his clipboard. "Can you tell Verhogan it's his turn?"

"Sure thing." The man went back toward the barrier.

"What's next?" Julie asked.

"The surface seems to be made up of a huge number of filaments, all running from the surface down to wherever they all meet, all fused together; we can feel the ridges, like a beaded curtain dipped in glue, only a lot smaller. Verhogan's built a very strong spreader. It's got tiny grippers meant to catch on those little ridges, so maybe we can pry a gap between filaments."

"You gonna go watch?"

"Yeah. This one I'm a little more curious about."

As Julie walked with Rudy toward the black wall, a truck backed up against the surface. On the rear of the truck was a device with wide jaws made from shiny metal. Julie aimed her minivid at the contraption, watching light glint from the fine rows of teeth.

Once the truck was parked tightly against the wall, the driver got out of the cab and walked around to where a big electric winch was mounted on the side of the truck.

Rudy lowered his voice slightly. "The winch will drive apart the two grippers, if we're lucky."

Julie couldn't see much with the truck covering the working area, but she left her minivid on. The driver of the truck looked at a small display screen as he adjusted two wheel-handled controls. When he finished, he pushed a button next to the winch, and then quickly moved back from the truck.

The winch made grinding noises for a few seconds before the noises dropped in pitch and the winch began to work harder. Several more seconds went by before there came a loud *sproing* as something in the mechanism gave way, and the winch began to race.

"Didn't sound real good to me," Julie said.

"Me, neither," Rudy said.

A few minutes later, after the truck had been driven forward, two workers verified that part of the mechanism had broken and the wall was unaffected.

"How many more ideas do you have?" Julie asked.

"Not too many," Rudy admitted. "But it's always the last one that works."

"Always?"

"Usually. 'Cause the cliché is that when you get something that works, that's when you stop trying."

The last one worked.

Rudy felt like he'd been working five days without sleep when he got word that the dipole oscillator was ready to try. He was having trouble working up enthusiasm, but he went for a look anyway.

Julie Kravine was back down in the tunnel, obviously eager to find out the results. She wasn't much younger than Rudy, but he felt like an old man in the face of her obvious energy. "What's this one gonna do, Rudy?"

"Well, it's a little like a microwave oven, except that what we're cooking is outside the oven. A microwave oven heats things by creating an oscillating field that makes water molecules want to line up with it as it changes polarity over and over. Once the water molecules start twisting back and forth like that, the friction with other molecules makes heat. It's the modern equivalent of rubbing two sticks together.

"This thing does it a little differently. It's set up to make magnetic domains twist back and forth, like an old bulk tape eraser, except much stronger and much more focused. The theory is that if we can generate enough internal heat and make enough molecules bounce around, then maybe we can weaken that stuff."

Julie looked pleased with the description.

Next to the black wall was a large machine with a cone-shaped extension pointed right at the wall, almost touching it. As Rudy and Julie watched, Dr. Brantower, a woman in her fifties, gave a go-ahead sign. A *click* sounded from somewhere, and an intense humming sound filled the tunnel. A spot on the black wall right in front of the cone began to glow brightly. It stayed bright for five seconds, at which time the same click sounded, the humming disappeared, and the spot on the wall faded back to black.

Dr. Brantower and a man Rudy didn't know went over to examine the spot. After a minute or so, Dr. Brantower called out. "Hey, Rudy! The surface texture is changed!"

Rudy felt a surge of energy, and suddenly felt younger than Julie. They went over to the wall, and Julie played her minivid over the surface while Rudy took a close look. Sure enough, instead of the black ridged surface, a spot the size of a fingernail was slightly gray and the ridges had been smoothed over. As Rudy watched, Dr. Brantower took a nearby flat-blade screwdriver and prodded at the surface. Particles flaked off like dust, and Rudy's heartbeat quickened.

"All right!" Rudy shouted. "You're a genius, Doctor."

Dr. Brantower laughed with delight.

Ten minutes later, Rudy and Julie and a crowd much larger than before watched from a distance as the cone slowly drew a plate-sized glowing circle on the black wall.

While the circle was cooling, a quick lottery picked a lucky winner for the person who got to swing a sledge hammer at the center of the circle. Fortunately the winner was a muscular man. He swung the sledge hammer so hard Rudy worried about the head flying off, but the head hit squarely in the center of the circle. The circle of material stayed where it was but it clearly vibrated in the second or two after the blow.

A cheer went up in the crowd.

As soon as they verified that the latest gas reading around the hole was safe, Rudy and several others went for a closer look. Around the entire perimeter, the black material had crumbled away. What showed in the gap looked like a sheet of dirty wires running up and down. As Rudy watched, one of the men pried loose a single fiber that had more give than piano wire. Someone else inserted a crowbar and tried to break the fiber. It stretched without breaking.

"Get a jack," Rudy said.

In minutes, a jack was in place, and one of the workers slowly notched it up one click at a time, pulling one end of the crowbar. When the strand had stretched about a foot, the man pushing on the jack began to strain harder, and just as it seemed the strand would prevent him from clicking the jack one more notch, the strand snapped and the crowbar clattered to the ground.

"That's it!" Rudy shouted. "That's it! This may take a while, but now it's just a matter of brute force and turning the crank." He took a deep breath and glanced at Julie, who looked as happy as he felt.

Just a few minutes later, though, as Rudy watched the crew start to cut a large door-shaped hole in the black wall, he realized that he was also a little scared.

He hoped they were really doing the right thing.

5

GRAY GOO

LIFELESS AUTOMOBILES LINED both sides of the street as though some nearby rich collector had long ago run out of space to house them.

Matt Sheehan's car dipped its nose as he drove south, moving into the left lane of the northbound half of the Battery Tunnel. The Manhattan digital audio station had been out of commission since they had been brought here, and the lone FM station currently on the air faded into static as he moved deeper. That was just as well; the song reminded him of a long hike he and Nadine had made outside of Rio. As he reached the column of cars and trucks parked in the right lane, a cop flagged him down, looked at his face, and told him about a parking space just ahead of a truck parked about thirty meters ahead.

On foot Matt passed through the decontamination station, where his skin and clothes were misted by a noxious combination of ingredients recommended by members of the board of public health, none of whom, as far as Matt could tell, had ever come through in person. He almost wished he was back in the WTC with Abby and the other linguists, but his help didn't seem needed there, and he was curious about the black barrier.

Beyond the decon station were a few more trucks parked on the right. Near the black barrier clustered a small crowd.

Matt came up behind Rudy and Julie, who sat together on a large box. He tapped Rudy's shoulder and exchanged hellos with the two of them, who both seemed in good spirits. Julie's minivid was inactive for the moment.

"Shouldn't be long now," Rudy said. He pointed at the large square outline in the black barrier. "They've weakened the base material all around that doorway, and they're cutting the individual strands holding the top in place."

"I'm glad I got down here before they finished."

"Any change in the transmission?"

"Nope. Bobby Joe doesn't know what to make of it. I don't understand, either. If they want to talk, what we're sending back should be a pretty clear hello." Matt rubbed the muscles at the back of his neck. "Bobby Joe's a strange bird, though."

"What now?"

"If he had his way, instead of transmitting the capture pictures, I think we'd be sending them Silly Sheila cartoons. 'Can't you just see the expressions on their faces when they decode this?' he says."

Julie smiled and said, "But he's a smart guy."

"No doubt about it. He's invaluable. He's just one of those guys who takes a little more supervision than average. I bet if he was married and had kids, he'd have them totally confused. But boy, would they have interesting expressions." Matt looked back at the crowd near the black barrier.

Rudy hesitated. "You look tired."

Matt took his gaze off the clump of workers and looked at Rudy. "A little. I guess we all are."

About the same time, someone in the crowd near the barrier called out, "We got it!"

Rudy and Julie got up, and the three of them moved forward. Julie turned on her minivid. Workers pried at the top of the square outline and slowly a very thin section of black material, still attached at the bottom, tilted out from the rest of the barrier like a drawbridge pivoting outward from a castle wall. Revealed behind the section was the same gray material they had seen covering the plain.

The black square tilted all the way down until what had been the top edge rested against the stained pavement. Along the hinged junction were exposed hundreds of tiny fibers. The sheet of black material looked paper thin, but it hardly flexed when a massive construction worker put his full weight in the center of it and bounced on his steel-toed work boots a couple of times. "Mighty strong stuff," the guy said.

Now that they had breached the barrier, Matt was more

interested in the gray material. If it had anything like the strength of the black sheet, they still had a long job in front of them.

A worker wearing gloves swung a hammer lightly at the gray wall, then looked carefully at where the hammer had silently hit. He swung again, harder, and Matt heard a soft dull *thud.* When the hammer came back, Matt could see a shadowed indentation on the gray wall, and he felt relief, convinced the gray stuff was going to be easier to deal with.

Rudy stepped onto the black sheet. He pulled out a pocket knife and put on a pair of gloves. The knife blade seemed to cut into the gray surface fairly easily. Seconds later, Rudy shook a small wedge of the gray stuff off his knife and into a beaker held by a woman in a long white lab coat. Rudy glanced at the faces of the work crew. "Good work. The chemists will tell us pretty soon how safe this stuff is, but so far it looks like it's going to be easy going from here on out. Take a break if you want."

Most of the group drifted away, but one man offered Rudy a very long screwdriver and said, "Want to see how deep you can go?"

Rudy took the screwdriver, put the point against the face of the gray substance, and leaned into it. The screwdriver buried itself to the handle. When he pulled it back out, the blade was clean. He looked toward Matt and said, "This stuff seems to have the consistency of modeling clay."

Matt took a closer look. An hour later, he was still standing near the exposed gray material, talking with Rudy and Julie, when the woman in the white lab coat came back and told Rudy that the stuff was safe unless anyone tried to eat it. The pH was neutral, it wasn't flammable or explosive, it didn't generate dangerous particulates like asbestos did, and it didn't give off any dangerous gases. Her summary was that it was as safe as modeling clay. She took some more of the gray stuff back to the lab with her, to do more extensive testing.

Rudy called the crew back to work and passed on the summary. He used his knife again and, as though the occasion were a bizarre wine and cheese party, cut small wedges for everyone to examine. "If we're going to tunnel very far, we've got to cut through quite a few meters of this," he said. "I'd appreciate your thoughts on the best ways to do it."

Matt held a sample of the gray substance in his hand. It didn't feel sticky. He squeezed it, and it flattened just like soft clay. He stretched it, and it thinned to the diameter of a pencil before it broke. The two halves mixed together easily, leaving no sign that they had been separated. He sniffed the material and detected no odor.

Other people nearby subjected the material to some improvised tests, like putting a glob on the floor and hammering it, and lighting a match under a piece. The hammered piece looked like flattened modeling clay, and the heated piece turned darker until it looked like discolored clay that was stiffer than normal.

Finally a man with a shovel stepped forward. He put the edge of the shovel against the wall and planted his heel firmly against the back end. Without too much trouble he removed a shovelful of the gray stuff and plopped it onto the pavement. "Maybe we just dig," the man said.

Abby came up behind Matt as he stared out the window of the World Trade Center command post and said, "How about dinner tonight?"

He turned and smiled. "You haven't found a hoard of real food, have you?"

Abby wasn't sure what there was about his smile, but it always made her want to smile back. "I'm afraid not. But we could picnic on the roof. That would be a change."

"Sure. Why not?"

They still had an hour of "daylight" left when they reached the observation deck. Matt carried a plastic liter jug of water, and Abby carried a jar of food pellets and a couple of paper cups. They walked up to the highest level of the deck.

"Would this table suit you, monsieur?" She gestured toward the nearby open space.

Matt looked around the empty observation deck and at the domes beyond. For just a second, his eyes took on that faraway look that she hated to see. "You sure you don't have anything with a view of the Hudson?"

"Don't I wish."

They sat. Abby looked at Matt, and thought more seriously about the question. "You think it's really possible that we may see the Hudson again?"

"I wish I knew. I'm not sure I can handle a steady diet of this stuff for the rest of my life." Matt gestured at the jar of food pellets.

"How's it going down below?" Abby asked as she took the cups and poured water for them both.

"By the time I left, they had dug a tunnel about two meters deep into that putty-like gray stuff outside. If everything goes well, I expect they'll reach the surface tomorrow."

Abby popped a foot pellet in her mouth. It was as tasty as a pencil eraser, as brittle as a calcium pill. "And then what? Whoever steps outside gets picked up and put back in the cage? Or gets sizzled by an enormous insect zapper?"

Matt took a couple of the food pellets. "I guess that's possible. We don't really know how closely they're watching what's going on. Rudy suggested spreading a tarp over a jeep and painting it the same shade of gray as the plain. I'm not convinced yet, and in any event we've got to get to the surface first."

"I want to go, you know." Abby looked at him over her cup of water. She felt surprisingly relaxed, enjoying the opportunity to be alone with Matt.

"On the trip to the other dome?"

"Of course."

"Could be dangerous." His gaze made her want to be in danger with Matt rather than perfectly safe without him.

"That's very true. That's why I thought you'd be especially eager to hear about volunteers."

Matt grinned.

Abby knew right then he'd been teasing her and that the answer was yes. She could read that message far easier than written words. God, why had she never met anyone like this before? "Well?"

"Well. Well, we have to have a linguist."

Abby felt a brief tremor pass through her body, but wasn't

entirely sure whether it was the result of knowing she could go, or knowing she could go with Matt. She covered her reaction by taking another drink of water.

"Thanks for not teasing me *too* long."

"Tease you? God forbid. You're teasing *me.*"

"Would you like that?" Without even realizing what she was doing, Abby moved closer to him.

Matt's expression was cheerful as she looked into his eyes from a closer vantage point. His expression slowly became more serious, as Abby said nothing, and she felt sure she could see the longing in his eyes. What she couldn't tell was whether Abby was at the front of his brain, or if his wife took that position. She found it more difficult to breathe.

Finally Matt said, "If circumstances were a little different, I'd like that a *lot.*"

Abby's courage suddenly faltered, and she didn't feel up to asking him *which* circumstances he was referring to. She could easily imagine how bad she'd feel if Matt went on to remind her that he was married.

Manhattan is home to over a hundred nationalities, most of which seem homogeneous only to the outsiders. One such diverse group is the Native Americans. Many of them rallied at the American Indian Community Home Gallery on Broadway north of SoHo.

From Arapaho to Iroquois to Sioux to Zuñi, they gathered at their island within an island for mutual support and to compare theories. At any time of day, there would always be at least a few groups of people talking, singing soft chants, or simply sitting near each other. More than a few of them made jokes about how first the white man stole Manhattan from the Indians and now someone else seemed to have stolen it again.

A cop let Rudy pass. Sometimes when Rudy walked from one place to another, he could let his thoughts drift, and for a brief time he could imagine everything was the way it used to be. He had worked hard to escape that tiny two-bedroom house in East L.A., and few things here reminded him of the small homes in the barrio. He'd told Matt and Abby his store of food in his office was because he spent so much time there, and that was partly true, but the main reason was one he seldom admitted to himself. After a childhood of competing with too many people for too little food, he had wanted never again to feel hunger for very long. The irony of now having to subsist on the alien food pellets was not lost on him.

Although he enjoyed its cosmopolitan life a lot, Rudy had never expected to wind up in New York. In fact, he had heard so much about it that he had once told Matt he'd never consider living in New York unless he had so much money he could afford his own zip code.

As soon as he stepped past the decontamination barrier the thoughts dissipated. He looked ahead, and he knew something was wrong.

He was early, as was his habit. None of the tunnel-digging crew had arrived yet. He reached the guard who'd been on duty and found the man asleep. Rudy walked closer to where pole-mounted trouble lights glared harshly near the tunnel mouth.

Actually it could no longer be called a tunnel mouth. Where yesterday a short tunnel had been cut into the gray material, now the square opening in the black wall was filled with the gray stuff, and gray goo had flowed from beyond the barrier into the Battery Tunnel. Looking a little like gray toothpaste squeezed through a square hole, the gray goo formed a thick alluvial fan extending over a meter from the opening.

Rudy knelt near the gray material and pressed a hammer into the stuff. It still possessed the modeling-clay firmness, but reason told him it must really be a fluid, albeit an extremely viscous one. He found a small pebble on the pavement and placed it about a centimeter from the edge of the gray goo. He watched the gap. He couldn't detect the gap actually shrinking, but several seconds later he could tell that it was in fact smaller than before.

He walked over to the dump truck and climbed up until he could see inside the back. What had been a pile of chunks of the gray stuff now looked more like gray cake batter poured into a pan. The high point was in the middle, but the stuff was obviously flowing slowly, gradually working its way into the corners. Another day and it would probably be level. Glass took years to fatten the bottom of window panes. On the viscosity scale, this stuff was much nearer cold molasses than glass.

Rudy remembered the piece of the gray goo that someone had burned the day before, and thought about how it had seemed stiffer. He retrieved an oxyacetylene torch, turned on the gas jets, and lit it.

At the edge of the gray goo that had now covered the pebble, he played the torch over the surface and watched it darken and shrink back. He found another pebble and placed it about a centimeter from the new edge.

As he moved around the fan-shaped spread of goo, heating the edge with the torch, he heard sounds of surprise as the construction crew began to arrive.

Nicholas showed up within an hour. By then the goo had spread no farther. Instead it looked like dough rising, confined by a darkened perimeter. Workers were just finishing the job of putting a panel in front of the opening and bracing it in place to minimize the flow.

"I got your message," Nicholas said. "I left Emile in charge. Fortunately things are going smoothly."

"Thanks for coming down," Rudy said. He gave Nicholas a quick summary. "So, you got any ideas on how to tunnel through this stuff safely?"

Nicholas shook his head and moved closer to the gray goo. He performed some of the same tests that Rudy had done, but Nicholas's tests were conducted at pencil length or with the aid of gloves. Finally he came back to Rudy.

"I may be thinking of some of the same things you are," Nicholas said.

"That's fine. I just didn't want to precondition you."

"Well, the obvious first. The tunnel walls have to be braced, just like we were working in dirt."

"Right." Rudy wasn't sure if it was his imagination or if Nicholas had shuddered slightly when he said, "working in dirt."

"Okay. This stuff seems about half as heavy as water, so that means the pressure at this point is about half of what it would be in water this deep. We're roughly, what, thirty meters below the surface. At one-half atmosphere for every ten meters—"

Nicholas pushed up his sleeve and exposed a wrist calculator. After pushing a few buttons, he said, "Eventually you're going to have something near fifty tons pushing on that panel."

Rudy nodded.

"But the depth is the only real nuisance. If we were to go back up top and dig just underneath the bottom of the bubble, you'd have a lot less pressure. You should be able to tunnel pretty easily there."

"True, but we've got a lot easier environmental control where we are. Plus, if we are being watched, this is a lot safer." Rudy thought a minute, then snapped his fingers. "I bet if we wanted, we could tunnel all the way to the next dome just below the surface without much trouble at all."

"Except for the nuisance of having to get rid of the stuff you dig out. And getting fresh air all that way."

"We might have ways around that. Near the surface, the pressure would be low enough that maybe we could just *push* our way through it. That way we wouldn't risk being seen on the surface."

"And bracing the walls would be a lot easier near the surface."

"Actually, we might not have to."

"I think you'd better explain, boss."

Rudy reached down and picked up a piece of the gray matter discolored from being heated. He rapped it against the wall, then handed it to Nicholas, who grabbed it with a handkerchief. "There's a chance that we already have the bracing material we need."

Bobby Joe Brewster leaned back and examined the close-up views of individual domes on the large display before him.

One window on the screen showed the first dome in what Bobby Joe thought of as the grand tour—the bubble about ten kilometers away, directly south of Battery Park. Whatever these people looked like, they must like the outside even less than Bobby Joe did. He hadn't seen any sign of activity since he started scanning. The dome looked to be only a tenth the size of the one over Manhattan, but the building inside dwarfed every human structure. The dome held but one giant building, a cube that must be half as tall as the World Trade Center towers. Irregular rows of large round windows helped him learn nothing about the interior of the building, because he couldn't see in. He stared at the patterns made by the windows, and wondered vaguely if they spelled anything.

Bobby Joe adjusted his controls, giving more power to the transmitters directed toward that dome. A scan of the receivers with antennas pointed at the dome said they still had detected no reply.

Bobby Joe absently reached for the plastic plate beside the console and grabbed the last couple of food pellets. He popped them in his mouth and took a drink of water from the soft-drink container. It would have been easier to use a glass, but the gaudy decorations on the triangular container made him feel less cut off from his normal diet.

He wiped his mouth and looked over at Abby where she sat at a computer terminal with the screen displaying the alien message. Before his conversation with Matt, he'd have been tempted to share his theory with Abby that the aliens took Manhattan, leaving behind a ransom demand, and that the Earth was refusing to pay.

When Matt reached the blocked end of the Battery Tunnel, he looked around for Rudy, but saw no sign of him. Even more workers than last time bustled about in controlled chaos. A faint rumbling shook the pavement, an indication that some of the subways were running again on a vastly reduced schedule, mainly carrying outpatients between hospitals and home.

The smaller tunnel through the black wall and into the gray goo looked different, more like a large mine shaft except for the gradual curve upward. Four-by-eight plastic beams lined the walls, floor, and ceiling. Three people wearing hardhats with lights came out of the shaft. Rudy was the third. He talked to a woman who jotted down notes as she listened, and then he looked up and saw Matt.

"I think we're getting the hang of it," Rudy said as he came closer. He took off his hardhat and scratched his scalp. "It's like tunneling through very slow-motion water. The cutting is easy, and as long as we're quick, the stuff doesn't rush back in. We're heating the sides as we go. Cooking the stuff makes it a little like very tough rubber. That alone might be enough to maintain the tunnel shape once we get high enough—where the pressure is lower."

"Great. I'm sure glad someone like you is in charge of it."

Rudy shook his head. "I sure didn't feel that way when I came back down here and saw that gray stuff flowing out. I should have thought about that possibility. If we had been digging fast enough, we might have wound up trapping workers at the end of the shaft."

Matt put a hand on Rudy's shoulder. "I'm confident you'll do everything right. I've always been more sure of you than you were."

"And vice versa, now that I think about it. Want to take a look inside?"

"Sure."

Matt followed Rudy to the mouth of the shaft. A half-dozen tubes and cables converged from various points and entered the tunnel along the floor. He didn't have to stoop inside the tunnel, despite his height and the hardhat.

They squeezed to one side as a worker on the way out hurried past.

Rudy pointed to the wall formed by adjacent vertical plastic beams. "Behind those beams is a fused layer of permaseal, and past that is the goo itself, heated enough to seal it. Some material-properties folks are conducting more tests right now, trying to see how the strength varies as a function of the temperature and duration of the heat. They're also trying to judge whether it's likely to change back. I think this section is safe no matter what, but closer to the surface we can probably get by with a lot less effort. We've gone to around-the-clock operation so the goo doesn't have time to make trouble."

They walked up the moderate incline, and Rudy said, "We would have cut it steeper, to get to the easier path earlier, but this will make it safer to get stuff in and out of the tunnel."

They edged past a worker maneuvering a wheelbarrow loaded with chunks of the goo. At intervals, small lights hung from a cord fastened to the ceiling beams. By the time they had passed ten of the lights and climbed what Matt guessed to be ten meters, they had reached the working end of the tunnel.

The final ten meters of tunnel were even wider than the section they had gone through. All the surfaces showed rough-hewn gray material. At the very end of the tunnel, a worker played a torch back and forth over the surface of the wall in a regular pattern. Just back from that point, a small team wallpapered the floor, ceiling, and walls with shiny sheets of material. Between the wallpaperers and the finished tunnel, another small team set plastic beams in place. The last couple of finished beams didn't look as even as the rest to Matt, and he assumed they would be pressed into final alignment by the goo itself as it pushed harder and harder from the outside.

As Matt and Rudy watched the goings-on, they had to make way for an empty wheelbarrow and then a pair of workers with a large drill.

One of the workers said to Rudy, "We're ready for the test hole."

Rudy said, "Good. Go ahead," then turned to Matt as the men moved past and began to set up their equipment. "They're going to drill to the surface so we can get an air sample from out there. You can stay if you like, but this is new, so we could be in for some surprises."

Matt said, "I'll stay. That's part of the reason I came."

A couple of minutes later one of the drillers gave Rudy a high sign. Rudy took a small box from his shirt pocket and pressed a switch on it. The lights in the tunnel winked off and then rapidly back on several times, then came back on steady. Rudy raised his voice. "We're about to drill a test hole to the surface, so anyone who's not involved should take a rest break."

As soon as a few workers had left the area, the drillers put on nose masks, aimed the long drill bit vertically at the roof of the tunnel, and turned on the drill. The drill moved fairly easily up toward the ceiling as gray grit fell slowly to the tunnel floor. When the drill got near the ceiling, they stopped it, freed the bit, and attached an extension, which they then tightened into the drill, and continued.

By the time they had gone through a stack of extensions, the drill finally began to turn faster. "I think we're there!" one of the workers shouted.

Running the drill in the opposite direction, and removing and stacking extensions for several minutes, left them with their original pile. As the bit itself finally came out of the hole and they shut off the drill, Matt could hear the whistling of air escaping just before a worker slapped a small silver square of permaseal over the whole. The sound stopped, and an indentation formed in the permaseal. Moving quickly, the other worker retrieved the rounded end of a hose. The permaseal cover came off the hole, and the pair of men ran the hose up the hole until a white ring around the hose met the ceiling, leaving about two meters of hose, capped with a threaded stem.

Matt could still hear a soft hiss of escaping air, but a worker stuffed what looked like real modeling clay into the small gap around the hose, and the sound died.

"Okay," Rudy said as another worker brought in a pump connected to a long extension cord. "Now for the interesting stuff." As soon as the pump and hose were connected, he moved closer and motioned for Matt to follow.

Rudy switched on the pump, and a light next to a gas canister lit. Over the throbbing sound, he said, "Right now, the hose is mostly full of our own atmosphere. I'm pumping gas from the hose into this canister, and I'll give it a safety margin."

The pump throbbed for a couple of minutes before Rudy flipped a switch. The light near the first canister went out, and a light next to a second, much smaller canister lit. After a few more seconds, he turned off the pump. "Okay. We've got a sample of the atmosphere up there. The only other thing we need now is the pressure." He flipped another couple of switches, and a lamp illuminated an attached pressure gauge. The black digits rose quickly to 0.60 and then climbed more slowly, settling on 0.642 atmospheres.

"Good," Matt said. The first report he'd gotten had said the pressure was probably between sixty and seventy percent of Earth-normal range, and it was comforting to get agreement. "And how soon does the lab say they can analyze this?"

Rudy detached the canister containing the outside gas sample. "A few hours. Part of that is just transit time."

Rudy gave directions to one of the workers who had brought in the pump. The woman disconnected the hose and sealed it, then wheeled the pump back down the tunnel.

"I don't know that there's much more to see right now," Rudy said.

Matt nodded and they started walking down the slope, out of the tunnel. They passed several workers returning to their jobs.

Back in the open Matt said, "You're doing great. Everyone seems to know exactly what to do, and everyone's efficient. But that's no surprise."

"Thanks. By the way, I should have a *real* surprise for you in a day or two."

Matt pulled the city car into the artificial sunshine and left the Battery Tunnel behind. He probably should have gone directly back to the World Trade Center, but people there knew their jobs, and they were doing all they could. He needed a few minutes alone.

He stepped on the accelerator, and the electric motor whine rose smoothly. Minutes later the car climbed the ramp onto the nearly deserted West Side Expressway. Matt pulled over to the right and stopped. He wondered how loud the honking would have been if he'd done that just a few days before. All the streets had at least one lane cleared for emergency vehicles. In places that meant abandoned cars had been forced onto the sidewalks.

He looked back at the mass of buildings. He was still pleasantly surprised at how well the residents had adapted. To be sure, the number of shouters was up a little, but street musicians and mimes and magicians and poetry readers were out in force, doing their part in giving the public something to take their minds off the situation. And they were probably getting far more attention than normal, which had to be rewarding. The political and religious cranks were out in force, and they all seemed to like the current situation even less than Matt did.

In the distance he could see some kids playing basketball. They'd had to fashion an extension from a pipe, so the hoop and backboard were two or three times their normal height. The kids bounced around the court as though it were a huge trampoline and they were in slow motion. The scene prompted a vague recollection of some kid's movie from long ago about basketball players able to jump three to five meters in the air.

For many people, the reason to continue their day-to-day routine was now gone. Crime had risen slightly to take up some of the slack, but the volunteer lists were overflowing for virtually every city function that needed more help than normal. A black market flourished, but since money meant nothing, the trading was limited to exchanging services or an ever-diminishing supply of luxury goods and consumables that were used up, worn out, ingested, or burned.

Matt looked through the dome at the bubbles beyond, and he thought of Nadine.

Sure, they'd had their share of arguments, but who hadn't? He realized now that having her abruptly say she wanted out when he had thought things were okay cut several ways. It made him question his judgment about everything. If he was that close to her and still couldn't see the inevitable, what did that make him? And why couldn't he drive her from his mind when he had a much larger problem to face?

Angry at himself, Matt looked back at Manhattan and tried to force Nadine from his mind. Several blocks away, a crowd had gathered at an intersection. He wondered vaguely what the attraction was.

Stuart Lund raised both arms to the crowd. He had found that although people looked away if they saw him in an everyday context, here the stump on his right arm was a virtual magnet for attention. With a deep, resonant voice, he said, "God is talking to us. Are you listening?

"He talked to me in the moments while he was taking us away. He took my hand, and he told me to repent." Stuart liked that line. God had taken his hand, in two senses. But he wasn't *too* proud of it. God wouldn't approve of that.

"Surely everybody here knows about Noah's Ark. Well, here we are on Noah's Ark Two. God will put us back on the Earth as soon as He's scrubbed it clean once again." Already Stuart saw comprehension flicker across a new face or two, and he knew he was gaining. God had, obviously, been all-knowing when He realized that Stuart could convey His message well. The streets held hardly any traffic now, so the crowd was free to spill into the intersection.

Quite a few of the people in the crowd watched Stuart intently, a couple of them unconsciously rocking back and forth as they stood. No doubt the crowd was every bit as agitated about recent events as Stuart was, and people just needed a direction for their energy to be focused.

Stuart didn't stop to count the faces, but as he maintained frequent eye contact with everyone who had stopped to listen, he was sure there were more than fifty people listening. People looked scruffier than New Yorkers normally had before, partly because of the rationing of non-renewable supplies like soap, partly because some of the people seemed to think this was some kind of vacation, that they had been relieved of their daily responsibilities. Most of these people listened attentively, possibly aware, as Stuart was, that this cataclysmic event had given them new responsibilities. Stuart drew a breath and continued.

"But not all of us are listening to God's word." Stuart gestured at one of the closest domes. "We're here, among God's other chosen people. All of us will be restored to our own sparkling clean worlds. But *not* if we tamper. Not if we're disobedient.

"God obviously wants us to stay here until He is ready for us to go back. God has obviously put His word over our heads. But there are people who are trying to escape this enclosure, trying to pretend they are on an equal footing with God. *And* they're trying to interpret God's word with no assistance from the religious community that surely is ready to help.

"Even as I talk to you, these people, with the mayor's consent, are putting us at risk. Their egotism, their sheer arrogance, is going to make God decide He has made a mistake—that none of us should be allowed to return to a pristine Earth. If they continue, they will *kill* us all!"

Abby walked beside Matt as he looked for Rudy. They found him finishing a conversation with a couple of workers.

Rudy looked up, saw them, and smiled. "We're just about at the surface," he said. "Come on and take a look."

Matt glanced at her, and she nodded. Matt said, "Lead on."

Rudy guided them past the motor-driven winch and toward the tunnel mouth. "Since you were here last, we added the winch to help bring out the stuff we've dug and to carry up more wall lining material."

"Wow," Abby said as they got into the tunnel.

"Some view, huh?" Rudy said. "This will take us a few minutes. You're looking at about a ten-story climb." The tunnel ran straight through the gray goo, climbing at a thirty-percent grade.

It reminded Abby of a long escalator tunnel, but this one was longer than any she'd been in. From here, the top of the tunnel was just a point of light.

The trio passed an empty wheeled cart as it rolled down the tunnel floor, bouncing lightly from one plastic beam to the next. Cables at both ends connected its handles to a line overhead.

Rudy said, "Walking up and down this kind of a grade without stairs will use some muscles you might not normally use. Don't be too surprised if you're a little sore tomorrow."

"That seems funny," Abby said. "With the light gravity it's hard to imagine anyone straining a muscle."

"Yeah, that's what I thought, too."

They finally reached the top of the tunnel, where it widened into a square room about three meters on a side. A horizontal brace at waist height spanned the room. One end of the brace met the plastic beams forming the wall. The other side of the beam braced a large square panel on the opposite wall. Protruding from the ceiling was a periscope. The level floor and ceiling were lined with plastic beams. At the base of two of the walls, steel beams rested on the floor.

Rudy went to the periscope and swung the eyepiece toward Matt and Abby. "Want to take a look around?"

Matt gestured to Abby to go ahead.

Through the periscope Abby got her first view of the Manhattan dome from the outside. By turning the periscope, she saw a ground-level view of the flat gray plain and a couple of other domes in the distance. She let Matt take his turn.

Abby looked back down the tunnel while Matt was occupied. It somehow looked even longer from this perspective.

"What are the I-beams for?" Matt asked when he finished with the periscope.

Rudy glanced at one of the beams. "To keep us from floating to the top. I didn't think about that right away, but when we first got this section completed, the ceiling was about a meter under the surface. When we checked again, the distance had shrunk to about ninety centimeters. Then I finally got smart. Especially with this top section having a bigger volume, we're essentially a big bubble in molasses. As long as what's in the bubble weighs less than the same volume of goo, we slowly float upward. If we load this place down too much, we'll sink. Get it just right, and we'll float at a constant depth."

An idle cable suddenly tightened, then started to move, and a pulley mounted to the ceiling braces began to rotate as the cable reeled, bringing something up from the bottom.

"Time for my surprise," Rudy said. "Help me move this beam."

As Rudy spun a handle several turns, the beam across the room loosened. Matt looked puzzled as he helped Rudy move the beam to the edge of the room. Rudy moved aside the plate covering most of one wall and exposed a large circle of gray goo almost as tall as the room itself.

Abby looked down the tunnel. Something large was blocking most of the light, leaving only the occasional overhead lamps to show where the tunnel was.

As the shape coming up the tunnel grew larger, Rudy said, "Okay. Now you've got two choices. We can cut through the roof here according to plan, and start walking on the surface. And then we run the risk of sinking slowly into this stuff if we're forced to stop for a while. And we run the risk of being detected.

"*Or* we can get there beneath the surface with the borer."

Matt looked as though he was about to start asking questions when Rudy waved him silent. Seconds later, an enormous contraption with a round plate on the front end swung slowly from the tunnel into the room. Rudy clicked a button on a small box in his pocket and the contraption came to a halt.

Abby and Matt walked slowly around the machine, in spots having to squeeze between it and the wall. The thing, a modified compact tank, was about the size of a car, but more boxy and windowless. At the front end were two huge disks, taller than the rest of the contraption, even taller than Abby, and about a half-meter thick, mounted adjacently like two large truck tires on the same axle. At the back Abby could see tanklike treads. Shiny tubing ran from a large tank forward into a maze of pumps and cables. Near the lower rear was a huge box labeled "Fuel Cell."

Rudy cautioned them to back into the tunnel for just a minute. He reached up and unsnapped a clasp, and the device settled onto the floor. He pushed some more buttons on his remote, and the tanklike thing went into action, moving toward the circular surface of gray goo. The huge round front of the contraption lined up with the exposed round patch of goo, and a long plunger slowly telescoped from the rear of the unit until it started to push against the braced wall and then halted. A mechanical whine grew louder, and Abby realized the outside disk on the front of the contraption was being pushed into the exposed goo.

Several seconds later, the front disk had pushed directly into the goo, and less than a minute later the disk behind it was covered, also. Rudy pushed some more buttons, and the plunger retracted into the body of the machine. Abby and Matt came back into the room.

As a couple of Rudy's crew silently joined them in the room, the contraption suddenly moved farther into the wall for half a meter, stopped, then resumed, again tunneling through the goo. She smiled at Matt's expression of wonder.

"Rudy, you're a genius," Matt said softly.

The borer was disappearing into the round tunnel it created. Someone had stuck a bumper sticker on the rear end: I BRAKE FOR ALIENS.

Rudy looked as pleased as a kid who'd just learned to ride a bike. "Thanks. We don't know for sure yet, but it should be able to do about a kilometer an hour. The front disk contains a piston. The back disk expands when it stops, to anchor the unit, *and* it heats the goo around the perimeter, making it tough enough, we think, to maintain the tunnel shape. While it's anchored, the piston pushes forward to make the tunnel slightly longer. When that cycle is complete, the piston retracts, the back disk compresses, and the treads take it forward for the next step. When we heat the goo, it oxidizes, turning darker and getting more dense. It also flows and expands very slightly, so I think we've found the best way to move through it."

"You're really a genius," Matt said again.

"I didn't do this on my own. I just helped design it. With the entire resources of Manhattan available, there isn't much we can't do. We *think* that with this size of tunnel, surrounded by the much denser rubbery goo that we get when we heat the stuff, the tunnel will float just below the surface. So, if you want, you can tunnel to the next dome. What we'll have to be a little careful about is not letting it sit in any one place too long, because it's so heavy."

Rudy grabbed a hand drill with a long bit, entered the round tunnel, which was already a few meters deep, and waved them in. It was darker since no lights had been installed, but Abby could see circles around the perimeter every half-meter or so. Rudy drilled straight up through the roof of the tunnel. Moments later came a *whoosh* of escaping air.

Rudy hurried back into the room and retrieved a gray pipe with a knobby end. He pushed the plain end into the hole, and then aimed his hardhat light at the end sticking out. "Since the atmosphere out there is tolerable, we'll put a pressure seal in this room, and all you need to do is every once in a while put in one of these ventilation fans so you'll have breathable air no matter how long the tunnel gets. We've got two models: a blower and a sucker. This one's meant to suck air into the tunnel. And it's got a built-in light. The pipe itself is a wrapped up sheet battery.

"The blower model is similar, but it has a tube that drops to the floor, so those will handle carbon dioxide exhaust. Even though carbon dioxide's heavier than oxygen, the air mixes enough that you won't actually have a carbon dioxide layer at the bottom of the tunnel. If we put these in a little closer together than necessary to get just enough oxygen, it should all work out fine."

The borer had continued to move while Rudy explained. Abby was sure it was moving at the equivalent of a very slow walk.

Matt's grin was infectious. "Rudy, you're a nuking genius."

He looked into the darkness of the tunnel the borer had left in its wake. "I guess we're about ready for the strangest journey we've ever had."

Abby looked at the disappearing borer and felt a tiny chill. "Or maybe the second strangest."

Ten days after the capture, Dorine Underwood gave the team a brief send-off. "I want you to remember that we'll have a large, heavily armed team ready to follow you if you run into trouble."

"We appreciate that," said Matt. "I know you'd like to send a larger team to begin with. In some ways I agree, but I have to admit, I'm a little glad the oxygen limitation forces us to go with a small number. That puts fewer people at risk, and it should lower the chances of our being detected." Despite some strong opinions among Dorine's advisors, he had successfully argued for his choices on the team, justifying Rudy on the basis of his having been the key designer of the borer, plus his general engineering and military skills. Contacting the residents of other domes without someone like Abby would have been pointless. Bobby Joe would be there for help with electronics and science, since some of the communication attempts might well need to tap a common understanding of how the universe worked.

Julie and several other journalists stood at the rear of the conference room, capturing events on video for the rest of the population.

Dorine looked at the map on her wall. It showed the intended route through the domes. With her concurrence, the path headed toward the dome that was transmitting, veering near some of the domes between Manhattan and the destination dome, mainly domes the telescopic survey had told them contained civilizations that looked the most similar to human life.

Matt used his walkie-talkie to tell the people back in Manhattan all was well. In the darkness ahead, the borer continued its jerky assault on the goo. Behind him was Abby, lit by the headlights of a small electric cart driven by Bobby Joe Brewster. And behind Bobby Joe was the longest pipe Matt had ever seen. Far in the distance, Rudy's hardhat lamp bobbed as he walked toward them, catching up fairly easily. The limited space overhead denied him the low-gravity lope, but he was doing fine with the lean-way-forward-and-keep-from-falling gait. Everyone wore a knife, to be used to cut themselves out if the tunnel walls collapsed. Their shirts and pants sported numerous small pockets, each with a snapping flap.

Abby's soft voice rose above the mechanical noises from the borer and the electric cart. "Too bad Rudy didn't design a borer that cut square tunnels. I keep turning my ankle." The tunnel walls absorbed the sound, unlike an actual pipe, which would have generated metallic echoes.

"You could drive," Matt said.

"And deprive Bobby Joe?"

Matt could feel her smile in the dim light. Driving for hours at parade velocity would be grating for him, too. But Bobby Joe had been an urbanite for so long that driving was a change of pace.

Rudy caught up and sat on the rear deck of the small trailer towed by the cart. He put the drill back in a tray on top. "Okay. The last air pump seems to be working fine. And the readings say we still have plenty of oxygen."

The smell of the air in the tunnel made Matt think of a clear, warm day high enough in the mountains that the pollutants were rarer than they were in the city. They had all adjusted easily to the reduced pressure, since the oxygen content of the gas outside was slightly higher than on Earth. Fortunately it wasn't enough higher to make fire a severe risk. The air temperature was a few degrees higher than the new Manhattan norm, but with short sleeves and limited exertion that wasn't a problem either.

"Great," Matt said. "Bobby Joe, how much farther?" One of the things Matt had learned so far was that Bobby Joe didn't like being called BJ.

Bobby Joe consulted a small display resting on a ledge near the steering wheel and added, "Just about a kilometer."

That meant they'd covered almost nine kilometers. Matt's legs felt tired despite the low gravity. He probably wouldn't have been that tired if they had walked briskly the whole way, but somehow the shopping-mall pace fatigued him more.

They could have let the borer continue ahead unattended and then catch up from time to time, but Matt didn't have enough confidence in it yet. If the heating element failed to operate for some reason, the borer might just start to sink into the depths of the goo, a submarine with no ballast tanks.

From time to time, Matt pushed hard on the tunnel walls to convince himself they were indeed the stiffer form of the gray goo, and that they wouldn't soon start closing in. The warmth left behind by the borer was comforting. The human body was heavier than the goo, so without that barrier they would eventually sink to the neutral buoyancy depth, however far down that was, but not before they were left trying to breathe gray goo.

Half a kilometer later, they stopped long enough to unfold the porta-potty for those in need and to drill another air pump hole. By the time they caught up with the borer, they were almost at the dome.

"How about if you let me take the lead?" Rudy asked.

That was fine with Matt. He and Abby followed as Bobby Joe called out distances and Rudy controlled the borer's path, trying to guide it into a curve that just touched the dome.

"I've probably got up to thirty meters of slop in these readings," Bobby Joe said.

Rudy said, "That's all right. If we have too hard a time, we can drill another air tube and take a closer look."

"Fifty meters . . . forty meters."

The tunnel began to curve noticeably over the next couple of minutes, bearing right, so they could graze the side of the dome.

Matt looked back and decided the tunnel had curved about thirty degrees and risen slightly. A moment later, the nearest light behind them winked out as they continued the curve. The cart's headlights illuminated Rudy and the borer.

"Thirty meters . . . twenty meters."

They curved still more.

"Ten meters. We're turned eighty degrees."

Rudy kept the tunnel straight from that point. Seconds later the noise from the borer shifted. It seemed to be slowing down for ten or twenty seconds, and then resumed its normal noise.

"I think we're there," Rudy called back.

Matt and Abby came forward. The tunnel curved slightly to the left, following the edge of the dome. Rudy stopped the borer and backed it up a couple of meters. Bobby Joe stopped the cart, and Matt and Abby crawled past the trailer and the cart to get up to where Rudy stood.

A couple of swaths of black showed at about shoulder height on the wall nearest the dome. Matt looked closely, and his hardhat lamp illuminated the familiar black barrier texture.

"Time to surface, Captain?" Bobby Joe asked.

"Actually it's 'Colonel,' " Rudy corrected.

"That's right? You're really a colonel?"

Matt said, "Yes, but I'm a little out of my jurisdiction. 'Matt' will do just fine. And, yes, I'd say it's time to surface."

"All right! I'll get the stuff."

Matt and Abby exchanged grins.

Moments later Bobby Joe was back with a kit of tools. Rudy put on a pair of goggles and then grabbed the drill. At the top of the tunnel, he drilled a vertical hole. Moments later, light filtered through the small hole. Rudy inserted a periscope and took a brief look. "Want to see?"

Abby and Bobby Joe took the next looks. When they were finished, Matt put his eye to the periscope. Directly in front of him, less than a meter away, was the edge of the bubble. "Great work, Rudy."

Rudy picked up a circular saw and plugged it into the extension cord from the power supply on the cart. The other three backed up as Rudy applied the saw to the tunnel ceiling. In less than a minute, he had a rectangular piece of goo cut loose, and diffuse light made the tunnel brighter. They could see the dome rising and curving out of sight from where they stood. Rudy applied a torch to the edge of the goo to keep it from spilling into the tunnel, and Matt had Bobby Joe get the cart so they could stand on it.

Matt pulled a gray tarp from a bag of supplies. When the cart was in place, he climbed up on it, holding the tarp over his head as he rose. A moment later, his head and chest were above the plain. He reached up and taped two corners of the tarp to the outside of the bubble, then pulled the other two corners away from his body. In the distance was the Manhattan dome looking quiet and calm. He heard nothing except his own breath. The sheer distance of flat nothingness felt eerie.

Rudy handed him a couple of rods. Matt took one, slipped it into a sewn pocket in one corner of the tarp, and stuck the rod into the gray goo. He did the same thing with the other rod and the fourth corner of the tarp, and they had a small square roof that should stay up for an hour or so before the rods sank into the goo.

Matt looked back inside the dome and experienced a renewed awe at seeing a structure not built by humans. The huge square building inside looked enormous now, where before in the monitor it had simply looked big. The building was bathed in deep blue light like moonlight. The video camera had corrected for light levels, but to Matt's unassisted eyes the scene was dim.

The large round windows held no hint of what might be inside. On the ground, an irregular series of planters contained vegetation that looked both alien and dying. Perhaps the plants were in fact perfectly healthy, but the tightly curled black leaves and the gnarled and wiry black branches looked pathetic. As before, Matt could see no sign of life aside from the pitiable vegetation.

Matt stepped down, and the others each took a turn. When Rudy finished, Matt said, "Okay, Bobby Joe, how about if you get up there and try out your communication toys."

"Sure thing!" Bobby Joe took a couple of boxes from the rear of the cart and climbed into the opening. He spent almost fifteen minutes making discouraging noises, and then finally came down.

He set the boxes back on the cart. "Nothing. I beamed in both light and RF, in a range of frequencies. I listened for everything I could. Either they don't hear us, or they're ignoring us."

Matt took a large wrench from the cart, and climbed up. He took a long look for any sign of activity before he finally tapped the wrench against the bubble. It made a *bong* like bouncing it against a battle-cruiser hull. He swung the wrench harder. Ten times he swung it, slightly harder each time. The last *bong* might have been heard back in Manhattan.

For several more minutes, he stared at the silent building, still seeing no signs of activity. He climbed back down into the tunnel.

"Very strange. Enough of these domes are so obviously populated, I'm having a hard time thinking our captors took an empty building, so I don't know what to think. Either these folks heard us and they're ignoring us, or maybe they're different enough that they don't even have ears. Or they don't hear in the same range we do. Or they've got some cultural thing about going outside."

"Or talking to strangers," Abby said.

"Does this all mean what I think it means?" Rudy asked.

"Probably," Matt said. "I think we need to know what's going on, and I don't see any alternative but to go inside and take a look around."

6

ANYBODY HOME?

ABBY SWALLOWED HARD as she gripped one corner of the square slab of solid-feeling dark-gray material Rudy had cut from the tunnel roof. Matt, Rudy, and Bobby Joe each took the other corners. The four of them pushed the slab back into place, as though fitting a very thick and stubborn ceiling tile into the lid of the world's longest coffin.

As the tunnel darkened again, Abby felt the claustrophobia tighten its grip on her lungs. When she was a kid, a friend of hers, Christie something, had closed a trunk lid while Abby was lying inside. The inability to stretch her arms and straighten her legs was even more frightening than the smothering darkness. Instantly she was afraid the trunk was soundproof and her friend wouldn't hear her cries for help. Abby screamed and nothing happened. She screamed again, pounding on the inside of the trunk lid. It was immovable. Panic electrified her and she suddenly imagined staying stuck in that position until she starved, or until she went crazy, which might happen first.

At the moment when she'd given up hope, her vocal cords rough from screaming, a line of white had appeared, and the trunk lid swung upward. Abby choked. She stuck her legs out the side of the trunk so the lid couldn't close again, caring not one little bit how her legs might get hurt if her friend tried to close the lid again. But there was her friend, helping her out, as startled by Abby's reaction as Abby herself had been.

"Good, good. That's got it," Rudy said finally, when the tough bottom of the slab came fairly close to matching the surrounding edges of the tunnel ceiling. He got a torch from one of the tool bins on the cart and applied the flame to the seam around the slab. The gray goo flowed together in the seam, like ice cream melting between counter-top tiles, and in places Abby could no longer see where the edges met. Rudy pushed a ventilation fan through a hole in the center of the restored area and sealed the goo around it.

"Kinda messy," Bobby Joe said of the uneven seam.

From what Abby had seen of the constant mess that seemed to follow Bobby Joe around, he was a fine one to talk. The only thing about him that always seemed clean was his bald scalp. Abby told herself Bobby Joe was probably the only one on the team not totally repulsed by the zipper-lock plastic bags they carried for emergency elimination.

Rudy put down the torch and turned to Matt. "When we cut through the wall and tunnel to the surface inside that dome, we're going to have to put the dirt somewhere. If we want to be able to bring the borer back through this tunnel at some point, we're going to want a small side tunnel to dump the dirt in. I guess it's about time we arranged that."

"How much time will that take?" Matt asked. "It's been a long day."

Abby glanced at her watch and realized Matt was right. It was already after eleven P.M., and they'd started early. Suddenly she felt tired.

"Shouldn't take more than fifteen minutes," Rudy said.

"Okay," Matt said. "What's involved?"

"We back up the borer maybe ten meters from where we stopped it, then turn it as much as we can while we tell it to go forward again."

"Let's do it."

Bobby Joe backed up the cart and the trailer while Rudy operated his hand control. The treads on the borer made a slightly higher-pitched noise when they moved in reverse, and Abby saw the back of the borer slowly come out of the darkness at the end of the tunnel. It got within a few meters of them before Rudy halted it.

Rudy pushed another button and the plunger, a head-sized circular plate on the end of a pipe, extended toward them. "This shaft normally forces the borer away from a wall and into the opposite wall, but we can use it another way."

Following Rudy's instructions, Matt, Abby, and Bobby Joe joined Rudy and they took positions along the plunger. When Rudy gave the signal and started the borer moving forward again, they all pushed as hard as they could against the side of the plunger, to curve the borer's path more sharply than it could handle on its own. Bobby Joe rested his back against the tunnel wall and pushed with his feet. Abby's shoulder bumped against Matt's and tingled even after the contact was lost.

The plunger moved a few centimeters deeper into the tunnel as the borer made labored noises. Abby was afraid the pressure they exerted wasn't enough, but a moment later she had to shift position because the plunger began to move slowly toward the opposite wall as it continued to pull farther into the tunnel.

"Looking good!" Rudy said.

Bobby Joe fell to the floor as the plunger moved too far away, and Matt, Rudy, and Abby strained harder to maintain the curve. Soon the plunger was against the tunnel wall, and for the next couple of minutes the four of them managed to keep the end of the plunger against the wall as the borer pulled forward.

In another minute Rudy said they could let go. They slowly followed the borer into a tunnel that grew darker and darker without the light from the cart adding to the small lights on their helmets.

Sure enough, the tunnel split into a Y. For a moment Abby felt as if they had been miniaturized and put inside an artery junction in a human heart. Rudy stopped and ran his hand over the narrowest section of the junction, halfway between the top and bottom. "I'd better get the torch. This section might be too weak to hold. And the tunnel face in the dead end hasn't been heated, so I'll have to torch that manually. We can probably leave the borer parked about eight hours without worrying too much about it sinking."

"Sounds good," Matt said. "When you're done with that, we'd better get some rest."

While Rudy was busy with the torch, Matt, Bobby Joe, and Abby retrieved sleeping bags from the cart. The sleeping bags and the flickering torchlight brought back a sudden memory of the one camping trip Abby had been on, a disastrous weekend when she was seven. Her parents had gone through a long series of vacation experiments, looking for something they would both enjoy, almost always finding out that one but not the other liked the most recent try.

When they'd tried sailing, Abby's father loved it, but Abby's mother got seasick and lacked the coordination to maneuver quickly as the boat turned. She had been dunked twice in the frigid water off the coast of Maine before they gave up on sailing. When they tried horseback riding, her father had been doing all right until his mount rode under a stout branch. Her father complained about back pains for months after the fall.

At first the camping trip had seemed like a success. Aside from being out of breath for about three solid hours as they hiked, all three of them enjoyed the clean air, glimpses of squirrels and birds, and the absence of the deep rumbling sounds of the city. It was only when they were setting up camp that things began to go wrong. When they'd loaded their packs with several tins of food, her dad had seen several pop-tops, so he didn't think to bring a can opener for the rest.

Trying to open cans by using rocks and keys and other instruments at hand managed to get tempers so high that no one paid much attention to the building clouds. Abby had been amazed at how quickly the weather could change from still, clear air to a drenching downpour. Trying to sleep and stay warm in a wet sleeping bag was a never-to-be-forgotten experience. By four the next morning they were all more than ready to get up and start back for the car. And then getting lost on the way back was a vocabulary-building experience that got her father angry enough that Abby worried that he'd have a heart attack.

Abby laid her sleeping bag and air mattress on the curved tunnel floor and pushed the switch on the pump. She sat on the floor next to it and watched as the mattress popped into shape.

Abby hoped this camping trip was going to be better than the last one.

Moments later she lay down on the air mattress and tried to go to sleep. Sleep normally came easiest if she was tired but not too tired, and right now she was too tired. Or too worried. She saw her parents' faces in the blackness, and she wished she could be with them again, even if they were in the same mood they were in on the camping trip.

She wondered if she'd ever see them again, and she wished that she had some way of telling them she was safe. For now.

The arched entrance to Temple Emanu-El at Fifth Avenue and 65th Street had set a new record for the number of people passing through in a twenty-four-hour period.

As with most places of worship, the crowd included a fair number of non-believers who were here for their first time, or their first time in years. The crowd also included a number of Jews who believed Elijah would announce the coming of the Messiah on a Passover. With the recent upheaval coming so close to Passover, many of those same people wondered if *now* was the time they had been waiting for.

Matt woke before his watch alarm went off. On the cart ten meters down the tunnel, the small utility light they had left on provided a faint glow that was just enough to highlight shapes of other sleepers on the tunnel floor. Matt touched the light button on his watch, and the numbers said it was ten minutes before they were due to get up. Matt sat up and crossed his legs, trying to be quiet, but impatient to be on the move.

The nearest sleeping bag rustled. Abby's soft voice said, "How are you doing?"

"Okay," he whispered. "You?"

"I'm nervous about going in there."

"Me, too. The three of us can go in first and get you on the second trip."

"No." Abby's whisper was intense. "I should be there, for all the reasons we've talked about. I just had to be honest."

She was right. When they encountered aliens, they still ran the risk of accidentally saying something like "Your food looks like rancid axle-grease" when trying to say "It's not safe for us to eat your food." They had to tread carefully when for all they knew a casual touch on the cheek might be tantamount to suggesting sexual relations. "You're sure you're going to be okay?"

"Positive. But thanks for being sympathetic. I wasn't sure if much of that went on in combat."

"Well, we're not in combat."

"Yet."

Suddenly Bobby Joe's voice carried through the tunnel. "Time for work."

Matt shook his head. He looked at his watch again and said, "Okay, Bobby Joe."

After breakfast, the first order of business was an air barrier across the tunnel leading back the way they had come, to prevent contaminants in the atmosphere here from interfering with anyone trying to reach them with medical help. If the earlier remote readings were right, the pressure in the dome they were about to cut into was slightly higher than that between the domes. Unchecked, the atmosphere from this dome would flow into the tunnel and out to the open space between the domes. And despite the fact that the oxygen content should be similar, letting the different mixture shunt into the open space could very possibly show up on their captors' sensors.

The barrier consisted of a frame built from four quarter-circle arcs, which, when fastened together, formed a circle just enough larger than the tunnel that it was a tight fit against the gray goo. Two layers of thin plastic were ample to keep the air flow negligible.

As Matt and Abby got the air barrier in place, Rudy drilled an air hole to the outside and placed one of the blower pumps in it so there'd be a dependable source of oxygen blowing in from the outside, no matter what the dome contained. After a few minutes the pump had built up enough positive pressure that Matt's ears popped, and the pump began to slow down.

Matt helped Rudy ready the dipole oscillator as Bobby Joe cleared off the tray on top of the cart, positioned it by the proposed opening to the dome, and scraped the goo off a square portion of the flat black barrier, a meter on each side, making a black window in the tunnel wall. The black surface leaned toward them, perhaps forty degrees from vertical. While Bobby Joe drove ahead and dumped the scrapings in the side tunnel, Rudy rolled the dipole oscillator into place.

With the device, Rudy drew a one-meter square on the black surface. The air in the tunnel grew noticeably warmer as the device traveled along the black surface, leaving a gray line behind.

When the gray line of weakened barrier material was complete, Rudy got out the tool he called "the cutter" and positioned it at one of the top corners of the gray outline. He switched it on, and it began to turn, strong tiny hooks snagging individual fibers, pulling them slowly around a spool, and stretching them until one by one they finally broke. The process was like cutting a very strong section of screen door whose wires ran only vertically, and sounded like fingernails run over the teeth of a comb.

Cutting the fibers along the one-meter line took almost a half-hour, so they all took turns holding the cutter. Near the end of the cutting, Rudy stood as far back as he could while cutting the final fibers.

With a crowbar Matt popped the top of the black square loose from the rest of the black barrier.

The black square tipped forward into the tunnel, revealing a square meter of hard-packed dirt. Rudy folded the black square down as far as it would go. Bobby Joe scooped out enough more goo from near the bottom of the opening so the black square would fold down toward the tunnel floor instead of sticking out into the tunnel. Matt applied a torch to the newly exposed goo.

Rudy got out the drill. "Okay. I guess it's time to check the air in there."

Matt unhooked the air pump at the top of the tunnel and inserted the periscope. "Still no sign of activity up there," he said moments later.

Rudy switched on the drill and slanted the long bit toward the surface. The bit tore through the dirt with little resistance, and dirt spilled into the tray on top of the cart. In less than a minute Rudy was pulling the bit back out. As the bit came out, a flurry of dust spurted into the tunnel, and Matt could hear the rush of air flowing through the hole. The barrier plastic billowed away from them and held, and a second later the air flow stopped. Rudy stuck a hose into the hole. Matt's ears popped again.

On the near end of the hose was the gas analyzer. In less than a minute, Rudy gave the other three a thumbs up. "We're in business. Nitrogen's a little higher than we thought, and argon's just a little higher, but we'll be fine. Best of all, it's about twenty-three degrees C."

Matt and Rudy took turns with the drill, making a series of slanting holes in a square pattern just inside the opening in the black barrier. Dirt spilled into the tray atop the cart, and dust swirled in the air.

When the outline was cut, Rudy and Matt attacked the dirt with shovels and within minutes had excavated almost a cubic meter of dirt. Bobby Joe drove forward and they dumped the dirt into the dead-end tunnel.

To Matt the dirt itself looked just like dirt on Earth. What was different was the network of black roots. One long root looked like a rope with knots every several centimeters, but was surprisingly easy to cut with the shovel.

By the time they could see a head-sized column of dim blue light filtering through the hole to the surface, they were all coughing steadily as the dust hung in the air.

Another twenty minutes was enough to dig a meter-square opening from the tunnel to the surface inside the dome, and by that time the dust was more manageable. A few more shovelfuls of dirt were enough to make a small ledge at waist level.

The tunnel section containing the borer had drifted a little lower in the goo, so Rudy moved it several meters from its old position. As he finished attaching adhesive mounts to the black barrier and to the door they had cut open, Bobby Joe came back from dumping the last load of dirt into the side tunnel, and Matt looked at the faces of the trio. Rudy seemed wary but ready. Abby appeared nervous and determined. Bobby Joe could have been ready to take his winning lottery ticket to claim his check.

Now that they were about to enter another dome, everyone wore a holstered pistol in addition to the scabbarded knife. In addition, from Abby's belt hung her computer, preloaded with communication aids she'd developed during the last week and with several language translation programs. It held only two gigabytes of main memory and a 400-gigabyte solid-wafer outboard memory, and she had complained several times about running out of storage. On her other hip hung her minivid recorder, and on her headband were affixed the minivid optics.

"Is everyone ready?" Matt asked.

They all said they were.

"All right. We've talked about this before, but I want to say it one last time: when we step past this barrier we are a military unit. What I say goes, and it goes instantly without argument. Is that clear?" Matt looked only at Abby and Bobby Joe. He knew Rudy didn't need this.

Abby nodded. Bobby Joe said, "Yes, sir. Absolutely, sir."

Matt looked suspiciously at Bobby Joe and decided he was hearing simple, genuine eagerness, nothing more.

"And if anything happens to me, Rudy is your leader."

He got more agreement. He had repeated this in hopes that the brief military orientation he'd given them would be enough to let the group function smoothly. If trained military people with the same skills had been available, he would have felt it necessary to use them instead, but adding more military personnel to the team would put that much more strain on the oxygen available through the ventilation pipes, and the larger the party entering the dome, the greater the possibility of them being viewed as a threat.

Matt used his walkie-talkie to tell guards at the Manhattan airlock they were about to enter the dome, then quickly double-checked the items on his belt. He removed his hardhat.

"All right. We're ready," he said. In the light gravity, he hopped onto the ledge, then slowly stood upright in the dim blue light. His shoulders came level with the ground, and he looked up at the nearby building. He could hear nothing but the faint rush of moving air, probably coming from the ventilation hoses attached to the dome. The air was comfortably cool but smelled unpleasant, vaguely sulfurous.

The building was several times wider than the biggest shopping mall Matt had ever seen. From this perspective, it could be as tall as the World Trade Center, but the height was harder to judge. The huge circular windows showed nothing but reflections. "Hello!" Matt yelled.

No sudden scurrying, no startled rustling. The building seemed as dead and silent as before. High overhead a dim blue light outside the dome shed moonlight. Matt looked around. In the direction of the Manhattan dome sat a closer dome obstructing the view.

Matt waited another ten seconds, then said softly, "All quiet." He jumped straight up. As his feet cleared the surface of the ground, he spread his legs. He landed gently on the surface, straddling the hole, then moved forward.

Rudy's head appeared in the hole, and Matt gave him a come-ahead signal.

Abby was next. She landed on the ground and looked around.

Bobby Joe was last. He didn't spread his feet quite wide enough. He almost fell back in the hole before Matt and Rudy each grabbed one arm and pulled him up.

Rudy grabbed the end of a cord and pulled on it. The black trapdoor they had cut through the barrier started to swing closed. As the gap narrowed, Rudy's feet slipped on the uneven ground, but he got the trapdoor completely closed.

Rudy fixed an adhesive cable holder to the end of the cord and stuck it against the interior wall of the dome. Matt armed the tension alarm, and they were ready. Anyone trying to leave the dome without entering the right combination should sound an alarm heard back at the Manhattan airlock.

"All right, people," Matt said. "Let's go."

Matt took the lead. Abby fell in behind him, with Bobby Joe behind her, and Rudy trailing.

The foursome walked toward the building. In the dim light, they cast dark-blue shadows that made Matt think of old cheap films that shot "night" scenes in daylight with a filter. Not far from them, a ramp led up to a water-filled bird-feeder.

They had walked less than five meters when the dirt ended and they stepped onto a smooth surface, a textured plaza surrounding the building. As Matt glanced to his left at a planter filled with the scrawny black growth he'd seen from a distance, a bright light switched on.

"Whoa!" said Bobby Joe.

Matt spun nervously, his heart beating faster. He looked for the source of the light, wondering if they'd triggered it or if someone within had spotted them and finally reacted. He relaxed when he realized that neither explanation was right.

The light came from the blue "sun," which had just switched from "night" to "day."

As soon as everyone understood what had happened, jittery expressions turned a little less nervous. Matt moved forward.

Now that Matt's eyes had adjusted to the brighter light, the pattern on the plaza floor no longer looked like random paint splatters. A variety of circle sizes covered the surface, but inside each little circle were markings that looked more like an unfamiliar language than haphazard marks. The surface no longer looked clean, either. Two long irregular cracks ran through the plaza floor from the edge all the way to the building.

Abby got out her minivid and captured several images. She startled Matt by jumping straight up in the air, more than five meters, but then Matt realized she was recording a large view of the patterns so she could try later to decipher them. She floated gently back to the ground and flicked off the minivid.

The black vegetation in the planters smelled vaguely like mint and rotten eggs. Matt kept his distance as he thought about Venus's flytraps and other strange vegetation on Earth.

Up close, the building seemed to be finished with a seamless, textured material resembling blue Astroturf except that the individual blades formed regular geometric patterns of boxes within boxes. It took Matt a moment to realize that all the little blades were positioned with their flat surfaces perpendicular to the rays from the "sun."

They approached the nearest huge entrance, a half-circle wider than a Manhattan block. At ground level was an alternating series of blue and gray vertical stripes, each a meter wide and three meters tall.

As they came nearer to the wide array of stripes, the closest gray stripe slid upward, a door opening. Matt could see nothing inside.

Matt walked through the doorway, followed by Abby, Bobby Joe, and Rudy. As Rudy stepped through the door, it slowly lowered into its original position. Matt was suddenly afraid of being trapped. He moved toward the door, and it opened again.

Inside it was just as quiet as it had been outside. Interior blue-tinged lamps set in rows high on the walls were so numerous that no one had a shadow anymore. Inside the huge building was another building. The "lobby" was a very tall thirty-meter gap between the exterior shell and the interior building, which seemed to be as tall as the outside shell. Ahead, an open corridor lined with blue lights led straight into the interior building and dwindled to a point. Along the wall of the interior building, a stairway with half-meter-wide steps and no guardrails zigzagged all the way up to the ceiling.

Halfway to the ceiling, one of the huge circular windows admitted blue light.

"Maybe there's no one here," Rudy said.

Bobby Joe said, "Maybe these folks have pretty strong feelings about drop-in company."

The team followed Matt into the interior, and they moved into a corridor with a ten-meter-high ceiling.

They walked twice the length of a football field before they found any break in the walls. A perpendicular corridor stretched into the distance in both directions. At the far ends of each hallway were squares of light no bigger than a fingernail viewed at arm's length.

"You see that flickering?" Rudy asked.

"Yes?" Matt said softly.

They all looked at the light spilling from a door cut into the cross corridor. They moved to the door. Inside, a big barber pole rotated slowly. From the pole extended horizontal one-meter rods, which dropped smoothly as they moved around the pole. At the floor, they disappeared into a slot, one every three or four seconds. A half-moon opening on the ceiling showed the level above, and the turning rods came through the opening above just as fast as they disappeared into the slot below.

"I don't think we have a word for it," Matt said finally. "My guess is the closest is 'escalator' or 'elevator.' Maybe 'escalifter.' "

Rudy said, "I'd go along with that. If that's right, this must be the *down* side. Maybe there's an *up* somewhere near."

They found the *up* on the opposite side of the main corridor. It looked just the same except that the rods rose as they turned around the central pole.

Abby said, "Maybe everyone is upstairs for some reason."

"Certainly possible," Matt said. "I think we'd better give it a try. Let's go. Be ready to get off at any time, but I don't plan on stopping until we see some indication of life."

Abby said, "I'm going to let my minivid run." She quickly snapped on a collar and attached the tiny black minivid optics to the front of it, pointing it straight ahead, its tiny lens looking like a jewel set in a square of onyx.

Matt said, "All right." He moved to a position where rods periodically passed overhead on their way up. He let the first rod go by, then grabbed at the next one to come along.

His body lurched into the air, putting pressure on his grip, but a second later the pressure relaxed and he felt nothing but the gentle centrifugal force as the central pole lifted him and the rod higher and higher. Cool air rushed at his face. He moved closer to the central pole and the force diminished.

The rod carried him through the open semicircle in the roof, and in the next half turn put him in a position where his feet would conveniently hit the floor if he were to let go. The 180-degree turn had showed him nothing but another empty corridor, though, so he held on.

He looked up and realized the semicircle cut into the next ceiling was oriented 180 degrees from the one he'd just come through, meaning that for someone who lost a grip, the longest possible fall would be only one floor—completely safe, given the light gravity.

The ride continued. He swung up into another deserted corridor. As the pole carried him upward and through the next semicircular opening, he saw below him that Abby was just being carried into the level he was departing.

Matt corkscrewed up through another empty corridor, and another. The corridors all looked virtually identical. He passed floor after floor, growing more and more puzzled at the lack of activity.

When finally his feet cleared the level of the roof, he said, "All off on this level," and released his grip. The corkscrew escalifter motion pushed him up in a gentle arc. He stumbled when his feet hit the floor.

Matt moved out of the way as Abby let go and windmilled

until she had her balance. Bobby Joe fell when he got off, but Rudy managed to avoid stepping on his head.

They stood under a small pavilion roof, with doorways on four sides. Matt helped Bobby Joe to his feet, and they all watched the top of the escalifter for a moment. As the rods neared the top of the rotating pole, they pivoted downward until they were vertical, at which time they seemed to melt into the rotating column. Matt turned away, and the four of them walked out onto the flat surface of the roof.

They could see another dome fairly close, probably the *down* version. In the distance they could see seven other pairs of escalifter domes, and by moving several meters, Matt could see an eighth set, so from above the nine pairs of domes would be centered in each of the squares of a tic-tac-toe grid.

In the distance was the top of the Manhattan dome, showing only the top half of the World Trade Center towers and the tops of some of the other tall buildings. The Manhattan dome itself seemed to clear the highest points with a margin of no more than ten percent of their height.

"Where *is* everybody?" Bobby Joe asked finally.

"It's spooky," Abby said.

Matt shook his head. "As long as we've got a clear shot at home, let me give them an update." He took the walkie-talkie off his belt and pressed TALK. "Manhattan base, this is Rover."

He released the switch, and listened. Nothing.

He tried again, and listened again. Still nothing.

Matt looked closely at the unit. The battery-charge indicator said it should be fine, and he couldn't see any sign of damage. He turned to Bobby Joe. "Any ideas? It doesn't seem likely they wouldn't be listening."

Bobby Joe made a quick check and confirmed that Rudy's and Matt's walkie-talkies could talk to each other with no trouble and that the batteries were almost fully charged.

"So," Matt said. "Are we out of range? We haven't gone *that* far since we left the tunnel."

Bobby Joe said, "My guess is that it's not the range. I bet it's the dome. I bet the dome doesn't pass RF in this frequency. We know it passes light, a lot farther up the spectrum, but we don't actually have any proof that we can transmit stuff like this through it. Maybe that's why we haven't picked up any RF signals from other domes. And maybe that's why we haven't gotten any answers to the RF we've been sending."

"Okay. But that still leaves us with quite a few questions. Like where is everybody?"

Abby unsnapped her minivid and pointed it at the dome above them. Matt looked up and saw what looked to be an identical copy of the message on the roof of the Manhattan dome.

Matt let Abby finish taking a few seconds of video before he said, "I think it's time we went back down. But let's take the center shaft." He pointed toward it. "Bobby Joe, how's your black box working? Any chance of us getting lost?"

Bobby Joe took a unit the size of a slice of bread from his belt and inspected the readings on it. People at Columbia had provided the inertial navigation unit and calibrated it for the lower gravity. "We should be fine. In case you're curious, we're a little over three hundred meters up."

"All right. Let's go."

Stuart Lund was actually enjoying himself more than he had expected to. God had dealt him a painful blow with the loss of his hand, but Stuart was making progress with his street-corner proselytizing, and that progress made him feel more worthwhile than he had felt in a long time. A couple of acolytes followed him as he walked toward his normal corner and tried to decide how to start his morning speech.

When he had wakened this morning, he'd interrupted a dream. In the dream, an old man with long white hair had said to him, "I am. Heed me. Soon all will be right."

The old man had carried a clipboard held to his chest with one arm, the way school kids in old Norman Rockwell paintings had carried their schoolbooks. Or, now that Stuart thought about it, the way Moses was illustrated carrying the ten commandment tablets.

Near the end of the dream, the old man had turned the clipboard so Stuart could see the front, which bore a copy of the strange message on top of the dome.

According to the news reports, the mayor had dozens of

people working on translating the message. Of course they had to be wrong, no matter what they decided in their ignorance. If even one of the team had been receptive, as Stuart was, they would already know what Stuart now knew. *I am. Heed me. Soon all will be right.*

Stuart reached the corner of Broadway and 12th Street and found a crowd already assembled, waiting patiently. The crowd was even larger than it had been when he quit the day before—another sign from God that Stuart was doing what was expected of him. In fact the crowd was starting to run out of space.

Stuart was ready to start making demands of these people. It wasn't enough for them to merely listen and exclaim agreement when it seemed appropriate. They needed to take actions just as Stuart himself did. He decided on a simple test.

He raised his arms. Voices rippled through the crowd as some of the regulars caught sight of him. Seconds later many faces had turned toward Stuart. "We are too crowded here," he said. "Follow me up the street to Washington Square Park."

Stuart began to walk south. He didn't look back, but he kept watching the store window reflections. Within seconds the glimpses he caught of the crowd told him they were in fact following.

Good. Next he needed to ask them for something larger.

Maybe the first thing he should ask was that some of them stop operations at the World Trade Center. If the Mayor's people trying to interpret God's word were left to themselves, with all the time in the world, they would eventually decide they had to say *something.* They wouldn't be able to interpret what the message really meant, because they were going about it all wrong. But they would have to save face. They would have to make up something that seemed plausible to themselves to justify their work.

This must *not* be allowed. Stuart would ask his people to disrupt activities there, to remind those people they were really trying to interpret the word of God. This was a good plan, he decided. And if his followers would indeed be willing to take this action on his behalf, that would tell him even more clearly that he *was* doing the work of God, and that God was helping him do what must be done.

And if that worked, then he would have to decide what the next step might be.

As the group approached the pair of escalifters in the middle of the roof of the huge building, Abby realized she was feeling more nervous than she had when they first entered the dome. She tried to figure out why.

It could be just that something was so very wrong here. If something bad had happened to residents of a city that had been here longer than Manhattan, maybe that meant Manhattan was soon to suffer even more badly than it had already. Or maybe it was her natural empathy making her imagine feelings that whoever lived here might have had. Unless they were hiding for some reason, a whole city of people seemed to have vanished. Had they known what was happening to them? Did they go one at a time, leaving the survivors to dread their turn, at the same time powerless to affect what was happening to their friends?

Abby shivered in the cool air and forced her thoughts back to the mission.

She stopped suddenly, wondering again why there was no sign of the residents. She had wondered if they were hiding inside. That could still be true. She realized she had stopped, and she started moving again.

They finally reached the dome covering an escalifter.

"Is everyone ready?" Matt asked. She hadn't seen that faraway look on him once since they had entered this dome. She wasn't sure whether the strangeness of this place kept him from dwelling on his wife, or if being in a "combat" role was enough to make him ignore everything else until his team was safely out.

Matt stood at the edge of the cutout in the roof and grabbed one of the rods as it swung past him, and he was on his way. Abby took a breath, and grabbed the next one.

She floated for a second as the rod pushed her down through the weak gravity field even faster than she would have fallen the first meter or two. Then her body was moving down at the same rate as the rod, and she felt the weak pull of gravity and the outward force as she spun around the central pole.

They went past several floors that looked exactly like the ones they had already seen. She was starting to assume they'd go all the way to the ground when Matt released his grip and shouted, "Let's get off here!"

Moments later the four of them stood in the deserted hallway next to the escalifter.

Matt looked down the hall. "This building just can't be nothing more than hallways and those few circular rooms, whatever they are. There's too much wasted space. I think we need to do a little more exploring."

They walked about twenty meters before Rudy said, "Wait a minute." He ran his finger down the wall. "What's this?"

When Abby looked closer and moved her head to just the right place, she could see a hairline crack running floor to ceiling, a seam narrower than the ones between adjacent wall panels in her parents' house.

Matt walked down the corridor about twenty meters and then came back. "There seem to be pairs of them. About a meter apart, a pair every couple of meters. Are you thinking they might be doors? Or just some construction artifact?"

Rudy looked at the floor, then at the ceiling. "Well, right about here, doors would make a lot of sense."

Abby pressed on the wall. She moved down the hallway, pushing on the wall every second or so, looking to see if the wall showed any other features. Aside from the thin seams, the wall was just like the sandpaper surface on the ground floor, apparently unbroken.

Matt said, "If these lines define the edges of doorways, I wonder if the doors are anything like what we came through on the way in." He put his palms against the surface and pushed upward.

A meter-wide section of the wall from floor to ceiling slid upward. Abby drew in her breath.

Through the gap she could see interior blue lights, smaller versions of the ones in the hall.

No sound came from within. Matt stepped cautiously through the doorway. Abby followed, her heart beating much harder than before.

A corridor ran straight back from the doorway. About ten meters farther along the corridor, it widened, but Abby couldn't see what was around the corner. Matt stopped and turned back.

"Bobby Joe, I want you to stay here, under the door. We don't want to take a chance on getting sealed in here."

Bobby Joe looked grateful not to have to go in. "Yes, sir."

As Matt, Abby, and Rudy went forward, Abby smelled a strong unpleasant odor, reminiscent of a refrigerator left unplugged and closed. The corridor opened onto what seemed to be living quarters.

This section was wider than the spacing between doors. If every door led to quarters, they must be jigsawed into place, some with the quarters closer to the main hallway than others. On a low pedestal was a one-meter-by-two-meter cushion. About a meter above it was a platform holding what could have been a chair and a desk. The chair was a cushion about as thick as Abby's wrist. Near it was a U-shaped desk mounted about a quarter meter off the platform. Against the wall was a column of small drawers. On the wall was a design with a big square beside a big circle. Inside the large square was a smaller circle, and inside the large circle was a smaller square.

"I'm going to get pictures of what's in the drawers, if anything," Abby said. She hopped up to the platform and reached forward to open the lowest drawer.

Inside it was a disk like a compact with buttons on the front. She pulled it out and set it on the desk. "Could be a remote control unit? Or a communicator?"

Abby made sure it was in the field of view of her minivid for a second, then tried the next drawer. It contained a red ball that felt rubbery. She showed it to Matt and Rudy, then put it back. As she checked the last drawer and found it empty, Rudy said, "I think you folks should see this."

Abby followed Matt into an adjoining room. In the center of the room was a circular stand covered with an uneven layer of solid brown fur. The unpleasant odor was stronger here.

"What do you think—" Rudy was saying as he moved around to the far side of the room. "Uh oh."

"What?" Matt asked.

Rudy pointed at the floor. Abby squeezed closer and saw that Rudy pointed to an oddly shaped knife, its blade almost covered with green foam.

"Oh, God," Matt said. "That's not just some covering of fur, is it?"

Abby's throat was raw, and she felt lightheaded. "You mean—"

Matt used one foot to prod at the fur atop the circular base. Abby felt she was going to vomit when Matt's toe moved a layer of the brown fur enough to reveal the glassy green eyes, mottled snout, and rictus of a creature with a head shaped vaguely like a badger's. The skin and fur were liquefying.

"God," Rudy said faintly.

"I've got to get out of here," Abby managed to say.

"Let's all get out of here," Matt said.

Matt quietly told Bobby Joe what they'd seen. About five seconds after Bobby Joe had moved from his position on the door, it slowly and silently lowered into the closed position.

In six more tries, Matt and Rudy encountered two more dead aliens, both positioned similarly to the first.

"Let's get out of here," Matt said.

As they started back toward the escalifter, Bobby Joe said, "Do you think they were murdered or they committed suicide?"

Matt looked at Abby and said, "Theories?"

Abby said, "I don't think I've really got any more than you have to guess with. If they were all murdered in the same place and the same way, that could indicate an incredibly busy murderer, or an organized approach, conducted by a team of murderers. You'd think at least a few of the victims might have struggled more or have been caught in some other location. And that would mean that maybe the murderer or murderers are likely the only ones we'll find alive.

"Suicide makes a lot more sense to me, but I'm really just wildly guessing. The fact that they each had their own weapon nearby, the fact that they all died in the same location, in the same way, suggests suicide."

Bobby Joe said, "Makes sense. But why? I mean *we're* not really happy to be here, but we're doing the best we can."

"Could be lots of reasons. Could be their religion predicted something close enough to what happened that they're doing what's expected of them in that situation. Could be they just couldn't handle captivity, being shut in. That one in particular is questionable, because a building like this would generate the feeling of being shut in all the time. I don't know why. I'd just guess that it was suicide."

Talking about it had helped Abby relax. By the time they reached the escalifter, she felt ready to descend. She followed Matt, and seconds later her body rotated smoothly around the central shaft as the device carried her deeper into the heart of the complex.

They passed more corridors on the way down, but when they were about halfway down to the ground level, she started to smell that horrible smell from before, and they came through the top of an enormous circular room, perhaps as wide as a football field. As Abby turned she saw a section of the wall covered with a large 2-D photo of what looked to be two buildings. They came closer to the floor, and she saw a sea of brown fur.

Her arms felt weak. She tightened her grip on the rod, suddenly afraid she'd fall. Dead bodies were everywhere. Hundreds of them, thousands.

Matt shouted up, "Abby and Bobby Joe, stay on and don't get off until the next floor. Rudy, get off with me."

"No," Abby heard herself shout. "I can handle it."

By then Matt had let go and hit the surface of the floor. The pole spun another revolution, and Abby let go. She skidded out of the way, and Bobby Joe got off, then Rudy.

She turned to Matt. "It's okay. I think I can handle it—"

Matt looked furious.

"Oh, come on," Abby said. "You don't have to protect—"

"That's not the issue." Matt's voice was harsh, cutting harder than she'd ever heard it. "We're operating on military rules. I gave you two an order." His gaze widened to include Bobby Joe.

"But I really don't . . ." Abby stopped suddenly, realized what he was talking about. She suddenly felt small.

Matt took a deep breath. Abby could see him willing himself to relax. He said, "Listen to me very carefully. This is not about power. This is not about protection. This is not about men versus women. What it *is* about is safety and surviving. When we're out here and I give an order, I want to know you'll obey it. When we get back to base, you can question it all you want, and you can quit, but out here I *have* to know you'll do exactly what I say. For all you know, I had just seen an armed enemy or something equally hazardous. If I don't phrase it as a command, you can ask questions. If it's a command, you've *got* to act on it. Right then. Any questions?"

Abby swallowed and shook her head. "None. You're exactly right."

Bobby Joe said, "Understood."

Matt visibly relaxed.

Abby said, "I really do understand. I realize why it's necessary, and I'm ready to cooperate. I guess it's taking me a little time to adjust to a military style, but I'm ready. Really."

Matt nodded. "Okay." He took a deep breath. "All right, as long as we're all here, anyone got any theories?"

Abby swallowed and forced herself to look at their surroundings. None of the furry bodies were closer than ten meters, but beyond that perimeter, there must have been thousands. The four humans walked in a small circle around the escalifter as Abby tried to ignore the nauseating smell.

Each body rested on one of those little couch things. This room could have been a huge meeting hall. Near many of the bodies she could see small cups on the floor where they had apparently fallen. Blue drops of some liquid showed near several of the cups.

"What do you think?" asked Matt after a long silence.

"I really don't know enough to explain this. But it looks like some horrible Jonestown or Tekafganton," she said softly.

Matt said, "You mean a mass suicide?"

Abby came around to where the huge picture covered part of the wall. It showed two huge buildings, judging from the relative size of the buildings and the two groups of small creatures standing in the foreground. One of the buildings was a very large cube, the other a big cylinder. As Abby stared at the picture for a moment, at the creatures in the foreground, she recalled the picture in the room several floors above, and suddenly felt very cold. "Oh, no. Oh, God."

"What?" Matt asked. "What is it?"

Abby hesitated. "I had a flash. I don't know I'm right, but it's one way of explaining what's happened. I might be just looking at it with a human point of view, but—"

"Go on."

"Look at the picture. That square building on the right. That's this one—the one we're in. Those creatures in front of the building. They all have solid brown fur, and that ruffling along the forehead, like the creatures here. Now look closely at the creatures in front of the cylindrical building."

"They look the same."

"No. Look closer. Look at their mouths, their snouts, whatever. Look very closely."

Matt was silent for a moment. "You mean it looks like there's some gray in the fur there? The ones in front of the cylindrical building have touches of gray fur the others don't? And none of them have those ridges along the forehead?"

"Yes." Abby's body shook as she said the word.

"I still don't get it," Matt said finally.

"You remember that picture up above? The one with the large square and the large circle?"

"Yeah."

"This is still just a guess, all right? There could be lots of other explanations. This is just one possibility."

"Yeah."

"It's possible that the gray fur around the snout and those forehead ridges distinguish one sex from the other. I think it's possible that the square and circle might represent something that distinguishes their sexes. Those are big ifs, but if I'm right, it could be this entire building housed only one sex, and that the circular building left behind housed the other sex. If that's right, those goddamned aliens who took us—who took *them*—took all of one sex and left the other sex behind."

7

A TREE GROWS

SURROUNDED BY DEATH and silence, Matt stared at the picture of the pair of buildings. The churning in his stomach said Abby's theory was probably right. The idea that members of one sex would kill themselves when stranded without the opposite sex was extreme, but it somehow fit with the idea that the sexes would live in separate buildings. Whether Abby's theory was right or not, the fact was the residents here were dead, and that probably wouldn't be true if they had been left alone.

In the stunned silence, Rudy said, "I bet you're right. Whoever captured us could lift one of those buildings, but taking both, separated by that much distance, would have been too much. I wonder if they know what they've done."

"Or if they care," Abby said. "The transmission we saw earlier made it look like they go in fast and remove all their targets just as fast as they took Manhattan."

"If they moved slowly, no one would be left in the city when they took it," Rudy said. "Except maybe a few crazies."

Finally Matt said, "Let's get out of here."

They lined up in their original order, and Matt grabbed an escalifter rod, letting it take him downward into the complex. He spun through floor after floor, almost numb with shock at the idea that their captors had taken citizens of only one sex. Either they had moved so quickly that they had no time to determine the magnitude of the mistake they were making, or they had known what they were doing and didn't care.

Matt spun through floor after deserted floor, the feeling of horror growing inside him. At last he reached the ground floor and released the rod. Seconds later the foursome stood together quietly. Matt no longer worried that the still building held a possible ambush, but he wished he could trade that former feeling for the bitter gnawing in his stomach that he now felt.

As they reached the corridor leading to the outside and Matt saw how long it looked, he sighed, staring into the distance. He wondered if being separated from Nadine would be any less painful if she had still wanted to be together.

They'd been walking for a few minutes when Matt became aware of the feeling of being watched. He glanced left and saw Abby's gaze on him.

"Are you doing all right?" she asked softly.

"Sure. I'm tough." Matt said the words with a light tone, bordering on self-mocking. He didn't feel very tough right then, and he knew Abby knew it.

Stuart Lund came down from the second floor just two minutes before the service was supposed to begin, and he found that once again they had outgrown the number of chairs. People stood in the back of the large room, leaning against the walls, and every chair was occupied.

The clamor of conversations died as Stuart walked from the back of the room, up the narrow aisle toward the spray-painted microwave packing box that was now his lectern. He took pride in recognizing it as a lectern when most people incorrectly called it a podium.

Stuart had a member of his congregation to thank for the space for the church. Warehouses had been gradually getting less and less useful at the same time Stuart's folk kept growing. Between services, Stuart still took to the streets, but now he took with him each time a different handful of people to act as a crowd seed.

Stuart had realized early that few people liked to be the very first to stop and listen, but if they could pause near the back of a small throng, they felt secure enough that they might stay ten or fifteen minutes, and by that time many of them were hooked. By having some of his congregation start the "crowd," the new arrivals assembled that much sooner.

Stuart reached the front of the large room and turned to look into the eyes of the closest people. The people here were excited, as excited as he was that in this time of need they had a chance to be a part of what God wanted them to do.

Today he would talk to them about the expedition outside the city, and he knew they would be as upset about it as he was, as soon as they understood that trying to get closer to God was no more acceptable now than it had been when the Tower of Babel was attempted.

By the time they left the large building, Abby's thoughts had cleared a little.

The horror she had felt earlier remained, but she now felt a little additional emotional distance from what she was more and more sure was the terrible fate of the residents here.

As they'd walked, she'd noticed Matt's faraway expression return several times, and she wondered if the division of the sexes was a particularly painful reminder of his wife being left back on Earth. Abby was irritated with herself because she couldn't deny that she was attracted to the man. Maybe it was because he seemed to be a mix of strength and vulnerability much like she saw in herself. Maybe it was something as stupid as the warmth she felt when he gave her that floodlight smile.

Even the blowup after she had disobeyed his order hadn't shaken her feelings. She'd known immediately he was right, and somehow she knew that if their positions had been reversed he would have been just as accepting of criticism as she had been.

The bright "sun" was still on as they walked to the opening they'd dug in the ground. Rudy's cord was still fixed to the metal disk stuck on the inside of the dome. Rudy sprayed a pocket aerosol tube on the edge of the disk, and moments later it slid down, then popped off the transparent bubble surface.

The black door into the tunnel opened. Abby took another look through the bubble as Rudy dropped into the hole and disappeared. The gray plain could almost have been a huge stagnant lake, unrippled in dead calm, a congealed sargasso sea. From the roof, Manhattan had looked much the way it had looked from the Staten Island ferry, except for being a little farther away and a little clearer, since the air between the domes was clean. Now Manhattan was gone again, hidden by the other dome.

When it was her turn to go down, she almost didn't want to enter the tunnel again, but she did. She put on her hardhat.

Matt stayed on the surface, and she could hear him calling Manhattan on his walkie-talkie. Several seconds later he joined the rest of them in the tunnel, where he tried his walkie-talkie again. This time the speaker crackled with a reply.

"Manhattan base. What do you need?"

"I need a comm check. Can you count to fifty for me?"

"You got it. One two three—"

As Matt moved back up into the cutout in the dome, Abby heard, "Four five six seven—" The "eight" faded, and she heard nothing more as Matt pulled the black door closed. Several seconds passed before Matt opened the door and came back into the tunnel. ". . . twenty-four twenty-five . . ."

Matt clicked his walkie-talkie, but the other end counted all the way to fifty before they took a break to listen.

Matt spoke into the walkie-talkie. "The clear bubble material cuts off your signal. Even with the squelch all the way down, I couldn't hear anything when I was inside the bubble. The black barrier material reduces the signal but doesn't stop it."

"Understood, Rover."

Matt gave the people back in Manhattan a summary of what they had learned so far, and what they suspected. A long silence ensued. When they finally acknowledged what Matt had said, he terminated the call, then helped as all four of them sealed the black barrier cutout back into place. Rudy stripped the protective layer off a length of supertape and carefully applied the material to the seam, giving the glue a few seconds to set.

The tunnel felt downright gloomy with only the hardhat lights and the light from the cart.

"What's next?" Bobby Joe asked.

Matt looked at Bobby Joe, then Rudy, then at Abby. His gaze still on her, he said, "We'd better start for the next dome."

"Those people are still out there!" Stuart Lund said. "Every day they spend on this foolish journey, the greater the risk that God will punish *all* of us." Stuart's voice was a little hoarse from trying too hard to project.

On faces in his congregation, Stuart saw anger and fear. And that was good. These people *should* be as angry and as fearful as Stuart was, because only when they *felt* would they begin to *act*.

"The Battery Tunnel no longer serves any purpose that benefits humankind," Stuart said in the deliberately understated style he'd adopted. So many pulpit-ravers had tried their vocal cords on the American public, Stuart was convinced that someone outside of the mold would be taken more seriously. "Once it led to Brooklyn, but Brooklyn is beyond our hearing, beyond our seeing, beyond our touching." Stuart continued to speak carefully, getting the crowd angry, preparing to divert that anger to where it would do the most good. A young boy perhaps ten years old sat between two adults, and the boy looked as angry as his parents did, which was a good sign that Stuart was really reaching them. He thanked God for preparing him with the techniques of persuasion.

In the row just behind the young boy sat an expressionless man, a short man with a crew cut. Stuart's gaze caught the man, and for just an instant the short man's eyes widened. A diffuse warmth spread through Stuart's chest. These people would do anything he asked.

"Now the Battery Tunnel leads to damnation. Now it points the way of the snake. We *must* stop this outrage against God."

Stuart kept working the crowd to a higher pitch of fear and anger. After the service, he was rewarded with a great honor; a group of about ten of the congregation members who talked among themselves at the back of the room came to him with ideas of how to discourage use of the Battery Tunnel. One of the ideas was just Biblical enough that it appealed to Stuart.

As the borer performed its slow-motion magic, Matt grew impatient. Fast cars and high-speed jets were more to his taste than this creeping assault on the gray goo. As a passenger, he'd once taken enough gees in an F-22 to drain a fair amount of blood from his brain before the automatic systems detected the same thing happening to the pilot and reduced the thrust. Here he was in danger only from accidentally falling asleep. Even the diet was tedious. The trailer behind the borer held a large supply of nothing but food pellets and water.

"What brought you to New York?" he asked Abby, who walked just ahead of him in the dim light.

"Feet."

"Okay, you don't have to talk about it."

"No, that's not what I meant," she said. "I went out for track when I was in school. I was already interested in languages and linguistics at that point, and my folks encouraged me to do something physical so I didn't stay cooped up with my studies all the time. Eventually it occurred to me that I could use running to meet more people from other countries if I was lucky enough to make the Olympic team."

"And did you?"

"No. I came close, but I just didn't spend enough time at it, for one thing. You don't get on the team unless you're pretty single-minded about it and work a lot of long hard hours. But I did get to the point that I liked running a lot. Manhattan seemed like a place I could run, and at the same time I could meet a variety of people. The melting pot is still bubbling in Manhattan."

Matt smiled.

"Once I got here, I started to get bored just running the same course all the time. I wanted to run wherever I wanted to."

"Could be a little dangerous, depending on where you wanted to run. A beautiful woman by herself in a deserted place."

"Well, I'm not beautiful. And a lot of times it doesn't matter whether you're a man or a woman as long as you're a stranger. But that's why I took self-defense classes."

Matt didn't respond to her inaccurate statement about beauty. "So that explains your skill when we were on the way back from the UN."

"Yes. No one's going to tell me where I can run and where I can't."

Matt could hear the smile in her voice even though her face was lost in the darkness ahead, and he smiled, too. Abby reminded him of a girl who had lived next door to him when he was growing up in Omaha. She hardly knew Matt existed, and at the time Matt had been gangling, constantly unsure of himself, while Tami had been poised, pretty, and popular. But what had been important was that Tami knew what she wanted to do, and she went out and did it. She was intelligent and funny and caring. She and Abby seemed to have a lot in common. After Matt's thoughts had strayed to the past and returned, he wondered how much damage is done because girls grow up faster than boys.

"So, what did you do when you were growing up?" Abby asked.

Matt hesitated. "I got into trouble a lot. I guess you'd say I was kind of wild."

Abby was silent.

Matt went on. "My dad was killed in an accident. He was on an Army training exercise when his helicopter crashed. I was eight. Mom idolized him. She didn't want anything to do with a 'replacement.' "

"So you grew up without a father?"

"Mostly. He was gone a lot even before that. But I'm not trying to blame my behavior on that. I don't really know why I did the things I did. Maybe I needed an outlet for my anger. Maybe I figured nothing mattered. Here a good man died in a senseless accident. I don't know."

"What kinds of things did you do?"

" 'Crimes against property,' the police called them. I never hurt anyone, but there were a lot of busted mailboxes and broken windows in my neighborhood. Things like that."

"But you grew up." It was a statement, not a question.

"Yeah, I did, I think. Maybe there's hope for Bobby Joe, huh?"

"What happened?"

"It's funny. One day I was feeling particularly angry. I kicked over a big section of a fence a couple of blocks from my house. I started to leave and I looked up. I saw the man who lived in the house. He'd been watching me from a window. He looked, I don't know, just sad. I went home that night, waiting for the police, knowing they'd be there at any minute. I'd had enough trouble with them already that I was sure I'd be sent someplace for a few years. I considered running away. I lay there the whole night, trying to decide what I'd do when they came for me."

"And?"

"And they never came. The guy didn't call them. I walked past his house the next day, and he was out there fixing the fence. I went closer—I mean, what could I lose? He looked up at me—he had a couple of nails in his mouth. I knew he recognized me, but he didn't say anything. I just stood there and watched. Finally he said, 'Something I can do for you?' "

Matt took a deep breath. "I still don't really know what changed right then—whether I realized that people did pay a price even though I didn't hurt anyone directly—or if I realized that things *do* matter—that just because my dad died in an accident that didn't mean the whole world was senseless, maybe."

"So?"

"So I said, 'Can I help?' He looked up at me and considered that for a minute. Finally he said, 'You can put that new post in that hole and then pour cement around it.' So I did. I worked a couple of hours with him, and he didn't say a word. I came back the next day and we nailed up the boards and painted them. When the whole job was done, I finally got up the nerve to ask him why he hadn't called the cops.

"He looked at the new fence, and he looked back at me. And then he said, 'Looks like I made the right decision, don't you think?' "

Abby was silent as they continued walking.

Matt cleared his throat. "I stayed real busy that summer. I patrolled the neighborhood, and whenever I saw anyone doing any work on their place, I stopped and asked if I could help. The first couple of people I asked turned me down, but pretty soon people understood that I wanted to do exactly what I said I wanted to do."

"I think that must have taken a lot of courage," Abby said at last.

Matt was trying to decide what to say when Rudy called from somewhere ahead of them in the tunnel. "Time for another air vent."

"I can do it this time," Matt yelled back.

"You got it."

Rudy appeared in the glow from Abby's hardhat light and he handed her the bag of tools. She passed them back to Matt.

"See you folks in a few minutes," Matt said as Rudy went back toward the cart.

"Any problem with me helping?" Abby asked.

"No problem at all. I don't need much help, but the company is nice."

Matt set the bag on the tunnel floor and made a quick check to ensure everything he needed was there before he started drilling. It all looked good. He took out the drill and inserted the long bit.

He reached up, aiming his hardhat light at the tunnel roof where the bit dug into it. Abby aimed her headlamp upward, too, and when Matt glanced at her, the reflected light spilled onto her face, and he could see that instead of looking at the drill bit she was watching him. It was so tempting to try to get closer to Abby, to help wipe away the pain from the way Nadine had left his life, but it wouldn't be fair to himself or to Abby. If he tried to use Abby to fill that gap, he wouldn't know if he was responding to her or to the situation. And it would just hurt Abby if it turned out he was reacting to the past instead of the present.

Abby's expression changed, as though she were about to say something, and Matt realized he'd been staring at her for several seconds. She looked so appealing, even with the hardhat covering most of her hair. He looked back up at the drill bit, which was almost all the way through.

"Abby," he said, unsure what he really wanted to say, "I'm glad you're on this . . . mission."

Her lips parted, then closed again. Finally she said, "So am I."

The drill bit quit giving resistance as it broke through to the top. Matt switched off the drill and pulled out the bit as a small rain of flakes of goo swirled to the tunnel floor.

Abby knelt and retrieved a new air tube from the bag, and as Matt took the bit out of the drill, she pushed the tube into the opening. The last tube had been for intake, so on this one they attached a flexible hose and taped it to the tunnel walls so it came near the floor. Matt attached a fan, and set it to exhaust. As it started to hum softly, he applied flame from the torch around the junction between pipe and the goo, sealing it against leaks.

Abby held the bag as Matt put the torch back inside.

"Thanks for the help," Matt said.

"Any time," Abby said. "Any time at all."

Twenty blocks north of the drug center of Manhattan, the Abyssinian Baptist Church, on 138th Street, was as crowded as every other church.

Over fifty people waited in a room filled with memorabilia from the days of Adam Clayton Powell, Jr.

Shirlee Bathcomb fidgeted as she waited with her parents for the people ahead of them to clear the sanctuary so they could attend a service and the people behind them could follow. The sound of voices raised in song reached her as she stared at a picture of Powell shaking hands with an old mayor of New York. Shirlee felt better knowing the current mayor was black, but she wasn't sure if it made much difference when whoever brought them here wasn't talking to anyone.

The idea that they had been brought here to be slaves had occurred to Shirlee, but she'd discarded the idea as being too horrible to contemplate.

Abby was getting really tired of the confines of the tunnel by the time they reached the next dome. Except for the fact that the smoothly bored hole was clean, the experience was like slowly traveling for kilometers through a sewer.

They had arrived after a long day, and they decided to wait until the next morning to cut through the gray ceiling. After dreams of rats so large they almost blocked the way, and of flying above an immense field of grass, Abby felt moderately rested but highly impatient as Rudy cut the square opening to the surface just outside the dome they wanted to visit.

The foursome got the slab of goo out of the way. When it was Abby's turn to look outside, she looked up and up and gasped.

Right next to their camouflaged cutout was a dome that might have been only as big around as a big city block, but it soared into the sky far higher, she was sure, than the towers of the World Trade Center. On the other side of the bubble material was a trio of huge trees whose bases sat in an equilateral triangle. Large circular leaves all faced the "sun," a yellowish bright light like the one over Manhattan.

Suspended by vines or ropes slung over stubby tree branches was a city with a far different texture than the previous one. Here and there in the webwork of ropes were woven structures vaguely like grass huts, but many of which were far larger. Figures moved high in the air, crossing on ropes, descending or ascending on larger, knotted ropes reaching from level to level, like ornamental strings used for decoration on the biggest tree in the universe.

None of the beings were close enough to see clearly with unassisted vision, but she had the impression of thin-limbed people, rather than apes or similar primates. She put on her minivid viewer, then cranked up the telephoto.

Centered in the jittery frame was a spindly alien tree dweller. As the alien's arms reached for a rope, light filtered through a fleshy web extending between the torso and the arm. Recording all she could see, Abby panned the minivid until she was startled by the much-larger image in her viewfinder.

She blinked, then started reducing the telephoto enlargement. One of the aliens had apparently noticed her. It was a child, judging by the smaller size compared to the other beings she'd seen.

The alien came closer, watching intently as it jostled down a rope. It stopped and cocked its head in the familiar posture of a human getting a different perspective on something it doesn't see clearly or doesn't recognize.

Abby directed her voice through the roof of the tunnel. "Someone's coming to investigate."

"Does it look hostile?" Matt asked from below.

Abby looked back to confirm her first impression. The approaching figure moved quickly toward her, not fast enough to be a predator on the run, not slow enough to be trying to sneak up. Nothing like a weapon was visible. In one hand the alien carried something vaguely like a whip, but it didn't seem to be using it as a weapon. The end of the cord seemed to want to naturally form a coil with several loops. Occasionally the alien would snap the cord toward a branch or rope just out of its range. The snapping motion would uncurl the end of the cord and it would wrap around the branch it had been aimed at. The alien would use the support provided by the weak connection to the branch, and when it had moved far enough that it no longer needed the support, it pulled the coiled section loose so it was ready to use again.

"No, it doesn't," Abby said. "And there are more on the way."

From higher up in the tree city another couple of the smaller versions of the aliens started down to look at Abby. Their bodies were all spindly, with taut skin over prominent bones. One alien from even farther up jumped from a limb, spread its arms, and glided about ten meters down to a grid of ropes strung between the trio of trees.

As the first couple of curious tree dwellers reached the ground and approached, at least a dozen more were on their way down to investigate. Abby didn't notice any of them calling to others, but the group kept growing.

Abby backed against the surface of the goo as Matt joined her. Within a few minutes at least a dozen short aliens and a couple of tall ones stood against the inside of the bubble, inspecting Abby and Matt, curiosity plain in their expressions, despite mottled skin that on a human would have probably denoted some terrible disease, and an emaciated look that for humans would mean death couldn't be far off.

"Think it's time for your computer?" Matt asked.

Abby nodded and took it from her belt. She snapped it open and unfurled the screen. She switched the power on, and a color 2-D startup image came up on the screen. She aimed the screen toward the still growing group of aliens and called up the first image.

The screen was thin enough that she could see the image through the back of the screen and verify that it was the right one. The image was a side view of Manhattan, one chosen to match what it looked like from this general direction. Next to the dome stood a human man and woman. Abby pointed to herself and to Matt, and then pointed at the couple on the screen. She pointed at Manhattan in the picture, and then pointed at the real thing in the distance. She watched the aliens as she pointed at Manhattan and saw eyes move, telling her these people knew what pointing meant. A cat would stare at your fingertip, but these people looked at *where* she pointed.

She triggered the next image, an artist's conception of a top view, showing Manhattan under a dome. The image began to shrink, and more domes came into view. Abby found the one with the small round shape, pointed to it, and pointed inside the dome.

The picture of the couple was superimposed on the screen near the Manhattan dome, and the couple began to move slowly across the screen, leaving a dotted line behind them. They stopped next to the small circular dome. Abby again pointed to Matt and herself.

The next image showed a side view of the edge of the dome. In a series of steps, a circular tunnel formed beneath the surface of the goo, a hole formed in the tunnel roof, and a human stood up showing half of its body. Next the human went back inside the tunnel. A hole formed in the tunnel wall, leading through the underground barrier and coming out on the surface of the ground inside the dome. The final image showed two people sitting opposite each other, an effort to convey the idea of dialogue.

As the sequence completed, Abby saw indecipherable expressions on faces beyond the clear barrier. Seconds later, one of the tallest aliens began to back up. Instantly everyone in the group was doing the same thing. They all backed up until they were perhaps ten meters from the barrier, and then all made gestures that were fairly easy to interpret as inviting. The aliens put palms down and mimicked pawing in the dirt, or perhaps scooping something toward them.

Matt said softly, "Does that seem as friendly to you as it looks to me?"

"I suspect so. I'd say they understand, and they're ready for us to come inside."

"Can you see any reason why we shouldn't proceed?"

"None. We don't have any guarantee that they're as peaceful as they seem, but I don't expect any warmer welcome anywhere."

"You want to stay here and keep them company? I think we can move a meter along the tunnel and cut through there."

"Sure."

Light filtered through the stubby tunnel to the surface. This time the air pressure inside the tall dome was about the same pressure as in the tunnel. The cutting and digging and sampling had gone well, much like going into the first dome. They had sealed the hole in the top of the tunnel as soon as they could see through the new hole.

Matt looked up through the gap and began to feel nervous. He trusted Abby to start communications as smoothly as possible, but there were so many unknowns.

Bobby Joe brought the cart back after dumping dirt in a new side tunnel, and Rudy and Matt cleared out a few more shovelfuls of dirt.

They were ready. Matt still felt uneasy, but he couldn't think of any reason to delay, so he moved down the tunnel far enough to get some quiet as he called Manhattan base and gave them a quick update.

Matt and Abby were again the first two out of the tunnel. They stood on the wiry grass next to the tunnel mouth, breathing in the sweet scent of growing vegetation, looking into the clear white eyes of a group of at least forty of the aliens. The mix of the group had shifted toward the adults. More tall aliens had arrived, and several of the shortest ones had climbed back up into the arboreal complex.

From here Matt couldn't help but think of Jack and the Beanstalk. The trio of trees extended into the inverted test tube, stretching far taller than Matt had imagined was possible. He couldn't remember how tall redwoods managed to get on Earth, but if this city had come from a lower-gravity planet, he supposed the limits to vertical growth would be less severe.

"Next," Matt called into the hole in the ground.

Bobby Joe Brewster came up as cautiously as a child on his best behavior at an adult gathering. Finally Rudy reached the surface. He fastened the "door" closed, and hopped lightly to the surface. The four of them stood together, all acting as carefully as innocent suspects facing a cop's loaded gun.

The tallest aliens were slightly taller than Matt. The few remaining shorter aliens all came at least up to shoulder height. All bare-chested, they were dressed below the waist in what appeared to be one very long turbanlike strip of cloth about as wide as a hand, wrapped in strip after strip, ankle to hips to opposite ankle. Their all-white eyes formed an uncomfortable reminder of cheap horror videos, but nothing about them seemed threatening. Their noses were darker than the rest of their faces, and their arms and heads showed no indication of body hair. Maybe Bobby Joe should have been the spokesperson instead of Abby.

As soon as the humans were all motionless, Abby said, "Hello." Alien heads turned to look at each other, but that was the only reaction until a gap formed in the wall of aliens.

Between the two small groups of aliens, a lone alien stood. This alien's nose was even darker than the others', and he looked even more fragile than the others. The alien made what Matt took to be a come-ahead sign. In accordance with the plan made earlier, Matt didn't react. He waited for Abby's direction. Only in the event that he felt defensive action was necessary would he resume control inside the dome.

Abby said softly to her human companions, "I think we're being invited in. Let's go."

Abby stepped forward in the lead, followed by Matt, then Bobby Joe, then Rudy. If they were stepping into a trap, that was too bad, but all had agreed earlier that the humans had to act as though the people they met were friendly until proved different. It would be all too easy to create hostilities when probably no one in the domes wanted to be here. Matt's exploration team had to be treated as expendable. If the worst happened, and they were killed, the base team in Manhattan would know which dome was hostile, and would keep any of the inhabitants from reaching Manhattan.

As the four of them walked, Matt was aware of the aliens inspecting him as carefully as he looked at them. The group of tree dwellers formed loosely around them, some walking by their sides, some ahead, some behind. Soft sounds of movement came from above them in webbing between the trees.

Their leader reached the base of one of the enormous trees.

At least a dozen knotted ropes or vines hung down low enough to curl on the ground. A couple of the tree dwellers grabbed ropes and began to pull themselves up. The leader made another come-ahead gesture and began climbing, too.

Matt and Abby glanced at each other and then followed the aliens up into the tree city. Climbing was easy in the light gravity, more like lifting a twenty-kilo weight with a rope and pulley than like lifting one's weight in normal gravity. The tree was probably as big around as fifty telephone poles bundled together.

Matt and Abby reached the rough equivalent of a floor in an Earth building. Ropes supported by the three trees were woven together in a loose cat's-cradle gridwork dense enough to break the fall of anyone dropping from a higher level. The area between the trees was about the same as a football field squashed into a triangular shape.

The tree dwellers above them continued climbing, so the humans followed. Matt couldn't hear any sound that seemed like voices, just the rustling noises of other climbers.

They came to the next level and here the gridwork of ropes was denser. In addition, several woven huts rested on the grid, each with a series of support ropes leading from the upper corners of the huts up toward the next level. They kept climbing.

At each of the next few levels the huts grew more numerous. When the aliens stopped climbing, they were on a level with one very large hut resting on a dense grid of ropes. The frail-looking tree dweller walked onto the grid, stepping on the thick ropes and grabbing occasional overhead ropes to keep balanced. Abby followed, and Matt followed her, relieved that the low gravity and frequent layers of grids would be forgiving if they happened to fall through one of the openings in the grid.

Matt glanced back and saw Bobby Joe and Rudy following. Bobby Joe looked as nervous as if he were treading a high wire without a net.

They reached the hut without Bobby Joe having a cardiac arrest from his obvious fear of heights, and they entered through permanently open cutouts. Inside was a smaller hut, with cutout doorways offset from the exterior doorways, perhaps to cut the wind, or to limit visibility. The floor was virtually solid now. Matt could see slices of light through it, but saw no danger of falling or even losing his balance. The floor swayed almost imperceptibly as people near him walked. Openings in the ceiling served as skylights. Each of the square cutouts had dark squares right next to it, as though the covers could be pulled closed when necessary.

In the center of the large interior hut was a low circular table at about knee height. Already seated at the table were three frail-looking aliens. The alien who had led them sat at the table next to them. Also around the perimeter of the table were four vacant cushions made of rope and leaves. Matt was impressed with them having exactly the right number, and wondered what might have happened if their party had contained five people or some other number. Maybe they'd accidentally brought the socially acceptable number of diplomats.

Their host gestured at the cushions.

Abby said, "Let's take seats, shall we?"

As the four humans sat down at the table, the rest of the tree dwellers who had accompanied them silently moved to the walls and sat on the floor around the perimeter. Matt wondered if they were observing or protecting.

Matt and Abby took the center two cushions on their side, with Bobby Joe and Rudy sitting on the two outside. The four people across the table from them didn't look friendly, but neither did they look hostile.

One of the four, the one with a mark shaped vaguely like an octagon on one cheek, leaned forward and turned over a square flap in the center of the table. On the reverse side of it was apparently a writing surface. The alien traced a fingertip along the surface, and a line formed, just like on an old magic slate.

The fingertip continued its travel, and the line turned into a tall, thin upside-down *U*. Next to it the alien drew a semicircle. Beneath the open ends of the two curves, the alien drew a long straight line forming a base on which both curves rested. The alien leaned back and gestured at the drawing.

Abby leaned forward and put a fingertip on the hemisphere. She drew her finger in a path from the inside of the hemisphere, under the long line, and then up into the tall upside-down *U*. The line her finger made was wider than the ones the alien had drawn. One of the tree people looked puzzled, and Abby said softly, "I think maybe they originally thought we might be the aliens who run this ship."

The tree dweller drew several horizontal lines in the *U* starting at the bottom. At the sixth line it added a small circle. Then it continued the line Abby had drawn, moving from the ground up to where they all now sat.

Around the pair of domes, Abby drew a very large circle. Then she continued the original line by moving her finger from inside the "U" and not stopping until her finger was completely outside the large circle.

All four aliens simultaneously rocked their heads from side to side. Matt glanced at Abby, and she looked puzzled.

With a slow, cautious movement, Abby removed her computer from her belt. She set it on the table and just left it there for a few seconds, as though she were trying to make it plain that it was not a weapon.

The aliens stopped their head-rocking motion and looked closely at the computer. Abby unsnapped and unfurled the screen, positioning it so they could see it. She snapped on the power switch.

Suddenly the air was filled with screaming. The aliens across the table put their hands to their heads and screeched like cats in pain. One of them keeled over backward. The aliens at the edge of the room were reacting, too. Some of them staggered to their feet, at the same time holding their heads in their hands.

"Turn it *off!*" Bobby Joe yelled.

Abby looked blank for an instant. As Bobby Joe moved to turn off the computer, Abby finally reacted and moved even faster. Her fingers hit the switch, and the screen went dark.

Around the room, the cries started dropping in volume. The aliens across the table looked stupefied. Ones near the edge of the room started to recover and began to approach, menace clear in their stance now.

Bobby Joe said urgently, "Don't touch the computer."

Matt said, "Move back slowly. Abby, tell us what to do to look as unthreatening as we can."

"Keep down," she said. "Keep your hands in front of you where they can see them. Don't move quickly."

"What the hell happened?" Rudy asked.

Bobby Joe talked quickly, quietly. "I think they're telepathic. That's probably why they haven't tried speech on us. That's why they all seem to decide the same thing around the same time. I bet when the computer turned on, whatever RF it leaks was enough to bombard the receptors they use for telepathy. We just did the equivalent of spraying them with sound or light way past their threshold of pain."

Matt said, "Abby, you've got to figure out how to convince them it was an accident."

Aliens from the perimeter of the room continued their angry approach. The aliens right across the table still seemed dazed, except for the one who had fallen. That one remained motionless.

"I think you're right." Abby slowly pointed at the computer, then made a gesture of sweeping it away from her, as though she didn't want it near her. Then she put her hands to her head and imitated the aliens' screams. She backed away from the computer and pointed at it again. "That's all I can think of for now."

Maybe it was enough. The tree dwellers from the perimeter managed to look less menacing, and halted their approach. They now seemed intent on the computer. A couple of them moved to the one who had fallen, gently picked up the alien, and moved carefully out of the hut. Slowly the three remaining at the table began to show signs of recovery. One of them tapped its temple a couple of times, and then shook its head.

Matt glanced at one of the doorways and realized that the emergency had attracted many more aliens. He glanced at another doorway. They were surrounded by a huge group now, but the group was still.

In the temporary calm, Rudy said, "But why didn't the computer bother them when—oh, we were *outside* the dome."

Matt said, "Score one for our captors' planning. If the domes didn't block RF, we might have pointed a directional broadcast at a race like this and maybe have killed them all. And in case it's not obvious already, don't *anyone* try to use a walkie-talkie inside this dome."

Very gradually the aliens in the room seemed to relax. Matt was very grateful they were dealing with an intelligent race; had this happened with people incapable of understanding the concept of accidents or unintentional results, the four of them might all have been dead by now. And the next party to come here could easily make the same mistake all over again.

One of the tree dwellers used a short loop of rope to pull the computer over to the opposite side of the table. Matt and the others made no objection. When things had calmed down a little more, Abby reached slowly forward to the drawing board. In an unused area she drew an outline of the computer on the outside of the dome. Radiating from it she drew a series of jagged lines in all directions. The lines that went in the direction of the dome stopped at the edge of the city.

She drew a jagged line through a stick figure inside the hemisphere. Next she drew a similar line through a stick figure inside the "U." Next to the stick figure she drew another figure on its side.

Matt thought he saw comprehension on the faces across the table, but he couldn't be sure.

A spindly tree dweller pushed through the crowd near the doors and entered the room. The alien sat down and took the place deserted by the one who had fallen. Matt realized there was probably no need for Abby to repeat what she'd drawn so far, not with a telepathic race.

One of the aliens took the pad and turned it over. When the pad was upright again, the previous drawings had vanished. The alien drew a large circle, and then proceeded to indicate that they had been cut loose from the surface of a planet and placed here. Abby traced a series of drawings that showed the same thing had happened to Manhattan.

When Abby finished, the alien again used a long, bony finger to draw. On the perimeter of the planet they had come from, it drew a series of cross marks.

"I don't know what that means," Abby said. "I think we're getting near the point where I'm going to have to generate some pictorial vocabulary."

Matt watched as Abby made a dot and wrote a numeral one next to it, then made two dots and wrote a two. He followed along with her, generally understanding what she was communicating, but his attention wandered when they weren't actually learning any specific information about their circumstances.

During the next several hours, Abby managed to learn that the tree dwellers had been in captivity for about a decade Earth time. Shortly after that, the session was interrupted.

"They want us to follow them," Abby said.

The four humans followed six of the tree dwellers out of the meeting room and up to the next level of cat's-cradle rope grid. There their hosts approached a raised, cross-shaped platform on which lay the body of a tree dweller who Matt thought was the one who'd been at their table earlier. With the aid of a small version of the magic slate, Abby confirmed the identity. God, the first city they entered that was occupied by living people and they'd already killed someone. He felt sick.

Another tree dweller approached with a small twig that burned at one end, and Matt suddenly realized how much damage fire could do to this city. He looked up and saw that on the level above them, a large group of tree dwellers stood around a huge ring of what looked like large water balloons made from skin or some translucent plant tissue.

The tree dweller with the burning stick reached the body on the platform. The alien applied the flame near the body's feet, and in moments the exposed surface of the platform was in flames. Inside the flickering brightness, the body darkened and burned.

The tree dwellers in a ring around the platform hung their heads, so Matt did the same. The fire burned for five or ten minutes, and when it died out, nothing remained except an uneven pile of ashes, not even bones.

Two tree dwellers approached, scooped the ashes into a small pan, and then poured water from a bladder into the pan and stirred the ashes. They poured the remainder of the water onto the platform, where it hissed and then grew quiet. The sludgy mixture of water and ashes was spread on the bark of the nearest tree.

When they got back to the meeting room, one of the tree dwellers made marks on the pad, at which time Abby said, "They say it's time to eat a meal. I think they understand we shouldn't risk trying their food without some testing."

Matt asked Abby, "Do they mind if we send someone to get our food?"

Soon Abby said, "No. That's fine."

Matt looked at Rudy. "Would you do it?"

Rudy nodded. He left in the company of a couple of the tree dwellers.

When Rudy got back, the four humans and the four tree dwellers ate a meal, each species using its own food. Matt was glad they had their own supply, not just because he knew it would be safe, but also because the tree dwellers' food pellets smelled like something that had been in the refrigerator too long.

Not long after lunch, Abby was able to determine that the tree dwellers had not yet been able to decode their message from the captors, either. She suggested that with only one language, and with a reliance on thought more than a written vocabulary, the tree dwellers might be the last to decode it.

By midafternoon, Matt's attention was beginning to wander. The tree dweller they had killed wouldn't have had to die if this expedition hadn't been undertaken. And all they'd learned so far was what they had expected—that other cities had received the same treatment as Manhattan.

Abby was leaning over drawing a couple of symbols on the slate when suddenly she jerked upright. "Oh, God."

"What's the matter?" Matt asked.

"Ah, ah, I don't want to say. Maybe it's nothing. I just remembered that the cremation platform was cross-shaped. The cross may be their symbol for death."

"So?"

"Let me try to find out something. I'll tell you as soon as I actually know anything."

Abby quickly scratched lines through everything she'd been working on and started a new drawing. Her fingers trembled as she drew.

The tree dwellers drew figures in response.

After about ten more minutes of interaction, the blood drained from Abby's face. On the pad was another version of the large circle with a series of crosses around its perimeter.

Abby turned toward Matt. "Oh, God. The rest of them were killed. I've been praying there's a chance I was wrong, but I don't think so." She took a deep breath. "They know this because they're telepathic. I'm still a little uncertain on time units, but as near as I can make out, something like twenty days after they were captured, while this ship was still near their planet, fire rained from the sky, and every single person remaining on their planet was killed."

8

ARMED AND DANGEROUS

TWO MEN PICKED their way through steam passageways and sewer tunnels beneath the southernmost section of Broadway. Flashlights powered by rechargeable batteries generated beams that cut through the haze, forming crude light-sabers whose points danced on the dark walls ahead.

Benny Kellermund, the man following, was a short man with a crew cut and a boxer's build. He'd wanted to be in the Mafia, but he wasn't Italian. He had earned a reputation for unpredictability.

Lucky Stiles, the man in front, had the body of a fighter and the charm of an IRS agent in the middle of a tax-evasion audit.

Benny took a long final drag and finished his last cigarette, which was probably to be nearly his *very* last cigarette. Instead of flicking the end into the scummy water filling the trough that ran along the center of the tunnel, Benny stuffed the last quarter inch of tobacco into his pocket. Later in the week, he'd assemble the remaining sections into the last cigarette he might ever smoke.

Benny cleared his throat. He'd been trying to breathe without paying attention to the stench, but he'd been unsuccessful. He wasn't all that crazy about opening his mouth, but he was curious. "How come you don't get lost down here? It all looks the same." His voice generated spooky echoes.

"Practice, practice, practice," said Lucky.

Benny shut up. His back was sore from having to bend forward to balance the bulky load he carried, but Lucky carried a similar load and he wasn't complaining. They passed dark side passages and turned corners from time to time, but only once did Lucky seem in doubt about which way to turn next. Occasionally, light filtered down from a grate high above, but mostly it was just dark. Benny didn't shine his light down any of the side tunnels or unexpected cavities. He preferred not to know what the darkest corners held.

Benny's adrenaline level was up, but his pulse was close to normal. Even though the Mafia wouldn't take him, he'd found his own ways to belong. He'd formed a street gang, and he'd done jobs like this often enough that it was almost routine, except for being underground. He felt good, knowing that when he was finished, the mayor would think twice about doing anything that might cause their captors to retaliate. People shouldn't be rocking the boat. They could all have a nice life in Manhattan. The island was all he knew of Earth, and all he cared about on Earth. The preacher was right; rocking the boat could only cause trouble.

Something moved in the water as Benny and Lucky moved along a new section of tunnel. Benny made a point of not looking, but he couldn't help think of the stories of baby alligators flushed down toilets. Alligators were mean enough as it was. What if they *remembered* being flushed down a toilet?

"Are we almost there yet?" Benny asked. His voice generated more metallic echoes.

"If you gotta take a leak, you can just turn left."

"I'm fine. Just curious." No way was Benny undoing his zipper down here. He wasn't even sure if he'd keep his shoes when he got back to the surface.

"We're close, okay?"

"Okay." Up on the streets, Benny felt equal to Lucky, sometimes maybe more than that, but down here he felt reliant on Lucky. Here Lucky was clearly the expert.

Benny started to shift his load to his other shoulder, but realized that would make walking in the curved tunnel difficult. Something behind Benny scraped against concrete. He didn't look around, but the hair on the back of his neck bristled. Benny could hold his own in any fight, but this place made him distinctly uncomfortable.

They passed a series of iron rungs set into the concrete, leading up into the darkness, and for a few seconds Benny regretted watching the *Aliens* films so many times. He almost wished he had a flame thrower.

The explosives in his shoulder pack seemed to grow more awkward by the minute. In the light gravity, the pack wasn't too heavy, but the bulk still made it hard to turn or stop instantly. He followed Lucky into another tunnel, this one with a huge number of pipes of varying sizes running along the length of the tunnel roof. His foot kicked a candy bar wrapper aside, and his next step generated the *crunch* of a beetle or a roach being ground into the cement. Benny wasn't about to stop and decide which.

After another few minutes, Lucky actually had to stop and consult a small map before pointing into a tunnel that seemed to slope perceptibly downward.

At the other end of the tunnel was a junction where six tunnels met, and Benny could feel vibrations through the soles of his shoes.

"Here," Lucky said as he unshouldered his pack and started to put it on the ground. At the last minute, he hung the strap on a bolt holding a pipe at chest level.

Benny acted as a nurse to Lucky's doctor impression as Lucky requested materials from the packs and he carefully set them into position. "Packet" meant Lucky wanted another greasy, plastic-wrapped brick of explosive. "Glue" meant Lucky wanted the glue gun to fasten something into place, once a fuse, once a timer.

This part of the trip made Benny the most nervous. Not many of Benny's friends called him things like "imaginative," but he sure was. He could see himself and Lucky getting blown to bits by just a quick accident: the wrong thing dropped, the timer being defective. For all he knew, accidentally putting the explosive next to a hot pipe would trigger it.

If Lucky shared Benny's fears, he kept them to himself. Seconds later Lucky finished his work, and they moved down another tunnel. A couple of minutes later, Lucky was again at work.

"Okay, that just about does it," Lucky said finally.

Benny realized he was sweating. "You're sure that'll do it?"

"Sure I'm sure. That huge pipe there? It's one of the tunnel ventilation tubes. When this baby goes—poof—it starts suckin' air from right here down into the tunnel. And that first job, back in the other tunnel? That'll rupture the biggest water line for blocks around. This whole tunnel will be flooded, and guess where the water's gonna want to go?"

"So, how much time do we have?"

Lucky looked at his watch. "About two, two and a half minutes."

"*What?* Let's get the hell out of here!"

"Fine by me."

Lucky hoisted his pack and started moving back the way they had come. Benny was right behind.

"Hurry it up, will you?" Benny said.

"Keep your pants on. Oh, did I say two minutes? I meant twenty minutes." Lucky laughed his screwy laugh, sounding like something halfway between a hiccup and a belch.

"You moron."

"Had you going. Am I right?"

"Get outta here."

For an instant, Benny considered tipping Lucky into the trough of scummy liquid flowing along the bottom of the tunnel, but he knew he'd never find his way out on his own.

He followed Lucky through turn after turn, thinking of ways to get even. A pair of red eyes illuminated by his flashlight took his mind off the problem temporarily.

"Hold up," Lucky said suddenly. He stopped so abruptly Benny almost bumped into him. Lucky turned so Benny could see he was looking at his watch. "Should be just about now."

Benny listened carefully, suddenly too aware of the creaks and slithering sounds and the soft buzzing that could have been flies caught in a big spiderweb nearby. "Why should I believe you this—"

"Shhh!"

And then it came. Two dull *cracks*, then silence, then a slow thundering noise as the rumbling made the tunnel walls vibrate. Grit fell from the ceiling, and somewhere a pipe *clanked* three times.

"Yes!" said Lucky.

"All right!" Benny turned to face the way they had come, and the rumbling seemed a little louder. He visualized the water flooding into the Battery Tunnel. That should give the mayor second thoughts about whether she should have people down there. "You're a wizard," he said softly.

"Tell me somethin' new," said Lucky.

The two men moved off into the tunnel. Occasionally Benny looked back nervously, a little worried that he'd see a wall of water coming toward them. If that happened, it probably wouldn't even matter that he couldn't swim.

Blood pounded in Matt's ears. "Their *entire* population killed?" he said, disbelieving.

Abby looked from the alien diplomats to Matt. "Yes. They heard the dying screams of a planetful of their race. A lot of what they heard wasn't coherent, but they got the strong impression of the whole atmosphere being on fire. From a live person there's always a residual amount of noise. Only when someone of their race dies does that person go completely silent. And silence is what they heard afterward. I'm amazed they haven't all gone mad."

"God above," Matt said slowly. "How sure are you that you're correctly understanding them? And is there any chance that the bubble being in place is what cut off the rest of the transmissions?"

Abby said, "I'm virtually positive I'm understanding them correctly, but I'll try to go at it a different way to make absolutely certain."

As Abby started drawing on the tree dwellers' slate again, Rudy leaned forward and caught Matt's attention. Softly he said, "As horrific as that sounds, we do already have some evidence that suggests what they're telling us is true."

Matt thought for a moment. "You're talking about the flashes of light over the horizon in the transmission we received? What we figured was a huge lightning storm?"

"Yes. If our captors really do destroy the planet after a city they take is off the surface, that lightning storm could have been caused by them. That lightning storm could have been something far worse."

Abby exchanged several more drawings before she said,

"What I've already told you has to be the right interpretation. These people could be lying to us, but I really think that's what they're saying."

Matt nodded. "Do these . . . people 'hear' anything from our captors?"

Moments later Abby said, "No. They've never been able to communicate with anyone who's not a member of their race. Apparently they can 'hear' electrical noise when it's generated, but to them that's all it is: noise." Abby hesitated. "God, I hate to even think this, but it's the obvious conclusion. If the people on their planet were destroyed after the city was captured, and that was what happened to the people who've been transmitting, that probably means the same thing—the same thing has happened to everyone on Earth. Or that it might happen *soon,* if it hasn't already."

Matt felt suddenly as if he'd been punched. He felt very old and afraid. The other three members of the human contingent were silent for a long moment, no doubt trying to get over the shock. Under his breath, Matt said, "Jesus, not Earth."

Finally Matt summoned strength and said, "But why would they be doing this? Why would they take a city and then destroy the rest of the population?"

Rudy said, "They could be killing the rest to make sure no one ever tries to get the cities back."

Bobby Joe fidgeted. "If all these cities constitute a gigantic zoo, then they could represent an investment. If you had a collection of anything, wouldn't it be worth more if it contained the *only* ones in existence?"

Matt looked at Abby. "These people say it took about twenty days between the city capture and the destruction of the population. But the transmission we received from the other dome makes it seem that it started immediately. I wonder why the difference."

Abby shook her head.

The aliens watched quietly as the humans talked.

Matt leaned toward Bobby Joe. "If the dome stopped RF from the computer, how does it transmit whatever frequencies are used for their telepathy?"

Bobby Joe spread his hands. "Can't tell for sure. If their

telepathy isn't confined to line of sight, it could be that it uses long-wave RF and the dome stops only short wavelengths. It could be telepathy uses spread-spectrum transmission, and again the dome cuts only part of that. Could be they were sending through the black base material instead of the dome."

"We've got to leave," Matt said suddenly. "Can you tell them we've got to get out of here right away? If there's a chance that Earth is still alive, we can't just sit here."

Abby hurriedly made more marks on the drawing board, and within seconds the humans were being escorted out of the meeting room.

As they descended the knotted ropes, Matt tried to imagine reasons their captors would destroy the remaining populations on their home planets, but he could think of nothing that made sense, at least nothing that would make sense if their captors thought like human beings. But there was no reason at all to believe their captors shared anything about the human outlook.

Large crowds of the tree dwellers watched from each of the layers the human team passed on the way down, no doubt as curious about humans as the humans were about them, and no doubt all aware the humans were leaving suddenly.

The team reached the ground, and Rudy moved to open the door into the tunnel. One at a time they dropped down into the hole and moved sideways into the tunnel. As Rudy and Bobby Joe folded the black cutout back into place, Matt walked along the tunnel toward the still borer for a full minute before he switched on his walkie-talkie, just in case the frequency it used was harmful to the tree dwellers.

"Manhattan base, this is Rover," Matt said into the mike.

"Go ahead, Rover."

"We've got bad news, and we're coming back. Please contact the mayor and request an emergency session in"—Matt made a quick estimate—"in about four hours."

"Will do. What's wro—hey, what the hell!" The Manhattan transmission cut off abruptly.

"Hello, Manhattan base. Hello!" Matt took his thumb off the TRANSMIT switch and listened. Nothing.

"Hello, Manhattan base. This is Rover. Do you read me?"

Still nothing. What the hell was going on? He left the walkie-talkie on and went back to the others.

"We've got more problems," he said. Abby, Rudy, and Bobby Joe stopped what they were doing and looked at him. "The transmission from Manhattan base was just cut off."

"What the hell is happening?" asked Bobby Joe.

"This is unbelievable," said Abby.

"True. But it's happening."

"What's the next step, then—go back?" Rudy asked.

Matt thought for several seconds. "Abby and I are going back. We need to get back to Manhattan and have a quick meeting to decide what we should do next. Rudy, I want you and Bobby Joe to keep the borer going as fast as you can. Keep heading for the dome that's been transmitting, and we'll catch up as soon as we can."

Rudy said calmly, "You already know what the meeting is going to decide, don't you?"

"Yeah, I think so. If in fact this ship does grab cities and then destroys the planets, the only way I can think of to keep Earth from being destroyed, if it hasn't been already, is to disable this ship."

St. Patrick's Cathedral was a bewildering mixture of calm and turmoil. As a round-the-clock prayer vigil continued, the crowds were heavier than ever before as five to ten thousand people vied for the space meant for 2,500. Around the perimeter of the church had been established prayer centers for people who couldn't fit inside the church, under its enormous vaulted ceiling.

A group of at least a thousand people sat in a huge circle around the statue of Atlas that stood between St. Patrick's and Rockefeller Center. The deacon who stood on the statue's base as she read prayers and talked to the crowd was convinced that well over half the crowd wasn't Catholic, but she didn't care. Sometimes it took extraordinary events to get people's attention.

* * *

Abby's legs were getting tired. She guessed that Matt was even more tired, but he hadn't complained and she wasn't about to.

They'd been running more than an hour through the tunnel back to Manhattan. The low tunnel ceiling prevented long, high strides and forced them into a leaning-forward-almost-falling gait that also made her neck sore. Fortunately, running in the tunnel was easy on the feet, like running on an endless strip of cork. Matt ran in front and Abby matched his pace. They'd still heard nothing more from Manhattan.

"Uh oh," Matt said.

Abby slowed as quickly as she could. By the time she was stopped, she realized that something was wrong with the tunnel floor. The entire stretch they'd run along had the normal circular shape, like a huge pipe. Here, the bottom of the tunnel was flattened.

Just as she realized what the problem must be, Matt confirmed it. "The tunnel must have a leak up ahead."

Abby's hardhat light penetrated the dark tunnel. Where they stood, the circular passage was flattened on the bottom, like a coin hit by a hammer on the bottom edge. The goo spreading along the floor looked deeper ahead. "It looks like the tunnel dips down."

Matt looked behind them, and then ahead again. "I think you're right. The extra mass of the goo that's in the tunnel makes it heavier than normal, so it's sinking."

"So that might pull the ventilation pipes below the surface."

"If it sinks very much, that's true. I just hope the tunnel isn't blocked completely."

Matt started moving ahead again, more slowly this time. Abby followed.

The level of the goo on the tunnel floor gradually grew higher. At the same time, the tunnel dipped slightly deeper. Within a minute, they reached the point where the goo filled the bottom half of the tunnel, and they had to start crawling on their hands and knees. Abby felt her lungs grow colder as they moved forward and the clearance diminished to not much more than a half-meter. She could no longer see past Matt to tell what it looked like ahead.

"Stop," Matt said. "It's getting even tighter ahead."

Abby stopped, extremely grateful they weren't going any deeper. Now that she was no longer moving forward, she was aware that her body trembled.

Matt reached for his walkie-talkie and started speaking. "Rudy, this is Matt."

A moment of silence was followed by, "I read you. What is it?"

"The tunnel has sprung a leak. We're maybe a kilometer from Manhattan. I'm guessing the breach is around one of the ventilators; that's what the odds suggest anyway. I'm hoping there's still enough clearance for Abby and me to get through it. If we get stuck, we can try to use our knives to cut to the surface, but it would be better if you could back us up. If you don't hear from us in fifteen minutes, get back here double-time and help us out, all right?"

As Matt spoke, Abby's chill began to spread again. She was already squeezed far tighter than she ever wanted to be. Wherever she looked, she saw the image of that trunk lid closing. She imagined getting stuck right where she was as the goo moved in ultra-slow motion to fill in the tunnel completely.

"You got it," Rudy said. "I can start now if you want."

"No, I think I can see far enough that the gap begins to get bigger on the other side of the leak."

"All right. Standing by."

"Thanks." Matt called back to Abby. "I'd suggest you hang your walkie-talkie around your neck, to make sure you can get to it. It's going to get a little tighter before we're through." Matt hesitated. "Are you going to be okay with this?"

Abby shut her eyes and forced herself to say, "Sure." Now she had a terrifying image of herself stuck in the tunnel, not totally unable to move, but too traumatized to go forward or backward.

"That's good. Depending on how tight this gets, I may need you to help pull me back out."

Abby bit her lip.

"All right," Matt said. "Let's go."

Abby followed Matt as they were reduced to crawling though the nearly blocked tunnel. Her head kept hitting the tunnel roof, and she imagined Matt was already meeting resistance from both the floor and ceiling. She closed her eyes and tried desperately to imagine she was crawling across a desert, sand below her, and nothing but miles and miles of sky above her. It didn't work. Her breath came in ragged spurts.

Ahead of her Matt grunted. "I think we're almost at the tightest spot. It *does* look like a leak from around a ventilator tube." He made audible straining noises as he pushed himself farther into the narrowing fissure. Abby's heart beat at double time. If he was taking this calmly, then she could, too. She had to.

Finally Matt said, "Yeah, here it is. I'm going to use my matches to try to seal it as long as we're here."

Abby could hear him hacking with his knife, no doubt clearing some of the leaking goo away from the pipe. She tried to think about a hot bath or a run through Central Park, but all she could focus on was one morbid thought. Even with the leak sealed, the extra goo in the tunnel might make the tunnel heavy enough to sink right here. The more the tunnel floor dropped, the more the goo could start pulling closer to the center of the depression, forcing the tunnel to sink even faster, and further accelerate the process of the goo flowing toward the middle.

A match flared ahead of Matt. Light flickered through the gaps around his body and off the narrow walls for several seconds. The match went out, and Matt lit another. After what seemed a long span of minutes, he finally said, "All right. I think that's got it."

Matt crawled forward again, his straining noises even louder. After moving another half-meter into the gap, he called back and said, "I think I'm almost through, but I can't quite make it. Can you brace yourself and put your hands against my feet so I can push just a little farther?"

At first Abby couldn't speak. "But what if you get stuck?"

"I'm hoping that won't happen. And I'm hoping that now the leak is sealed, if I do get stuck, it'll only be a matter of time until the goo flows far enough that I can get free. Just make sure you don't go so far that you get stuck, too. One of us has to have our hands free."

"You're certain you want to do this?"

"No," Matt admitted. "But I've got to. And I really think we can make it."

Abby wanted to scream, but she couldn't. She was petrified, her muscles suddenly locked in a terrifying self-imposed rigor mortis. The image of Matt stuck ahead of her in the tunnel and the tunnel closing in behind her as she struggled to get free was horrifying.

"Abby! Abby!" She finally heard Matt's voice over the ringing in her ears. Suddenly she was able to breathe again, and she took in a gasp large enough to make her feel even bigger in the confined area.

She deliberately bit her tongue and the pain cut through the haze. She tried to force everything but Matt out of her mind and did her best to ignore her fears. She moved forward and felt Matt's shoes. "Okay," she said a moment later, her voice shaky.

Matt's shoes pressed into her hands, hard, harder. She tried not to think about dying. And finally the pressure went away.

"I think that did it!" Matt shouted.

Abby craned her head and saw Matt's feet move ahead another half-meter.

"I'm through the worst of it. Come on ahead!"

Abby didn't need that request repeated. She scuttled forward, having to pull in her elbows to clear the worst of it, wondering how tight Matt had felt.

She crawled forward, her arms outstretched, pulling herself along by sticking her knife in the goo, and pushing herself forward, sometimes with the tips of her shoes on the tunnel floor, sometimes with her heels against the ceiling. She was smaller than Matt; surely she would be able to get through a space he had managed.

The ceiling was low enough that she was sure she was forming grooves as she pulled herself along. The roof and floor felt like the jaws of a vice, and for an instant she was completely unable to speak, unable even to draw air into her lungs. Oh, God, please no, don't do this. Please let her breathe again.

With her eyes squeezed closed in fear, she tugged herself forward, trying to breathe, but afraid that if she filled her lungs she'd be stuck here forever in a sweltering, dark coffin. She started to cry, but controlled herself as soon as she had sobbed only once. Her body was hot, far too hot. No air could circulate around her. She gritted her teeth and made herself keep moving forward.

She traveled a meter and then another. Thank God. He was right. The tunnel *was* getting slightly wider again. Suddenly she moved even faster, afraid there might somehow be *two* leaks and that somewhere ahead the tunnel would begin to narrow again, and they'd never be able to back out all the way though that closing gap.

The tunnel grew wider and taller until before she realized it the passage was a half-circle, the leaked goo blocking only the bottom half of the tunnel, and the top half was totally clear. She kept following Matt, willing her heart to slow down. When finally the tunnel was two-thirds clear, giving them almost enough room to stand up and run, her hardhat light revealed a perfectly round tunnel ahead in the distance.

Matt stopped. Abby stopped right behind him and put her head down so he couldn't see her face. Her body shook for a long moment, and finally she felt herself getting back in control.

When she looked up, Matt was sitting cross-legged, his back to the tunnel wall, breathing deeply, his hands over his face. He put his hands down and looked at her. "Are you all right?" he asked softly.

"Yeah," Abby said.

His voice shuddered. "I haven't been that scared in a long time. Damn!"

Abby moved closer and sat beside him. "I thought it was just me."

"No, it wasn't just you." Matt's breathing finally started to relax. He picked up his walkie-talkie and pressed the TALK switch. "We're through, Rudy."

Rudy acknowledged, and Matt leaned his head back against the tunnel wall.

Abby said, "I figured you never got scared."

"I probably get scared every day of my life. That's just a little worse than normal."

"What do you get scared of?"

"Lot of things. Growing old alone. Making the wrong decision."

"I didn't know you were scared until we got here."

Matt looked at her now. He seemed to be feeling much better. A glimmer of his smile had returned. "I'm the designated leader. I've got some responsibilities."

Abby nodded. "Well, I was scared, too. Scared—I was terrified. I just knew I was going to die back there."

Matt nodded, then reached one arm around Abby's shoulder. She leaned toward him and for the first time was aware that she was trembling. Gradually she relaxed.

They sat there fifteen or twenty seconds before Matt squeezed her shoulder. "We've got to get back. Are you okay now?"

"Are you?" she asked.

"Yeah. I think so."

"Then let's go."

They duck-walked for a few meters until the floor was low enough to allow running again. Matt in the lead, Abby following, they ran. The rhythm of air filling then leaving Abby's lungs moved into a familiar pattern, and within a minute or two she realized that she felt very good. Good to be alive. Good to be running. Good to be with Matt.

Seeing the airlock door in the distance filled Matt with relief. "We're almost there," he called to Abby, who ran behind him.

"Thank God."

Matt was tired of the lean-forward gait, but he still wasn't as tired as he would have been if he'd just run several kilometers in Earth gravity. He slowed down, and by the time he neared the chamber housing the airlock doors he was walking.

The first airlock door frame was jammed to fit into the gap defined by the chamber walls and ceiling. It held a half-width sliding door that could be opened from either side regardless of the relative pressures.

Cautious since communications had been cut off so abruptly, Matt unlocked the door and slid it open just a millimeter. Air whistled through the gap for a few seconds, then slowed. Matt slid the door all the way open.

Matt and Abby stepped into the airlock, and Matt slid the door closed and locked it. Matt unlocked the inner door and slid it open just a crack. Air whistled in.

"That's funny," Matt said, worried.

"What is?"

"When I opened the outer door, air was forced out. I assumed that meant the space between the doors was at Manhattan pressure. So when the inner door to Manhattan opened, there shouldn't have been any change. But the air on the far side of the door is at a higher pressure."

Matt put a hand near the gap and felt the air blowing in. A moment later his ears popped. Finally the inrush of air slowed and stopped. Matt looked at Abby, then opened the door all the way.

They stepped through the opening. Lights on the other side were still on. They walked a few steps to the end of the chamber and stopped at the opening to the tunnel leading downward to where it joined the barrier outside the Battery Tunnel.

The tunnel didn't look right. The string of lights led downward just the way they had the last time Matt had seen them, but now just this side of where Matt had expected to see the opening to the Battery Tunnel, a dark barrier cut across the tunnel.

"What's going on?" Abby asked.

"I don't know. Let's take a look."

Matt and Abby walked down the tunnel, stepping from one plastic beam to the next. They were almost to the dark barrier before Matt realized what it was.

"It's water," he said. "The tunnel is flooded."

"You're right. God, I wonder what happened."

They came even closer and a discoloration on the surface finally became clear.

"It's a body," Matt said.

He moved closer. Floating face down in the dark liquid was a uniformed body, probably the guard who'd been in this tunnel when it flooded, the man who'd been talking with him at the time. Matt stepped on the lowest dry beam and braced himself against the wall. With his free hand he was able to grab the victim's belt.

He pulled the body from the water, and Abby helped drag the victim up the tunnel until the man's feet cleared the water by a meter. They let the body down gently on its back. The man's forehead showed a vicious bruise, but the water had washed away the lost blood.

One glance at the wrinkled face told Matt the time for artificial respiration was long past. The man had probably drowned about the same time they lost communications with him. "I'm afraid there's nothing we can do for this guy," Matt said.

Abby took several deep breaths and finally said, "Well, we know why this man quit talking to us. But what happened?"

"You got me. Maybe our captors found out about our tunnel. Maybe one hell of an accident."

"I guess I'd prefer an accident."

"Me, too." Matt lay down on the sloping tunnel floor, his head near the water level. Submerged lights still shone dimly in the water. A moment later, Matt said, "The level's going down."

Abby knelt next to Matt. "Any idea how fast?"

Matt watched a little longer. "It looks like about a centimeter every five seconds." He stood up and thought. "I'd guess a couple of hours."

"Maybe we're low enough and near enough that our walkie-talkies will reach inside."

"Good thinking." Matt took his unit from his belt. "Rover calling Manhattan. Do you read?"

After a few seconds the reply came. "This is Manhattan. Are you all right? What happened with the aliens?"

"We're all fine, but the guard you left in the tunnel up to the airlock is dead." Matt decided to say nothing about what they had learned until he saw the mayor.

"God, that makes four. Some crazies flooded the Battery Tunnel. Some of the water is draining naturally through the drains that still work. We're also pumping it out as fast as we can."

"How soon do you expect we can get through?" Matt asked.

"A few hours from now."

"We have to schedule an emergency session with the mayor to start just as soon as we get out of here."

"No can do. She's announced that she's going on the air to talk about this at eight P.M."

"Patch me through to her. It's *important.*"

"More important than this? Guaranteed?"

"Guaranteed."

Several minutes passed but finally Matt heard Dorine Underwood's voice on his walkie-talkie. "This is the mayor."

"This is Matt Sheehan. It's vital that we talk."

The mayor's conference room in City Hall was packed with almost every senior surviving member of city government. At the perimeter of the room were numerous journalists, including Julie Kravine.

From where Julie watched, she could see Matt Sheehan, Abby Tersa, and Dorine Underwood engaged in a private conversation. As soon as they finished, Dorine made her way through the crowd toward Julie.

"Miss Kravine?" Dorine said.

"Yes, Ms. Mayor."

"The ground rules have changed. Live coverage of this meeting is no longer possible. I'll make a statement at the conclusion, but I don't want the meeting itself on the air. I anticipate some strong arguments, and I think at this point it's better to wait until we can show everyone a united front. You're probably as aware as I am that just in the last day we've had as many suicides and new admissions to mental clinics as we had in that first day. People already have enough stress. Waiting an hour on this meeting will add to it, but not as much as getting a direct connection to what I expect will go on in here. Is that clear and can you and the others abide by those terms?"

Julie hesitated. She knew a "no" would mean expulsion. "Well, I'm not real happy about it, but if that's the way it's got to be, I'll pass the word."

"Thank you. I think you'll understand soon enough." Dorine looked tired as she turned and went back to take her seat. Julie wondered what was going on.

A minute later Dorine rapped her gavel on the table top. In

seconds the room was quiet. Dorine and Matt and Abby and another eight people sat at the rectangular table, and several front rows of seats were filled to capacity with senior members of city government.

Dorine looked out at the audience and said, "This emergency meeting is now in session. We have some big decisions to make tonight, and some of what you're going to hear is no doubt going to be disturbing. I ask you to remain as quiet as possible unless you have the floor.

"The exploratory team has encountered new information about our situation. If the information is to be believed, we may have no choice but to act on it. We're here tonight to evaluate this information, and then to make decisions. This information will be presented by Matt Sheehan, Colonel, U.S. Army. I've reviewed his military record and suffice it to say that he has a reputation for honesty and effective action. Colonel Sheehan."

Matt scanned faces in the crowd briefly. Julie knew her own team was recording, even though they didn't have permission to transmit yet.

Matt said, "What I'm going to tell you is going to be difficult to accept at first. I'm going to give you the bottom line in just a minute, and then I'm going to backtrack and show you the evidence we have to back this up. You'll have a chance to ask questions when I've finished. In the meantime, I ask you to try as hard as possible to remain quiet so I can finish. Time is critical.

"We have very strong evidence about the aliens who brought Manhattan here. We think their actions fit a pattern. The real bottom line is that shortly after they snatch a city, they exterminate the population remaining on the planet. Therefore, the entire population of Earth is either already beyond help, or they need our help very much right now. I have recommended to the mayor that we embark immediately on a mission to find a way to disable this ship to the extent that it cannot be used to destroy what remains of the human race."

Julie sagged against the wall behind her and shivered. Her ears rang in the stunned silence.

The silence lasted only a couple of seconds before the yelling started. Dorine rapped her gavel on the table several times, and the noise abated.

Matt continued. "The evidence for the conclusions I just mentioned come from two sources. One is subjective, and requires us to take the word of another captive alien race. The other is more objective, although still open to interpretation, and comes from the transmission we received from a different captive city."

Matt first explained about Abby's communications with the telepathic, tree-dwelling race, who claimed to hear the dying screams of the rest of their race. Then he turned on a video unit connected to a large wall screen behind the table. He played the recording Julie had seen earlier, but this time when it reached the section where the city was about to disappear into the ship and the lightning showed over the horizon, Julie knew that couldn't just be lightning from some enormous storm.

Now the room was nearly silent, except for the sounds of two or three people sobbing.

"There you have the evidence for what I've told you tonight. In addition to that we have evidence in this same recording that thousands of people died as their city was cut loose. And added to that, we know that when Manhattan was captured, many people died in the process. I believe this undeniable disregard for life is fully consistent with the belief that whoever was left on the planet would not live much longer anyway."

Julie had felt horror as Matt talked. Now she felt the beginnings of anger, anger that their captors had come so far to so callously kill so many people they'd never even had contact with.

"So, what are we going to do about this?" Matt asked. "That has to be the next question. And my answer is this: as soon as possible, I, or anyone you appoint, will take a team and leave Manhattan. We will be equipped with the most powerful explosives and weapons we can find. Our goal will be to, as fast as possible, break out of the area these cities are imprisoned in, locate the propulsion system, and damage it to the extent that this ship cannot be used to destroy the Earth."

Dorine had to use her gavel again to quiet the sudden outbursts.

"Why the propulsion system? Why not power or something else?" asked Dorine.

"For one thing, we figure the propulsion system will be easier to identify than other subsystems. If we keep the ship from being able to move, we're hoping that would buy us enough time to be more selective in what we damage. If, for instance, we tried to destroy the power plant, whatever and wherever that is, we might harm ourselves, too."

Another flurry of questions made hearing impossible.

When calm was restored, Matt said, "That's all I had to say. How about if we deal with questions, but one at a time?"

Dorine controlled the question process. A man in the back said, "What if we're too late? What if—if the Earth has already been destroyed?"

Matt said, "Then all we can do is prevent this ship from harming other planets, other civilizations."

A woman asked, "But what if you accidentally destroy the ship, or if you destroy the life-support systems that Manhattan is dependent upon now?"

Matt hesitated. "Very good question. For Manhattan that's the worst-case scenario, but it's one that we have to acknowledge. When it comes right down to it, for every single person in Manhattan there are, what, two to three thousand people on Earth. If you had to choose between a couple of million people here in Manhattan, and five or six *billion* people and the Earth itself, which would you choose?"

It took Dorine almost a minute to get the group under control again.

"But maybe we're guessing wrong," a man said. "Maybe they only do that to some of the planets."

Matt said, "Perhaps. But we have evidence for a sample of two, and so far the evidence suggests a hundred percent."

"Isn't it possible that our captors will find the team before it does any damage and decide to destroy Manhattan because we're dangerous?"

"Yes," Matt said.

"What do you think the odds of success are?" a woman asked.

"I honestly don't know," Matt said. "I *think* I know what the odds are for Earth if we do nothing."

"What makes you think there isn't another ship that actually does the damage? Maybe this is just one ship in a small fleet."

"If this isn't the only ship, then perhaps there's no hope. If it is the only ship, and it certainly seems large enough to be the only one, then we can only hope that doing significant damage here will delay their plans and give us more opportunity to stop the slaughter."

"How big a team should we send?" asked a woman in the back.

That question brought the biggest argument. Matt recommended one small team, partly to minimize the risk of being detected, partly because they had only one borer and the oxygen supply coming into the tunnel was limited. People on opposite poles of the argument wanted either several large teams sent, or no one sent. Dorine sided with Matt, partly because of trust in his judgment, partly because of the obvious limitations. As a further compromise, another two borers would be built, and a large armed troop would be readied. A member of the press would accompany the team, to let people on both extremes of the argument get unbiased reports on what was happening.

As the heat finally began to diminish, a man in the front row asked, "Mayor, do *you* really think we should do this?"

Dorine took her time as a few tremors in the crowd died down. "I think that unless someone comes up with a brilliant idea in the next ten minutes, yes, we should. We should equip this team with what they need. And then, in whatever manner is appropriate for our various religions, we all should pray."

9

MECHANICAL FAILURE

On the way back out to Rudy and Bobby Joe and the borer, Abby rode on the back of a new cart. This one made her nervous, because it was completely filled with plastic explosives, timers, detonators, and the other paraphernalia gathered overnight by a new member of the team.

Richard Welkon, an ex-Army demolitions expert, sat beside her. The man made Abby almost as nervous as the explosives did, mostly because he was so quiet. Abby hadn't yet seen him joke or smile, not that now was the best time for joking and smiling, but an occasional release of the nervous tension she felt was probably a good thing. Richard seemed like a bomb himself, silently ticking.

A small trailer behind the cart carried a supply of weapons, ammunition, and explosives. Abby hadn't seen that big a cache since a newscast had documented the fall of a teen gang on the Upper West Side. In fact, she wouldn't have been surprised if some of the boxes of explosives had orange spray-painted logos saying PROPERTY OF THE TAIL GUNNERS.

Matt drove the cart through the tunnel, covering ground almost as fast as he and Abby had moved when they were running the opposite direction. Beside Matt sat Julie Kravine, her minivid apparently active even though one kilometer of tunnel was much like another. Julie had argued successfully that if they were possibly going to destroy a significant amount of technology currently unknown to the human race, the least they could do was save images of it. In addition to that, having six on the team instead of four allowed a greater chance that some of the team could sleep while the others worked, without getting the team so large that its size caused oxygen-supply problems. The networks had hastily proposed a list of journalist candidates, and Matt had picked Julie because she was a known quantity who would require no learning curve.

They had already passed the area that had caused Abby and Matt so much grief on the last trip. Matt's efforts had indeed stopped the leak, and the goo had flowed enough that they were able to drive over most of it, having to shovel only the few meters nearest the ventilation tube.

Abby felt herself pushed gently sideways as the cart started a turn, and seconds later they passed a sealed opening in the tunnel wall. She pointed at it as it vanished in the darkness that kept pace with them behind the trailer. "That's the opening to the dead city we explored earlier."

Richard nodded and said, "Mmm."

Abby wasn't sure why she had bothered.

When they curved past the sealed entrance to the tree dwellers' city, Abby didn't say anything.

They caught up with Rudy and Bobby Joe just as Rudy was directing the borer in an arc that took the tunnel right past another domed city. As long as they were limited by the speed of the borer, Matt wanted to take a quick look at the city. Rudy and Richard continued ahead, and Abby felt measurably better as soon as Richard was out of sight.

Matt drilled a hole to the surface, but before he put in the ventilator tube, he pushed the periscope up through the hole.

As Matt took a look through the periscope, Bobby Joe jerked his thumb in the direction of Richard and the cart and said to Abby, "That's a great idea, bringing a robot. Food will last us that much longer."

Abby smiled, feeling better that she wasn't the only one bothered by Richard's icy demeanor.

Matt stepped away from the periscope, and said, "Who's next?"

Julie took a turn. "These guys have sure done a lot of decorating."

When Abby took a turn she understood what Julie had meant. The bottom two or three meters of the dome were virtually covered with drawings. She saw occasional glimpses of motion through untouched slivers of the dome, but couldn't get any clear view of what was inside.

Bobby Joe took his turn, then shook his head.

Matt looked at Abby. "Any guess as to what that's all about?"

Abby took another look, this time noticing that several of the patterns were replicated. In fact, at least half of the drawings seemed to be duplications. If the drawings were some sort of visual history, she wouldn't expect that much duplication. She pulled back from the eyepiece and shook her head. "I don't really have enough information to make an intelligent guess, but if I had to make a totally wild guess, I'd say these people could be trying to communicate with our captors, or they could be worshiping whoever brought them here."

As soon as the team was safely on its way, Dorine Underwood held a press conference. She had resolved to make the broadcast as unemotional as possible, in hopes of instilling a little calm in the middle of the new storm of bad news, but she had to pause during her description of what had happened to the race occupying the huge square building. She swallowed hard and went on.

Despite the risk the team was taking, she felt more comfortable about explaining their new mission, stressing that it was vital that they stop the ship from moving to destroy yet another planet.

"This was a difficult decision, and I'm asking you to accept it. This is a time for courage, a time for all of us to act as heroes, not a time to crawl into a hole and hope the problem will go away. This action has risks. Inaction has even larger risks."

Dorine paused for a drink of water.

"The final item for now is the Battery Tunnel incident. I can understand that our actions outside the dome scare some of us. But we will not tolerate further interference and destruction. There's a chance that we will be the only survivors of the human race. That we are killing each other when we should be focused on survival is contemptible. And it *will* stop."

* * *

"We cannot stand by and let the forces of darkness march over us!" Stuart Lund called out. His voice felt especially smooth today, and the growing crowd gave him hope.

Stuart paused for a breath and looked out over his "congregation," which nearly filled the open section of the warehouse. He saw renewed fear and anger on the faces in the crowd, the same fear and anger that he felt. People in authority were always making bad decisions, so in one sense today was like every other day. But it wasn't really. The mayor's decision to send out a team with explosives and weapons was simply too much. Too many lives, too many souls were at risk.

He resumed his "Make a Difference" speech, exhorting his followers to do anything in their power to reverse the decision, to help make the mayor see the wrongness in her plan. He talked another ten minutes. He had enough material to keep going for another several hours, but he could sense the restlessness in the congregation. The people wanted to do something. They believed, too, and if he kept talking now, he'd be less and less effective. So he stopped. He had little doubt that the tunnel flooding had been the work of his congregation; they'd certainly find fresh ways to hamper the new effort.

"God will know who among us stand idle and allow this so-called expedition. Talk to your friends. Take a stand. Make sure they know you feel this is wrong. Make a difference."

The people cheered and clapped, most of them in obvious agreement. Something had to be done. Stuart felt a little uncomfortable with the lack of decorum, but the immediate feedback was tremendously encouraging.

As people filed out, a few stayed to ask questions. The next to the last in line was a short but stocky man who introduced himself as Benny Kellermund. The man behind Mr. Kellermund was obviously with him, but he didn't volunteer his name. The silent man looked as if he'd been in a number of fights. Stuart was suddenly nervous that his preaching was somehow cutting into someone else's line of work and he was about to be warned.

Mr. Kellermund waited until the few people in the congregation were out of hearing, then said, "Reverend, you're exactly right."

Stuart felt surprise and a quick sense of relief.

"The mayor's got a hair up, er, the mayor is an idiot. We've got to stop her before this expedition stuff ruins everything we have here. Me and my friend, we're on your side."

The friend nodded when mentioned, but he still didn't speak.

Mr. Kellermund glanced around. "Look, can we talk somewhere a bit more private?"

Stuart took a look around, too. A few of the congregation members lingered near the door. Under different circumstances, these two men would have made him uncomfortable, but now they were on his side, and of the people Stuart had seen today, these two seemed more likely to get results than most.

"Upstairs," said Stuart. "I have a small office on the second floor."

The men followed Stuart up the stairs, through a small maze of construction materials, and into a small office that contained a cot and a table and a chair.

"Is this better, Mr. Kellermund?"

"Much. But call me Benny." Benny still didn't introduce his companion. "Anyway, we're on your side. In fact, we're responsible for the flooding."

"No," Stuart said in surprise. He realized that he'd been hoping the flood was an act of God, a pipe that suddenly burst of its own accord, or some other sign that God was clearly on their side.

"Yes. My friend here is very handy with tools."

"Well, I'm very grateful." Stuart fell silent, unsure of what to say.

"Anyway, I think I can do something to stop the team," Benny said. "I think my friend can do something about convincing the mayor to change her mind."

At another time the man's intense stare and his dark eyes might have made Stuart a little nervous, but the team needed to be stopped, and the mayor had to be convinced, so he didn't feel the need to question the man further. "Thank you," he said finally. "Whatever assistance you can lend, your help will be rewarded by God."

* * *

"I don't care about any reward from God," said Benny Kellermund. "I just don't want to die." He sat on a straight-backed chair in his apartment, a modest place on the Upper West Side.

Lucky Stiles leaned back in a stuffed chair that almost swallowed him. "I don't know. You'd think the tunnel stuff was enough."

Benny thought about Lucky's hesitation. "You know Stella, that little blonde who hangs out at Spacey's? She owes me a couple of big favors. I already talked to her about you, and she's waiting for you tonight." The currency of the day was favors, labor exchanges. This was the only thing he had to offer that he thought might be enough.

"Stella? Yeah, I remember her."

"Did I ever tell you Stella can tie a knot in a cherry stem with her tongue? She knows lots more exciting tricks."

"And she's waiting for me?"

"If you'll do this. It's what you want, too. You don't want Manhattan squashed because we're doing things we shouldn't be doing."

Lucky said, "Well, I can probably convince the mayor of the error of her ways." He laughed, a smoker's laugh that turned to a cough.

Rudy raised the periscope near another dome, this one containing what looked like a large grassy hill rather than a fabricated city.

The large hill reminded Matt of a wasp's nest, constructed by sticking on little sections one after another. Here and there on the hillside were cave openings. Near several of the caves, small creatures frolicked in the grass. They were mostly green, and apparently had hard shells, like armadillo hide, covering much of their torsos. Matt couldn't tell if they could retract the limbs or head. Matt found himself grinning as he watched the little creatures roughhouse with one another, like cats at play.

"Those little guys sure are cute," he said finally, relinquishing the view to Julie, who agreed with him.

When it was Abby's turn, she watched for several minutes

before she said, "Is it my imagination, or do those creatures stay in almost the same place all the time?"

Matt took another look. After a couple of minutes he had to agree. "You're right. I wonder why that would be. Maybe they're extremely territorial?"

Bobby Joe took another look, and then Julie took a second turn. She held her minivid optics up to the periscope. Shortly she said, "I see the reason. They're on leashes."

When Matt got a chance to look through Julie's viewfinder, he could see clearly with the magnified view. Attached to the rear legs of the small creatures were clear straps, short enough that they couldn't get tangled up, and long enough that the creatures could get to each other.

Bobby Joe said, "It's like letting your dog outside and making sure it doesn't go too far. Maybe they're pets, or maybe that's just the way they do playpens."

Matt trained the lens on the cave opening nearest the frolicking group of creatures. The hair on the back of his neck stood up as the lens revealed glimpses of two or three huge creatures hiding inside the cave. About the only thing Matt could see clearly were wide rows of teeth. Something moved at the edge of his field of view. Two fast-moving yellow-green creatures were approaching the small, tethered creatures. The following seconds were full of activity.

The yellow-green creatures moved so quickly Matt never did get a good picture of them, except to see large sharp talons as one of the creatures cut loose one of the tethered youngsters. At almost the same time, large versions of the youngsters erupted from the nearby cave. When the fight was over, one of the invaders had fled with his catch, and the other invader was dead.

Matt sucked in his breath. "It looks to me like those little guys out there are bait."

Abby looked through the lens next, and Matt told her what he had seen and which cave to look at. Seconds later she said, "I bet you're right. But this isn't quite the normal version of using bait, not like, say, humans using worms to catch fish. I think those are adults using their own young for bait."

Matt peered through the periscope after Julie finished making a short recording. The semi-dark tunnel felt even more uncomfortable as he looked through the dome at the glint of wide rows of teeth in the cave on the hill. "I wonder why our captors would have brought this hill. Everything else we've seen is fairly clearly a city of some kind."

Abby spoke up. "Hard to say. One possibility is that our captors are more like these creatures than any other captives. Maybe *their* cities look like this from the air."

Matt scratched his ear. "Oh, that gives me a chilling thought. I can imagine a city that's mostly underground, like an iceberg at sea. Depending on how deep these people cut when they extract a city, they could cut right through the center of a city, or not even take very much of it."

"Sounds terrible but possible," Abby said. "If they left behind half of the first city we saw, I suppose they could have even done the equivalent of swooping down on a body and removing only the heart."

Bobby Joe stepped forward from the semi-dark in the tunnel. "But this all makes it sound as if they're dummies. Or maybe kids who've just got their first chance to play with their parents' starship."

"It *is* puzzling," Matt said. "Maybe they're just in a terrible hurry for some reason."

Bobby Joe said, "Maybe they have a quota. Or maybe they're on a huge scavenger hunt. Can you just imagine the list? 'One island city, one hill city, one enormous square building.' "

Matt shook his head. "Implausibility aside, I don't know that that's consistent with destroying the rest of the planet after they've got a city."

"Sure it is. That way the competition has to look even longer to get the one for *their* list. Can you imagine how long it might take them to get another smoggy island city with internal combustion engines still in use?"

"This is nonsense," Julie finally said. "These guys aren't gonna go racing around the universe to play games."

Abby said, "You're probably right. But an intelligent species that would go around destroying lives and worlds just so they can build a bizarre zoo with intelligent captives is hard to accept, too. We obviously need to stay open to the possibility that they don't think like us. For all we know, what they've done is perfectly reasonable and kind, from their point of view."

Matt suddenly jerked away from the periscope. "Jeez!"

"What?" Abby said.

"Something just jumped at the periscope. I didn't even see it coming." Matt had his eye back on the periscope. "It looks moist and formless, and it's just oozing down the inside of the dome."

The others took turns looking.

"One more reason for not going in there," Abby said.

Julie recorded a few seconds for posterity. "It looks like it's pulling itself back into shape."

Matt took one last look. At first the gooey mess on the inside of the dome had made it seem that the creature had been moving so fast it had ruptured against the hard surface, but now the creature actually seemed to be recovering. Matt caught glimpses of tissue that alternately suggested squid suckers and fur, but he never got a look at the entire creature. His stomach felt queasy. If they had cut an opening in this dome . . .

"Come on," Matt said. "Let's get the ventilator in place and catch up with Rudy and Richard."

In East Harlem, called Spanish Harlem by some and El Barrio by far more, nine-year-old Manny Garzón sat on the steps in front of his apartment building.

Heavy booming from several car stereos and boom boxes almost made the morning seem normal, but Manny knew it wasn't a normal day.

He wished his family had stayed in Puerto Rico. Then they'd be safe. His mom complained so much that only white people were Americans, Manny had been surprised to learn that Puerto Rico *was* part of America. He still didn't understand why then they'd had to move from one part of America to another just to live in a slightly nicer place.

He looked up at the dome over the island and said to himself, "No doubt about it. We shoulda stood at home."

By the time Abby and the others caught up with Rudy and Richard, the borer had almost reached the city that was transmitting the video they had all seen. Rudy curved the path the borer took so that it went past the dome very closely.

"Are we going inside this one?" Abby asked Matt.

"I want to if it looks safe, but it's also a function of how much time we have to spare." Matt raised his voice. "Let's have a short planning meeting, everyone. Rudy, let the borer just go on ahead for now."

The six of them sat in a line on the tunnel floor, Matt and Rudy in the center, Abby and the others on the ends.

"How long will it take the borer to reach the wall we're heading toward?" Matt asked.

Rudy tapped a few buttons on his watch. "I think we've probably got another twelve to fifteen hours at the rate we're going. And there's no way to speed that up."

"Okay. That gives us enough time to explore this dome and at least try to get a clue as to why no one's responding to our return signal. The more we can learn, the better, as long as it doesn't slow us down. Rudy, you and Richard stay with the borer, and trade off enough to get whatever sleep you can. Unless we see anything that changes my mind when we take a closer look at the dome, I'd like Abby and Bobby Joe with me. Julie, you've got your choice."

"I'd like to get pictures of the city," she said.

"That's fine, but especially when we're outside this tunnel, we have to act like a military unit. Abby and Bobby Joe can probably fill you in if the lecture last night wasn't enough."

Abby smiled ruefully and nodded.

"Can we ever," said Bobby Joe.

Matt, Abby, Bobby Joe, and Julie moved as quickly as they could into the alien city. In the sky on the far side of the city, a dim reddish "sun" sent out weak light. The air smelled of burnt leaves.

The silhouette of the city was an erratic graph, peaks and valleys formed by a collection of cone-shaped buildings of varying sizes and distances from Matt. One of the taller and closer cones was topped by a light that varied irregularly in color and intensity; Rudy had deposited them close to the building that was still transmitting a signal to the world outside the city's bubble—a signal that had been answered with no apparent effect.

They passed by a couple of cones that were approaching Matt's height.

As they reached a few cones that were about five times Matt's height, the tall tip of a cone near the center of the city began to pierce the "sun." Moments later they entered shade.

One of the nearest cones reached what had to be a hundred meters into the air and had an exterior spiral staircases. Matt could still see the cone with the beacon, slightly deeper into the city, but minutes later they walked through what felt a little like a mountain valley, with sharply pointed hilltops all around.

"I still don't see anything that looks like a door," Abby said. "Do you think we have to go up those staircases to get inside these cones?"

"I was hoping you'd tell us," Matt said.

The group made another turn, and Matt saw their destination cone. They reached the bottom of the spiral stairs and started up. The spiral was a gentle rise, looping around the cone six times as it rose. Soon they got an aerial view of the surrounding city and could see domed cities in the direction of Manhattan. In the opposite direction was visible the nearest wall of the chamber enclosing the collection of cities. Almost directly opposite Manhattan, a faint vertical line showed at the junction of two flat surfaces, and Matt remembered a graphic image Bobby Joe had generated, one showing that from above, the chamber outline was a huge octagon.

Two-thirds of the way to the top, Matt suggested a rest stop. He looked back toward the hill-city and Manhattan, imagining he could see the route the tunnel had cut.

"You and Rudy were in the Army together, weren't you?" Julie said unexpectedly.

Matt took his gaze away from the route they had traveled and looked at her. "Yes. Mostly in Brazil and Argentina."

"What's he like?"

"Like he is now. He's one of those few people I'd want to have on my side if I were starting a small company. Whatever he's paid, he's worth more."

"Why'd he get out of the Army?"

Matt hesitated. "He got into a situation where he either had to blow the whistle on a respected colonel who had some unsavory habits involving young boys, or live with his conscience and let it go on."

"So he got out?"

"He blew the whistle and then got out. Rudy was born in East L.A. and a lot of his friends were Hispanic, so maybe he took the colonel's transgressions a little more personally than some other outsider might have." Matt looked at the horizon. "South America is a mess right now. The internal politics are a cesspool, and the career potential for whistle blowers isn't very good. One of them ran into a bad accident in the jungle."

"But you stayed in."

"Yup. I was angry, too, but sometimes you can do more from within the system. A couple of months later, after the charges had been dismissed for lack of evidence, the colonel got himself accidentally photographed by surveillance cameras that had been undergoing testing before being sent out to remote airstrips suspected of servicing drug runners. And copies of the film were accidentally duplicated and sent to several organizations along with routine test photographs."

"You're saying you're responsible for those accidents?"

"Oh, no. Rudy did most of the work. I just signed a few requisition forms, stuff like that. Rudy told me later that he and the colonel came back on the same flight. Rudy was amazed at how many martinis a person could consume between Rio and New York." Matt looked at the view for a moment. "I told you all of this in your role of being a friend of Rudy's, not as a reporter. I assume you understand that."

"I do. That's why I was curious."

"He's a good guy. He's a little possessive, in the good sense. New York is *his* city now. This team is partly *his* responsibility. He works hard to make sure that no one hurts anything that's partly his."

"What would Rudy say about you?" This question came from Abby.

"About me? I don't know. That I'm a bad gambler because I don't know when to give up, cut my losses. That I repeat my mistakes. That I have a tendency to stop along the way and look at the view. That I've been doing it too long now." Matt smiled.

The time it took to walk around the cone grew significantly shorter as they moved farther up the side.

Bobby Joe said, "Do you realize how slow the sun is moving?"

Matt looked down to where the tip of the shadow of the cone they were climbing hit the ground, and he realized Bobby Joe was right. It had hardly moved in the whole time they'd been climbing. "These folks must be used to very long days, huh?"

"Good guess."

A final quick revolution brought them to the top of the cone. Inside a low wall was a meter-wide path that formed a nearly complete circle, and inside the path was a short cone, only three meters tall, flattened on top. Sitting on the flat top was the transmitter, which here was too bright to look at directly as it flashed purple then green then crimson.

Matt made a quick communications check with his new light-spectrum walkie-talkie, and Manhattan base responded.

Bobby Joe spotted a cable going from the bottom of the broadcasting light, down the surface of the cone for several centimeters, and then vanishing. By pushing on the right spot, a section of the cone moved as a doorway formed in its place.

Dorine Underwood found a near-riot when she reached the conference room five minutes before the morning status meeting. She hadn't heard the crowd so agitated since the abduction of the city.

Her throat was dry, not because of anxiety, but, she suddenly realized, because she had kept taking her allergy medication after arriving here. Now that the air contained far less dust and pollen, she could probably stop.

She stepped into the meeting room. The conversation level dipped for an instant, then rose even higher than before. She could guess what the concern was already: second thoughts.

Several times during the night, Dorine had found herself awake and worrying about the same thing. For the past several days, Manhattan had been functioning smoothly enough that she had started going back to her home at Gracie Mansion on the Upper East Side at night. She felt more relaxed in her own bedroom than she had been sleeping on a cot in City Hall, but back at Gracie Mansion were more reminders of Rafael. She said another quick prayer that he was still alive, because despite her fear that the team outside could cause the destruction of Manhattan, she was convinced the evidence was right. Something terrible was going to happen to Earth, or it had already happened.

Dorine took her seat and called the meeting to order. The room quieted. She made no attempt to sidestep the issue. It wouldn't go away on its own, and she knew no other issue would get much real attention until this one had been dealt with. "All right. Who wants to start?"

First up was Tony Robinson, the council president, a short man whose eyelashes were so long Dorine sometimes wondered if they were real. "Ms. Mayor, you've got to stop Sheehan and his team. All they're going to do is get us all killed."

"I understand that we are all at risk, but are you telling me you're prepared to let the whole Earth die to save yourself?"

Tony snorted. "That's not the issue. The video from the aliens in those huge cones showed their planet being destroyed right after their city was taken. The Earth is probably already dead."

A flurry of murmurs took several seconds to die down.

"That's only one data point," Dorine said. "The other one we have from the tree city says the people on their planet survived for between three and four weeks. If Earth is on the same schedule, we still have somewhere between a few days and more than a week to make a difference."

"But there's no way to know the Earth is still alive right now. We could be taking this risk for nothing."

"You'll get no argument from me on that. But there's also no way we can tell the Earth *isn't* alive and healthy. For the time being."

"But, Ms. Mayor, you've got to—"

"Just a minute, Mr. Robinson." Dorine scanned faces in the room. "I want to get a sense of the attitude here, by having a show of hands. I'm not saying I'm going to reverse my position, but I do want to see how people's feelings run. Everyone who thinks we should continue our efforts to prevent this ship from harming Earth, please raise your hands." Several hands rose, and Dorine counted them. "All right, everyone who thinks we should stop and play safe, raise your hands." She counted fewer hands. "Undecided?"

"All right," she said. "By my count, we've got about sixty percent in favor of continuing, twenty percent who think we should stop, and twenty percent who just don't know. Out there, where people don't have as informed an access to the facts, TV polls report thirty percent think we should stop, but I don't think that should prevent us from doing the right thing."

Dorine took a breath and looked closely at faces of the people she could normally count on for unequivocal support. On two of the five faces she saw traces of doubt. "Of the people in this room, only a couple have had the bravery and the unselfishness to be willing to serve as police officers. I can't imagine a lot of things scarier than walking into a dark warehouse where there's some reason to believe the shadows hold danger, danger that could take your life in the next five minutes. For a short time, we've all suddenly been called on to show that courage, and I'll be the first to admit I'm scared. I'm scared bad. But we've got to do this. We can't just turn our backs and let someone else do it. There *is* no one else. If we can all be brave for a short time, maybe we'll find out there's still time for us to make a difference, maybe not. Maybe we'll find out the Earth has already been destroyed, but at least we'll know we tried to help them. And if we're too late, we can bide our time and wait for a better opportunity to do something about our situation. No matter what, I promise you no one is going to do anything that will put us at risk without a damn good reason."

Lucky Stiles felt hot in the cool apartment, his body slippery with sweat. This was the part he hated the most.

Seeing the news story after the fact, watching the horrified expressions on the faces of the people who had been close but not *too* close was the best. He folded a section of paper into place with fingertips covered by latex gloves. He didn't bother with any safety equipment like goggles, though. If he made a mistake, he'd be beyond the reach of cosmetic surgery. Maybe the boys in white coats would be able to scrape some of his cells off the refrigerator door and clone him, but Lucky wouldn't be around to lie down personally on some operating table.

He was glad his upstairs neighbors had been out of town when Manhattan moved. Ever since then, he had no longer heard the bass throbbing through the ceiling, and right now he was especially glad not to have the irritation. Lucky's fingers trembled ever so slightly as he wrapped the last flap of paper into place and slipped the packet carefully into the preaddressed envelope.

He took a deep breath. At the sink he sprinkled water on the flap glue and sealed the envelope shut. A drop of sweat fell off his forehead.

He could sure use a beer right now. This certainly qualified as a special occasion. In the refrigerator were his two last cans of Coors, bought by a buddy on a recent vacation. Lucky was convinced that the beer canned in Colorado tasted better than the stuff in the local stores. When Lucky finished the can, he went down to the street and dropped the envelope in a nearby mailbox. The envelope looked funny without a stamp, but the mayor herself had announced that mail without stamps would be delivered.

That served her right. What happened next would be her own fault.

Matt was relieved to see no sight of a threat on the other side of the door.

Inside, above eye level, Matt could see straight through the wall on the far side of the cone. They followed the cable into the interior, down the internal stairs, which curved in a corkscrew arc. Above them, virtually the entire cap of the cone was transparent, including the floor they had first stood on.

As soon as they passed the floor they'd been on, he could see an even greater distance down into the cone than they'd been able to see before. The other stairways and the one they were on wound downward in long graceful spirals that eventually stopped at another circular floor perhaps a hundred meters below. At two or three points on each stairway were boxes the size of a small room suspended in the air, as though glued to the side of the stairway.

The group descended, following the cable, until they reached a room containing a small pedestal supporting a black cube and a black cone, both about as tall as a coffee cup. On one side of the cone was a moving image, the same image they had received in Manhattan.

Bobby Joe picked up the cone displaying the picture. As he twisted the cone, Matt realized the back of the cone was also displaying an image. Bobby Joe rotated the cone until the other image was clearly visible. "Well, looky looky."

The picture was the video Julie had put together, showing Manhattan's experience.

"So they *are* receiving us," Matt said. "And that doesn't just mean that our signal is getting through; it means they *wanted* to be able to receive. So where are they? And why haven't they replied?"

No one had an answer.

They descended, exploring the small rooms, and ten minutes later they found a room that was occupied. In a clear, coffin-shaped box lay an alien body that looked like the ones in the transmission. The body was humanoid, a Cyclops. The single eyelid was closed. The alien's skin was brown and leathery, with the worst case of varicose veins Matt had ever seen. Thin black lips surrounded a small mouth, and the piglike snout showed one nostril. Flat against its chest was something that looked like a hastily performed skin graft with tendrils reaching into the larger creature's chest. No one had the slightest idea whether it was a pet, a symbiont, a medical implant, or something else entirely.

Stuart Lund surveyed his congregation in silence. He was ambivalent about the latest news. On the one hand, the idea that the people who had ventured outside the dome could bring down God's wrath terrified him. On the other hand, since the latest news of the trek had been made public, new arrivals had been accumulating faster than Stuart's helpers could count. Obviously the dome contained a large number of people who were uncomfortable with the idea of sending out people to damage the structure holding Manhattan and those other cities.

Stuart knew that the team had absolutely no possibility of

success, but the sooner he could organize something that would stop the effort, the lower the risk of retaliation. Flooding the Battery Tunnel had been a good idea, but the police had been able to drain it too quickly. There had to be something else they could do. Something that would stop the craziness outside and bring everyone back inside.

The moment of silence had stretched long enough, so Stuart opened his eyes and said, "Please be seated."

The congregation filled the warehouse floor. People way in the back were too far away for Stuart to make out distinct faces, but Stuart knew his words reached that far. Congregation members had collected an adequate supply of public address system components, and wires ran in six directions from the pulpit. The only concession to having mixed and matched several PA systems was that no one had found a cable that let one microphone drive an array of amplifiers, so Stuart spoke into a collection of microphones that made him feel he was giving a press conference for the entire known world.

A wave ran through the congregation from front to back as almost two thousand people settled into their chairs, the ones in front moving first, and row after row following. For just an instant, Stuart saw an image of water parting before him.

"I'd like to welcome anyone new to us this morning," Stuart said when the rustling quieted down. "I don't think it's news to anyone here that we are in the middle of the greatest test we've ever faced. God is undoubtedly watching us closely, measuring, judging, testing. And I think we need to make sure we get a good report card."

Within fifteen minutes, Stuart had his followers hoarse from screaming.

10

ON THE LOOSE

MATT BACKED AWAY from the unmoving alien and rapped his knuckles on the wall.

The alien didn't react. The single gray eyelid remained closed. The other three came closer until they surrounded the body.

Matt slowly reached out and prodded one arm, then touched a hand. "I don't know about heavy sleepers, but I'm remembering the 'sun' that hardly moves. Maybe their days and nights are extremely long, like weeks or months for us. Maybe this is the middle of the night, and maybe during the night they hibernate."

Abby looked at Matt. "That makes a whole lot of sense. They could have started their transmitter a long time ago. If we had responded during the 'day' they would have replied. But now they'll sleep until 'morning.' "

Matt touched the alien's wrist. "I can't feel a pulse, but that doesn't tell me anything, I guess." He put a hand on the alien's neck. After a moment he said, "I can feel something. It's more like a slow vibration than a heartbeat, but I think this . . . person is alive."

Abby reached forward and put her hand on the alien's neck also. "I think you're right. I can feel it, too." Abby put a hand on the coffinlike enclosure. "And I can't feel anything here, so I don't think it's vibration from somewhere else."

Matt said, "Let's get out of here. I think we've learned enough here for now, and besides, we've got more pressing business. The borer should be getting closer to the outside wall."

They walked back through the valley between cones, and Matt suddenly felt envious of people who could sleep a long time. He looked back at the "sun." "It's been about four hours since we were here. How far do you think the 'sun' has moved?"

Bobby Joe moved a couple of steps sideways, then tapped a few buttons on his watch. "This is just a really crude estimate, because I didn't get any good reference before, but it looks to me as if it's only moved two or three degrees. If that's true, that would make their night"—he pushed some more keys—"somewhere between twenty and thirty of our days."

"No wonder we didn't get a reply yet," Abby said.

Back in the tunnel, Matt called Manhattan base with his RF walkie-talkie and told them why their return transmission hadn't been acknowledged.

Matt switched channels. "Rudy, this is Matt."

"Go ahead," said Rudy's voice a moment later.

"We're out and we're safe. We should be able to catch up with you in an hour or so."

"No need to hurry. The borer just broke down."

Abby easily kept up with Matt as their long, slow leaning-forward strides carried them through the tunnel just ahead of Julie and Bobby Joe. Besides Abby's talent for running, being several centimeters shorter than Matt helped her get slightly longer strides without coming too close to the tunnel ceiling. Her hardhat light bounced back and forth with the motion of her body.

She was still breathing comfortably ten minutes later when they caught up with Rudy and Richard. They slowed to a halt and for a moment the only sounds were a mechanical *tap tap tap* from ahead and Bobby Joe's gasping for air from somewhere behind. For being a basically healthy person, Bobby Joe was in the worst shape of anyone Abby knew.

Rudy lay on his back, his hands busy twisting something on the end of a socket wrench. Richard sat on the cart. Abby nodded to him and he nodded back.

"What's up?" Matt asked.

"What's down is more like it," Rudy said. "The tread on the

right side vibrates enough when it moves that it wore through a bracket supporting some control lines. I think I caught it before it did much damage. I should be ready to give it another try in ten or fifteen minutes."

"Great. You need anything?"

"I'm fine. Maybe you should put in another ventilation hole and take a peek. According to the inertial navigation unit, we're getting pretty close."

"Will do."

As Matt moved back to do that, Julie came forward, followed by Bobby Joe. Bobby Joe's breath still came in audible drags.

"How're you doing?" Julie said.

"Good," Rudy said. "I think we're almost back in business. How was the tour?"

"Stranger than Macy's in late December. But interesting. Fascinating. Apparently everyone's asleep." Julie started to describe what they'd seen.

Abby started back toward Matt and moved past Bobby Joe, who was still panting. She said, "This trip is probably the best thing that could have happened to you. I think it's good for you to get out and get some exercise."

Abby reached Matt as he started drilling a hole in the tunnel roof. Minutes later she was looking through the periscope. They were indeed near the edge of the huge enclosure that housed all the domes. The enclosure wall seemed no farther away than a few hundred meters. The vertical line where two wall surfaces met now resolved into two parallel lines.

"What do you think those lines in the corner are?" she asked.

Matt took another look. "Maybe the sides of an elevator shaft."

"One that would stop on this level?"

"No idea. It probably wouldn't be a good idea for us to try it even if it did stop here. I can imagine some warning bell ringing on the bridge if we did."

"So you're thinking we'll cut through the wall?"

"That's the first thing to try. I expect the wall to be strong, but I don't know that it needs to be any stronger than the one we already came through."

"And if we can't get through?" Abby said.

"Then we'll try the next thing and the next thing and the next thing."

"You sound like nothing can stop us. Why are you so optimistic?"

Matt took his gaze away from the periscope and looked at Abby. His hardhat light was angled high enough up that his eyes were visible. "I haven't run nearly as much as you have, or run with your class of athlete, but I'd be willing to bet that back in your racing days, once in a while you found yourself halfway through a race, and you felt like dying. You felt that at any second you'd pass out, or you'd have to stop and throw up. Ever feel like that?"

"Yes, a few times."

"But you kept going, didn't you?"

"Yes."

"And, for those races, what were the smallest stakes?"

Abby thought back. "I guess the most trivial was the time I was running against three of the fastest boys in high school. I wasn't actually competing with them in the strict sense, because they separated boys and girls for actual competition. But one of the boys had teased me about being slow."

"So you felt like dying but you kept running, whether you won or lost, and the only thing you stood to lose was your pride. Is that an accurate description?"

"Actually I did win," Abby said with satisfaction.

Matt smiled. "I think you also answered your own question. If you did that much for ego, how hard would you fight when the stakes were survival—survival of an entire world?"

Abby was silent for several seconds and then she smiled. "You're saying the people who brought us here picked on the wrong folks?"

"Yeah, I'd say that. What do you think?"

"I think you're right. If I weren't so angry, I'd almost feel sorry for them."

"Now you're talking." Matt pulled out the periscope and inserted an air hose and pump.

Abby hesitated. "But we aren't really invincible."

"That's a fact. But we're not going to give up easily."

"You know," Abby said, "your wife is a very lucky woman."

"I don't know about that," Matt said, but the words were muffled because Abby suddenly turned and started walking back toward the others.

How could she be so stupid to say something like that? Matt's wife was probably already dead, dead with everyone else on Earth, and Abby had to go and say she was lucky. Her brain was mush. And then she realized she had just walked away from Matt while they'd been in the middle of a conversation. What excuse could she offer? She could think of nothing that wouldn't make her sound brainless. And she couldn't just go back right now, because she had no idea what she should say. She hadn't felt this flustered in a long time. She felt like a dumb teenager all over again as a flush warmed her face.

Abby moved past the trailer and found Julie, Bobby Joe, and Richard still watching Rudy. For an instant she expected they would all turn and stare at her for acting so stupid with Matt, but of course they didn't. They hadn't been anywhere close.

"I think that's got it," Rudy said. He collected several tools, then deposited them in the trailer.

At about the same time, Matt got back.

"I think we're back in business," Rudy said before anyone else said a word. "I'm going to give it a try in a couple of minutes."

"Good," Matt said. "The ventilator seems to be working fine." As he moved past Abby to get closer to Rudy, his hardhat light was directed at the back end of the borer, and Abby's body was in darkness. With a gesture guaranteed to be invisible to the others, Matt gently squeezed her shoulder.

Abby didn't know what the touch meant, whether it was "That's okay; we all say stupid things," or "I understand; I'm nervous, too," or what, but she realized almost immediately that she felt better. Much better. Her shoulder tingled.

At the same time, Matt continued talking. "It looks like we're only a few hundred meters away from the wall, so the borer doesn't have to work for very long."

"Good," Rudy said. "That's consistent with the readings." He picked up the borer control and punched a couple of buttons, saying, "Here goes."

The borer moved forward just enough to notice, then stopped. Seconds later, it moved forward slightly. After a minute of watching it, Rudy said, "I think it's operational again."

Everyone but Richard said a word or two of congratulations and thanks.

When the inertial navigation unit told Matt they were within twenty meters of the wall, he warned Rudy to slow down the borer.

"Okay," Rudy said. "You still want to curve so we wind up running parallel to the wall for the last few meters?"

"Go for it."

From behind him in the tunnel, Matt heard Bobby Joe say something about parallel parking. "Hey, Bobby Joe. Why don't you do something useful? When we go through this wall, we could be going into a different atmosphere and pressure. Go back about fifty meters and put in another air barrier."

"Will do." Bobby Joe grabbed equipment and headed back.

Matt held the inertial navigation display where Rudy could see it as he controlled the path of the borer. They were approaching the intersection of two walls that met at about a 135-degree angle. The display showed two lines meeting at a point. Near the intersection, an orange dot with a tail like a comet showed their current position and most recent history. Superimposed on the display was a dim grid currently showing one-meter squares.

In the upper right corner of the display were their actual coordinates relative to the ground-floor lobby of the World Trade Center, shown in rectangular and polar coordinates. One of the polar coordinates said they were 48,912 meters from home. One of the rectangular coordinates said they were 17.4 meters below where the inertial navigation box had been zeroed out.

They slowly moved another four meters as the range gradually slowed and the angular displacement crept up in very small increments. The comet-tail image on the display confirmed that they were curving left toward the wall. Matt looked behind him and saw Abby, Julie, and Richard walking slowly behind them in the gently curving tunnel. Just before Matt looked forward, Richard stumbled, then caught his balance again.

Soon the tunnel straightened out as the borer moved next to the wall, closer and closer to the intersection. Occasionally the borer's whine would increase in pitch as it dragged against the wall. A lighter gray streak at about waist height on the right wall showed where the borer had scraped against it.

Finally, as the borer neared the intersection, Rudy turned it away from the surface, curving its path more to the left so that minutes later, according to the display, the borer was going parallel to the adjacent wall.

"That should about do it," Rudy said. He shut off the borer and for an instant all was quiet in the tunnel.

"Good," Matt said. "Before we do anything else, let's make sure we've got a good seal."

Under Matt and Rudy's direction, the team retrieved tape from the trailer and applied sections of tape wherever the borer had come close enough to the wall to leave gaps or thin sections of solidified goo, just to make sure no goo leaked into the chamber. Bobby Joe got back in time to help them finish.

"What next, boss?" Bobby Joe asked.

Matt rubbed the back of his neck. "The next order of business is to dig the goo away from the intersection of these two walls. Rudy thinks wherever there's a seam might be the easiest place to try to get through the wall, and that will also let us find out if that elevator shaft or whatever it is will be useful."

"We're not going to just blast our way through?"

"Nope. This wall might be a divider between our compartment and the bridge, or it might be a hull between us and the outside. If we don't use a little caution, we could all wind up sucking vacuum."

"It could be this chamber isn't actually in the ship any longer. We could be hidden away on the back side of the moon or something."

"That's possible, but their pattern seems to be pick up a city, add it to the collection, and move on. Anyway, even if we were on Luna, we could still be a meter from vacuum."

"Okay. I just thought if we were ready to use some explosives, then Richard would get a chance to talk."

"I am quite able to carry on a conversation when it's appropriate, thank you very much," Richard said. Suddenly everyone was looking at him.

"Dick, it's really great to hear you talk," said Bobby Joe.

"People call me Richard." His tone almost made his breath frosty.

"How can you be sure?" Bobby Joe asked innocently.

Richard's eyes narrowed, and Matt moved in to divert the energy into something useful. "All right. We need to clear the goo away from the wall, especially near the corner. Bobby Joe, you and I will take the first shift."

Matt and Bobby Joe attacked the goo, both cautious not to let their shovels clang against the wall. As they worked, the other four used the borer to make a small side tunnel to use for storage of discarded goo. The soft clattering noise from the borer's treads was comforting in its regularity.

In an hour they had exposed the intersection between the walls. The walls did in fact meet at a 135-degree angle, but two short walls jutted out from the two long walls and met in a vertical seam, as though a diamond-shaped shaft ran vertically along the intersection.

Matt finished installing another ventilation tube as Rudy played a torch over the rough edges of the goo left after the excavation. Behind Rudy, Richard, Julie, and Abby sealed strong tape over the junction between hardened goo and the wall surface now revealed, so no goo could leak in. The team had cleared an area about a meter high and eight meters wide. The walls around the elevator shaft, if that's what it was, didn't look any different than the other walls.

Rudy came back from the trailer with a stethoscope connected to an amplifier and headphones. "If everyone can be quiet for a minute, I'd like to see if I can hear anything from the other side."

Rudy knelt on the tunnel floor and stuck a suction cup against the cleared wall surface. He put on the headphones and turned on a small switch on the amplifier.

He turned a dial, then scratched again, then listened intently for fifteen seconds. Finally he took off the headphones and said, "Nothing." He moved to retrieve a drill from the trailer.

Rudy put a bit into the drill and said, "Let's start small. If it *is* vacuum on the other side, or if there are people close enough to notice, this probably makes the most sense. Plus, we can stick a small fiber-optic probe through and do some snooping before we decide what to do next."

"Sounds good to me," said Matt.

The wall looked like brushed aluminum or steel in the glare of the hardhat lamps. Faint lines defined large equilateral triangles, a meter on each side, as though the wall had been built from triangular plates that had then been welded together, or molecularly bonded. Rudy positioned the drill at the center of one of the triangles and pulled the trigger.

At first the bit just spun on the surface, like a spinning toothpick held against a plate of glass, but then it started to form a dimple in the metal.

An extremely fine powder sparkled in the light from the hardhats as the tiny particles slowly fell away from the bit. After a minute or so, Matt could tell that the bit had moved slightly into the surface.

Rudy leaned on the drill for several minutes. Matt's mind had begun to wander, and he was unsure whether they might break through in seconds, hours, or days.

The drill suddenly lurched forward several centimeters. At the same time, a red gas began to escape from around the perimeter of the bit.

"Everyone but Rudy, get out of here!" Matt shouted. "On the other side of the barrier. Now!"

As Abby, Julie, Bobby Joe, and Richard scrambled to get away, Rudy pulled the drill bit out of the hole and Matt stuck his thumb over the opening.

"I've got some tape," Rudy said. "Just a sec."

Rudy scattered small tools as he pawed through the tool box. A moment later, he and Matt were alone in the tunnel and he pulled out a roll of tape.

"Okay," Rudy said. "Move it."

Matt pulled his thumb away, and Rudy slapped a piece of tape against the wall surface, cutting off the tiny jet of red gas.

Both he and Matt held their heads as far away from the opening as they could. Matt tried not to breathe.

In the East Village, a small group of Hindus gathered for mutual solace in the apartment shared by two of the group.

Gerard Ghendl desperately wished that if he were near death, somehow he could travel to Benares to bathe in the sacred river Ganges to cleanse himself of his sins.

Gerard knew the trip was impossible, though, so he tried not to think about it. Instead he thought about karma, and wondered what, as a group, the inhabitants of Manhattan had done to deserve this.

Matt held the ends of the tape in place as Rudy stuck several more pieces over it. When they pulled their hands away, the tape held, and they couldn't see any gas leaking out.

"Let's move away," Matt said.

The two men came to a stop about ten meters from the taped hole. Rudy coughed a couple of times.

"You feel okay?" Matt asked. He looked closely at his thumb but saw no indication of damage.

"Yeah. Nervous, but okay. You?"

"I'm okay. At least that apparently wasn't some fast-acting poison."

"Not that affects us, anyway."

"Can you hook up the gas analyzer?"

"Right away." Rudy went to the trailer and retrieved equipment. Minutes later he had an intake tube positioned near the taped hole, and the sampler pump was running.

"It'll need to sample for about ten seconds," Rudy said. "I can hold the tube."

"No. I've already been exposed. No point in risking both of us."

Rudy shook his head, but went back to the pump. "Any time you're ready."

Matt peeled edges of the tape back until he had exposed the small hole again. He put the end of the tube over the spurting red gas.

"Okay, that's enough," Rudy said finally.

Matt pushed the tape back into place, sealing the hole, and put another couple of strips over the rest. He went over to watch over Rudy's shoulder. "So, what have we got?"

Rudy was silent for a moment. "Mostly oxygen. Some nitrogen. And a smaller amount of some compound I can't identify. That has to be what's coloring the gas. But I can only hope it's not harmful in the quantities we inhaled. It probably wouldn't be much good for our lungs, though, if we had to breathe a lot of it. The good part is that nothing in this stuff is emitting radiation."

"Right," Matt said. "I'm going to call the others back. We need to talk."

Minutes later the six of them were once again near the cleared portion of the wall.

"So, what *was* that stuff?" Julie asked.

Matt looked at Rudy, who explained.

"Is that what our captors breathe?" asked Bobby Joe. "Maybe we need to go back and get scuba gear."

"That's not the only problem," Abby said. "I don't know if we'd be able to see through that stuff."

The group was silent for a long moment.

Finally Matt said, "I'm not sure our captors breathe that stuff."

"I may be thinking the same thing you are," Rudy said.

"A fence?"

"Could be."

"What *are* you talking about?" Richard asked.

Matt turned to Richard. "When Rudy was drilling, the bit cleared the wall, and the drill pushed forward several centimeters, and it stopped again, but the bit wasn't sunk in all the way. There's another surface just behind the one Rudy drilled through. This red gas may be confined to the gap between these two layers."

"For what purpose?" Julie asked.

"To make it easy to find out if anyone breaks out, and exactly where it happened. If we had used explosives just now, we might easily have blown a hole so large and jagged that we couldn't seal it. If we'd been using a really high-power laser, we could have drilled right through the second surface at the same time, and that gas would be filtering out the other side even though we patched this side."

"That seems kinda low-tech," Bobby Joe said.

"Maybe," Rudy said. "But the advantage is that it's very easy to implement. They've got hundreds of square kilometers to protect, and instrumenting the entire surface with sensors or setting up enough lasers and mirrors to let them check for breaks that way would be a hell of a lot of work. This way they just build two boxes, one inside the other. They periodically measure the pressure of the gas between. Easy."

"It makes a lot of sense to me," Matt said. "But what other theories should we explore? One possibility that's been mentioned is that it's our captors' natural atmosphere. What else?"

"Maybe we drilled into a duct," Bobby Joe said. "A duct that's carrying this stuff to a particular location. Or we hit a tank of the stuff."

"A tank would probably be at a lot higher pressure," Rudy said. "And a duct going from somewhere to somewhere implies some other need for red air."

"Any other possibilities?" Matt asked. After a moment of silence, he said, "The first theory still makes the most sense to me. So what do we do next?"

Julie said, "Well, if we can't get through here, maybe we can get through someplace else."

"I bet the whole perimeter is protected this way," Rudy said. "But I think maybe we *can* get through anyway."

Abby watched nervously as Rudy used the saw to cut slowly through the wall panel. The job was complicated by bad visibility and the layer of plastic.

On Rudy's suggestion, they had taken a large sheet of the clear plastic material used for tunnel air barriers and taped it over the triangular panel Rudy intended to cut loose. The sheet of plastic ballooning out from the wall was significantly bigger than the proposed opening, and they had taped it so that several of Rudy's tools were on the inside. Rudy gripped the saw through the plastic, as though he were operating some equipment in a sealed environmental chamber. The red air filling the balloon made it hard to see what was going on inside. They had installed a blower pump in the tunnel ceiling to keep the pressure on this side of the plastic as high as possible.

"I want your hardhat for just a second," Abby said to Rudy. She took it, replaced the lamp battery with a freshly charged one, and put the hardhat back on Rudy's head. "Okay."

"Thanks," Rudy said.

Abby had just finished trading recharged minivid batteries when Rudy said, "That's almost got it. I need help holding the cut-out so it doesn't fall between the two walls."

Matt and Richard moved closer. Matt reached through the plastic and maneuvered a screwdriver up to where he pried out one edge of the cut-out. Minutes later Rudy completed the cut and, hampered by the plastic barrier, Matt and Richard lowered the plate against the wall.

In the large triangular opening the red air made visibility difficult, but there did indeed seem to be another surface just centimeters away.

Rudy and Matt reached through the bottom of the plastic and grabbed some of the goo they had put there before taping the plastic in place. Slowly they pushed pieces into the gap around the triangular opening.

"I think we're just about ready," Rudy said finally.

"Okay," Matt said, turning toward Abby. "We're going to need to move quickly. Abby, you and Bobby Joe get your torches ready. Rudy and I will cut out the center of this plastic. Richard, you and Julie are ready with tape?"

Julie said, "Yes," for both of them.

Abby and Bobby Joe started their torches.

"All right. Take your last few breaths," Matt said. "Three—two—one." With their knives, Matt and Rudy quickly cut out the center of the taped plastic and forced the edges into the gap with the goo, being careful to stay out of the way of the torches. Red air swirled into the room, and Abby could see a few tiny jets of red air escaping from leaks between the wall and the goo stuffed into the gap around the perimeter of the cutout.

Abby moved forward and quickly played the flame over the goo. She watched with relief as it darkened and expanded to seal the gap. A couple of small red spurts of air cut off. She choked as she finally had to breathe, but by then the red cloud was dissipating.

As soon as Abby finished a section with the torch, Richard slapped some tape over the gap as an additional barrier.

Everyone in the chamber was coughing for several minutes as they raced to complete the seal. Even after they finished, it took a while for Abby's breathing to return to normal. She wasn't sure if the problem was just the red air or if her adrenaline reaction might have made it worse, but finally she felt all right again.

Matt surveyed the sealed gap around the edge of the triangle. "Looks good. Everyone did a great job."

The view was clear now, and the tinge of red in the air finally vanished. Beyond the triangular opening was indeed another similar surface, as though they had just cut through the first wall of a car door.

Rudy held up his drill. "Shall I?"

Matt grabbed a roll of tape and said, "Go ahead. I'm really curious. Let's play a little safer this time, though. Everyone but Rudy, please go back down the tunnel. Richard, you lead the way back. Be cautious."

Abby didn't like this part much better than the earlier wait. As she walked down the tunnel with the others, she realized that she didn't mind taking a risk along with Matt, but that she didn't like the idea of him taking a risk that she didn't share.

Abby, Bobby Joe, Julie, and Richard reached the air barrier, took it down, and then put it back up when they were on the other side. Abby sat down on the tunnel floor, leaned back against the curved wall, and flipped her hardhat light off to conserve the charge. The business end of the borer sat facing them only a couple of meters away, and she felt nervous to be on this side of it.

Bobby Joe stood and paced. After a couple of minutes, he said, "So, Richard. What's a bomb guy do?"

"I am *not* a 'bomb guy.' "

"Oh, sorry. Demolitions expert. So, what's your background?"

"Twenty years in the *real* world. In the world where if you make a mistake, someone scrapes the pieces of your body into a cigar box and buries you like a pet in the back yard."

"You sound a little bitter. Why do you do the work if you hate it so much?"

"I don't hate it. I love it. I just don't like people to trivialize it."

"You love it?" Bobby Joe said.

"Yes." At first Abby thought that was all Richard was going to say, then he added, "Perhaps it's like a drug addiction, but I feel so *alive* when I'm working. The rest of the time, I'm just waiting to get back to work. Like right now."

"They're coming back," Julie said.

The hardhat light on the far side of the air barrier came closer, and Rudy called out, "All right. It's safe to come back."

In the chamber everything looked much as it had before except that now a small hole penetrated the second wall.

"The other side is air, just about like here," Matt said. "And the pressure is about the same. But we can't see much; it's dark."

Rudy proceeded to use the saw to cut a triangle slightly smaller than the one cut in the first wall. As he finished the cut, Matt and Richard maneuvered the piece of metal into the tunnel and set it on the floor. Beyond the opening was nothing but blackness.

"Leave your lamp off at first," Matt said as Rudy started to lean his head into the opening.

Rudy switched off the lamp, then took off his hardhat entirely before he stuck his head into the darkness and looked down then up. He pulled back into the tunnel. "I don't see anything at all," he said softly.

Everyone on the team got a turn. Abby couldn't see anything when she looked, either, except possibly a very faint glimmer, which might or might not have been imagination, directly across from the opening.

"All right," Matt said finally. "I guess there's no harm in using our lights."

Rudy switched on his hardhat lamp and now Abby could see a vertical wall about a meter away from the triangular opening they had cut. The surface of the wall was flat black, absorbing so much light that despite its being illuminated Abby had to move her head back and forth a couple of times to convince herself the wall really was close.

"Whoa!" Bobby Joe said when it was his turn to look.

Abby understood his reaction when she looked down. She felt the vertigo coming from standing on top of a tall building under construction. The gap between the two walls receded into the depths, broken only by staggered rows of large beams extending between the pair of walls, a beam every two or three meters. She could see at least fifty rows down as the reflections grew weaker and weaker. The invisible bottom could have been a hundred meters away or a million.

A similar view showed to the right and straight up. To the left, the intersection between the wall they had cut through and the one next to it blocked her view, but she supposed the view around the corner would be much the same. The air between the walls was significantly cooler, and Abby suddenly felt very small.

"What now?" Bobby Joe said softly.

"I'm not sure," Matt said. "I suppose we see what's beyond that next wall."

Abby turned and saw that Rudy had already retrieved a rope from the trailer and was tying a loop around his waist. "I'm ready," he said as he picked up the drill and a roll of tape.

Matt looked like he was going to object, but then said, "Just a minute. Let's get some tape over this new edge so we don't cut the rope or anyone's hands."

Minutes later Rudy climbed into the dark opening as Matt and Bobby Joe held on to the rest of the rope. Rudy got his balance on one of the beams running between the walls, moved slowly toward the far wall, and straddled the beam. He brushed his fingers against the far surface. "This wall is *cold.*"

Rudy locked his feet together under the beam and put the drill against the wall. He switched it on, and Abby realized how nervous she was that someone beyond the wall would hear them this time. She deliberately relaxed her breathing.

The drill noise sounded for at least five minutes before Rudy switched it off. He moved his head close to the wall and aimed his hardhat lamp toward the point where the drill bit had been. He turned back to the group watching through the triangular cutout and said, "I don't know that we're going to get through here very easily. I can't see even a scratch."

Bobby Joe looked at Matt. "If that wall is really cold, it could be an outside wall."

"True. Just a second."

A moment later Matt came back from the trailer with a long flashlight topped with a wide reflector. He aimed the lamp down into the space between the walls, then up.

After Rudy crawled back into the tunnel, Abby got a chance to see what the powerful flashlight revealed. Looking down, she could see a faint glimmer that suggested a floor. To the right side and straight up, there wasn't even a hint that the surfaces ever stopped—just a never-ending forest of black beams shrinking in the distance and sucking away the light.

Matt took another look into the chasm. "I think the closest surface must be down there. I think our next step is to get to it."

Abby took a deep breath and told herself this would be no worse than the tunnel had been. Probably.

11

FIRST ENCOUNTER

"IS EVERYONE READY?" Matt asked. He felt nervous about entering the hole between the walls. At the same time he was excited that they were finally getting closer to being able to do something positive, and worried that they might be too late.

"Except for one thing," Rudy said. "I'd better park the borer."

"I thought it *was* parked."

"It is. I should have said, 'park it more securely.' " Rudy walked down the tunnel toward the borer. "We're going to be leaving it parked a lot longer than normal. I just don't want it sinking to the bottom. Besides the fact that I don't want to lose it, I also don't want it pulling this section of the tunnel down with it. We don't need to have goo start pouring into the hole we just made, and I don't want it to snap the tunnel and flood it, either."

As Matt followed Rudy toward the borer, he realized that the tunnel floor was in fact dipping down as they approached, even though it hadn't been all that long since they had parked the borer here.

"So, what are you going to do about it?" Matt asked.

"Balloon," Rudy said. "I'm going to give it some flotation support, so it's closer to neutral buoyancy."

As Matt watched, Rudy retrieved a dozen small pipes, gas canisters, and inflatable bladders. Rudy hammered the pipes into the walls, then sealed each pipe with a torch. Finally he attached a small gas canister to each bladder and stuck the limp bladders into the pipes. Each canister had a small lip that hooked over the pipe it fit next to. Rudy twisted the valves on each of the gas canisters.

"Okay," Rudy said. "I'm almost set. The goo flows slowly enough that it will take a while for those balloons to fill, but I think it'll go fast enough that the borer won't sink very far before it starts to rise again."

Finally, Rudy took a huge balloon and connected a larger gas canister. The balloon expanded to fill the entire tunnel. Rudy let the gas keep running until the balloon formed a tight fit, then turned off the gas. "One more layer of insurance," Rudy said, "in case the tunnel springs a leak."

Matt and Rudy went back to the hole in the wall. "Okay. Is everybody armed and ready?" Matt asked.

Abby and Bobby Joe patted the Glock 17s at their hips and said, "Yes." Everyone else said "Yes," without needing to double-check. Canteens hung opposite their holsters.

"All right. Let's get on with it." Matt picked up the end of a long coiled rope and snapped the hook onto his belt. He climbed up and into the dark space between the walls. The black surfaces absorbed much of his helmet light. Matt climbed onto one of the beams that ran between the walls. Richard hooked the next clip onto his own belt, then climbed into the hole and let the slack in the rope fall into the blackness.

"Hand me the lamp," Matt said.

Richard gave him a utility lamp. Matt took it and stuck the suction base to the wall, well away from the opening. Matt set the lamp to flash once every five seconds so the battery would last a long time.

"All right," Matt said. "I'm going to another beam."

Richard said, "Okay. I'm hooked up, and so is Abby."

Matt nodded. He took a breath and leaped for the beam closest to the nearby corner intersection. His body felt weightless as he arced through the darkness toward the beam three meters away. His hardhat almost hit the beam in the row above. His feet hit the next beam, and he steadied himself against the walls.

He leaned into the blackness, and he could just see around the corner. The space between the two parallel walls looked the same as where he was—just an unending series of beams between the surfaces.

Matt leaped back to the beam he had been on and prepared to jump diagonally down to the next row. He looked at the beam he was bound for. It was almost three meters below him, and about half that distance away horizontally. He checked the slack in the rope to make sure he wouldn't get almost all the way and then get sprung back like a dog on a leash. Fortunately the low gravity made a jump of that distance much easier than it would have been otherwise.

He made his best guess as to how fast he'd fall, and he pushed himself away from the beam. He dropped deeper into the darkness.

The beam rose to meet him, but he wasn't moving sideways fast enough. Instead of hitting the beam with his feet, he was falling past it just as his arms got close enough to grab it.

He held on more easily than he had expected. He pulled himself up to the beam. Seconds later, he jumped to the next beam down on a diagonal. This time he pushed harder and hit the beam with his feet. He bounced and steadied himself against the walls. His backpack was large but not too heavy, and contained part of Richard's supplies.

Matt looked up toward Richard and called softly, "Next."

Richard moved onto the beam near the hole, then followed Matt to the beam he had just been on. Richard also misjudged the jump, but he managed to scramble up onto the beam seconds later.

Within minutes the rest of the team were all in the gap. Behind Richard were Abby, Bobby Joe, Julie, and finally Rudy. Lengths of rope stretched between each adjacent pair. Matt was so far down into the darkness that he felt as if he was in a tall elevator shaft, and the hole above looked like a dim opening onto a poorly lit floor some five stories above. Flashes from the lamp next to the opening were much easier to see than at first.

The team made another series of jumps, bringing each member lower into the chasm. As Matt watched the group catch up, they looked like giant fireflies with a purpose. Abby must have landed wrong, because Matt heard a sudden "Whoops!" but when he looked back she was all right.

They worked into a pattern where each person would jump

just after the person ahead in line jumped, and soon Matt figured they were moving down one level about every ten seconds. The cycle was interrupted occasionally, once by Bobby Joe missing his beam entirely, but fortunately his weight in the low gravity was only twenty or thirty pounds, and Abby and Julie were able to support their ends of the rope while Bobby Joe climbed up to the beam he had missed.

Richard's only reaction during the incident was a muttered "Klutz." Shortly after that, Richard himself slipped and had to climb back up.

They'd been going on and off for an hour when Matt called a slightly longer halt. "How is everyone holding up?" he asked. He could see the five other hardhat lamps but couldn't make out anyone's face.

No one complained.

"How deep are we, Bobby Joe?"

"The box says eleven hundred sixty-two meters."

Matt took the big flashlight from his backpack and aimed it at the floor of the chasm again. The floor seemed brighter this time. "We're making significant progress, it seems to me. I'd guess we've gone at least a quarter or a third of the way."

"How about if I drop a dollar and we time it?" Bobby Joe said.

"Go for it," Matt said.

A moment later the sparkle of the silver coin lit the beam from Matt's hardhat lamp. "Everyone be quiet for a minute or two," Bobby Joe said.

The silence lengthened to almost five minutes, and still Matt had heard nothing.

"Something's wrong," Bobby Joe said finally. "It had to have hit by now."

"Let's get moving again," Matt said. "We'll figure it out later."

Abby's soft voice came to him clearly in the darkness. "Be careful, Matt. Maybe the coin hit some barrier."

"Will do."

The team resumed hopping diagonally down into the darkness. They had been jumping for another half-hour when Matt realized he had misjudged the last several beams, overshooting each of them. He called a halt. "Has anyone else been misjudging their jumps recently?"

Everyone but Richard admitted they were having the same trouble, and finally Richard admitted it, too.

"I feel fine," Matt said. "I don't think I'm getting tired or anything. Any theories? And how deep are we now, Bobby Joe?"

No one had any theories.

"We're about two thousand three hundred thirty-nine meters down," Bobby Joe said. A moment later, he added, "Uh oh."

"Uh oh what?" Matt asked.

"I'm not sure. But the depth reading is still increasing. And I'm just sitting here."

"Are we moving?" Julie asked.

Rudy said, "You mean the ship? I don't think we'd be able to tell. Since we haven't felt any acceleration other than gravity since we've been inside, my guess is that somehow they've got the technology to shield the interior of the ship from the ship's motion."

"That's lucky for us, too," Matt said. "If this ship can accelerate as quickly as those smaller black ships, we'd probably be dead. Bobby Joe, how does that box work?"

"The inertial navigation unit? It's got a three-axis sealed unit with guts that stay oriented the same direction all the time. Accelerometers in all three axes feed into a microcomputer that integrates the input and computes how far the box has been moved. The vertical axis had to be recalibrated for the lower gravity in here. Right now it assumes a constant reading of about one-sixth gee means we're staying level. If we go up, the increased acceleration tells the box what's happening, and it knows we're going up. If we go down, the decreased acceleration tells the box that, too." Bobby Joe was silent for a moment, then said, "Ah!"

"Ah?"

"If we're in a lower-gee field, it could be tricked into thinking we're descending. And that would explain why we're overshooting beams."

"True," Rudy said. "And if that's the case, then the box is no good for telling how deep we are anymore."

"Any better explanations that occur to anyone?" Matt asked.

No one said anything.

"Okay. Let's get moving again."

They continued their descent, angling down as though following a huge excavated cavern in a deep mine. Within minutes, Matt was convinced the gravity was lower. His leaps took longer, and the lateral push required grew smaller.

"The gravity is definitely lower," Bobby Joe said. "And the box is saying we're dropping even faster."

Soon the gravity was even weaker. Matt felt a tightening in his throat and a queasiness in his stomach. He had to hold on to the beams to avoid floating upward. He looked back down into the dark chasm, and realized that "down" was no longer as easily identifiable as it had been. He looked behind him. Far in the distance behind him he thought he saw something small and shiny traveling up, but an instant later it was gone.

"This is getting a little crazy," Matt said after moving past a few more beams. "If anyone has anything in a pocket that's not snapped, you'd better fasten it down. This is virtually zero gee."

From beam to beam, Matt now just gave himself a gentle nudge in the right direction and glided straight to it. Moving between beams over the blackness was like walking from log to log as they floated on the surface of the water in a dark bottomless pit.

The air grew dusty, and several times Matt sneezed.

The first time he missed a beam, he realized the rules were continuing to change. He had floated straight toward it at first, but then slowly curved "up," missing the beam by centimeters.

Matt floated until he hit a different beam, one in the same row he had started from. "We've passed zero! What used to be 'down' is now 'up.' "

He positioned himself on the top of the beam, what five minutes ago would have seemed the bottom, and leaped again for the beam he'd been going for earlier. This time he made it. He looked back and saw the pinpoint flashing light in the distance, and the line of climbers behind him. They were still on a straight path from their starting point, but now it felt as if they were climbing out of the chasm instead of going deeper into it.

"Can you point your big light back that way?" Bobby Joe asked.

Matt got out the lamp and aimed it behind him. Very far in the distance a small silvery object moved slowly "up."

"That's my dollar," Bobby Joe said. "It's just oscillating through the zero-gee point. Eventually air resistance will slow it down enough that it just hovers in this region. And that's why it's so dusty here. This is kind of a bizarre gravity well, where everything gathers."

Matt directed the flashlight toward the "floor" he had seen earlier. No reflections returned. "Uh oh," he said. "The floor we saw earlier must have been just the dust in the air in the region we just passed through."

"Does that mean we should stop?" Bobby Joe asked.

"No. Just that the environment is stranger than we expected."

They resumed their trek. After several minutes Matt began to get more comfortable with the idea that they were now traveling "up." Each time he jumped from one beam to the next, he had to jump just a little higher.

They kept climbing. The gravity was still lower than what they'd been used to lately when Richard said, "Lucky the gravity has varied smoothly. Otherwise, we might risk jumping into a ten-gee field."

Matt had a sudden image of dragging the other five behind him to their deaths.

Matt kept climbing through the rows of beams, feeling like a child in a huge jungle gym. When he cleared the next beam, he looked back to make sure he could see the flashing lamp they had left at the hole. It was still there, but very faint.

After another break they reached a region where the gravity seemed as strong as it had been when they started out. Finally the scenery ahead changed. They were apparently nearing another corner of the huge octagon-shaped level of the ship.

Five minutes later that suspicion was confirmed. The wall met another wall at a 135-degree angle. Matt gave the command to stop, and he stuck another small flashing light to the wall.

"So, what now, boss?" Bobby Joe asked. "Try to go through the wall?"

"I think the first step is to explore the boundary," Matt said, then pointed. "Look up there. It seems to me there's a break in the row of beams."

"I think I see what you mean," Abby said.

Julie took advantage of the break to pan with her minivid, capturing more video.

"Quiet!" Matt said suddenly.

In the stillness of the semi-dark gap, Matt could hear the others breathing shallowly. In addition a hum from somewhere around them grew louder and louder. Rapidly the hum grew to a peak and then started to fade again, but Matt couldn't determine which direction the sounds came from.

"Elevator?" Rudy whispered.

"Possible."

Several seconds after the hum was no longer audible, Matt said, "Let's go."

Matt in the lead, the group jumped from beam to beam. Minutes later they halted as the hum came and went again.

After five more minutes, Matt was convinced there was some kind of irregularity in the spacing of the beams above. When they finally reached the area, he felt more encouraged than he had been in more than a day. Set into the inside wall was something that had to be a door. They waited without speaking for a minute as the elevator hum rose and then faded.

"Maybe we're in business," Matt said.

The others gathered around on the nearby beams and looked. They each sat on a beam, their legs hooked together beneath the beam. Abby recorded video of the unintelligible markings on the door.

The door was octagonal, about two meters across. On four edges were octagonal handles.

"The size suggests that our captors are approximately as big as we are," Abby said. "That's good."

"Why's that good?" asked Bobby Joe.

"How would you want to try to establish communications with a flea or a whale?" she asked.

"Are we going through?" said Richard after a moment of silence.

"Yes, but cautiously. On the other side of the door might be atmosphere we can't breathe. There might be aliens coming down a transparent elevator every five minutes. There might be alarm bells going off."

Matt hesitated. "All right. We've heard the elevator pass by here a couple of times in the last ten or fifteen minutes. That's good and bad. Bad because it means we may have our first confrontation soon. Good because it means the elevator is in use often enough that if *we* use it, we have a chance of remaining undetected."

"Do you think the door really will sound an alarm?" Julie asked.

"My gut says no, mainly because the protection around the enclosure is pretty thorough. If we wind up getting split up, though, you know what to do. Rudy's second in command, followed by Richard."

"What about another atmosphere on the other side?" Rudy asked.

"We play safe. If *this* section contains breathable air, my guess is that the living quarters do, too, but again, we can't assume that. Bobby Joe, can you get out the analyzer?"

Bobby Joe brought out the gas analyzer and unwound the flexible tubing extending from it.

"All right," Matt said. "Let's try to open the door." He was closest, so he edged nearer and gripped one of the four handles. He turned it, and it rotated easily under his hand. He kept turning, and the knob kept turning without reaching a stop. He turned it the opposite direction until he was sure it was well past its starting position, and he still felt no resistance.

"This isn't encouraging," he said. He reached for another knob. It reacted the same way.

"I wonder if that means the door's been disconnected somehow," Rudy said. "Maybe it was just here when this ship was built, and now it serves no purpose."

"Possible," Matt said. "But I wouldn't do that aboard a human ship. Things like emergency exits don't get used all that often, but when there's an emergency, you *want* them to work.

And you don't want people wasting valuable time trying to get through a dead end."

"Maybe they don't think like we do," Bobby Joe said.

"I think Bobby Joe's right," Abby said. "But that doesn't mean the door won't operate. Maybe they just operate doors differently than we do."

"All right," Matt said. "I'm open to discussion."

Abby said, "For starters, there are four handles instead of one. Maybe that means they have to be turned in sequence, or simultaneously."

"What sequence?"

"I don't know. With four handles there are only so many possibilities. Since up and down tend to get confused in space, my guess is that they rely on something that doesn't depend on orientation, other than facing the door."

"So that would be clockwise or counterclockwise?"

"Or some pattern, like a combination that's independent of the actual starting point?"

"Seems reasonable," Abby said.

They spent several minutes trying combinations. Nothing worked.

"Well, Abby?" Matt said.

Abby was silent for a moment. "Maybe," she said slowly, "maybe you have to turn all four knobs simultaneously."

Matt looked back at the knobs. "That's pretty demanding for an emergency exit. You're assuming they require the buddy system? Two people working together?"

"Not necessarily. The people who built this ship might have more limbs than we do. And this might not be an emergency exit. It might just be a door that they wanted to make difficult to open accidentally."

Matt thought about that a moment. "Rudy, can you give me a hand?"

Rudy moved from beam to beam until he was on the beam adjacent to Matt. "Okay, I'm ready."

Matt grabbed the two handles farthest from Rudy. "Can you reach those other two?"

Rudy locked his ankles underneath the beam and leaned out into space. He was just able to reach the two handles.

"All right," Matt said. "Turn them clockwise." He did the same. Nothing. They tried counterclockwise. Nothing.

Suddenly Matt had an image of standing at a sink and simultaneously turning on a hot and a cold water tap. "Turn the one in your right hand clockwise, and the one in your left counterclockwise." He did the same.

A muted *click* sounded from somewhere inside the door.

Dorine Underwood stopped at the office door and leaned in. "Anything hot, Tim?"

Tim Adjmati looked up from sorting mail, his black eyes reflecting pinpoints of light from the overhead lamp. "Nothing so far, but one marked *personal.*" He was building three stacks of opened mail that Dorine really wasn't keen on starting yet.

The last three envelopes marked *personal* that Dorine had received were all from Raphael. He never gave her cards at home. Instead, he had liked to think of Dorine and her routine suddenly interrupted by a smile.

From the door she could see the small package that Tim pointed at. It was a little larger than a book, wrapped in brown paper and heavily taped.

"There's nothing personal in that stack," Dorine said. She tried to keep the sadness out of her voice. Besides the image she had to maintain, she didn't want anyone feeling sorry for her.

Tim nodded.

"I'll stop back in a couple of minutes on my way back from Lamar's office and grab anything that looks hot."

"Yes, ma'am."

Lamar wasn't in his office when Dorine got there, so she found a piece of scratch paper and left a note. She could have used the electronic mail system, but trips to various offices constituted almost all the exercise she was getting lately.

She turned back down the hall toward Tim. She had covered about half the distance between the two offices when the building suddenly shook and a deafening blast started her ears ringing. A discharge of papers and wood splinters and smoke exploded from the office Tim had occupied.

Dorine stumbled, then regained her balance. She moved closer. The doorframe was bent and splintered. On the wall across from the office was a darkened surface roughly the same shape as the doorway. The air was thick with smoke and swirling paper fragments.

Dorine took a glance through the doorway and sank to her knees, oblivious to the sounds of approaching people.

"All right," Matt breathed. The unlocked door stayed in position. He pushed gently on it, and it gave. Good. At least they had no pressure differential to deal with. "Bobby Joe, hand me the nozzle."

Bobby Joe tossed the loose end of the tubing connected to the gas analyzer. Matt caught it. With it held in his left hand, he unsnapped his pistol and removed it from his holster. He flipped off the safety. Next to him, Rudy also readied his weapon.

Matt pushed the tube toward the thin crack that had opened on the left edge of the door. Bobby Joe started the pump, drawing gas into the analyzer. The sound felt far too loud.

Soon Bobby Joe said softly, "It's safe."

Matt stood up on the beam. With his free hand, he unsnapped the rope from his belt. He pushed the edge of the door with his foot, and it pivoted inward. Light flooded into the cavity between the walls, and Matt's eyes adjusted.

Matt crouched and moved through the door and into the empty room beyond. He stayed low. In front of him was a short wall, maybe a meter tall, topped with a clear observation panel, through which he could see distant tubes running from the chamber ceiling down toward bubbled cities.

To his immediate right was a solid wall about three meters tall and about three meters to a corner. He moved to the 135-degree corner and peered around. The other half of the observation deck was identical, except that what seemed to be an elevator door broke the surface of the wall. Set into the outer wall beyond the elevator was another door like the one he had just come through. The matching door had the same pattern of four handles, two on top, two on the bottom. It bore identical legends, meaningless to Matt.

Matt moved back to the doorway. Quietly he said, "Come on out, but stay low."

Moments later all six team members crouched in the observation chamber. Matt pushed the door shut with a soft *snap,* and with Rudy's help made sure they could open it again. Finally Matt closed it again, on the off chance that some status light might attract attention.

"God, this place is big," Bobby Joe said softly.

Matt peered over the low wall, through the bottom of the transparent surface. They were high enough to make out easily the octagonal shape of the enormous gray floor far below. More than a dozen strange cities sat under individual clear domes. Spires in a city near the far wall reached almost as high as they were now. From this distance some of the cities resembled elaborate old-fashioned paperweights. Life-support hoses ran from numerous ceiling ports down to sides of the bubbles. In one of the nearest domes, a huge irregular building with parapets slowly rotated.

"I don't see Manhattan," Julie said.

"It's not down there," Rudy said. "We're turned around because of the gravity switch. We're looking at what's *underneath* the plain we tunneled into. If we'd known, we could have tunneled right through and come up on the other side of the world."

"Elevator," Richard said.

"Quick," Matt said. He pointed toward the side of the observation deck concealed from the elevator door.

Everyone moved quickly and quietly. They waited thirty seconds, but never heard the hum they had heard before.

"Maybe it was my imagination," Richard said finally. "Maybe my nerves are a little tight."

"All right," Matt said. "We're all a little jumpy. No harm done."

Back at the observation window, Julie used her minivid as she said, "You're saying these people have built a huge pancake? We're looking at one side, and the other side looks just like it?"

"Exactly," Rudy said. "Except that this side looks less populated."

Richard had dug out binoculars from his backpack. "I can't see any windows near the other elevator shafts."

Matt said, "So maybe this is one-way material?"

"Makes sense," Abby said. "These people haven't shown themselves to anyone that we know of. That would be consistent with them wanting to keep it that way." She turned to use her minivid on the legends on the doors.

Rudy looked up. "Those small circles on the ceiling could be observation ports, too. Maybe the elevators are mainly being used by people who want to get from one side to the other, rather than by people who may stop on the way."

"Interesting theory," Matt said, "but I don't know that we can count on it."

In the silence, Julie, who had been looking at cities through her minivid telephoto, said, "The city by the right wall on the right looks vaguely like an old castle. I guess they didn't just take people from high-tech worlds."

"True. They took us, didn't they?" said Bobby Joe.

"All right," said Matt. "We need to get out of here. The basic question is whether to try the elevator or go back to crawling between the walls. I'm for the elevator. Anyone have a good reason why we shouldn't try it?"

No one spoke.

"All right." Matt drew his pistol again. "Let's do it."

The elevator door was octagonal, about three meters from top to bottom and from side to side, with a single pull handle on the left. Next to the handle was a set of four buttons in a vertical line. The inner two were circles. The top and bottom were ellipses aligned so the long axis was vertical.

"Any guesses as to what the controls do?" Matt said. He tugged lightly on the elevator door handle, but it didn't budge.

The silence lasted several seconds. Abby said, "Beyond the obvious, that maybe the top pair says we want to go up and the bottom pair says we want to go down, I don't know."

Rudy said, "The ovals suggest speed to me. Maybe the circles are the regular up and down buttons and using the ellipses says you're in a hurry and you want an express."

Matt said, "Or maybe the circles take you to the top of the chamber and the ellipses take you to the floor or floors beyond that." He reached forward and pushed the bottom button.

A bright line formed around the perimeter of the ellipse, and it began to blink. "Why down instead of up?" asked Rudy.

"This side is less built up than the side Manhattan is on. I'm just guessing that means the bridge is on the Manhattan side. I figure the odds are no worse than fifty-fifty." Matt looked at the five other faces around him. "I want everyone armed when the door opens, but be careful. Don't shoot unless it's absolutely necessary to protect yourself or to prevent one of our captors from escaping."

Moments later the blinking line around the ellipse stayed on steady.

"Could mean we'll have company," Abby said. "Or it could mean the elevator has started on its way here."

As they watched the indicator, the bright line around the outside grew wider as the interior dark ellipse shrank.

"That's *got* to mean it's getting closer," Abby said.

"Why only one handle here and four on the other door?" Matt asked.

"My guess is the other door isn't an everyday access door the way this one might be. They didn't want anyone accidentally opening it."

By the time the dark ellipse had nearly vanished, Matt heard the hum of an approaching elevator. Seconds later, the dark spot vanished as the oval indicator completely filled with light. As the hum died, the ellipse started to blink, and a *click* sounded from the elevator.

Matt gripped the handle with his left hand and aimed his pistol into the elevator. He yanked on the elevator door, and it swung open smoothly.

The interior was empty.

Behind Matt, Julie said, "Thank God."

The interior fit all six of them comfortably. It seemed more like the interior of a subway car than a normal elevator, though, because it was ringed with several rows of handles, one at eye level, one at chest level, and one at waist level.

Matt got in last and pulled the door closed. An iris closed, concealing the unreadable markings on the inside of the door, and just as a red circle began to glow next to the entry, the elevator lurched into free fall and Matt grabbed a handle with one hand.

"Oh, God," Julie said softly.

After a few seconds of free fall, Rudy said, "We're turning. The elevator is rotating."

Matt realized he was right. Over a period of about ten seconds, it seemed the elevator turned end for end, still in free fall. Seconds later, he felt a gentle nudge of gravity as the elevator accelerated slightly.

A couple of minutes passed as the elevator noises rose in pitch and Matt imagined them whipping past stop after stop. Gravity began to grow stronger.

Rudy said, "Either we're speeding up more, or we passed the zero-gee midpoint, and what we're feeling is additional gravity instead of acceleration."

They hurtled through the elevator shaft, the elevator shuddering perceptibly, but the apparent gravity didn't increase past what they had been used to for their days aboard the ship.

Bobby Joe said, "They really should leave some airsick bags in here."

Matt glanced over his shoulder, and he caught Abby's gaze. He looked at her for a long moment without speaking. She seemed worried, which was natural, but she also gave him a nervous smile that for an instant cut through all his fears and made him wish this mission were long in the past.

The pull of gravity seemed to lessen, and the vibrations began to drop in pitch.

"We're getting ready to stop," Richard said.

The elevator cage slowed more and more, finally coming to a complete stop. The iris dilated and exposed the interior of a different door with still different unreadable markings. Matt readied his gun. "On your toes, folks."

He pushed open the door.

Matt left the elevator quickly. "We got lucky. I don't see anyone around. Let's get out of here pronto."

He made sure everyone was behind him as he started moving toward a trio of large cylinders about fifty meters away. From near the elevator door, a track bed with a single wide rail reached into the distance in the direction of the center of the ship. Two more monorails vanished in the distance along the walls. The ceiling here was maybe fifty meters high, and from the open space all around, Matt could believe this level was just as wide as the city chamber below their feet. Far in the distance the floor and ceiling converged along perspective lines, and Matt was unsure if they'd be able to see all the way across the hundred-kilometer span if the ceiling was only a half percent of that distance or an even smaller fraction. With the current tension, he didn't care too much about stopping and doing the math.

At seemingly random locations ahead were tall and bulky equipment housings, some with unrecognizable machinery exposed, like one that could have been a huge oil derrick as visualized by someone on a bad drug trip. Others were simple boxes or upright cylinders. The air was filled with the soft sound of gas being expelled, as though a thousand tire pumps were running just on the threshold of hearing. No individual lights showed anywhere. Instead, the ceiling emitted a uniform yellow-green light.

They reached the cover of the trio of cylinders without hearing the sounds of discovery. Of course Matt didn't know if they'd even be able to hear the aliens' voices. Perhaps they were telepaths like the tree dwellers, or they could have batlike voices pitched high enough to be inaudible, or use something other than sound.

Matt felt uneasy even in the comparative cover of the cylinders, each several meters in diameter, ranging in height from twice as tall as Matt to maybe five times his height. No matter where they moved, they were still visible from at least one direction. At least they could make sure they weren't visible from the monorails, which Matt figured were the most likely sources of trouble. Abby captured legends from the sides of the cylinders on video.

"What the hell is all this stuff?" Julie asked quietly. No one answered.

Matt took a long look in the one direction he could see and could detect no signs of motion. He jumped straight up, just far enough that his head and shoulders cleared the top of the lowest cylinder. He reached out and made sure the flat top was firm before he fell back to the floor.

"Rudy," Matt said softly, "I want you to come with me on top of this cylinder so we can take a look around. Everyone else stay down here and stay as hidden as you can."

Matt and Rudy jumped to the top of the cylinder and crouched. The surface felt quite solid. Matt pointed to the next-higher cylinder, and he went first. Rudy joined him seconds later and they both lay flat as they crept toward the edge that would give them the best view of the interior of this level.

Matt made a slow sweep with binoculars as Rudy did the same. He could see almost all the way across the ship; near the center there seemed to be a section walled off from the outside. Spread out around the area they could see were occasional massive concentrations of strange equipment. Their size and placement suggested that each major concentration of equipment was directly above a captured city or over a berth for one not yet here. Matt supposed the devices would be doing things like driving air and water and food down the tubes they could see vanishing through the floor, and pulling waste and used air back up for recycling. From each concentration of equipment seemed to be a monorail running to the walls of the central enclosed area.

What they could see of this octagonal level seemed to be split into pie wedges by monorails that came from the enclosed midpoint out to each of the corners. Centered in each pie wedge, about five kilometers from the outside walls, were enormous red cylinders probably as big around as a city block, extending from floor to ceiling.

Between the largest concentrations of equipment were smaller enclosures in a variety of sizes, dotted irregularly across the floor of the ship. Matt decided they might provide enough cover to let the group pass undetected.

Beside him, Rudy said, "Uh oh."

Matt took his eyes away from the binocular eyepieces long enough to see where Rudy was looking. He turned that direction and held up his binoculars. Just as Rudy said, "We've got company," Matt saw the approaching monorail car.

"They may not be coming because of anything we did," Matt said.

"True. It just makes me nervous."

As the car approached, Matt was able to start resolving more and more details. By the time the car was a few hundred meters away, Matt could see two riders.

Rudy saw them at the same time, because he said, "God, they look like giant spiders."

Dorine's daily telecast had begun on a more somber tone than usual. The police still had no clue to whether the letter-bomber was a lone crank or someone stirred up by one of the several rabble rousers vying for public attention. She now had people watching all the major dissident groups, but that small added sense of security barely diminished the pain of losing Tim Adjmati.

As she explained the circumstances surrounding Tim's death, she couldn't help thinking about the fact that on the other side of the camera lens was someone who wanted her dead.

"And now I'd like to address the person who did this. If you believe that an incident like this will change my policy, you're sadly mistaken. If you think that, had you succeeded, the person stepping into my spot would do things differently, you're an idiot. My only concern is the welfare of the citizens; more than a million people in this dome want to get out of here, or at the very least to know why we're here.

"If you object to the quest for knowledge and control over our lives, then that's too bad. But the path we're on is far too important for us to be swayed by fear and intimidation. We're not on a playground where one kid with a handgun can intimidate the whole class.

"It's a damn shame that Tim Adjmati died because someone within the sound of my voice thought things would change if I was dead. That's just plain wrong. We owe it to Tim, and we owe it to ourselves, to do everything we can to save ourselves.

"And nobody with a letter bomb is going to take that from us."

12

ARCHIES

ABBY HEARD THE soft *whoosh* of air from somewhere on the other side of the cylinder just about the same time that Matt called softly down from the top of the highest cylinder.

"Abby, I need you up here, but you've got to move quietly. The rest of you stay alert, and stay hidden from the monorail that goes toward the center of the ship. We've got company."

Abby jumped to the top of the middle cylinder and her feet landed softly, making her glad she was getting better at judging distances. She turned to the one Matt was on. He lay flat on the cylinder top.

Matt said, "Don't jump up here the same way. Jump just high enough to reach me, and let me pull you the rest of the way."

Abby gauged the jump as well as she could, and leaped. Matt had to have a good reason for the request.

Her jump brought her head and shoulders just above the top of the cylinder Matt lay on. Matt grabbed her hands and held on. Matt's body slipped slightly toward the edge, but with Matt's help Abby was able to crawl to the top of the cylinder.

Matt held a finger to his lips, then turned his body around until he and Abby both faced the opposite side of the cylinder top, where Rudy lay quietly next to his backpack and Matt's. Matt put his lips very near Abby's ear and said quietly, "We spotted some of the residents. I want you to get some video of them in case that will help you understand their language. Take off your backpack so your profile is low. And so you don't make any sounds of surprise when you see them, they look like big spiders."

Abby turned her head until she was looking directly into Matt's eyes, not more than a few centimeters away. His pupils dilated for a half-second, and then settled back to normal. Despite the tension, she had time to be aware of the desire to be this close to Matt at some time when survival wasn't as immediate an issue.

She eased out of her backpack and slithered toward the far lip of the cylinder, her minivid already recording. She touched the control at her temple and cranked the lens as far up as it would go. The telephoto image jittered wildly as she moved.

As soon as she peeked over the edge, she saw motion. A monorail car was slowing down as it neared the outside wall.

In the car were two aliens who really did look a lot like large spiders, the way a cat would look like a dog to someone who'd never seen anything but dogs. The monorail car pulled to a stop, and the aliens got out.

Their elongated and segmented bodies were about a meter above the ground, maybe a meter from front to back, and perhaps only a third of a meter wide and high. The rear segment was slightly larger than the front segment, and they were joined at a spot where the segments narrowed to a diameter no larger than a human neck. Both segments sported stripes of light fur that showed where their clothing didn't reach. She couldn't tell if their clothes served the same purpose as human clothes, or whether they just happened to be elaborate holders for the tool belts circling the forward segment. The clothes, if that's what they were, were black bands around both segments, covering about half of each.

The segments in front bore single eye-stalks. Fortunately, their eyes seemed to be directed toward their destination, rather than at this trio of cylinders. Of course they could have a much wider field of view than humans did, so Abby stayed cautious. As they walked, one of the two aliens waved its eye-stalk back and forth a couple of times, perhaps helping it judge distance, or perhaps some body language Abby had no way to decipher. Abby got a glimpse of one of their mouths and saw dark teeth.

Each alien had eight long, multi-jointed furry legs, thicker than large crab legs, and Abby thought about all the octagons contained in the ship's design. The four front legs swiveled from joints under the first segment; the rear four were attached to the back segment. The aliens walked on their middle four limbs, making the two in front and two in back available for other purposes.

At the end of each limb was an appendage that looked vaguely like a monkey's hand, with dark fur but short individually articulated digits.

As they walked, Abby realized that she must have subconsciously expected them to move with slightly jerky actions, as though drunk or uncoordinated, and she realized that impression must have been generated by too many old films in which creatures unlike humans were photographed with stop-motion or animation. These creatures walked fluidly, gracefully, with almost all the joints bending smoothly and in unison. In their own way, they were very pretty.

The creature in front reached the elevator door and pressed one of the buttons with a graceful motion. The elevator door opened almost immediately. The two spiderlike aliens went inside and pulled the door closed behind them. Abby hadn't seen any indication that the aliens had been aware of their presence.

To Abby's right, Rudy let out a sigh. To her left, Matt said, "Wow. Let's get out of here."

The three of them slowly backed away from the edge. When they were near the opposite side, they put their backpacks on. One at a time, they swung over the edge of the roof and dropped gently back down to the floor.

Matt described what they had seen to Julie, Richard, and Bobby Joe. "I want to get away from the monorail while things are quiet. Abby's got video we can all look at when we get someplace a little safer."

Richard pointed toward the nearest huge red cylinder. "I suggest we head toward that cylinder. It's the largest thing around, and the only thing that reaches the ceiling, so from what I can see here, it's got the best odds of being associated with the propulsion system."

Matt considered that for a few seconds. "All right. I'll take the lead. After me, Abby, Bobby Joe, Richard, Julie, and Rudy. You know the drill."

Matt took a quick look around, then headed for a pair of

boxy cabinets not far off. He moved quickly and smoothly. From there, he signaled for Abby to follow. She ran, the mechanical nature of all the surroundings giving her the feeling that she was running across bare space on a hugely magnified circuit board. She reached Matt at the integrated circuit without tripping on a resistor or capacitor. "What if they've got monitoring cameras on the ceiling?"

"Then we're dead," Matt said. "But if they're monitoring the ship in such detail that they could see us, they'd be running the risk of information overload. This is a huge place. As long as they don't know we're out, we've got a chance. As soon as they suspect they've got problems, then we could have a tough time staying undetected."

Bobby Joe reached their side and gave the go-ahead to Richard.

Matt said, "Bobby Joe, make sure you've got the coordinates of that corner noted."

Bobby Joe nodded. "The vertical measurements are all screwed up, but I can get the X-Y."

The next spot of cover was a curving U-shaped fencelike barrier formed by a series of vertical dumbbell-shaped uprights. From there, the group worked their way over the strange terrain, moving from one structure to another as the equipment housings grew more numerous.

Almost thirty minutes later, they reached a structure that reminded Abby of an oversized doghouse. The six of them huddled inside.

"All right," Matt said. "I think from here on we can risk going a little faster, and moving in a group."

"We're really up against spiders?" Richard asked suddenly.

"Yes. Abby, you want to let people take a look at the video you took? It's probably for the best that anyone who's going to be shocked get it over with here in private instead of the next time we see them up close."

Minutes later, Bobby Joe said, "They're not exactly like Earth spiders. Real arachnids that look like this have all eight legs attached to the forward segment. And these guys—'Archies' is easier to say than 'arachnid'—their mouths are different."

"I assume the 'hands' are different, too," Richard said.

Julie said, "I'm glad they look like spiders. I'd like this even less if they turned out to look like cuddly bunnies or something."

Abby didn't say anything, but she realized she actually felt the opposite way. If appearances were part of the equation, she wished their captors *were* cuddly and cute, making it as difficult as possible for anyone in the group to pull the trigger or light the fuse or do whatever one did. They had to be absolutely certain they were doing the right thing.

Stuart Lund walked up Broadway feeling agitated. There had to be a way he could force the mayor to call back the expedition team.

The wide street stretched almost twenty blocks ahead of him before the curve near Times Square hid it from view. Occasionally Stuart's gaze would drift up the lengths of the tall buildings ahead, and then he'd notice the overhead dome, and then he'd get even more agitated. God had called on Stuart, and here he was, apparently ineffectual.

His congregation understood. And as much as he was saddened by the death of the man sorting the mayor's mail, he took pride in the fact that they had sent her a message. For the mayor to believe that her view was the only correct interpretation of the situation was just maddening. How could she be so blind that she could think she understood the one true way?

There had to be a way to convince her, a way to show her the mail-room incident was a real expression of the will of the people—thousands of people, millions of people.

Stuart walked for blocks lost in thought. Occasionally he'd almost bump into someone and then pay more attention for a few seconds. Quite a few people were on the street, but the pace was decidedly slower than on Earth. Many of these people must have been out for a walk or just people-watching. They didn't move with the same fervor they had possessed when they had been on the way to work, to see a Broadway show . . . to have a life.

Stuart reached 33rd Street and crossed against the light.

Normally he was one of the few people who waited on the corner when the traffic was clear, but when traffic was almost nonexistent he felt no harm was done.

He neared 34th Street and saw that the recently reopened Macy's was closed. The fact made perfect sense, but it was still unsettling. Macy's of all places.

Stuart started to cross 34th Street against the light. When he was halfway across the street, he took another look both ways for traffic. A second later he stood motionless in the middle of the street, looking up and to his right. There on the south side of 34th Street was the Empire State Building, reaching, it seemed, all the way to the dome above. Stuart stood mesmerized, his thoughts racing.

Stuart still remembered his first visit to Manhattan. His parents had brought him, and on their first day they went to the top of the Empire State Building. The building had seemed to Stuart to *be* New York. It was somehow a symbol of the whole skyscraper island for him. He never thought of New York as the Empire State, but whenever he thought about the Empire State Building, he was instantly reminded of the congregation of tall buildings and midtown Manhattan and pretzel vendors and seeing the Statue of Liberty in the distance and seeing the wake of the Staten Island ferry. The Empire State Building *was* New York.

Seconds later Stuart realized he was standing in the middle of 34th Street as people passed him on either side.

Suddenly he knew he had to go to the top. He turned and walked back to the curb, then down 34th Street toward the Empire State Building. From here he couldn't tell if any people were on the observation decks. He didn't know if the elevators were running. But he had to go. He had an idea.

Abby gave Matt a head start and followed. Behind her came Bobby Joe.

She felt filthy, sweaty. The men were probably even filthier by now, and they all looked like unshaven bums. Except Matt. He, too, was unshaven and ragged, but somehow he didn't look like a bum. Bobby Joe's combination of bald skull and facial hair made him look vaguely as if someone had twisted his head upside down.

She desperately wished for sleep. They'd taken a short break that seemed no longer than ten minutes, and then it was over.

They scurried across the floor from one piece of cover to the next. In the distance ahead was the tall red cylinder stretching all the way to the ceiling. About midway between it and where they were was a large collection of equipment cabinets and big machinery of unknown purpose.

They skirted a small field that looked like a graveyard with metal posts instead of tombstones. As Abby forced her body to keep up with the long, slow strides, she thought again about how tired she was. And if she was this tired, the odds were that Bobby Joe and Julie were even more tired. They weren't complaining, though, and neither would she.

After almost a half-hour they reached a structure with a roof so low even Abby had to duck. Poles at each of the four corners supported the thin roof, and stubby walls on two sides rose about a meter off the ground. It vaguely resembled a carport, but Abby had no clue as to what it was really for.

The group took cover as Matt and Rudy scanned the horizon. Abby leaned back against the low wall and stretched her legs. Julie sat nearby, rubbing her ankles and calves.

Julie and Bobby Joe groaned when a few minutes later Matt informed the group it was time to move again, but they didn't actually object. Within minutes of being on the run, they encountered another monorail track, this one running crosswise between the radial tracks.

They crossed the track and kept going, the large collection of structures growing steadily closer. The dark shapes projecting above the horizon grew higher and more numerous, giving Abby the feeling she was approaching a huge oil refinery.

Their path cut through the center of the deserted tract of equipment, and Matt slowed the pace. They passed under arches and through cutouts in the buildings. On Abby's left was a large transparent tube that came through the floor and curved to meet the side of a huge octagonal cabinet. Sludge resembling rocky road ice cream moved slowly through the tube, upward and into the cabinet.

Five minutes later Matt signaled for the group to slow down. Ahead was something that at first looked like a pond, but as they approached more closely Abby could see it was a window built into the floor, an observation port through which they could see the world below. She could see the city of cones beneath its dome far below, miniaturized by being seen from several times the height of the tallest cone, an airplane-window view rather than a bird's-eye picture.

The transparent port was at least ten meters across, surrounded by a raised lip. Suspended over the observation port were strange instruments aimed down through the port, some of them mounted on articulated supports like dentists' drills, others running on sets of tracks like small construction cranes. Capping the whole array of equipment was a suspended and inverted transparent bowl. The lip of the bowl extended several meters out from the perimeter of the observation port, but hung a couple of meters in the air, allowing access to the port.

Matt cautioned the team to stay clear of the edge of the observation port as they navigated around it. A moment later, Abby got a glimpse of Manhattan far in the distance toward the center of the octagonal area below.

Matt must have seen it, too, because he stopped and held up his new walkie-talkie and spread the silvery antenna into a flashbulb reflector. "Manhattan base, this is Rover."

Seconds later, a female voice said, "This is Manhattan base. How are you?"

"We're all right. We should be able to take action soon." Matt explained what they'd found after cutting through the wall.

"Well, you'd better move fast. The streets are full of protesters not too happy with the plan. They're marching toward Gracie Mansion, and they're busting up cars all along the way. Some preacher's got them stirred up. Says we're on the way to heaven and you guys are just going to blow it up."

"We're maybe a kilometer or two higher than you are, and from here I've got to say this doesn't look like my idea of heaven." Matt released the *talk* switch and suddenly motioned Bobby Joe to come closer.

"Can we transmit some of Julie's video down there? Seeing actual pictures of the Archies and this level might slow down the protests."

"Okay. Tell them to get set to receive some video at ten percent of normal speed."

Matt continued the walkie-talkie conversation as Bobby Joe asked Abby and Julie if he could use their minivids for a few minutes. Abby and Julie cued their recorders to the start of what they thought would be the best sections.

Bobby Joe opened a small compartment on the side of Matt's walkie-talkie and uncoiled a small cable from inside. The plug on the end of the cable went into the side of a minivid. He fingered the minivid controls, then said to Matt, "All right. It's sending. The walkie-talkie was optimized for a lower bandwidth than video, so we can't transmit at normal speed, but they should be getting it."

Abby moved so she could get a clearer view through the observation window. Standing near the lip of the port was a little like standing near the edge of a tall cliff. Distance turned one of the domed cities below into a cake under glass. Julie quietly gave her report along with the video.

Matt scanned the horizon a couple of times during the time the minivids were connected. Finally he told Bobby Joe to stop. "Manhattan base, we'll check in again if we get a chance."

"Roger, Rover."

"Let's get out of here," Matt said as he folded up the reflector antenna. "We've been out in the open too long."

The group continued toward the large red cylinder in the distance. They had been angling through the equipment-littered landscape for no more then ten minutes when Matt unexpectedly fell slowly forward and scrambled almost flat on the ground. He gave an urgent hand signal to take cover. He got as close as he could to a narrow, low wall. As Abby and the others scrambled into position behind the same structure, she got a glimpse of a distant monorail car approaching, running more or less parallel to the wall they were hiding behind.

Abby quietly took her pistol from the holster. The Glock 17 felt slightly oily, and she blamed that on sweat. The semi-automatic was loaded with a seventeen-round magazine containing nine-millimeter bullets. The pistol was light to begin with; in the low gravity it felt like a toy gun in her hand.

Abby had thought the sound of a gun being fired was one of the scariest sounds in the world. Now she was aware of a sound that chilled her even more—the soft *click click* of a gun being cocked.

Over her heartbeat, Abby could hear a soft *whoosh* of air grow louder as the monorail car came closer. She didn't breathe again until she was sure the sound was starting to grow softer. It was only then that she let herself think about how good it felt to lie down for a couple of minutes.

Matt waited several minutes before he cautiously raised his head over the wall. "They're gone. We'd better keep moving."

The group stayed closer together as they threaded their way through what resembled a grove of telephone poles, hundreds of shiny blue poles that reached halfway to the ceiling, spaced far enough apart that an obstacle course driver could have driven a compact car between them.

Rudy said, "I just had a thought. With all the monorails running either radially or on transverse runs from radial to radial, you know what it would look like from the air?"

"A giant spiderweb," Abby said.

"And," Bobby Joe said, "it probably won't be long before we're heading straight for the center."

Julie said, "To think that I could have gone on vacation about a week before this all started. I was considering going out to Colorado with a friend."

"Yeah, but then you might be roasting more than just wienies right now," Bobby Joe said.

Benny Kellermund was leaving the warehouse church with the rest of the congregation after one of the two daily services.

The preacher was at the main door, and he seemed to be looking for Benny, because he gave a big sigh when he caught Benny's attention.

"I need to talk to you," Stuart Lund said.

"Sure, okay," said Benny.

"It concerns your friend, too. Could you stop by in about an hour?"

"Yeah, I guess we could do that."

"Thanks *very* much. I think I've got an idea that will interest you."

"This is encouraging," Richard said. "They wouldn't build something this sturdy if all it did was recycle air for one of the prisons below."

Abby suspected he was right. The closer they got to the red cylinder, the more obvious it was that the massive structure was a product of heavy-duty engineering. Here the floor, which had supported the numerous pieces of large equipment they had already passed, was braced.

"I'm beginning to think you're right," Rudy said. "This really does look more like something designed for propulsion than anything we've seen so far."

The group moved closer, picking their way through stuff that a giant might have strewn around while working on some enormous automobile. Monstrous valves, levers that didn't move but looked as if they were ready to do so at any moment, glowing cubes that pulsated with greenish light, none of it made the slightest sense to Abby. She continued taking video whenever she saw markings on equipment or noticed anything that cried out for being immortalized on video. On the way, she put in a fresh battery.

The red cylinder seemed like a huge storage tank at an oil refinery, except for one thing. Small doors were scattered over the surface of the cylinder. Ladders led to many of the doors, ladders unlike the ones Abby was used to. These ladders were more like pairs of back-to-back ladders, probably designed so the Archies could use one set of legs on each side.

At four locations Abby could see gantrylike structures rising next to the base and meeting the cylinder wall at a door.

Finally they squatted under a T-shaped structure not twenty meters from the base of the cylinder. Matt looked at Richard and said, "Are you ready to put some explosives in place?"

Abby cleared her throat deliberately. "I'm nervous about

this. Suppose this isn't really the propulsion system? I still can't make much sense of the symbols I've seen."

"It's a calculated risk," said Matt.

"Even if it is the propulsion system," Julie said. "That's still no guarantee that blowing it to pieces will help us."

"Again, it's a calculated risk. We could be doing the wrong thing, but this is one of those times that doing nothing is doing the worst thing." Matt looked at Abby and back at Julie. He turned to Richard. "Get started."

"Sure," said Richard. "The whole works?"

"Whatever's appropriate, but I don't want to use it all yet. And I want it on a long timer, say ten hours. I want to have time to be a long way from here, and I want time to change our minds if we learn more during those hours. This definitely *feels* like propulsion to me, but I understand the possibility that it could be some vital piece of life support for the entire ship."

"There's another reason for making sure we disable the ship's propulsion," Rudy said.

"And that is?"

"It'll make it that much tougher for them to take us somewhere harder to escape from, and farther from home."

Matt nodded. "Makes sense." To Abby and Julie he said, "I hope you're satisfied with this, but we're not a democracy right now." He scanned the area ahead and said, "All right. Let's go."

They moved quickly to the octagonal door at the base of the cylinder. It opened smoothly. Matt stepped through, and the team followed. Abby stepped through, very happy to see handles on the inside of the door, too.

Abby looked up and had to catch her breath. Several years ago, she'd been on a tour at Canaveral and had seen how large the thrusters were. What was contained in the cylinder didn't actually look like a thruster, but the enormous funnel reminded her of one. The funnel sat with its narrow end almost touching the floor, the large end not far from the ceiling. Gigantic coils wound around the underside of the funnel. The individual coils must have had about the same diameter as a manhole cover.

Lights ringed the cylinder wall in rows about ten meters apart. Here and there inside the huge cylinder, catwalks led from the cylinder walls to work areas near what looked like huge gray barnacles on the coils.

Richard pointed toward one of the barnacles nearest the ground. A double ladder led to a small platform just under it.

Richard took Rudy's backpack and his own and went up the ladder. From the floor below, Abby watched as Richard took out slabs of a puttylike substance and tucked them between coils so they didn't show from the ground.

Abby caught Matt's attention. "Why would the Archies wait before they destroy the planet?"

"I really don't know. Maybe it's a function of how interesting the planet itself is. Maybe they save more video images if it's something unlike what they've seen before."

Rudy said, "Could be lots of reasons, probably most of which we wouldn't even understand. Maybe sometimes they have to charge up their weapons from a nearby sun, and that takes a while."

"All done," Richard said as he climbed down.

"Good. Let's get out of here," said Matt.

Matt pushed the door open slowly. Abby was sure they'd see a huge spider blocking the entire doorway, and despite her rational awareness that these aliens had nothing in common with Earth spiders other than an unusual similarity in appearance, she suddenly thought about spiders that ate their mates.

Outside the door the way was clear. Matt stepped through and the rest of the party followed.

They didn't stop moving until almost an hour later when they took cover in a small clearing surrounded by rectangular equipment cabinets about a meter high.

"God, I'm tired," said Bobby Joe the instant he sat down.

Abby was tired, too, more tired than she'd been in ages. Her eyes hurt, her legs hurt, her shoulders hurt.

"Rest well," Matt said. "We're moving on in ten minutes."

Abby leaned back against one of the cabinets and closed her eyes. She imagined she was back in her apartment in bed, in the most comfortable bed in the world.

She turned on her right side and saw the morning sunshine streaming through the window. She turned to her left and saw

Matt lying next to her. Matt's eyes opened suddenly and he said, "We've got to go."

"What?"

"We've got to go," Matt said again.

Abby felt a hand gently nudging her shoulder. She opened her eyes and saw Matt kneeling beside her. He was dressed in his multi-pocketed expedition shirt. Above his head was the ceiling of the Archies' ship. Abby blinked.

"All right," she said. "I'm awake."

Moments later the team resumed the trek. Ahead in the distance was the center of the web, where walls from floor to ceiling concealed what lay inside. The horizon seemed even more cluttered than before with equipment cabinets and machines of unknown purpose.

Hours dragged on until Abby no longer cared whether they were spotted, no longer feared capture, as long as it would afford her the chance to sleep or die. Matt had obviously been hesitant to break out the stimulants, but a little earlier everyone on the team had popped a couple of pills. They seemed to make almost no difference.

They grew closer to the walled area in the center of the ship. And then, when they had traveled so far that the wall was only another several hundred meters away, she got her second or third or fourth wind. Reality still had a mildly dreamlike quality to it, but she felt more energy, more aware of her surroundings.

A series of doors was set along the bottom of the wall. At each door, a monorail track stretched out toward the perimeter of the huge floor they were on. Next to the nearest monorail door was a smaller octagonal door, possibly intended for foot traffic or emergencies.

Matt signaled them to stop and take cover. Seconds later, Abby watched through a crack between two cabinets as a monorail car with one Archie aboard approached a door farther down the side of the wall. About ten seconds before the monorail reached the door, the large door swung open silently. The monorail car sped through without slowing, and the door swung closed again as soon as the car had vanished.

From that point on, everyone carried their pistols in their hands instead of in their holsters.

The group snaked forward, threading between more equipment cabinets and strange structures, until they all crouched not thirty meters from a monorail door and the smaller door next to it.

"I suppose we need to see what's on the other side of the wall?" said Rudy. Rudy volunteered to go check. He took off his pack and set it on the floor. He moved forward, pistol ready.

Rudy scanned the area before him briefly, and then he ran, faster than Abby had expected. Just a few seconds later, he was at the door. He gripped the handles and just as he was about to pull the door open, the larger double doors over the monorail track began to open. Rudy flung himself sideways, getting as close to the base of the monorail track as he could, and seconds later a monorail car sped outward, occupied by two Archies.

Abby held her breath, afraid the Archies would see Rudy, but the car kept going without slowing down and coming back. The door on Rudy's side swung closed over his head. Rudy stayed motionless where he was for a full minute before he got back up and moved to the smaller door. He put his pistol in his belt and twisted the handles. As soon as the door pulled forward a little, Rudy retrieved his pistol.

He pulled the door open a little more and peered through the gap. Finally he pulled it open farther and leaned inside. Seconds later he turned toward the rest of the team and gave a *come on* sign.

"Let's go. *Fast!*" said Matt.

The team moved faster than they had in hours. Less than a half-minute later, they were all through the door and it was closed behind them.

Abby suddenly felt heavier as she ran behind Matt and they moved farther into the enclosure. The gravity must be higher in this section somehow. Another wall, perhaps a kilometer away in the distance ahead, formed part of what must have been a still smaller octagonal enclosed area. Between the inner wall and the outer wall lay a forest of large enclosed kiosks. Through the maze of kiosks Abby could see short sections of monorail tracks continuing in toward the center of the complex.

The kiosks were octagonal, about two meters on a side and about three meters tall. Their placement seemed to be random.

Abby and the others followed Matt until they were hidden from the nearby monorail track by two or three kiosks.

The kiosks were almost all a uniform gray, except for a few nearest the monorail track, each of which had a dark band around the base. Matt approached one of the kiosks. Abby saw that it seemed to have an entry corridor rather than a door. A little like park restrooms, the kiosk was a solid enclosure with an extra short wall that came directly out from the wall, then bent at an octagonal-corner angle and continued for a couple of meters. Apparently, one could walk right inside, but the interior couldn't be seen from outside.

Matt moved closer to the kiosk with a dark band around the base. He slowly entered the short corridor and peeked around the corner into the interior. Just as softly, but obviously more tense, now, Matt backed up and motioned the team to get away.

The team moved quickly and quietly past several more kiosks, one with a band around the base.

Matt cautiously entered the corridor around another one of the kiosks, this one a plain one. Just about the same time that Matt peeked around the edge of the interior doorway and motioned the rest of the team to come ahead and join him, a dark band appeared around the base of the kiosk.

Abby followed him. Inside the unoccupied kiosk was an octagonal room about three meters across. Against one wall was what was probably a bed. Set into the opposite wall was an unfamiliar-looking console. The ceiling glowed a soft blue.

"What did you see back there?" asked Rudy softly.

Matt kept his voice very low, too. "A sleeping Archie. These must be quarters."

Abby said, "I think you're right. And I think we must have just turned on the *no vacancy* sign."

13

TRAPPED LIKE BUGS

"YOU WANT TO blow up the Empire State Building?" repeated Lucky Stiles.

Benny, Lucky, and the preacher were in the upstairs office at the warehouse. Benny was having as much trouble shifting gears as Lucky was.

Stuart Lund had a glow to his eyes Benny hadn't seen before. This guy was *excited.*

"No, no, no," said the preacher. "I don't really want to blow it up."

"But you want I should put a bunch of explosives up there and rig them to go off?" asked Lucky.

"Yes. But as a *threat.* Not that we'd actually do it."

Benny sat silently, just observing Lucky and the preacher.

"I don't understand," said Lucky. "I either do something or I don't do something. You're talking about not doing something, or you're talking about doing something?"

"I'm talking about threatening to blow up the building if the mayor doesn't cancel the expedition."

"Okay. So what if she doesn't?"

"But she will. She won't want the Empire State Building blown up. She'll *have* to realize that if people feel so strongly about stopping the expedition, that it should be stopped. She'll call them back."

"I mean," Lucky said, "what if she doesn't?"

The preacher looked as if this was a brand new idea to him. "But I'm telling you, she will."

"Let's say I'm not convinced. Actually, I kinda like the idea.

But I don't understand. You say if she doesn't cancel, you'll do this. That means you gotta be ready to do it."

"Right. Exactly. We'd be ready to do it. We just wouldn't need to actually pull the switch."

"But if she says no, then I can pull the switch, right?"

"Er—" The preacher was quiet.

"I mean, if we're not prepared to follow through with the threat, there *is* no threat, am I right?"

"I see what you're saying," the preacher said slowly. "It's just that we won't need to follow through because the mayor will give in."

"Okay, okay," Benny said suddenly. "I think I can straighten this out. Lucky, you can pull the switch if the mayor says no. The preacher says she won't say no, so as long as the preacher is right, you don't pull the switch. If the preacher is wrong, which he says he isn't, then you can pull the switch. But the preacher says that won't happen."

Lucky scratched his head. "Thanks, I think."

The preacher sat there saying nothing, like some robot given unclear directions.

"But there's still a problem," Lucky said.

"And what's that?" asked the preacher.

"There aren't enough explosives in the world—or at least here—to do the job."

The preacher frowned. "I thought you did the job with the water in the Battery Tunnel with explosives."

Lucky nodded. "Yeah, but this is different. We're talking about a *huge* building. I mean, in World War II, a *bomber* flew right into the side of the building. Somewhere near the top, too. The bomber isn't there anymore. The building is. What does that tell you?"

"Gee," the preacher said. "I hadn't thought about it. But I do remember that story." He leaned back in his chair and looked depressed. "So this whole conversation's been for nothing?"

"Depends. I can do a lot of damage. With some luck, I might even be able to blow off the top section, along with the antenna tower. If that thing came crashing down, it'd do a lot of damage.

And that would get the mayor's attention. 'Course, if I never pull the switch, none of this matters anyway."

"Well, it does matter. If the mayor doesn't believe the threat is real, then she won't act."

"Like I say, I can do a lot of damage. I could put stuff close enough to the observation towers that they'd be gone, or they'd be closed forever. And every time anyone looked at the skyline, they'd see what a dumb move the mayor made."

The preacher brightened at that. "Maybe this will work. So you'd have to have some kind of remote control."

"That's for sure. They haven't made a fuse long enough for me to get out of the building in time. Plus which, we don't want it going off automatically. I've got to be in control, so when the mayor says okay I don't push the button."

"And you could rig it so that anyone tampering with the explosives would set them off?"

"Piece of cake."

The preacher leaned forward in his chair and looked into space for a minute. "I think it will work. Will you do it?"

Lucky hesitated. He looked at Benny. "What do you think?"

"If that expedition keeps going, they're going to stir up a hornet's nest. We only have to push the button if the mayor doesn't listen to reason. The preacher says she will. And if she doesn't, it's her fault. We got nothing to lose."

"I don't know. We're talking about a lot of trips to the top with backpacks. You willing to help?"

"Sure. The preacher says the elevators are still going."

Finally Lucky said, "What the hell. At least we don't have to worry about rats and alligators this time."

"Rise and shine, Bobby Joe."

At first Bobby Joe's eyes felt as if they were glued shut. A hand jogged his shoulder, but it took him several seconds to get past squinting in the light. Matt Sheehan knelt next to where Bobby Joe had fallen asleep on the floor of the kiosk.

"You've had your two hours. That's all we can afford."

"Oh, God." Bobby Joe pulled himself upright and leaned back against the wall. If he had been trained in anatomy, he probably could have identified by name the one or two muscles that weren't sore and the one or two joints that weren't stiff. Matt helped him up.

Richard, Julie, and Abby still slept on the floor. Rudy stood guard by the door. Light-headed from sleep deprivation and low gravity, Bobby Joe moved to the wall and ran his finger along the desktop that supported what had to be a computer and communications console, if the Archies worshiped the same technology god.

Matt's voice came from over Bobby Joe's shoulder. "I think it's time you earned your keep. You think you can figure out how to use the system?"

"Too early to tell. If our being here was one of the things they had in mind when they designed the system, I'd have better luck teaching Richard to be a public speaker. If their race is one hundred percent honest and respectful of property rights and 'need to know,' then I've got an outside chance." Bobby Joe's generation had begun by manually programming VCRs for their parents, so he had more faith in his abilities than he let on.

"I can't expect miracles. Just do your best. I suppose you and Abby will need to work together, so she can try to interpret while you do your computer stuff. Wake her up as soon as you think there's something for her to start on."

Bobby Joe ran his fingers over his bald scalp. "Will do."

The first puzzle was how to sit down. The Archies might just stand when they used the computer, but then again maybe they didn't. Bobby Joe knelt and looked closely at the wall below the console. If he were designing living quarters meant to be as space efficient as possible, he'd go for built-in furniture that folded out of the walls. Maybe the Archies did, too. They were a lot different from humans in appearance, and perhaps in thought, but both humans and Archies had to function with the same rules of space and time. If the Archies wanted to fit ten units of materials in a five-unit kiosk, they had to live with some of the same constraints humans would have.

The two square meters of wall surface under the desk showed no obvious blemishes, deformations, or knobs. Bobby Joe pushed on a series of points anyway, just in case human color vision didn't pick up everything the Archies' eyes could see. No results.

Bobby Joe stood up, wondering if perhaps some action at the console would activate a device that would move a chair into place. He didn't want to touch the console yet, though. When he found out how to turn it on, for all he knew he might start transmitting video to a central location. *That* should get a reaction from the Archies.

Besides that, a console switch would imply some powered, mechanized method of getting a chair in place. Again, if he were designing a setup like this, he wouldn't want to rely on motors and actuators when a simpler system would be cheaper and more reliable.

Kneeling again, he inspected the two walls adjacent to the console. Nothing obvious there, either. Crap.

Matt told Rudy it was time to trade places. Matt took over the guard position, and Rudy lay down on the floor to sleep. The place looked like Bobby Joe had imagined summer camp to be, only more octagonal. And some of the campers had new beards.

Bobby Joe stood up again, puzzled. Maybe the Archies did just stand while they used the console. He ticked off possibilities on his fingers and stopped abruptly when he hit "ceiling."

The kiosk roofs were peaked, reaching a point about a meter above the seam where the roof met the wall. But the ceiling was flat. A close examination of the ceiling showed a set of eight small squares forming a ring about a meter wide. Bobby Joe reached for the square set in the pie slice above the console. He couldn't reach it.

Bobby Joe jumped and pushed the square. It clicked. Slowly in the light gravity, the ceiling pie slice began to pivot, the point in the center swinging down into the room, bending at a hinge along the edge where the ceiling met the wall.

As the ceiling segment swung down, a segmented sheet above it unfolded like Japanese origami or whatever they called that stuff when you fold a piece of paper into some 3-D shape. Finally eight segments touched the floor. Bobby Joe felt an inordinate amount of pride in the accomplishment, despite the fact that the chair didn't look like it would be very comfortable for a human. The "chair" was more like a short ladder with only two wide steps. Apparently an Archie would rest on it with the rear body segment supported by the lower step, the higher step supporting the forward segment closer to the console.

Bobby Joe put some weight on the bottom step. The structure stretched a bit, but held. Bobby Joe wondered how heavy humans were compared to the Archies. Finally he sat on the rear shelf and leaned forward on the upper shelf. His posture was a little like that of someone sitting backward on a chair and leaning forward to rest on the chair back. The position was slightly more comfortable than standing.

He glanced back at Matt, who gave him a thumbs-up. Bobby Joe felt a small surge of pride in pleasing him. As he averted his gaze, he noticed another faint square set into the floor.

Bobby Joe knelt beside the chair and fingered the square on the floor. Finally he pressed his thumb against the square and it sank into the surface. As it did, a larger octagonal outline appeared next to the square hole. Gingerly, he pushed the octagon sideways and revealed a similarly shaped dark opening. He looked up at Matt and said, "Maybe this is how they get rid of trash."

Matt nodded and looked impressed. Bobby Joe slid the cover back into place and stood up. Now for the hard part—figuring out the console.

On the surface of a trapezoidal shelf about a half-meter deep was an octagon split into eight pie wedges. In front of it was a much smaller octagon, about the size of a dollar.

On the wall above the shelf was a much larger octagon. To the left and to the right of the octagon were much smaller octagons, about the size of a thumbnail. The one on the right had a glassy sheen to it, and the one on the left was perforated with a few hundred tiny holes. Bobby Joe felt good to have a starting point. The odds suggested that the two small octagons were a camera lens and a microphone.

Bobby Joe dug through his backpack and found some tape. He tore off two short sections and applied the pieces to the two small octagons. If he accidentally turned on console communications, he didn't want a bunch of Archies showing up to find out why one of their kiosks was infested with apes.

Nothing on the desktop looked like an on-off switch. Bobby Joe touched the small octagon at the front of the desktop. Instantly the large octagon on the wall lit, displaying eight pie wedges, each with an image.

Bobby Joe stared at the eight images. They could have been icons, or they could have been actual text in the Archies' language. Bobby Joe looked at Matt and said, "I think it's time I woke Abby."

"Okay."

A couple of minutes later, Abby and Bobby Joe stood on opposite sides of the chair and looked at the screen. Abby's minivid optics module sat on the chair, angled so it could record whatever images they summoned on the console.

The images themselves surprised Bobby Joe by being of lower quality than he'd guessed was likely. They were granular, the individual pixels easily discernible. In addition, they flickered, like TV screens shown on old films, and the flickering was even worse when he looked at the screen from the corner of his eye instead of straight at it.

Abby rubbed her eyes and said, "This may tell us something about their eyes. They may not see as well as we do, and their persistence of vision may be longer than ours."

"So this might look just fine to them?"

"It's possible. This ship wouldn't have been cheap to build. I'd bet they could have higher resolution if they wanted it. And it could be they don't see in stereo since the display is flat. Having only the one eye-stalk suggests that they have either no stereoscopic vision, or stereoscopic with fairly limited depth perception since the separate views would have to be pretty close together."

"Well, it may be okay for them, but I bet it'll give me a headache in an hour."

"Mmm," Abby said.

"Any ideas so far?"

Abby pointed to the pie wedge on the left. "That image there reminds me of a side-view silhouette of their mouths. It looks a little like a spider's mouth, but with no mandibles."

"Yeah, it does. So maybe that indicates communication, speech?"

"Could be."

"If that's true, we don't want to activate that function."

"How would we if we wanted to?" asked Abby. "Touch the corresponding wedge on this control panel?"

"That's my first guess, but I didn't want to try anything like that without a clue as to what it might be turning on. Showing a mouth might not mean speech or communication, and I didn't want to be ordering a pizza."

"Don't talk about real food, all right? I'm getting so very tired of green pellets."

"Sorry about that." Bobby Joe hesitated. "Do spiders have good vision?"

"I don't know, but that's probably just as well. If we think of the Archies as just big spiders, I think we're bound to make mistakes. As much as possible, we should focus on what we can learn about the Archies and extrapolate from there. For instance, we shouldn't expect they lay eggs unless we get some direct evidence for that assumption."

"Okay. So what next?"

"I've got several video images stored. Language or symbols from things like the elevator door and several machines. I need to create a small catalog of them. I want to use more space than a computer screen." Abby looked at Matt. "Any problem with writing on the wall? It'll make it tougher to cover our tracks."

"Go ahead. It won't be long before that's less important."

Abby and Bobby Joe went to work, with Abby locating images and Bobby Joe transcribing them on the wall, along with a brief note about where they came from. When they finished, a dozen images decorated the wall next to the console.

To Bobby Joe several of the images looked more like Rorschach ink blots than characters. Abby's image collection included the sign on the dome over Manhattan, and images from the emergency exit door, the elevator, the monorail car, the location Richard had planted explosives, and several other unidentified equipment cabinets. Now that they were all together on the wall, Bobby Joe could see a similarity in most of the images except for the sign on the dome. On the right-hand side of all the other images was a distorted octagon and a square with a vertical line at its center.

Abby must have been looking at the same thing, but she was ahead of Bobby Joe. She pointed to the octagon and square from the message on the emergency door. "You know what? I'm beginning to think these symbols on the end are location references. This octagon is almost whole. But look at the ones from places farther inside. They're smooshed in."

"That's a technical term, right?"

"Right. The one from near the observation port is smooshed in maybe ten percent. The one from what you guys guessed was part of the propulsion system is smooshed farther in, and the actual location is physically closer to the center of the ship. The octagon we found on the elevator is almost whole. I think the smooshing says where you are, what direction from the center of the ship, and how far out from the center. And the thin line in these squares shows elevation in the ship. Everything on this level looks the same, but the one from the emergency door says we were closer to the middle of the ship."

Bobby Joe scanned the images, looking for any inconsistency that could disprove the hypothesis. He didn't find one. "So are you saying the Archies have a pictographic language?"

"I'm betting they don't. If their history is something like ours, separate groups developed their own languages, and pictographs are an easy solution that allows a group of people who don't all use the same language to quickly understand the message. Even if they do all use the same language now, pictographs are still convenient shorthand."

"So all we need to do is figure out what these other seven pictures mean? How do we do that?"

"That's the first step. And all I can say for now is keep your mind as open as you can, and be prepared for the possibility that we just won't be able to decipher everything. Think about the *I Love New York* bumper sticker with the heart symbol for the word 'love' and what the Archies would need to know to understand it. The heart is an internal organ, so they're not going to know what it looks like without a dissection or a scan. Then they would need to know that our stylized shape correlates to the heart, and they'd need to know the historical basis for believing the heart is the source of emotion. Plus they'd need to know that in that context, red is good. The symbol is actually a ideogram, not a pictograph."

"They'd never figure that out without a lot of help. So you're saying we're going to have that tough a time, too?"

"With some of the figures, maybe. Then again, we might get lucky and find the equivalent of a side view of a stairway used to show where the stairs are. Some pictographs should simply be a small picture of what they represent."

"So we're back to making guesses as to what these things represent?"

"Yes."

Bobby Joe and Abby stared at the eight pictographs. Finally Bobby Joe said, "The one that looks like a 3-D octagon. Could that be the ship we're on?"

"Could be," Abby said slowly. "But they use octagons so frequently it could be other things, too." She looked at the picture of the message on the dome ceiling. "The first symbol in the message is the same one."

Bobby Joe looked back at the symbols on the screen. "That one on the right looks a lot like a dome."

"Yeah, it does. How about if we try it?"

Bobby Joe turned to Matt. "Any problem if we try out some of the console functions?"

Matt shook his head. "Give it a shot."

Benny Kellermund and Lucky Stiles entered the Empire State Building from 34th Street. Benny felt instantly dwarfed in the two-story passage surrounding the banks of elevators. He also felt a sharp twinge of guilt. This grand old building was coming up on a hundred years old.

The building was much quieter than he'd seen it in the past. Apparently the bulk of the normal visitors were from out of town. Now the supply of out-of-towners was pretty limited. A large sign said no admission fee was being charged and for people to use the elevators whenever they wanted.

Benny walked with Lucky, trying to look casual. Both men wore maintenance clothes. Lucky had explained that would be their best camouflage, and Benny had seen the wisdom. They both also wore bulky backpacks. They had talked about suitcases and cardboard boxes and other options and finally settled on this plan.

No one seemed to be paying them any attention as they passed elevators meant for people who worked in the bottom two-thirds of the building and reached the express elevators that would reach all the way to the eightieth floor. For the first time in Benny's memory, an elevator was waiting for them. They got in alone, and Lucky pressed the button for eighty.

"Seems slow," Lucky said as they began to rise.

"It's the low gravity," Benny said.

"I knew that," Lucky said.

Benny smiled, but he didn't say anything.

"What?" Lucky asked.

"Nothing. Nothing." Benny blanked his expression, but he still felt good about knowing things Lucky didn't. Lucky was good with explosives, but he wasn't smarter than Benny.

Benny's ears popped only once on the way to the top. He was sure they had popped two or three times on the way up in the past. He was suddenly sure it was the result of the lighter gravity, but he wasn't exactly sure why.

The doors opened on the eightieth floor. Benny and Lucky moved down the hall to the pair of elevators that would take them to the eighty-sixth floor. On previous trips on windy days, Benny had been able to feel the building shudder slightly with the gusts. Today the building hummed with air-conditioner noise and the vibrations of elevators and other machinery, but the floor felt rock solid under his feet.

One of the elevators to the eighty-sixth floor was ready for them when they reached the door, and going these six floors seemed to take half the time it had taken them to rise the first eighty floors.

On the eighty-sixth floor, Lucky was all for going directly to the elevator that led to the 102nd floor, but Benny convinced him they should go out on the observation deck first. "After all, it might be a long time before anyone's allowed up here again, if you know what I mean."

They went out to the open-air observation deck, and the view took Benny's breath away for an instant. The air inside the dome was totally clear. Beyond the security barrier, the World Trade

Center towers looked so close they could have been only twenty blocks away. Benny looked up at the remaining dozen or so floors rising from the center of the observation deck. The antenna tower on top of the domed building, just above the higher enclosed observation deck, rose even taller, so high that it seemed to almost touch the transparent dome overhead.

Benny's surge of pride in Manhattan and the sense of familiarity generated by his previous trips to this point were displaced by an emotion he refused to identify as fear. Those domes outside: from here Benny had the best view he'd ever had of those outside domes, and he felt cold. Just past the tip of the Chrysler Building with its curves and points was an incredibly tall and thin dome that for no obvious reason reminded Benny of the ant farm his aunt Martha had given him when he was five or six. He had a sudden image of the way the ant farm had eventually looked in the trash, the glass cracked, the ants all dead.

Benny got as close as he could to the edge and looked down on the closest buildings. "You remember those Letterman reruns where he dropped watermelons and stuff off a big building?"

"We should go," said Lucky. "We got things to do."

Benny followed him silently, more nervous than he wanted to admit about whether they should be doing this. He kept telling himself the explosives would never actually be used.

They took stairs up a floor and got on the elevator that would go all the way to the top—the 102nd floor. Lucky pressed the button for the ninetieth floor. Benny was still amazed at not having to wait for elevators.

At the ninetieth floor the men got out on a floor much smaller than the first eighty-six floors. Benny said, "Did you know they built this entire building in a year and a half?"

"Get outta here." Lucky clearly didn't believe him, but Benny was sure he remembered right.

"That's *true.* I wouldn't make that up."

"You couldn't build something like this in ten years. You know how long the Farber Building's been under construction? You can't even get a bridge fixed in a year and a half."

Benny let the subject drop. "Why here?" he asked as he followed Lucky. "Why the ninetieth?"

"Compromise. Much lower, and we wouldn't have a hope of doing any real damage. Much higher and all we'd do is take down the antenna. This should be just about right."

They made a complete circuit of the floor without seeing another person. Finally Lucky tried the knob on a door near the elevator. The door was locked. Lucky set his pack on the floor and knelt next to the door. From his jacket pocket he took a small tool and started playing with the lock.

"What's in there?" Benny asked.

"Shhh."

A half-minute later Lucky had the door open. He found a light switch inside, and the lamp revealed a janitor's closet. He motioned Benny inside, then shut the door. "This is close to the elevator, so it's one good location to blast. Later on we can put stuff near the outside wall, 'cause there'll be support beams running up through the walls."

"You really think you can cut the whole thing off here?"

"I don't know. But they're gonna know they were hit."

Benny nodded. For the next twenty minutes he did what Lucky told him. When they finished, a beige box occupied a corner between the ceiling and two walls. On the box was a large official-looking sign saying AIR QUALITY MONITORING. DO NOT TOUCH.

Behind that sign, which would come off without much effort, was another sign saying HIGH EXPLOSIVE. TAMPER ALARM ACTIVE. DON'T EVEN THINK ABOUT TOUCHING THIS.

Bobby Joe turned back to the console and pressed the octagon wedge corresponding to the dome. The eight images on the screen vanished, replaced by eight more.

"Well, *this* is easier," Abby said.

Bobby Joe agreed. The eight new pictographs were body types. One showed a silhouette of a humanoid, another something like a badger. Others showed a body shape suited for swimming, a generic-looking eight-legged creature, and a many-legged creature.

Abby pressed the wedge associated with the humanoid creature. This time only six of the wedges were occupied, all with variations on the humanoid form, one with a huge head, another that looked very much human. Abby pressed the one that looked human.

The screen changed from its normal eight-wedge octagon. A circular image formed in the center, surrounded by smaller icons on eight trapezoids that showed around the perimeter of the image. The image itself was an overhead shot of Manhattan.

The icons were less meaningful now. Bobby Joe pressed one at random and the view changed to a false-color image. "That could be infrared," Bobby Joe said. The icon corresponding to what he had pressed was now inverted. He pressed the same wedge again, and the icon returned to normal at the same time the central image returned to normal.

Abby pressed an icon that looked like a megaphone, and the central view grew in magnification as long as she kept her hand on the surface.

Bobby Joe tried an icon consisting of four double-headed arrows that formed a snowflake octagon. The image in the center began to move to the side. He moved his finger on the wedge and the direction of motion changed. He moved the image until it was centered on midtown, then pressed the magnification image Abby had used.

The image grew until they could see that Fifth Avenue was crowded with people. What seemed most unusual was the complete absence of steam rising from any below-pavement leaks in the normal heating-steam supply lines. Bobby Joe moved the image until it was centered on Fifth Avenue and kept magnifying it. The image grew until they could see individual people holding signs saying STOP THE EXPEDITION and GOD WILL PROTECT US. They could see only the signs held by people getting a little tired and letting the poles rest on their shoulders. The vertical signs were nothing but narrow slits.

Bobby Joe increased the magnification until he could see a small portion of the pavement when it wasn't obscured by the heads of protesters. A Baby Ruth wrapper grew until it filled the screen. Seconds later the image was large enough that he could read the ingredients, and then someone's blond head filled the screen, dark roots showing along the part.

"How do we back out of this and get to some other information?" Abby asked.

"I'd guess this small octagon." Bobby Joe touched the symbol at the front of the desktop. The image of the blond head vanished and the screen returned to the one showing the several forms of humanoids. Bobby Joe pressed it again until they were back at the original eight icons. "I wonder if escape keys are universal."

"Let's try this one." Bobby Joe touched an icon that looked like an octagon connected by a curved line to an eight-pointed star. The next display showed icons in only two wedges. He picked the one that looked like a dot next to a circle. The next eight symbols were all nearly identical, and he picked the one on the bottom. For another minute or two he kept pressing switches as a series of images flashed on the screen. Abby thought he repeated his course a time or two, but he was hard to keep up with. She had a sudden image of Bobby Joe as a computer vandal, impatiently and furtively breaking into some bank computer system. Finally he slowed down and gave her a summary of what he had learned. "I'm impressed," she said softly, and Bobby Joe beamed.

The center of the screen suddenly filled with a slowly moving video image of a forest, seen from airliner altitude. Abby backed up and picked another image, this one showing an ocean coast dotted with small villages. The next image was one Bobby Joe recognized. Portions of England and France divided by the English Channel moved slowly south.

Abby pushed a wedge and the image began to magnify smoothly. She let it continue until they could see ships bobbing in the English Channel, and traffic on both sides of the Chunnel. "Thank God," Abby said softly. "They haven't started the destruction yet."

"If these are live."

"Right. If they are live, then maybe the Archies are making a complete record of Earth before they destroy it?"

"Could be. But why? So they can show before and after shots to their buddies?"

"Or for posterity."

Matt said from behind them, "Or to show to potential adversaries, to demonstrate their power."

Abby backed out of that section of information, shutting off the image of Earth. "I can't watch this right now." She selected the 3-D octagon and another set of icons appeared.

"Hey," Bobby Joe said, "if they can't see in stereo, why would they have a 3-D icon?"

"Take a look at a ball with one eye closed. You can still see that it doesn't look like a two-dimensional circle."

"Gee, if they only have one ear, they could have saved a mint on hi-fi equipment."

Abby picked another icon, and the center of the screen filled with what looked to be plans for the ship. She skipped around and found a top view of the octagonal floor on which Manhattan lay.

Bobby Joe knew roughly how large the ship was, but seeing the tiny noodle-shaped image in the octagon that formed the sides of the ship still took his breath away.

Abby picked a side view of the ship. According to a blinking dot, they were on the uppermost floor. The ship was divided into the two back-to-back levels containing cities. On each end the view showed a thin floor. The floor they were on looked more cluttered than the floor on the opposite side of the ship. Further in toward the center of this floor were two more concentric octagons.

Another view showed the eight huge cylinders highlighted. A different view of them from the side showed dotted lines extending to a point in space as though the cylinders formed a giant lens.

"It still looks to me like the cylinders are associated with propulsion," Bobby Joe said.

"Good," said Matt. "The timer should go off in about an hour. Try to find another target we can reach quickly. Armed with the views of the ship, if we can keep them off guard long enough, we might be able to find the bridge and plant some explosives."

"Blow up the bridge?"

"No. That would probably guarantee we'd all die. But the threat might give us leverage."

"Maybe you should call for the second team to bring out more explosives and weapons?"

"I've thought about that a lot, but I don't think it's worth the risk right now. If we can thoroughly understand the situation, and know for sure what to damage, what not to damage, maybe it will make more sense. But right now, not knowing any more than we do about how well the ship is monitored, having more people moving around just increases the odds that they'll capture us." Matt hesitated. "As soon as you can find out from that console where the bridge is, we'll head for it."

Bobby Joe nodded and turned to Abby. "Can I take over the search for now?"

"Sure. Having this access has helped a lot. I think I'm closer to decoding the message on the dome ceiling. So far, I'm pretty sure that two of the pictographs mean 'ship' and 'city.' "

Bobby Joe went back to the data on the ship itself. An icon resembling a tic-tac-toe grid led him into a set of overlaid displays where each segment showed interconnections of one type or another, but with no clues he could easily recognize as indicating whether the currently highlighted web represented communication lines, power lines, pneumatic tubes, water or air supplies, waste disposal, or lines that had no counterpart on Earth.

It didn't take him long, though, before he was able to start making some assumptions that seemed reasonable to him. A web that all funneled into a central area of the ship was more likely to be communication lines than waste disposal. A couple of networks that focused on an enormous circular structure well away from the populated area of the ship were more likely to be air, water, or waste. Abby helped him discover that the Archies' directional indicators were half-octagons pointed opposite to the direction Bobby Joe's intuition said they should be, and that helped eliminate possibilities. Waste disposal, for instance, presumably wouldn't be *sending* material all over the ship, unless the Archies were really pretty disgusting creatures.

"I think I've got it," Bobby Joe said a few minutes later.

Matt woke Richard and asked him to stand guard, and then he was looking over Bobby Joe's shoulder.

"All right," said Bobby Joe. "The lines highlighted right now are what I suspect are communication lines for two-way traffic and monitoring. I suspect that where they converge is the bridge." The display looked a little like a street map of Washington, D.C., showing a mass of lines radiating out from one point, a point inside the innermost octagon. "And this overlay is what I think is power lines." The power lines radiated from a different point, a large cylinder about halfway between the center of the ship and the edge, in the wedge adjacent to the one they had moved through.

Bobby Joe pointed. "I think that must be the power plant. You can see the pattern of large supply lines spreading into smaller lines as the grid stretches out to the smallest systems. There's extra shielding here and here. This thing shows four lines, so you wouldn't need that if this was the water supply. And you can see that the bridge is supplied by some large lines. We could try to cut the power to the bridge."

"Or we could threaten the power plant itself. It doesn't look as hard to get to as the bridge."

Matt's alarm beeped, and he looked at his watch. "It's time Richard's explosives were set to go."

"Will we be able to feel anything here?"

"Count on it," said Richard.

Bobby Joe, Abby, Matt, and Richard waited in silence. Rudy's snore was audible.

Two minutes came and went. And a third.

Suddenly the floor began to vibrate. In a couple of seconds the vibration stopped, and a second later it started again, even more intense, and lasted almost half a minute. In about the middle of the period, an alarm started, at least that was what Bobby Joe figured. It sounded more like a musical doorbell than an alarm. A sequence of eight to ten notes repeated every second.

"Sounds awfully complex just to say 'trouble,' " Matt said.

Abby said, "I agree. That might be enough to say not only what kind of trouble, but where it is."

Matt turned to Richard. "Good job." To everyone he said, "They're probably going to be stirred up for a while. I suggest we wait here for a couple of hours, and then make a break for the power plant."

Abby said slowly, "From the feel of things, we've already done a significant amount of damage to the ship."

"True. I wish we had a way to assess the damage. Maybe you'll be able to make a guess from here."

Bobby Joe was about to turn back to the console when he noticed Abby's eyes. She looked puzzled, and her gaze was fixed on Richard's shoes or something near them. Bobby Joe looked that direction and saw nothing special.

Matt had noticed, too. "What's up, Abby?"

"What's that?" She pointed.

Richard raised one foot. "Did I step in something?"

Bobby Joe saw what she was looking at. A small bug stood motionless in the crack formed by the junction of the wall and the floor. "An insect?"

"I don't think so," Abby said.

Matt moved closer as Richard backed away. With his toe, Matt brushed the bug away from the wall, and then hit it toward the center of the room.

"I don't like this at all," Matt said. "Get Rudy and Julie awake."

Bobby Joe got a closer look at the bug, which was sitting still. It looked vaguely like a spider, but it had twice as many legs, and the whole thing looked too regular, too symmetrical to be a typical insect.

Matt crushed the thing under his sole, and when his foot moved away, what was left was a small pile of rubble, not a greasy stain. "They know we're here."

Julie and Rudy were up in seconds, squinting in the light. Three pistols clicked at almost the same time as their owners readied them.

Matt looked at Rudy. "I want you to—"

A tennis ball, or something that looked a lot like one, bounced into the kiosk. As Matt scrambled to get to it, maybe to throw it back out like a hand grenade, two more bounced in. The first one exploded before Matt reached it, and the other two exploded a second later.

From the one Bobby Joe could see, dozens of tiny streamers shot out in every direction. Several of them touched his pants and shirt and stuck. He tried to pull one of them off his shirt, and his hand stuck to it firmly. As he pulled back toward the wall, he pulled Julie off balance. Julie fell over, and the streamers linked between her and Bobby Joe went taut and pulled Bobby Joe off balance.

He didn't fall all the way to the floor, though. A couple of the streamers had hit the wall, and so he dangled there, unable to get loose.

14

TALK TO ME

"JEEZ, ARE MY legs tired," Benny complained.

"What a wimp," Lucky said. "People *run* up these steps every year. Don't you watch the news? And that was in regular gravity."

"Yeah, but those are trained athletes. We're not running some race. And those guys don't carry big packs."

The men had reached the seventy-second floor of the Empire State Building. On their last two trips, they had encountered a building guard who apparently didn't have enough to do. This time they had taken the stairs to vary the pattern. Only a couple of floors earlier Benny had realized that walking up the stairs carrying packs was probably at least as suspicious as being seen a third time in an elevator. Lucky was insistent, though.

They climbed the remaining floors to the ninetieth in silence, except for the sound of Benny's panting. Fortunately they didn't run into the guard again.

This time Lucky planted more explosives along the outside walls of the ninetieth floor. When Benny had asked Lucky where he was getting all the explosives, Lucky told him he had a stockpile. Benny asked why he had such a big stockpile, but all Lucky would say was that he liked to go fishing a lot. Benny let the subject drop.

Unable to move, Abby was loaded onto a cart as though she were a side of beef. She could see through only one eye. The other was sealed shut by one of the sticky streamers. Thankfully, the streamer had stuck to her cheek and forehead, too, so she didn't have the other ends of the streamer tugging directly on her eyelid. Another streamer sealed her lips closed, and she thanked

God nothing had blocked her nostrils or stuck to her eye before she blinked.

Someone else was piled on top of her, but she couldn't tell who. She assumed all six of the team were stuck together by the streamers that had exploded from the balls tossed into the kiosk.

"Watch where you—uh!" Bobby Joe started to moan.

Another body hit the cart in front of her, and her view was partly cut off by someone's sleeve. She felt chilled, and the claustrophobia closed in on her as she realized how little she could move. Her right arm could move forward and backward a few centimeters before a sticky strip curtailed the motion. Her left arm and leg felt immovable. Sections of the sticky strips had probably stuck to the bottom of the cart on either side of her leg. She could turn her head only a few degrees.

An Archie moved past her field of vision, and she peered at it under one squinting eyelid. This close the Archie seemed enormous, but she told herself that was only because it resembled something humans expected to be small. Its abdomen sported a mat of short black hairs as thick as the hair on a human head. As it passed by, she realized it had a short tail. She couldn't imagine how a tail would be useful to creatures like the Archies, but then, she still possessed an appendix that didn't seem very necessary. She was suddenly aware of an odor like that of lemon-scented laundry detergent.

A chattering sounded from somewhere out of sight, answered by a higher-pitched chattering from behind her. Their voices reminded her of dolphin sounds she'd heard, except for seeming more purposeful, as though a deliberate conversation was taking place, but it was in another language. Question, reply, command, response.

She was dimly aware that their treatment implied the Archies didn't necessarily want to kill them, but she hoped they weren't just left this way for much longer; otherwise she'd probably prefer almost any alternative.

The cart moved forward. Everyone must be on board, all six of them stuck together like flies on wadded-up flypaper. Abby suddenly thought about the barbaric way humans treated lobsters about to be consumed, and forced her thoughts elsewhere.

The roof of a kiosk moved past her field of view. Abby was

suddenly more nervous as she realized that she'd heard Bobby Joe speak a couple of times, but not anyone else. Were the others silent because they had nothing to say, or because the sticky strips prevented them, or because they were smothering to death? Abby had no idea whether the Archies would take a close look at the humans and bother to free nasal passages for anyone in need, even if they understood what was happening.

The roof of another kiosk drifted past. Not being able to move her body was driving Abby crazy. She tried hard to straighten her right leg, and suddenly it moved, her leg moving inside her pant leg. Just as her foot moved several centimeters, it came up short as it hit something, and from that direction came an "Ooof." At least that said someone else was alive for sure, although she couldn't tell if the voice had been Rudy's or Richard's. She bit the inside of her lip and forced herself to get her mind off being immobilized. Think of anything else, anything at all.

She closed her eye and imagined herself on a cinder track. She was seventeen again. It was a spring morning, the air crisp and clean. She crouched in starting position on the track, and for a second or two her fingers pushed into the small gravel.

The starting gun fired, very loud despite the fact that it fired only a blank. You'd think they could load a little less gunpowder if they knew the blast didn't have to propel the normal bullet. She hurtled into space and began to pump her legs.

Her ears recovered from the blast, and all she could hear were cleats scattering gravel as they hit the ground, and the beginnings of lung sounds, other runners breathing routinely, not the gasping agony of the 440 finish line.

Abby was on the inside, where she liked to be, starting out behind so just pulling even with another runner before the final curve meant she was ahead, and the other runner knew it, too.

She and the other three runners hit the last curve, Abby in second place but knowing the inner curve gave her an advantage now, both physical and psychological. Her breath burned through her lungs as she hit that final stage where she was committing all her energy until she passed the tape. Whatever penalty her body had to pay for the effort would be put off until the race was over.

From ahead and behind came gasps for breath mingling with Abby's own, the crunch-crunch-crunch of compressing and scattering cinder, the swish-swish of arms moving forward and back, and legs pumping forward.

The runner Abby slowly overtook never turned her head, but Abby knew the instant the other's peripheral vision and hearing told her Abby was next to her. The runner pushed into a higher gear, and somehow Abby did the same.

They were even.

They held even for another second or two, then Abby began to edge ahead. The first centimeters were the hardest, but by the time Abby was a half-meter ahead, suddenly she knew nothing could stop her and she widened her lead, still widening it when she broke the tape.

She kept running, slowing gradually for fear she'd tip over and fall forward now that her body knew it could shut down the blast of energy, entering recovery mode and now letting her know how much her stomach and lungs hurt. Seconds later she was able to slow to a stop and before she bent forward to get as much air as possible into her lungs, she caught a glimpse of her parents in the stands. Her father was on his feet, cheering, more animated than she'd ever seen him, loud enough that she could even make out his individual voice in the crowd.

In that moment she realized how much she wanted to please him, to please the man who once too often let it slip that he'd really wanted a boy.

Her chest hurt. She knew she was far too young for trouble like that, but for just an instant she felt the pain had come from her heart.

The cart carrying her shook. Abby opened the one eye that she was able to, and she saw the roof of another kiosk. The bumping increased and part of the ceiling was obscured by a closer dark lip of something shorter. For a terrible moment she visualized them being levered into a large trash compactor to be disposed of like useless debris.

They weren't in a trash compactor, though. Seconds later she recognized the roof of one of the monorail cars. Before long they accelerated smoothly in an unknown direction.

They must have been heading inward, because if they'd been

going outward, they would have passed through a doorway soon after they started, and she saw no signs of that. They traveled for five minutes or fifteen as Abby tried not to think about being unable to shift position.

Near the end of their monorail journey the car did pass through a doorway into a new area, after which time the ceiling was lower than it had been, now only about ten meters high. The cart was unloaded from the monorail car, and passing through her field of vision were two more Archies, chattering to each other.

They passed through another doorway and the echoes changed. They were in a smaller space now. The cart came to a halt.

Some chattering began behind Abby's back. From the sounds, three or four different Archies were present. She wished she'd had the minivid on before all this started so she would have at least the voice recording. From somewhere came a spraying sound and Bobby Joe said, "Well, it's about time."

A few seconds later Abby realized one foot was free to move. She straightened her leg, feeling a strong sense of relief. Behind her bodies shifted. Something hard fell onto a metallic surface. The air carried the scent of paint.

A weight that had been pressing on her shoulder lifted. An Archie entered her field of view. It was holding a small object like a balloon. It squeezed the balloon, and a fine mist sprayed toward the cart. The sticky strips over Abby's mouth and eye turned limp and fell off. She was able to move. She took a deep breath and slowly got up.

Two Archies stood silently on both sides of the only door in the room. Both carried in their forward two arms what had to be weapons. The gray devices bore unrecognizable knobs and attachments, but they also sported unmistakable gun muzzles that easily sliced through the language barrier. Two more Archies were engaged in getting the sticky mass of humans separated. On the floor sat a stack of minivids, pistols, and stuff from their backpacks.

Abby was the last to get free. Matt was safe, and he gave her a look that said he was relieved that she was all right. He sat against the far wall. Rudy and Julie and Richard sat nearby, also looking nervous but all right. As an Archie pushed Bobby Joe toward the others, he sat down and joined them. Abby did, too.

As the six humans sat against the wall, two Archies pawed through the pile of equipment in the center of the room. Abby patted her hip and realized she no longer had either pistol or holster.

The Archies were forming two piles in the center of the room. Into one pile went holsters, empty backpacks, the minivids, computer, canteens, and things like the resealing plastic bags and rope. Into the other pile went the pistols, a power drill, flashlights, and Richard's plastic explosives. The weapons pile then went onto the cart, which one of the Archies, one with stripes of yellow in its clothing, pulled out of the room. The other Archie near the center of the room backed up so it was nowhere near line of sight between the armed Archies and the humans.

The Archies all wore two utility belts, one around each body segment, and Abby couldn't help but think of old pocket protectors and saddlebags. Their heads met their forward segments with not much opportunity to swivel. When one wanted to look in a different direction, it either moved its entire body, or just the eye-stalk that protruded from what would be the forehead on a human. The knobby legs were wider near the body than at the ground, like tripod legs. At the end of each limb was a four-fingered hand. The rear two hands were idle at the moment, and she briefly wondered what joke Bobby Joe would make from that.

Abby glanced at the room itself finally. Rather than being octagonal, it was actually square. What could have been a sink stood in one corner. In the opposite corner was a console like the one in the kiosk.

The Archie who had left returned with two flimsy drawings, unmistakably drawings of the ship. It set the drawings on the floor, then took a small marker from a belt around its forward segment. On an overhead view of the plain below, it drew a short line from the Manhattan dome. On the top view of the floor they were on, it drew a small line from a kiosk out to a huge cylinder, no doubt the one they had damaged. Finally it tossed the marker onto the floor between itself and the six humans.

No one moved or said anything for a moment.

"It wants us to draw the path we took, wouldn't you say?" Abby said.

Matt stood up and moved forward. He reached the marker, picked it up, and approached the Archie, whose eye-stalk tracked him all the way. Calmly Matt handed back the unused marker. He returned to the wall and sat down.

Bobby Joe laughed softly and said under his breath, "Go spawn yourself, Archie."

The Archie stood there a moment with the marker in its hand, and then it jumped straight up in the air just high enough that Abby could see clearly that all four center legs had left the ground simultaneously. Abby tentatively cataloged the response as annoyance.

The Archie stood there for several seconds, motionless except for its eye-stalk, which scanned the row of humans. Finally, it turned and chattered at the other Archies, and they all withdrew, the armed Archies at the rear. The last thing Abby saw before the twin doors slid closed together was a pair of eye-stalks watching as if the Archie were worried that the humans might dash to the door.

It was a legitimate fear, Abby understood then. For all the Archies knew, humans might have far quicker reaction times than they did. Suddenly she decided the Archies probably had even more backup nearby, just in case.

"All right," Matt said. Abby could hear the discouragement in his voice. "They've left us with a console. If it hasn't been disabled, at least we can continue learning about the ship and the Archies. Abby, can you and Bobby Joe get started?"

Abby hesitated. "Can I take a ten-minute break first?"

Matt looked at her. "Sure."

What Matt didn't say, but Abby read into his expression, was, "No hurry." The Earth was probably already doomed anyway; they couldn't have done enough damage to prevent that. Exploring with the console was a busy-work request that was probably most useful in just keeping them occupied. Once the Archies decided what to do about them, the humans would probably all be killed anyway.

Abby let her eyes close for just a second, and she took a few deep breaths.

Matt and Rudy sifted through the pile of possessions the Archies had left behind and began to tape up a privacy curtain in front of what looked something like a sink. Julie retrieved her minivid and began recording. Abby was surprised at how accurately the Archies had divided their equipment into threatening and non-threatening piles.

Abby hadn't felt this tired in a long time.

She and Bobby Joe stood at the console as Matt and Rudy and Julie watched over their shoulders. Julie had her minivid active most of the time. Bobby Joe had actually had a joke-free hour, and he'd been invaluable in helping interpret drawings of the ship. Richard slept. He also snored.

Abby held less hope than before that they'd done adequate damage to the ship. The console showed that the floor opposite the one they were on also held eight huge cylinders, one in each slice of the octagon, and the other set was even larger. Maybe they had a completely redundant propulsion system.

Their efforts at the console had concentrated on two areas—finding out what else they could damage, given an opportunity, and finding what escape routes might exist. Abby was a little surprised the Archies hadn't disabled the console, but the team's best guess was that the Archies figured the humans had already had access to a console so there was little to lose. Besides that, the Archies could easily have disabled specifics they were nervous about allowing access to. Abby wondered if allowing access was a way of saying they were not hostile.

Their examination of the current screen content was interrupted by the sound of the two doors opening. Two armed Archies entered, followed by two more, and two more after them. Julie aimed her minivid at the new arrivals. After the six armed Archies formed a barrier in front of the door, a seventh Archie squeezed between two of the others. This Archie may have been the one they'd seen earlier, because its clothing looked similar, yellow stripes in the material.

The Archie brought two things. The first was a transparent bowl of familiar food pellets, which it set on the floor as though a pet dog were nearby. In addition it carried a small box with eight switches on top of it. It set the box on the floor near the bowl. It moved toward the console, then stopped, apparently waiting for the humans to get out of the way.

Abby and the others stepped back, and the Archie used one graceful limb to touch the console switch that let it back out of the information they had been exploring, and then it chose another area. Eight new icons came up on the screen. The Archie made a point of pressing one of the wedges slowly enough for the humans to see which one it had touched, and the screen changed again. One of the icons looked like the box on the floor.

The Archie then backed up and left the room. Two at a time the armed Archies departed until the humans were alone again.

"What was that all about?" asked Matt.

"I don't know," Abby said.

Rudy picked up the box and they examined it. Each of the eight switches was a rotary switch with eight positions.

A brief chattering from the console turned their heads back to the screen. A picture of an Archie came up on the screen. At the same time a chattering sound like the previous one, but subtly different, came from a speaker on the console. The screen changed and showed a top view of an Archie with the two front limbs highlighted. Another sound came from the speaker.

"It's language lesson time!" Abby said. "I need the computer. And can someone set up my minivid and just let it run?"

As quickly as she could she readied the computer, and as the sequence of sounds and images continued, fell into a pattern. Each time the computer produced a snippet of the Archies' language and showed an image, she had the computer record the sound bite and immediately afterward spoke and recorded her best guess as to what was being described.

After cataloging several snippets, Bobby Joe interrupted to show her what he'd deduced about how to slow down the flow, or speed it up, or reverse it. Touching the left and right side wedges on the keyboard put the sequence into forward or reverse, and the distance from the center determined the speed. Abby went back to the beginning and recorded the sound associated with the image of an Archie.

She made no attempt at first to break the collection of words into categories or try to deduce anything about speech patterns, phonetics, morphology, semantics, or syntax. Almost every word she heard sounded like the previous three words. All she could hope to do for a start was build the collection of sounds linked to human best-guess expressions.

The sequence of images continued, some of them looking like photographic images, others looking like artists' conceptions, still others just icons.

If she had been studying the individual sounds, trying to replicate them or understand them, she'd still have been on the first two or three sounds. Instead, after a couple of hours, she reached the end of the sequence, and her computer said it had recorded 884 sets. She leaned back, feeling drained.

Bobby Joe pushed another one of the keyboard wedges, and the console spoke for a couple of seconds, probably five or six words strung together.

"Do that again in just a minute," Abby said, suddenly feeling more energetic. She told the computer to start listening for foreign words in its vocabulary and to play back the English version after each word it found.

Seconds after that, Bobby Joe played back the sequence. From Abby's computer came her recorded voice speaking the sentence, "Ship Archies dome human city." Since the intonation on each word was similar, her voice sounded like a spelling checker.

Bobby Joe looked at her and said, "Me smart now."

From the corner of her eye, Abby saw Matt give Bobby Joe a come-here signal, and Abby was just able to make out his words as Matt said, "Abby is our best hope of communicating with these guys. Slow her down, and you and I are going to have a little talk."

Abby reached forward and triggered another phrase. This time her computer said, "Ship Archies two human."

She shook her head and played more sentences, slowly realizing by analyzing sentence after sentence that earlier she had made a series of small errors, like saying "two" when the symbol probably had meant "with." Each time she was able to reach a conclusion about a specific word, she went back and changed her recording and rethought some of her assumptions, as though she were working a 3-D crossword puzzle. She hit an easy stretch, a series of dots obviously meant to represent numbers—first one dot, then two, then three and so on, and then the images went back to more difficult ones.

A long time later, what seemed like days, she was aware of Matt standing nearby. She turned to him. "I think I'm getting pretty close to a basic working vocabulary. It's still bound to have errors, but it's starting to make sense."

She played another Archie sentence, and her computer said, "Mouth Archies box two one three four five six seven eight." Abby looked at the box the Archie had left, and Matt retrieved it.

"You think it's a combination?" Abby asked.

"You're the expert."

"I think it's a combination."

"And if I set the combination on these switches?"

"Then maybe that's a signal that we're ready to talk. Probably what I thought meant 'mouth' actually means 'talk' or 'speak.' "

"Are we ready?" Matt asked.

"We're as close as we're going to get for a while longer. I've been using Archie-to-human look-up, but I can also set it to human-to-Archie."

The others came closer as Matt turned the switches on the box, lining the points on the knobs up with the right number of small dots drawn at each position. As he set them he said, "Two, one, three, four, five, six, seven, eight. I don't know if they use left-to-right or right-to-left, but I guess we'll find out."

A few minutes later the double doors opened again, and armed Archies moved cautiously back into the room. The Archie with yellow stripes in its clothing moved forward and stopped. Matt stepped forward and handed it the box, which it accepted. The Archie's hand was dark-skinned, like most of its body. The hand was smaller than a human's, with no sign of the equivalent of fingernails. The hand swiveled as the Archie placed the box into a small pouch on the belt on its rear segment. Abby glanced back and saw that Julie had her minivid recording again.

The Archie's head was so big Abby found herself comparing

it not to insect heads, but to animal heads. It was a little like a sightless buffalo with a large dark nose and gray teeth. The eye-stalk protruding from the forehead seemed terribly vulnerable to Abby, but perhaps it was much stronger than it seemed, or perhaps the Archies' regenerative mechanism was more thorough than humans'. Suddenly she had to suppress a grin as she realized what the large worm-like eye-stalk vaguely resembled.

The Archie chattered briefly, and Abby's voice came from the computer, saying "Archie." Abby touched a switch on the computer and said, "Human." The computer chattered, and suddenly the Archie sat down in the middle of the floor, its center four limbs folded underneath it, the back two and front two extended. Its eye-stalk pointed toward Abby. The armed Archies didn't change position. Matt and the others sat behind Abby in a semicircle. Abby was again aware of a scent like laundry detergent.

The Archie pulled a small egg-shaped device from its forward belt. It spoke and again the computer translated. "Archie ship explosion one." As it spoke, it manipulated the egg, and a couple of meters away the console screen changed. The new screen showed damage to the huge red cylinder. Then the Archie spoke again. "Archie ship explosion two." The console screen changed and showed a top view of the ship.

Abby turned to Matt. "I think it's asking if we planted more explosives, and if so, where."

"I want some information from them before we answer that. Ask them why they took Manhattan."

Abby turned to the Archie and tried to figure out how to phrase that, given her limited vocabulary with almost no verbs. Finally she decided on trying to use a sequence as the Archie had and said, "Planet city two. Dome city ship three. One," and the computer chattered.

The Archie was silent for almost a minute, then said, "One planet city fall. Two dome city not fall."

Abby said to Matt, "I think I got a couple of words wrong. I think it's saying the city is safe now. That now it's protected."

"What about the Earth? Is it all right?"

Abby turned and thought. She'd correct "fall" to "unsafe"

later. She gave the Archie a choice. "Human planet fall. Human planet not fall."

"Human planet not fall."

"Thank God." She hesitated. "Human planet not fall. Archie human planet fall."

"Human planet not fall. Archie human planet not fall."

"I think it's saying the Archies are not going to hurt Earth."

"Why should we believe them?" Matt asked. "We know they destroyed the world the tree people lived on. And we've got evidence that at least one other planet was destroyed."

"Tree people planet not fall. Archies tree people planet fall."

"Tree people planet not fall. Archies tree people city dome not fall. Tree people planet fall."

Abby tried several times to phrase the question another way and got several variations on the answer. Finally she turned to Matt and said, "I *think* it's saying that the Archies didn't destroy the tree people's planet. Someone else did."

"Someone else? So they—they're just rescuing cities before someone else comes along and wipes out the planet?"

"I think so. If I'm interpreting all this correctly, the Archies are trying to preserve a little bit of each civilization before someone else destroys it all."

"Can you find out how much time there is before whoever is destroying planets destroys the Earth?"

Abby turned back and thought. Finally she phrased her question. She thought she knew what the answer meant, but she tried to ask it another way.

"I've asked it twice, in different ways. I got what I think is the same answer both times."

"So when is it? When do they say the Earth will be destroyed?"

"I'm still unsure of time units, but I think it could be any time now."

Dorine Underwood was finally talked into taking the call. "This is the mayor," she said.

"It's about time," said a male voice that made Dorine think of a large rodent.

"You want to speak to me or not?"

Hesitation. "Yes," the voice said suddenly. "Cancel the expedition. You're going to get us all killed."

"I can't do that. The expedition is our only hope of survival. Look, it's been nice talking to you, but—"

"Wait! A lot of people are going to be killed if you don't stop. The Empire State Building is wired to explode."

"Look, I'm really very busy."

"I'm not joking. There are two hundred kilos of plastic explosive, all ready to blow if anyone touches them, or if I send the signal."

"Has anybody ever told you you're a son of a bitch?"

"I don't think you're taking me seriously. And I don't like that. I'm the one who climbed through the sewers and did the Battery Tunnel job, and you took *that* seriously. Do you only get excited when it's too late?"

Dorine had received crank calls a number of times in the past, but somehow this one didn't seem to fit the pattern. The man might be telling the truth. "What are your terms?"

"That's better. Have the expedition called off by midnight. Or else the—"

Suddenly the phone on the other end clattered.

"Hello?" said Dorine. "Hello?"

Several seconds passed before a voice came on the line, a different voice this time. "Hello. Mayor?"

"Yes."

"Sergeant Wilkins here. He was calling from a public booth on Broadway. We're searching the area now, and we'll keep you posted."

"Okay. Thanks."

Dorine immediately called the commissioner. "Barnaby, I just got a call saying there are two hundred kilos of plastic explosive in the Empire State Building. I want the building evacuated, and I want an estimate of how bad the damage could be, assuming it's been placed in the most effective spot. Then see if you can find qualified bomb squad volunteers. Use your own judgment on how much else needs to be evacuated. I think the guy's for real, but I don't know for sure."

"You got it."

Dorine hung up the phone and wondered what to do. There was no question about halting the expedition, but the idea of someone destroying the Empire State Building made her sick.

15

DAMAGE REPORT

MATT RUBBED HIS forehead and looked at the Archie who sat just a meter in front of Abby. Its brown head looked hard, like chitin on a magnified ant's head. The Archie's eye-stalk swung toward Matt, looking far too much like a penis with an eye on the tip. The eye didn't look like a human eye; it was faceted, like a fly's eye.

"I'm still having a little trouble shifting gears," Matt said. "What this Archie is saying, essentially, is that we're an endangered species, and that they grabbed Manhattan so they could preserve what little they could?"

"That's the way I see it," Abby said.

The Archie spoke again, and Abby's computer said, "Human Archie ship. Human human city."

Matt raised his eyebrows, and Abby said, "I think it's saying it wants us back in Manhattan."

"No." Matt thought for a moment. "Tell them we cannot sit by and do nothing about the Earth. Tell them we've got an explosive a thousand times larger than the one that went off already, and that it's hidden on the ship. It will explode unless we command it not to. As long as they cooperate fully and answer all our questions, we will not damage the ship. But if they do not cooperate, we will have to assume they are lying to us, and we'll let the explosion destroy the ship. We insist on staying here and finding out what's going on."

Abby looked at Matt without expression for a second. "That's pretty complicated, but I'll give it a try." She and the Archie talked via the computer for several minutes, as the Archie got more and more animated, its eye-stalk twitching, and its body quivering. Finally Abby turned to Matt and said, "The Archie obviously is unhappy with that—angry, indignant, insulted, I don't really know how to characterize the feeling, and I don't know if it really has a human counterpart, but the Archie has agreed to let us stay here and learn more."

"Good. Ask them who's destroying all these planets and why."

Moments later Abby sighed and said, "This isn't working. I need to know more about their language."

"Okay, can you tell them that and tell them we don't want to be captives here? We want free run of the ship, and we promise not to do more damage if they're telling the truth."

"Truth is going to be a tough idea to get across right now."

"Then just say we won't damage the ship."

Abby spoke and her computer translated. She and the Archie went back and forth, the Archie growing more agitated at first, and then finally relaxing a little. The Archie's eye-stalk pointed first at Matt, then Abby. The Archie's oblong mouth was ringed with what looked like tiny hairs.

This time the Archie apparently had to consult with its peers. It rose smoothly on its center four legs and left the room.

Abby said, "This is really hard to calibrate, but I'm getting the feeling these Archies are acting less like what I'd imagine a starship crew to be like, and more like I'd expect a group of civil servants or bureaucrats to act. If I'm reading this right, the objections were more along the lines of this being against the rules, rather than objections that our having more explosives here might damage the ship or injure people."

Rudy shook his head. "These creatures are acting more like labor unions than a starship crew."

Julie nodded, then asked, "If they want proof of this explosive we claim to have, what then?"

Matt said, "I don't know. Maybe we can show them file recordings of nuclear testing."

"Yeah," said Bobby Joe. "And if they're willing to trust images, we could show them the death-star blowing up Princess Leia's home planet."

"I hadn't thought about how easy it is to fake images. I guess we just have to act tough and cross our fingers. Certainly the fact that we got here and set off one explosion must have helped convince them we can be real trouble if we don't get our way."

As they waited, Rudy asked, "Do these Archies have names?"

Four Archies remained standing against the wall next to the door, their weapons still trained on the humans, their eye-stalks still directed at the humans.

Abby shook her head. "I don't know."

Bobby Joe looked around. "You could try 'dickhead.' "

Abby turned away and Matt couldn't see her expression, but her shoulders shook slightly, and he got the feeling she was trying to hide the urge to laugh.

Minutes later the Archie returned. It spoke to the four others, who all lowered their weapons and left the room. It chattered briefly, and Abby turned to Matt and said, "If I'm understanding correctly, we can go where we want as long as an Archie is nearby. I think you're right; having detonated the explosion has made them take us more seriously. And Rudy's right, too. I'm getting the feeling the Archies are having trouble adapting to this new situation. They seem to be trained to do their normal jobs, but they have trouble dealing with change. As long as we tell them clearly what we want, and refuse to negotiate, my guess is that we can do quite a lot."

"Interesting. Tell them we want to be on the bridge and for you to be able to continue your language lessons. I assume by now doing that in person would be quicker than at a console."

"That's true."

"All right. Tell them that, and tell them we won't damage the ship any more as long as they do what we ask."

Abby spoke again, and the computer chattered.

The Archie responded, clenching and unclenching its front two hands as it spoke, and Abby said, "I think it's still pretty unhappy about all this, but it seems willing."

The Archie rose and this time the humans all rose with it. "Rudy, help me grab the stuff we've got left," Matt said.

The six humans followed the Archie through the door, where they were joined by five more Archies, all armed. The procession turned down a hallway and walked about fifty meters before passing through another doorway.

This was the bridge. Matt had no doubt at all. The room was octagonal, maybe fifty meters across, and it had no ceiling.

Matt knew there had to be some surface covering the top of the room, whether it was a totally transparent layer, or a clear force field, or simply the very best holographic display screen he'd ever seen. Whatever the actual mechanism was, the bridge held a comfortable atmosphere while appearing to be open to the night sky.

The view was dazzling.

Roughly in the center of the display or directly above the ship were the Earth and Luna. They were far enough away that Luna was the brightest star in the sky, one with its circular disk just visible. The Earth was a blue marble streaked with white. The Milky Way angled across the sky, hints of reds and blues and yellows in pinpoints almost too tiny to make out, against what seemed to be a band of white clouds stretching out of sight at both ends of the window.

Julie gasped. "It's kind of a cosmic ticker-tape parade."

Matt could suddenly see the similarity—stars so dense that there had to be a legion of stars hidden by the closest ones. The swath of stars spread through the sky like ticker tape filling the gap between the dark buildings bordering a parade route.

Matt was finally able to tear his gaze away from the starry sky. The room itself was dimly it. Directly in the center of the room sat an Archie in a reclining chair tilted back far enough that it looked straight up into the expanse of distant suns.

"Abby," Matt said. "Ask for your language lesson now. And try to get it quickly. I don't know if there's anything we can do, but if there is, it's got to be done quickly. Maybe we can transmit a message from here to Earth if you find out enough about what's going on."

Abby nodded and spoke to the Archie. They moved off toward a corner while the other five Archies stayed with Matt and the others.

Rudy said softly, "I don't think there's much reason to communicate with Earth. They don't have any defenses that could help against something like this. If they are still alive and we can't stop what's happening, all we do is give them a few hours or days of hell instead of five minutes."

"That's probably true, but maybe a few people could survive in orbit if they get enough warning. It's a tough call."

Rudy nodded.

Matt scanned the room. Eight other Archies on their own recliners surrounded the central Archie in an octagonal pattern, each looking up at the sky. Farther out sat still more Archies, but the ones on the perimeter sat in chairs that allowed them to face the walls, on which display after display showed views of the interior of the ship from various points of view, and magnified images of the stars. A couple of screens showed views of Earth, one of them showing the whole globe, the other showing a low-orbit scan of a brown and vermilion land mass.

"This is the mayor," Dorine said into the phone.

Barnaby's voice was calm as he identified himself, and Dorine felt grateful even before hearing his message. "The bomb squad's located the explosives in the Empire State Building. The guy was telling you the truth."

"And?"

"And I think we've got a good shot at disabling them. The control mechanism is an old, discrete job, and I've got a couple of guys with experience."

Dorine knew anyone who had that experience and who was still alive must have avoided a lot of mistakes, and that was a comforting thought. "You'd better give them a chance at it then," she said. "I'm not backing down."

"You got it." Barnaby didn't say it in so many words, but the pride in his tone of voice said, "That's exactly what I would do."

For a few seconds, the starry scene overhead reminded Matt of a night long ago when he had lain on his back past midnight and stared up at a sky filled with stars. The air had been filled with the sound of crickets and unidentified snaps and creaks as the wind flowed over his body. Far in the distance, a train had sounded its whistle, and the faint rumble of the cars sounded almost like distant thunder.

"Matt." Abby was next to him again, and the Archie was next to her.

"Yeah."

"It doesn't sound good."

"Go ahead." Rudy and the others moved nearer so they could hear.

"I talked with her some more—"

"Her?"

"If I've got the sexes correctly identified. Anyway, I'm getting more confidence in what they're saying. I think I understand the vocabulary we've got so far correctly. The message on the domes is meant to say, 'The ship is moving the city to safety.' She says they had expected the message would be easier to figure out than it was. And she says the Archies are in fact scooping up cities to protect them. There's another ship, built by someone else, that's apparently on a programmed course of locating worlds that fit various criteria and converting them for their own purposes. It's completely automated—no intelligence aboard."

"Converting. Like we would terraform another world? Change its climate and atmosphere so it would be convenient for us?"

Abby spoke to the Archie, then turned back to Matt. "Yes, something like that, except that whatever this planet-shaper does also kills the indigent life so it doesn't interfere."

"God. A robot ship converting planet after planet for their own purposes, and not caring what happens to anything living there?"

Julie said, "Sounds a lot like us and the rain forests."

"And who are the people who built this planet-shaper?" Matt asked.

After consultation Abby said, "They don't know. Some other alien race. To the Archies we're an endangered species. They're preserving what life they can. If they're able to locate another Earth-like world, they'll eventually plant us there."

"But that won't help the Earth, for God's sake." Matt turned abruptly and looked at the screens showing the Earth from space. "There are billions of people down there. And it's our home. We can't just let some ship come along and do whatever they do to it."

Rudy said, "Not only that, but the same thing could still happen again for all we know."

Abby stood there silently.

"Where is this planet-shaper?" Matt asked. "How far away?"

Abby talked to the Archie again.

"They don't know. It's at least several hours away because it hasn't showed up in our solar system yet. Apparently the ship jumps through space when it's going a long distance, but when it gets here it moves more like we would expect it to."

The Archie said something to Abby and she listened for a moment as the computer analyzed it. "Apparently the Archies' ship has the same choices—moving fairly normally around the solar system, or, if the ship is well away from the sun, it can jump long distances. What we heavily damaged was their ability to make those long-distance jumps."

Matt said, "I'm sorry we damaged their ship, but I don't see that as an immediate problem."

Abby traded more words. As she did, the Archie scratched its rear with one back leg.

"*They* see it as an immediate problem. A major problem. If I'm getting this right, when the planet-shaper gets ready to jump, they can watch which way it's going and then jump ahead to beat it. Without the ability to jump, they can't save anyone from the next place the planet-shaper goes. They'll all be killed. It might take them long enough to fix the drive that the planet-shaper will have time to destroy several more planets before they can resume rescue operations."

"Oh, God," Matt said softly. Finally he said, "Please tell them that was never our intent. We thought we'd be preventing the destruction of Earth."

Abby relayed that information and turned back to Matt. "They understand that now."

"Why don't they fight the planet-shaper? Stop it now, and none of this would be necessary."

Moments later Abby said, "They can't. This ship has no weapons. It's designed specifically to rescue cities. That must be part of the reason the Archies seem uneasy with the changed situation. They're trained to do a specific job, and we're asking them to do a different one."

"No weapons? There's nothing they can do to stop the planet-shaper?"

Abby talked again, then turned to Matt. "On or near their home planet, they are designing and building a ship, a destroyer, to eliminate the planet-shaper. But the destroyer won't be ready in time."

"How soon will it be ready?"

"There's a chance I'm getting time units wrong, but I think she's saying a couple of years. I know it's more than a couple of months. Obviously far too late to help Earth."

"Unless the planet-shaper isn't actually coming here after all. Maybe they made a mistake. Maybe that's why it hasn't showed up yet."

Abby talked to the Archie again.

"She says they haven't been wrong yet."

The Archie spoke to Abby again.

"She says even if the ship did have weapons, the crew is trained specifically for saving cities, not waging war. That's got to be why they seem more like bureaucrats than warriors—could you imagine a small group of Greenpeace activists going up against the entire U.S. Army?"

Matt was silent for almost half a minute, furiously thinking of options. "I see two choices. One, roll over on our backs with our feet in the air like the Archies. Or, two, do something about it. We're going to do something about it."

"What?" said Richard. "We have no weapons. Haven't you been listening?"

Matt swiveled to stare at Richard. He moved one pace toward Richard and very quietly he said, "If I want complaints or negativity from you, I'll ask for them very clearly. Right now, I don't want them. Is that clear?"

Richard swallowed hard, then nodded. "Yes."

Matt turned to Abby. "Tell your friend we need an escort for Bobby Joe and Julie. They're going to the closest observation port."

As Abby spoke to the computer, Matt looked at Bobby Joe. "I want you to contact Manhattan, first to tell them exactly what's happening, and second to get an inventory of anything they can think of that might be useful. It's pretty unlikely anyone was transporting nuclear weapons through Manhattan when it was grabbed, but who knows? The Mayor is going to have to go on the air and ask for anything that can help. Take Julie with you and get enough of what's in her minivid sent down there so we won't have anyone wasting time not accepting this as fact. As soon as you've made the initial transmission, get back here. If I'm busy, try to set up a link between this room and Manhattan."

Abby touched Matt's arm. "She's agreed."

Matt looked at Bobby Joe and Julie. "Go."

Bobby Joe nodded. He knelt by the pile of their remaining belongings and picked up the new walkie-talkie and two old ones. He and Julie left, followed by one of the other Archies.

To Abby, Matt said, "Tell this Archie that we want to know everything there is to know about the capabilities of this ship, and how many smaller ships it contains, what they're capable of."

Abby spoke, then listened.

"She says it's useless."

"Tell her we don't care. The damage they've suffered to the ship so far is nothing compared to what we'll do if they don't cooperate."

As Abby spoke, Matt said to Richard and Rudy, "I want you two listening closely to whatever we learn about the Archies' capabilities. I'll want any suggestions you can think of for options, no matter how peculiar, as long as they're serious."

Abby said, "I don't think she feels it's of any help, but she'll tell us everything about the ship."

"That's fine. I don't care what she believes as long as she cooperates. Oh, and tell her I'll want to talk to the captain soon."

After a moment Abby said, "She *is* the captain."

Matt glanced back at the Archie occupying the central chair on the deck. "Oh. I had assumed the captain would be sitting up there."

"Apparently she feels this is more important."

"All right. What do we have to work with? Those lasers on the ships that cut Manhattan loose sound like they can be used as weapons, for instance."

Abby spoke to the captain and moments later turned back to Matt. "Aboard this ship are twenty smaller ships. If I'm getting this right, they have sixteen ships with cutters—I suppose those are the lasers—and they have two spares. Then they have two lifters, much bigger ships."

"What weapons are aboard the lifters?"

The Archie's eye-stalk dipped a couple of times as it answered Abby's question.

"No weapons."

"Well, we have to find a way to stop the planet-shaper."

After a moment, Abby said, "They really don't want to fight. The captain is sure they can't damage the planet-shaper and she doesn't want to risk damaging the smaller ships. She's pretty clearly not equipped to deal with a military operation."

Motion to Matt's side caught his eye and he turned to see Bobby Joe and Julie returning with their Archie escort. Matt raised his eyebrows.

"It's going to be easier than we thought to set up a comm link between here and Manhattan," Bobby Joe said. "The nearest observation port is about a minute from here. I've got your optical walkie-talkie set up for line-of-sight transmission, and it's cross-connected to a regular walkie-talkie. You can talk directly from here, or we can relay anything you want. They're getting the Mayor now, and she should be online any time. We can transmit some video as soon as you want. And if you like, later we can set up one of the minivids so it transmits a frame every ten seconds from here in addition to voice."

"Perfect. Rudy, keep going with getting a summary of what's available. I'll talk to the Mayor."

Matt picked up one of the walkie-talkies and snapped it on. "Matt Sheehan here. Who am I talking to?"

"Barnaby Jolliet. The mayor should be on the line any second now. It may take her a minute or two to get fully awake."

Matt looked at his watch and realized for the first time that in Manhattan it was a little after one in the morning.

"Dorine Underwood here," came her voice clearly.

"Matt Sheehan. Good news, bad news, and a request for help."

"Shoot."

Twenty-eight minutes later, Dorine Underwood blinked at the camera lens as a hyperactive crew got ready for an emergency telecast. A police car permanently assigned to Gracie Mansion had sped her downtown as fast as the driver could safely travel in low gee. The siren wailed as traffic lights automatically turned green in the path ahead. Others in her office had arranged the emergency TV crew, who knew nothing about what Dorine was going to announce.

Still others had switched on air raid sirens all over the island, the signal for everyone to turn on their television sets. As Dorine had sped through dark streets in the police car, she had occasionally heard the air raid wailings over the siren, and she felt she was in another dream, a dream like the one on the morning Manhattan had been lifted into the air, a dream like the one the morning she'd found out her son Terry had died in a traffic accident, broadsided by a drunk.

In the studio, Dorine still felt not quite *real* somehow. Some of the things Matt Sheehan had told her were still spinning through her brain, edging their way from knowledge to fear. She didn't disbelieve anything he had said; it was just taking her a while to convert the information into reality.

On a monitor in front of her was a still frame of a starry sky with Earth near the center. The frame changed and she saw the ship's bridge with the human team and several of the huge spider creatures. On a monitor next to that one was her live image, looking far too pale for her heritage. She pushed a lock of hair behind one ear.

A technician finished the countdown.

"Hello, New Yorkers," said Dorine to the camera lens. She always started with a few words that could be missed by people suddenly saying or hearing, "Shhh. She's starting to talk," as the audience came to attention. "Obviously I wouldn't have scheduled this telecast for two A.M. if time were not critical.

"I'm going to give you an overview, and then I'm going to

tell you what we must do next, and finally I'm going to show you some video that will leave no doubts about what I'm saying.

"Put very briefly, we in Manhattan are all safe. No harm is going to come to us. The Earth itself is in danger, however. Sometime in the next hours or days, the Earth is going to be under attack, faced with weapons it has no defense against. That is the reason I am talking to you now. It's possible that we may be able to help in some currently unforeseen manner."

The view in the second monitor changed to show an airplane-window view of Manhattan under its taco-shell dome, and Dorine lost her next thought until she looked back at her notes.

"This is going to be a little difficult to accept, but perhaps no harder to accept than our current home. The alien race who brought us here did so *not* to keep us like zoo specimens or to experiment on us. They brought us here because the Earth itself is in immediate danger. A huge, automated alien ship built by yet another race is on a programmed course of destruction, converting habitable planets into planets that will one day comfortably support their own life. One of the things the ship does is clear the planet of other life-forms.

"The ship we are on has as its purpose taking a city from each planet about to be destroyed, so they can eventually relocate the cities to other planets that will support life. For that reason, this ship is unarmed, except for the lasers used to cut cities loose from their planets, and the people who 'rescued' us do not believe the lasers are a sufficient weapon against this other ship—the planet-shaper ship. An armed destroyer being built to overcome this . . . planet-shaper will not be ready in time to help the Earth."

Dorine carefully avoided saying outright that everyone still on Earth was probably doomed.

"We're at a turning point. We can either do nothing, in which case we'll never see the Earth again, and we'll eventually be deposited on some other planet to live out our lives. Or, we can fight. We can try to destroy the planet-shaper. If we're successful, the Earth and everyone on it will be safe. We might not be successful. Certainly the odds are against us. But we cannot stand by and not try.

"What we need now is a weapon. We need something that can help us change the odds, to help us destroy the planet-shaper. If you know of anything that is here with us in the dome that can help, I want to know about it.

"What I don't want to know about are conventional weapons. Rifles, even assault rifles, and things like bazookas are not going to help us defeat a huge, armed ship. But if, for instance, any nuclear weapons were being transported through Manhattan when we were taken, or if, God help us, a group of terrorists had a weapon ready to use as a threat, we need to know about it. If you know of any hugely powerful weapon of any kind, call nine-one-one right now. The nine-one-one system operators are ready to funnel emergency calls like this into a staff standing by right now. Do *not* call nine-one-one during the next hour unless your call clearly pertains to exactly what I requested, or it's an emergency that threatens many lives. Anyone abusing the nine-one-one system during the next twenty-four hours will be dealt with harshly, under martial law provisions. The lives of billions of people are at stake.

"Now, for those of you who are having trouble accepting all of this information, or are simply curious about the ship we are on—and I assume that's almost everyone—I'm going to show you some still-frame video that's been sent back by Matt Sheehan and his team, who are at this moment on the ship's bridge high above us, at the center of the level that forms the roof of this giant chamber we're in."

Dorine pressed the switch the technicians had rigged, and the first still-frame replaced her image on the monitor. Matt Sheehan and Abby Tersa stood next to a spiderlike creature almost as tall as they were. Above their heads was a view of space that made it seem as if the roof of the bridge had just been ripped away.

When Dorine had finished showing the still frames, her image came back up on the monitor.

She took a breath, wanting her audience to be able to catch their breaths also. Finally she said, "I don't know how much time we've got, but right now I don't have any more information. The station is going to keep this channel transmitting around the clock until we know the fate of the Earth. Until we get additional information, or need to make more requests, the transmitted sound will be turned down all the way. I suggest you just leave your televisions on and don't turn down the volume. The crew here will show a series of still-frames sent down by the exploration team, and I will be back on the air as soon as we know anything more.

"Perhaps a miracle will occur. Perhaps the planet-shaper will not arrive. Perhaps our 'rescuers' made a mistake about which way it is traveling. Whatever happens, I think this is another one of those times when Manhattanites who are so inclined might do well to pray in whatever manner you're comfortable with.

"I honestly don't know what we're going to do, but I do know we can't just do nothing."

Stuart Lund stopped in the street, watching a huge array of television screens on display as they all moved in unison, showing what the mayor said had been transmitted from the exploratory team. He suddenly felt tired.

Stuart turned and shouted to his followers who nearly surrounded him, "These images must have been falsified. You all know how easy it is to generate pictures like this. You see it every day in the movies."

In the portion of the crowd near enough to see the pictures for themselves, people turned to their neighbors and whispered. A few people turned and started to walk away. A man at the back started to shout, but the guy next to him shut him up.

Stuart began to speak again, but suddenly stopped in mid-sentence. Abruptly he felt tension in his stomach as he realized what was wrong. He was having trouble working up the enthusiasm he'd had before. The pictures were extremely unsettling. If Stuart and all the others were indeed in God's house, awaiting God's decision, these images of giant spiders didn't square with Stuart's expectations. Not at all.

The earlier pictures had been easier to accept as fakes, mainly because only one of the images showed a spider, and that really had looked like a fake. These pictures showed more than a dozen of the creatures, most of them sitting in chairs obviously designed for their strange bodies.

As Stuart stood at the side of the street, he realized it was *over*. He scanned faces among his followers. Many of them seemed to accept his denouncement of the video, but his followers weren't the problem. Stuart was the problem. He realized then and there that he no longer had the conviction he had started out with. The videos could all be fakes, but he had a terrible feeling they weren't.

So it no longer mattered what the crowd believed. Stuart's enthusiasm and conviction had carried them this far. Without that certainty in his voice and manner, they would know he had changed. The fire he had felt could not be faked. The crowd would know within minutes that the fire had died.

Stuart stood there, numb, and his followers looked at his face, and they began to whisper among themselves as they looked from his face to the television monitors and back.

The crowd began to dwindle slowly at first, but within ten minutes the stragglers were clearly disgruntled, distraught, and dispersing. Stuart no longer had the will to try to stop them. He sagged. He sat on the curb, watching most of his followers spread out along the dark streets. Maybe a tenth of the people stayed behind, most of them looking expectantly at Stuart, obviously still willing to believe. But Stuart wasn't sure he had anything appropriate to say.

A burly man in a plaid shirt came forward through the diminishing throng. He stopped in front of Stuart long enough to say, "Maybe we should all repent for all those bugs we've stepped on, huh?"

A young mother with two children at her side walked up to Stuart. The woman said gently, "We still believe you, Reverend."

Stuart waved her away.

As he sat there watching most of the people disappear, two boys in their late teens or early twenties came up and stood facing Stuart, their feet spread wide in a hostile stance.

The taller boy wore a conventional Mohawk, and his companion sported a twin Mohawk. They both wore left-hand-side-only mustaches made popular last year by Twisted Sabbath, and both had tattoos on their upper arms.

The taller boy said, "You made us look stupid. We *really* don't like to look stupid."

Stuart was sorely tempted to tell them they looked pretty

stupid anyway, but he just turned his back and walked away. If they wanted to follow him and attack, let them. Stuart didn't care anymore.

"That bastard," Benny Kellermund said as he watched the screen relaying pictures from the bridge of the ship. "Man, do I feel stupid."

"That's 'cause you are stupid," Lucky Stiles said.

"You thought he was right, too."

"Yeah, maybe."

"Well, we know we're nowhere near heaven. And those spider things aren't going to come down here and kill us. They would have killed us already if that's what they wanted."

"Right again, brain surgeon."

"So, what are we going to do?"

"You mean are we going to pull the switch? Explode the Empire State Building?"

"Right."

"Well, it's pretty tempting."

Benny knew he looked shocked. He was speechless.

"Just kidding," Lucky said quickly.

"So, do we go back and get the stuff?"

"Are you kidding? They'll have cops all over the place. And I'm not lugging that stuff back down. They can have it."

"Yeah?"

"Yeah. I'll find a pay phone and tell the mayor how to get it out safely."

"Man, we came pretty close."

"Too close." Lucky rose suddenly. "I'm gonna go out for a while. I'll be back."

"It doesn't sound good," Rudy said. "Not if the lasers won't do any good against the planet-shaper."

Matt rubbed his eyes. "True. But there's got to be something we can do."

"Even if the Archies aren't willing to fight?" Richard asked.

Matt glanced at the Archies at their positions on the bridge. "We'll just have to persuade them."

Abby took a break from her conversation with the Archie

captain. She came over and sat down next to the group of humans. "So far I haven't found any inconsistencies in their story. You want what I've got now or later?"

"Go ahead," said Matt. "We should hear pretty soon if there's anything in Manhattan that might be useful. And the more we know about the Archies' ship, the better."

"All right. Some of this will be repetition. When the planet-shaper finishes with whatever planets it damages in a solar system, it starts up some kind of interstellar drive that I'm just going to call warp drive. I *think* what happens is that the ship somehow jumps from one location in space to another one far away, and it has to make sure it's far from the sun—several times the distance we're at now. The planet-shaper makes a series of these jumps, and eventually arrives in a new solar system, and starts doing whatever it does again. Apparently the planet-shaper doesn't distinguish between inhabited and uninhabited planets.

"Anyway, the Archies' ship is better at this warp drive, if I understand this correctly. By watching which way the planet-shaper jumps, the Archies can see what solar systems lie on that course, and then make a single huge jump, getting to the destination before the planet-shaper does. If the solar systems are close together, the Archies don't gain much lead time, but if the planet-shaper has to make a long series of jumps, then the Archies usually have more time. When the planet-shaper jumped toward us, the Archies knew it would take several jumps, so they're not surprised the planet-shaper hasn't arrived, but it could be here any time. It all sounds fairly inexact, but I guess that's because they can't predict exactly what intermediate steps the planet-shaper will make."

Rudy looked up. "So that's why the destruction on the planet with the city of cones started even before the city was secure. The Archies didn't have much of a lead."

"Exactly," Abby said. "And that's why we're still here in our own solar system. The Archies have to wait until the planet-shaper is finished here before they know which way to go next."

"God, I hate that sound," Bobby Joe said. "They sound like teenagers when they eat."

Not far away, one of the Archies was eating as it sat at its station. The Archie apparently sucked its food into its mouth, sounding as if it were trying to get the last dribble of malt through a straw. Then, for a change of pace, it made a sound like it was sucking strands of spaghetti.

Abby grimaced. "I take back that last sentence. The Archies don't have to wait here until they see which way the planet-shaper goes; they have to wait here at least until they fix the warp drive. Oh, and on the other side of the ship, the other set of eight huge cylinders—they're the main components of the normal drive. They can still get around inside the solar system with the normal drive. They just can't make the long-distance jumps until the damage is fixed."

"And how long will that take?" Matt asked.

"They think about twenty to thirty days."

"I don't understand. If they can fix it in that long, why do they say they'll be unable to help the next few planets?"

"Because they think it may take them quite a while to find the planet-shaper again. Incidentally, no more than one out of ten of the planets it converts has life on it; they figure it will hit another fifty or sixty planets before their search will locate it again."

"How can they transform an entire planet that fast?"

"They don't. The initial barrage kills most of the native life, but the total transformation takes many years. Part of what the planet-shaper does is deposit machinery—I don't know what size they're talking about—that slowly finishes the job."

Motion overhead caught Matt's eye. Thin arcs formed in what Matt now realized had to be a display rather than a window on top of the bridge. A gray line intersected the Earth and curved out of sight on both ends. Six more gentle arcs formed in the display, two of them intersecting what looked to be stars, one yellow, one red. Six of the arcs seemed to all fall in a plane, but the most distant arc cut through the plane at an angle of maybe twenty degrees. In addition, the outside curve cut inside the nearest curve for part of its arc.

"Those must be orbits," Bobby Joe said. "We're a little above the plane of the ecliptic. I bet those curves represent the orbits of Earth and the other planets." He pointed. "Those bright 'stars' on the lines near the center must be Mars and Saturn. The other planets must be behind us or at our side."

"Makes sense," said Rudy.

"Of course it—whoa!" Bobby Joe's mouth dropped open as elements of the display changed. The two "stars" representing Mars and Saturn suddenly grew until they were perhaps a quarter of the size of the Earth in the display.

Mars was a reddish disk with few blemishes. Saturn was large enough to show its rings.

"What happened?" Richard asked. "We can't have moved. The Earth looks the same."

"Display enhancement," Bobby Joe said. "I like it. They magnified small elements in the display, just enough to show details. If they'd zoomed the whole display enough to show that much of Saturn, they would have narrowed the field to something less than one percent of what we can see. By doing it this way, we still get the big picture, but we can see what's what. Very elegant."

The display suddenly shifted, as though the ship were turning. Enormous cross hairs formed in the display, and the lines spread into filmy translucent planes, dividing space into four quadrants. Grids formed on both of the planes, and then two dotted lines emerged from the Earth, each one extending toward one of the grids. Matt was sure the two points where the dotted lines intersected the grids defined the Earth's position relative to the ship.

Jupiter, its streaked clouds visible, and Venus, a yellowish disk, appeared in the screen, obviously made to look close by the display enhancement.

Suddenly several of the Archies on the bridge chattered. Abby turned to the captain as a star near Jupiter began to blink. More dotted lines appeared between it and the grid planes. Dotted lines sprouted from Jupiter, and Matt realized the new object was roughly midway between the orbits of Jupiter and the next planet out, which Bobby Joe reminded him was Saturn.

Matt felt the adrenaline rush and a brief, sharp pain in his chest even before Abby turned from the captain and verified what they were all assuming.

In a hushed voice she said, "The planet-shaper has arrived."

16

THROWING ROCKS

ABBY FELT THE hush in the room as human eyes turned and Archie eye-stalks swiveled toward the new pinpoint of light blinking against the backdrop of stars. After the initial flurry of whispering and chattering, the bridge was suddenly as quiet as an early morning run. Even Bobby Joe was still. Then Abby was aware of Julie speaking quietly into a walkie-talkie, calmly feeding details to Manhattan. At the moment, Abby envied Julie's calm acceptance of recent events, no doubt aided by her experience in covering tragedy after tragedy in the past. Then again, maybe she was just like Abby, striving to be calm on the outside, but inside, a furious whirlpool of questions and fears.

At times Abby felt like moving off to a corner and going quietly and seriously insane. In Abby's place, her mother probably would have done exactly that. Her mother had been frightened just to think of Abby living on her own in New York.

Several times Abby had been on the verge of panic, despite her outward calm. Each time she had felt that fear tightening her throat, the experience had been something like feeling really out of breath halfway into a long run. And each time she had miraculously found her second wind, just as when she ran.

She couldn't freeze now; she couldn't give in to the panic. Now that the planet-shaper had actually arrived, she had a sudden image of her parents sitting out on the back porch, waiting in quiet anguish, wondering what had happened to Abby. Unless the team could somehow find a way to divert or destroy the planet-shaper, her parents would be gone, without even knowing why. An image from an old nuclear holocaust film jammed in her brain and wouldn't go away until she pinched herself so hard the pain brought her back to the bridge.

The area surrounding the blinking light in the display shimmered, and a larger image formed in its place, as though the planet-shaper had suddenly moved much closer than it had been seconds earlier, or the Archies had magnified its image, the way they had with the planets.

The planet-shaper looked more like a shiny piece of jewelry than a starship. Not quite a four-leaf clover, the planet-shaper brought to mind a cluster of four silvery teardrops, all joined at their narrow ends. At that central junction was a small sphere, the glob of glue holding the four sections together. Two teardrops opposite each other were slightly elongated, so together the teardrops formed a diamond. Distorted star fields reflected off the shiny surfaces.

Suddenly the star images slid aside and new ones replaced them as the planet-shaper changed orientation. Abby was struck by how beautiful the ship was.

"God," Richard whispered.

Abby glanced at Matt. She couldn't read his expression. He could have been in the middle of a poker game or a war. And this really *was* war, she realized.

A line began growing from the planet-shaper. The Archie captain said something Abby's computer transformed into "Direction."

The line continued growing until seconds later the destination was obvious: Venus. The line kept lengthening until it intersected the image of Venus.

"Maybe they don't want the Earth," Abby said suddenly. To the captain she said, "One planet? Not Earth?"

The Archie's four support legs flexed for just an instant, and its entire body dipped. It chattered and the computer said, "Two planets."

Bobby Joe said, "Earth and Venus must both be close enough to whatever profile they're using to pick planets. Venus is close to the size of Earth, and close to the same distance from the sun."

"What about Mars?" asked Rudy.

Bobby Joe shook his head. "Mars has about ten percent of

the mass of Earth. Venus is more like Earth, except for the heat and atmosphere, and I'm guessing this thing can deal with those little problems."

"Now what?" Matt asked.

Abby asked the question of the Archie captain.

"Wait. Watch," came the answer.

Julie approached Matt. "The Mayor wants to talk to you." She offered him her walkie-talkie.

Matt held the unit to his mouth and answered. A moment later, he said, "Yes, ma'am. Maybe I can get Bobby Joe to set up a second link so Julie can continue feeding a steady stream and we can still talk." Matt glanced at Bobby Joe, who thought for a couple of seconds then nodded. "Yeah, apparently it's possible."

Matt listened for a long moment. "No, I don't think that'll help much, either." Pause. "All right. We'll do our best."

Matt listened a moment longer. "I understand. I was about to ask the Archies to make sure we know as much as they do about the planet-shaper, and we've still got some questions about their own capabilities. If there aren't any supplies in Manhattan that will help, maybe ideas can help. Would you put out a call just the way you did for materials? If there are any experts with useful suggestions about space warfare or any useful ideas triggered by what we learn about the planet-shaper, pass them up to us fast. Right at the moment, we're a little short on options. We need creative, devious ideas. There has got to be a way to stop that ship."

A moment later Matt handed the walkie-talkie back to Julie. To Bobby Joe he said, "Okay. Get a second link set up as soon as possible, and give me a walkie-talkie on the second channel as soon as you're finished."

"Will do," said Bobby Joe. He hurried off toward the nearest line-of-sight point without even a smart remark.

Matt glanced at Abby, then at the others in the small group. "The mayor has set up a technical team to help get answers to questions that may come up. And I'm officially in charge of the war effort. By the time anyone else could get here from Manhattan, it might all be over anyway, plus we're the Archie experts now." He looked at the overhead screen. "First item of business:

Abby, tell the captain we want to intercept the planet-shaper. About *there* if we can." He pointed to a spot about a third of the way from Venus to the location of the planet-shaper.

Abby nodded. This would be pushing the limits of her speech translation, so she grabbed a marker, sat down, and began to write directly on the floor of the bridge. She made sure the captain was watching. She drew an octagon and said, "Archie ship." She drew a four-leaf clover and said, "Planet-shaper."

As she drew, the Archie captain folded her legs underneath her and sat on the floor, tipped forward so her eye-stalk could point at the drawing on the floor. Her mouth hung open, and Abby tried not to look at it.

Abby drew a line from the planet-shaper to a dot she called "planet." From the Archie ship to the intercept point she drew an arrow. From the planet-shaper to the same point she drew a second arrow. Finally she said, "Move," and retraced the arrow from the Archie ship to the intercept point.

The Archie's eye-stalk wiggled from side to side, then she chattered. The translator said, "Waste."

Abby went back and forth a couple of times trying for clarification as her anger built up and she had to work harder to conceal it. Finally she looked up at Matt. "She's saying it's a waste of time or energy. She says this ship has no weapon that can damage the planet-shaper. I'll show her two choices—either moving this ship or having this ship explode." Matt nodded.

Abby drew a picture of a fractured octagon, then what she thought was the "or" symbol, then retraced the line to the intercept point again.

Finally the Archie brushed its mouth with one of her forward legs, then chattered to her nearest compatriot, who in turned chattered at the Archie in the center of the bridge. That Archie's eye-stalk swiveled to point at the captain, who proceeded to tap one hand against the floor.

Moments later the image overhead changed as a series of concentric circles formed, centered on a point about a third of the way from Venus to the planet-shaper. The set of circles began to expand slowly. The display reminded Abby of scenes in movies showing the cockpit display as an airliner came in for a landing. Each circle disappeared as it reached a diameter of about a meter, and at the same time tiny circles appeared in the center of the smallest circles. "I think we're moving," Abby said.

Abby wasn't sure why she'd had to go through with the threat again. It was almost as if the Archie captain didn't believe anything that had been said only once or twice. Maybe the team was now closer to being taken more seriously.

The rate at which the circles grew increased, as though the ship were moving faster and faster. Julie directed her minivid at the display.

"What next?" Abby asked.

Matt stared at the expanse of stars above as he spoke. "If they're unwilling to fight, or unequipped to fight, they're only good for one thing: following our directions. Can you tell the captain that she's going to have to be *prompt* about doing what we ask? Tell her that we won't take any action as long as she cooperates quickly, but keep reminding her that we still have the power to destroy this ship."

"I'll give it a shot."

Abby spent more than ten minutes trying to get the concepts across to the Archie captain. As she was still working on it, Bobby Joe came back and handed Matt a walkie-talkie, saying the second link was all set. Abby drew on a new section of floor, trying to get across the idea of an undamaged ship, and finally, several minutes later, the Archie captain verbally agreed to the request and confirmed Abby's suspicion that tapping a hand on the ground meant "yes."

"Okay," said Abby. "I think she's still having a hard time accepting the idea that we would deliberately destroy the ship that's keeping us alive, but I tried to convince her we think differently from them. It's odd, though. A couple of times I've gotten the feeling they actually *like* having someone telling them to do something more than save cities and watch the planets be destroyed. Maybe they're feeling guilty about not being able to do more. What next?"

Matt said, "Next she's got to tell us everything she knows about the planet-shaper's weapons and its defenses."

That request took almost a half-hour to complete, but Abby's hope grew as she was able to add more vocabulary to her computer's translation bank as she did it. Communication ease was accelerating. The planet-shaper's hull was mirrorlike as part of its defense. The surface would apparently easily reflect the cutting lasers employed by the Archie shuttlecraft. And beneath the reflecting layer was a very hard material, so hard that the Archies felt no projectile would penetrate it. Small projectile weapons like human rifles and even antitank weapons would be useless.

"But muzzle velocity is meaningless," Bobby Joe pointed out. "The weapons we're talking about have muzzle velocities measured in thousands of meters per second at most. If we're going to reach where we're going any time soon, we'll be traveling at millions of kilometers per second. Just dropping a bullet in empty space and veering away would leave the bullet traveling a thousand times faster than we could shoot it."

Matt said, "Good point. But what about the planet-shaper's offensive weapons?"

The Archie captain was less sure about what weapons the planet-shaper carried. Apparently they hadn't had much reason to care. Abby finally decided the Archie captain was telling her the planet-shaper did in fact carry a weapon that could strike at a distance, but she didn't have the vocabulary to pin down what it was.

"Well, we've got to damage the planet-shaper somehow," Matt said finally. "We've got to find a way of turning something into an offensive weapon."

As Matt talked to the others, Abby realized she had finally obtained a large enough sampling of Archie-speak that she could load it into a language program that would start to extrapolate additional data to fill in the gaps.

If only it could help.

Dorine Underwood couldn't avoid a yawn. She wasn't at all bored, but she'd been awake for too long. She was exhausted. She held up a hand to the camera operator to say, "Just a couple of seconds more."

Finally she nodded. The camera light came on and she saw the "on the air" signal.

"Hello, New Yorkers. By now many of you have been watching what's happening on the bridge of this ship we're aboard. Now that the planet-shaper has arrived, our captors are telling us there's less than a day before the ship reaches Venus, and then perhaps only another eight hours before it reaches Earth. We were lucky that, thanks to where the planet-shaper appeared, it happened to be closer to Venus than to the Earth. That bought us an extra half-day.

"We need to make sure that gift is not wasted. We need to find out some way of crippling or destroying the planet-shaper before it reaches Earth. I want to be very clear on this point. If the ship we're in takes offensive action against the planet-shaper, there is a risk that it will strike back. By trying to save the Earth, we ourselves will be at risk.

"I believe the risk is one we have to take. I say this as someone who has a husband still on Earth, but I would say it anyway. I don't honestly know how to evaluate the risk, any more than someone running into a burning building to save a child knows exactly what the odds are. I think for the most part you will agree with me that we have to take the risk. If the worst happens to us, and this ship is damaged while stopping the planet-shaper from destroying life on Earth, then at least we will know that for every life in this dome, we saved a thousand lives on Earth, and the Earth itself."

Dorine pinched the bridge of her nose, then looked back at the camera. "I also have to say I've lost some of my optimism. We may not find a way to save the Earth. We're in a ship built for comparatively peaceful purposes, up against a ship built by people who probably expected it to run into massive opposition.

"But I also have a strong belief in human ingenuity. If there is a way to fight the planet-shaper, we will find it. If none exists, then we will have at least done everything possible to help.

"The nine-one-one lines are open again, this time for suggestions or tactics we could employ against the planet-shaper. As before, abuse of the nine-one-one system will be dealt with harshly. If you've got a legitimate idea, call. If you don't *know* that it's useful, call anyway. We'll filter the ideas down here, and pass as many as we can to the team on the bridge. Keep watching the telecast from the bridge, in case any new information triggers more possibilities.

"Thank you, Manhattan."

Rudy said, "We could have the Archies ram the planet-shaper with a shuttlecraft."

Abby asked the Archie captain about that and got the answer that even if she were willing to try, which was unlikely, she was pessimistic about the impact being large enough to do significant damage.

Bobby Joe's eyes opened wide. "Between Mars and Jupiter are lots of asteroids. What if we could grab a big one and throw it at the planet-shaper?"

Matt nodded to Abby. "See if you can get an answer to that." He clicked on his walkie-talkie and asked the mayor to run the same question by the technical team that was now standing by.

Within a few minutes Matt interrupted Abby's discussion with the captain. "The technical team says it's feasible, but the answer depends on the maximum acceleration the Archies' ship can attain. We'd have to go through three acceleration phases. One to get up to a high enough speed to approach a suitable asteroid long enough before the planet-shaper arrives, a second to slow down to match speed with the asteroid, and a third to get the ship and the asteroid up to ramming speed."

Abby shook her head. "I don't think it will work. She was trying to tell me the ship couldn't move fast enough, and now I know what that means."

Matt relayed that information to Manhattan. Seconds later, he said, "All right. They're ready to relay some of the initial suggestions that they've recorded and that the technical team thinks are at least adequate to pass on to us. I think if we all get close to the walkie-talkie I can crank up the sound enough that we can all hear so I don't have to relay everything."

Matt sat down next to Abby. Bobby Joe, Rudy, and Richard huddled close by as Julie kept transmitting. "Go ahead," said Matt.

The sound was tinny but audible. What sounded like an old man said, "Warn Earth. They can use atomic weapons on that sucker."

A young girl's voice said, "Squirt acid on the ship. Dissolve it."

"Fly out of the sun. Surprise it," said a male voice. A different voice, presumably one of the technical team, added, "This one makes sense not just because of the obvious visual difficulty the planet-shaper would have. Besides that, the sun gives off a huge amount of broad-spectrum noise that might interfere with other kinds of sensors, too."

A nervous man said, "I think perhaps . . . perhaps we should just ram the planet-shaper with this ship."

For the last twenty hours, the largest display in Times Square had been showing live video from what residents had dubbed The Mayor Channel. At the moment, the screen showed the bridge of the Archies' ship, along with Matt Sheehan and Abby Tersa.

Herb Abjernal watched the screen intently, wishing he had a cigarette, ignoring the jostling of the huge crowd. At the corner of Seventh Avenue and West 43rd Street, a tall pedestal supported twelve huge speakers that carried the audio to go with the video. Herb was close enough to the speakers that when the Mayor or someone else spoke, the sound hurt his ears, but he didn't move away because sometimes the crowd's excited reaction almost covered up the words.

At the moment, the speakers were silent, and Herb heard the loud voice of a man on the south side of the intersection. "What the hell do we owe Earth? All the rest of the world ever did was complain about New York. They're probably glad we're gone. Why should we risk our lives to help those idiots?"

Even if Herb hadn't had a daughter in Hawaii and a son in Arizona, he would still have been angry. He considered moving from his chosen spot, but the angry reactions from the people nearest the speaker said there was no need to move. The man was being cursed in three languages.

The man started up again, saying, "We're all safe. No one is going to touch us if we don't interfere. I say—"

Whatever else the man had to say was interrupted by the meaty sound of a punch. Voices rose again, but Herb didn't hear the complainer say anything more. Who said New Yorkers just stood by and let crap happen?

"You know," Matt said, "we do have something really massive we could throw at the planet-shaper. And we wouldn't have to go anyplace to get it."

Rudy cocked his head. "And what might that be?"

"A city. The dead city we explored."

Abby sensed the first glimmer of hope she'd felt for hours.

Richard nodded, and Bobby Joe said, "I like it!"

To Abby, Matt said, "Ask the Archies if that's possible, and if it is, to get started removing the city as fast as they can. We won't want to match speed at the intercept point; we'll want to be moving as fast as we can relative to it."

Abby nodded and turned to the Archie captain. She tried to get the question across, being extremely careful to identify the correct city.

The Archie captain seemed to get excited. Her two front legs twitched as Abby completed the first question. Finally Abby turned back to Matt and said, "She thinks they can do it. And she seems to think it might work. They'll start now."

One of the wall screens showed an overhead view of the huge square building they had searched earlier, and Abby identified it as the correct city.

"Tell them about setting a course so the final approach has this ship directly between the sun and the planet-shaper," Matt said. "We can't assume they know anything about fighting."

"Let me help, will you?" Bobby Joe said to Abby as he reached for the marker.

Bobby Joe drew on a new section of floor, showing the straight line between the planet and Venus and the straight line between the Archies' ship and the interception point. He scratched through the straight line and next to it drew a curve that ended at the intercept point. He drew a tangent to the final portion of the curve and drew a straight line directly into the sun. Bobby Joe suggested what Abby should say, translating from technical to layman as Abby completed the translation.

Finally she was convinced the Archie captain understood.

The captain chattered to a nearby Archie. Seconds later, Bobby Joe said, "Terrific!"

Abby followed his gaze to the overhead display, which had changed. The series of expanding concentric circles had stretched out so they were no longer concentric but instead formed a transparent shape like the old-fashioned curved cone of an early mechanical record player. Instead of heading directly for the intercept point, their path curved closer to the sun.

"Hello?" Lucky Stiles called.

His voice echoed in the warehouse, but no reply came. Lucky moved quickly up the stairs and through the maze to the preacher's office.

"Hello?" he called again. Still no answer.

The office was unoccupied. The preacher must have been out someplace, getting more idiots to follow him.

Lucky withdrew a package from his coat pocket and quickly did what he needed to do.

Jamie Fahred carefully pushed the buttons on the portable phone. Nine-one-one. Seconds later a woman's voice said, "Please state your suggestion concisely. Go."

Jamie hesitated, then let the idea burst forth. "I think we should move the Earth so it's on the other side of the sun so they can't see it."

"I don't think we're going to be able to contact Earth," Abby said. "At least not in time to help. With Bobby Joe's help, I've tried to describe radio, and as best as I can tell, they use some other method of communication."

Abby didn't know whether to be disappointed or not. There was nothing the people on Earth could do to avert disaster. If her parents were doomed to die soon, maybe it would be best if they didn't have their final hours filled with panic and frustration.

"All right," Matt said. "We've had some suggestions for taking parabolic satellite dishes and modifying them so they could be used to feed signals toward Earth. People in Manhattan are working on the modifications, but there's probably not enough time to finish and move the equipment to someplace it could be used."

Abby sighed. "All right. You ready for the inventory?"

"Shoot."

"Each shuttlecraft has a high-power laser. The Archies say they've got power to run them almost continuously for a long time. I didn't figure out what a long time was except that it's at least longer than a month."

Rudy looked up. "Even if we can't cut through the outside surface, we might be able to heat the interior enough to cook whatever's inside—depending on the reflectivity of the surface."

"Okay," Matt said. "What else?"

Abby looked at the short list she'd written on the floor. "Enough bubble material to cover another hundred cities."

Richard had been lying flat on the floor with his eyes closed. He opened his eyes suddenly and said, "That could make a good defensive barrier for this ship if it's impervious to the planet-shaper's weapons."

Matt shook his head. "The point is not to defend this ship; what we need to defend is the Earth. We'd need a lot more. What else?"

"They've got more of the black material they inject in the cuts to go under the cities. Again enough for another hundred cities or so. They're more concerned about using it up than they are about using the lasers."

"That's because they don't think we can destroy the planet-shaper. Can we just get close to the planet-shaper and push on it? If this ship has more thrust, we could just keep them at bay until some other weapon is available?"

Abby talked with the captain again. "No luck," she said finally. "The captain is sure that if a ship this large gets close to the planet-shaper it will be fired on. And even all the shuttles together don't have the combined thrust of the planet-shaper."

"How big is that thing anyway?" Bobby Joe asked.

After conferring with the captain, Abby said, "Apparently it's about a tenth of the size of this ship. Oh, and she also says they have virtually unlimited fuel for acceleration for both this ship and all the shuttlecraft."

"Take a look," Bobby Joe said suddenly. "The movers are here."

Abby looked at the large screen Bobby Joe pointed at. The huge octagonal port on one wall of the huge chamber below was open, revealing the stars beyond. Eight black shuttlecraft in formation moved slowly through the opening, several of them visibly shaking in the fast-moving air that shot toward freedom. The port slowly dilated closed as the shuttlecraft formation drifted carefully inward.

An adjacent screen showed the dead city, its life-support tubes separating from the dome and retracting into the ceiling.

Fawn Terricole called nine-one-one on an antique Mickey Mouse phone so old that it had to have one of those interface boxes so it could be connected to the phone line. She could feel her heart beat louder as the ring sounded in her ear. She rubbed a smudge off the white in Mickey's eye.

When it was her turn to talk, she said, "What if we were to disguise the Earth, so it already looked like whatever those people want it to look like? Then they wouldn't have to change it."

"Any way to tell what the odds of success are?" Matt asked Rudy.

Rudy shook his head. "Apparently this city should have a mass that's no more than a few percent of the mass of the planet-shaper. But a bullet is a smaller fraction than that when you compare it to a human body. Relative speed and internal shock waves are the key, and that's what we're taking advantage of."

"But we're firing a bullet at a tank."

"Right. But penetration isn't the only way we can win. Ever see a picture of someone without an air bag who hit the windshield but didn't go through? Even if all we can do is suddenly slow down the planet-shaper, that might be enough to do a lot of damage to whatever's inside. If we've got enough kinetic energy, we might slow it down the same way a brick wall slows down a car."

Francesca Abdalla spoke precisely and slowly into the phone. "Use the bubble material to cap as many cities on Earth as possible before the ship arrives. That way at least the people inside could survive."

The eight black shuttlecraft had surrounded the dead city and hooked support lines to points around the perimeter. Abby held her breath as the eight ships rose until the lines were all piano-wire tight.

They held that formation for almost thirty seconds, and finally the domed city started to move slowly upward. Abby realized she'd been holding her breath the whole time. Oh, please, let this work.

On the star field above, the planet-shaper was much closer, and the set of expanding circles was cycling even faster than before, no doubt indicating they were moving faster and faster. The path through the circles was closer to a straight line again. The Archie captain had explained that once the city moved outside the ship, it would no longer be subjected to the gravity/inertial field established inside the ship. From that point on, the city would fly an independent path, a straight line at constant speed determined by the ship's motion at the release point.

By that time, the Archies' ship had to be on a perfect trajectory. The ship could swerve away from the impact point, but the city would be a bullet in a vacuum. If the planet-shaper's instruments picked up the approaching mass and changed its course, the bullet would be wasted, the chance forever lost.

The Archie captain sounded more optimistic than she had earlier. The dead city emitted no signals that might help the planet-shaper detect it, and the black material absorbed signals that might be generated by the planet-shaper.

Abby felt a strong sense of accomplishment that, aided by the computer, she was getting better and better at understanding the Archie captain. Communication had passed beyond the essentials, and she was learning even more about the Archies, who called themselves something that translated to "omni sense."

On the Archies' home planet, the competing life-forms usually had one or two prominent senses, but the Archies were the only species to possess vision, hearing, and smell. Abby was relieved that "omni sense" didn't rhyme with "dickhead," or Bobby Joe's designation would be tougher to ignore.

The city rose still farther, and Abby could see part of the black cone beneath it. Below it in the goo was a deep cone-shaped depression that might take days to fill up.

The dead city continued rising, and the bottom point of the black cone rose past the level of the plain. The domed mass rose smoothly until minutes later the entire city, looking vaguely like a monstrously large snow cone, began to drift sideways, maneuvering through the maze of life-support tubes carrying nutrients to the still-living cities.

The overhead display showed the set of circles concentric once again. The sun was no longer in the display. If the Archie ship was on course, they would be speeding into their own shadow as they raced closer and closer to the planet-shaper.

Once again the huge octagonal opening on one side of the ship dilated. The dead city and its eight pallbearers slid into space. The eight shuttlecraft moved into a ring surrounding the lip where the bubble met the black cone, and they pulled the city through the portal. The dark point of the cone was aimed directly at the planet-shaper, and the dome over the city was lit by brilliant sunshine. The octagonal portal dilated closed as the eight shuttlecraft started to drift away from the motionless mass.

The Archie commander chattered to one of her compatriots. A view of the city appeared on another wall screen and abruptly began to shrink as the ship veered away. The bullet was on its own trajectory.

17

URBAN DISINTEGRATION

STARS SHIFTED IN the huge overhead screen as the Archies' ship veered away from the path of the dead city. The planet-shaper was an immense silvery mass consuming the central quarter of the screen. Reflections of stars rippled across its contours. At the edge of the view, the dead city floated into view, accompanied by four Archie shuttlecraft assigned to give any necessary last-minute course-correction nudges.

From near the center of the bridge, Matt watched the screen, and for the moment nothing else in the universe mattered. He wished he could view the action from a point along their previous trajectory, so he could watch as the dead city approached the planet-shaper head on. The drawback was that, had the Archie ship stayed on the same course, it would not survive. It was a big enough target that the planet-shaper would probably see it too soon as it flew out of the sun, since it would eclipse the sun in plenty of time for the planet-shaper to notice it. Right now, the Archie ship should be small enough to be nothing more than a comet as far as the planet-shaper was concerned. And even if the planet-shaper didn't react to it in time, a collision would probably destroy the Archies' ship with no real guarantee of destroying the planet-shaper. Matt felt as if he were trying to win a battle against a tank while equipped only with a passenger car.

The rest of the team watched the screen without speaking as the Archie captain chattered into her control panel. She had taken the central chair, and the other nine Archies had all changed positions in series, as though the eight seats surrounding the captain were in pecking order rather than assigned to specific functions. The Archie who had been the last one ejected from a chair had left the bridge.

Abby stood next to Matt, near enough that her shoulder bumped his upper arm. Matt looked at her and she deliberately edged slightly closer so their arms touched. Abby looked at him and held his gaze without moving away.

Matt put his arm around her shoulder. In response, Abby leaned against him for a moment.

Motion on a large wall screen riveted Matt's attention, as it suddenly presented the view Matt had wished for earlier. Without being consciously aware of the action, he moved away from Abby and toward the screen. The planet-shaper was dead center, growing noticeably. The view must have been coming from one of the shuttlecraft escorting the dead city. He hoped the craft could get free safely.

The planet-shaper grew larger in the screen, the bright sun reflecting off a half-dozen curved stretches of the ship's hull. As the image grew larger, a small dark spot formed near the center of the brightest reflections, and Matt realized the spot was the shadow cast by the dead city. The planet-shaper just kept getting bigger and bigger, as though a specimen under a microscope. Its surface showed no features, just seamless reflectivity, as the mirrored star field continued to distort while they grew closer. Matt thought of a knight in shining armor faced by a pencil hurtling through the dark. And he remembered pictures of straws of hay shot into oak trees during tornadoes.

The Archie captain spoke, and a louder chattering response sounded from speakers somewhere in the room. The view in the wall screen suddenly began pulling to one side faster and faster as the shuttle pilot veered to safety.

On the ceiling screen, the four escort shuttlecraft split off from the dead city, which seemed to be only seconds from impact with the planet-shaper. The planet-shaper turned, or seemed to turn, but when Matt saw the star field behind the planet-shaper moving more quickly he realized that they were almost even with the planet-shaper, watching it from the side as they passed. Matt held his breath.

The black cone of the dead city occulted a strip of stars as it sped toward the planet-shaper, its dome gleaming in the sunshine to its back. The cone was no bigger than an arrowhead about to hit a body. At just about the same instant that Matt felt the Archies' ship was directly even with the planet-shaper, the gap between the dead city and the planet-shaper closed to zero.

Matt had watched enough movies that he was expecting an enormous explosion with billowing clouds of flame and fireworks sparklers spinning off in all directions. That never came.

Total silence accompanied the view. The impact point was out of sight, occurring between two of the cloverleaves, but suddenly there was no doubt about whether the city hit. The planet-shaper suddenly began to turn like a giant pinwheel.

"Yes!" Bobby Joe shouted as a spray of material jetted out of the gap where the impact must have occurred. Bits and pieces in the spray glinted brightly on the sun side and started to fade as the Archies' ship's velocity carried it past the planet-shaper.

The Archie captain chattered and received two replies. The view of the planet-shaper magnified until it nearly filled the screen. As they watched, the ship's rotation slowed, then stopped.

"Oh, God," Rudy said softly, and Matt knew exactly what he meant. The only way the ship would stop rotating like that was if it had been powered to a stop, with thrust applied in the right direction for the right amount of time. The planet-shaper was obviously still operational.

Within minutes they had confirmation that the planet-shaper was still decelerating at just about the right rate to bring it into orbit around Venus.

"Decelerate," Matt said to Abby. "We've got to stop and go back. To catch up with the planet-shaper."

It took Abby a moment to get the captain's attention. The captain's first response, relayed through Abby was, "Waste. Why bother?"

Matt's first reaction was to threaten the captain that he'd twist her head off if she didn't. He tightened his self-control and forced himself to say, "Tell her we'll explain later, but to just do it." Maybe later Matt could think of a good reason. At the moment, he felt like he was David and had just found out Goliath was wearing full body armor.

"Okay." Abby exchanged several sentences with the captain

and she finally sighed, then said, "She's agreed. At least she's lost nothing irreplaceable and this ship suffered no damage."

As the view from a returning shuttlecraft showed the enormous dark octagon of the Archies' ship, the planet-shaper was already just a dark speck against the sun.

Stuart Lund flipped on a light as he moved toward the stairs. Climbing the stairs gave him the impression that full gravity had returned, he felt so heavy as he moved.

On the second floor, he navigated his way through the leftover construction materials and entered his office. He felt like lying down on the cot and sleeping for a year.

On the table was a gift-wrapped present with a card. The pink paper with small pictures of babies was almost certainly inappropriate for any gift for him, but supplies like wrapping paper were scarce, and the choice didn't bother Stuart.

He picked the card off the top of the present. It was snagged on something, and a hair-thin fiber snapped as the card came away in his hand. He opened the card. The sloppy handwriting said, "You almost made us blow up the Empire State Building. You've got ten seconds."

Stuart instantly knew what the note meant, but he made no effort to run. Instead, with a tired sigh, he sat down in the chair next to the table and rested his face in his hands.

When it came, the explosion shattered windows three blocks away.

Kay Arknette turned down the sound on The Mayor Channel and moved to the utilitarian black desk phone. She felt self-conscious as she called nine-one-one. This was not the kind of thing a grade school teacher did. Finally, after the go-ahead, she said, "I think if it's either us or the Earth, we should ram the planet-shaper with this ship. If we're not sure this ship can do enough damage, wait until the planet-shaper is close to Venus or Earth and ram it from above. It might survive hitting us, but I'll bet it won't survive the impact when we both hit the ground."

It wasn't until Kay had hung up the phone and let her breathing slow down that she had a sudden additional thought. If they did run this ship at a very high speed directly toward the planet-shaper and the planet below, and if the planet-shaper was able to suddenly move out of the way, then they would lose everything.

It took several hours to lose the velocity that it had taken them several hours to gain, but finally the Archies' ship was moving toward the planet-shaper again. By that time, the planet-shaper had almost reached Venus.

Abby had been doing a terrific job of getting more information out of the Archies. One of the mysteries she'd recently found an explanation for was the lack of Archie response to their earlier transmissions. Having only one native language, the Archies were extremely inept—Abby's word, not the Archies'—at communicating with other species. Their monitoring equipment checked for physically observable problems associated with the life-support systems, such as the water supply flooding a city, but they hadn't been listening for any transmissions, figuring they wouldn't be able to understand them anyway.

It seemed to Matt that they could have done better than they expected. Their expectations were chains more effective than any prison could be.

As Abby continued to talk with the Archie captain, Matt approached Bobby Joe. "There's something I don't understand. I've been thinking back to school and seeing diagrams of transfer orbits. In this ship we don't seem to be paying any attention to stuff like that. What is it that I'm not getting?"

"Energy. This ship can accelerate so fast that orbital mechanics are noise-level concerns. When it takes you months to go from one planet to another, you have to factor in where the planet's going to be when you finally show up. When you can get there in hours, the planet has hardly had time to move."

Matt nodded. He had a stiff neck from looking up at the overhead screen so much of the time. Centered in the display were the magnified images of the planet-shaper and Venus. Venus was a yellowish ball of gas whose image suddenly transformed into something more like Jupiter's. The image now showed what seemed to be huge spirals of light clouds over a darker planetary body.

"I didn't think the planet-shaper was close enough yet to start doing anything," Matt said.

"I don't think it did anything," Bobby Joe said. "I bet the Archies just added ultraviolet conversion to the spectrum they're viewing with."

Beyond the planet-shaper and Venus was a bloated reduced-intensity image of the sun. The surface brightness had been decreased so it was only marginally brighter than Venus, and a huge sunspot showed near the equator. A slow-motion prominence had erupted near the bottom of the disk and was arcing out from the sun to what seemed to be half the radius of the sun itself. The diffuse halo around the sun, what Bobby Joe had identified as the corona, billowed out to about twice the sun's radius, transforming the sun into a cosmic fried egg, its yellow yoke surrounded by translucent egg-white.

"Oh, God, no," said Bobby Joe. "It's feeding time again."

Matt saw the first Archie leave its chair and head for the meal cart that had appeared in a small doorway. As soon as the first Archie had retrieved its small bowl of what Matt labeled porridge, the next one up in the pecking order fetched a meal until finally the Archie captain went to get a bowl.

By that time, all the other Archies on the bridge were making that awful sucking noise as they drew the porridge into their mouths. The substance must have had enough water content on its own, because Matt saw none of the Archies drinking. Bobby Joe grimaced at the sounds. At periodic intervals, the Archies disappeared one by one to take care of elimination, but as far as Abby had been able to tell, the Archies did not sleep. They had occasional naps or rest periods during which they were very relaxed though fully aware. She hadn't yet been able to communicate the notion of sleep.

Matt wished humans had the same trait. He had taken a short nap when he reached the point that he just couldn't stand it any longer, and even now he felt extremely fatigued, his eyes gritty. A light-headed feeling persisted with the constant hypertension symptoms of rapid heartbeat and shortened attention span.

On the display above, the line that had recently been pointing from the planet-shaper just past Venus changed. It turned into a circle that surrounded Venus. Matt knew even before Abby confirmed the fact that the planet-shaper had entered orbit around Venus. The Archie ship was still several hours away from catching up. The idea that, since they were past the midpoint of their catchup journey, they were now deliberately slowing down even as they tried to catch up with the planet-shaper as fast as possible was enormously frustrating.

At least, thanks to the inertial shield system the Archies' ship must have according to Bobby Joe, they didn't *feel* like they were slowing down. When Bobby Joe had talked about the acceleration, he said that for the ship to move from a stop near one location and arrive at a stop very far away in a matter of hours, the ship had to be accelerating at enough gees to squash everyone inside if it weren't for some kind of protective field. He supposed that however the ship isolated the interior from the acceleration, that process had to burn almost as much energy as the acceleration itself.

A wall screen began to display a closeup view of Venus, showing just enough space around it that the planet-shaper was visible as it began to curve around to the far side of the planet. At ten-second intervals, what looked like tracer bullets fired downward from the planet-shaper into the cloud cover surrounding Venus.

In the ship's wake was a series of brilliant but diffuse flashes underneath the top layer of clouds, as if a lightning storm was speeding across the planet's surface at an enormous rate. The flashes turned the clouds slightly greenish and made them bubble, disrupting their patterns. The images weren't all that different from a series of depth charges exploding after being dropped from a mine-sweeping helicopter, except that the depth charges affected an area less than a kilometer wide, while each of these explosions had to be covering hundreds of kilometers.

After every eight or ten tracer bullets came a brighter flash, as though the series of shots included a mixture of devices. Within minutes the natural swirling patterns of clouds in the atmosphere were visibly disrupted.

"God almighty," Bobby Joe said softly.

Abby came back from a conversation with the captain. "She says the planet-shaper has started on the first phase of its conversion. This phase is designed to destroy all surface, atmospheric, and aquatic life. If I'm understanding correctly, the planet-shaper deposits some material that absorbs massive amounts of oxygen and maybe carbon dioxide, traps it for a long time, and then starts to slowly release it back into the atmosphere."

"Venus doesn't have much free oxygen," said Bobby Joe, "but if I remember right, it's got a lot of carbon dioxide. If they get rid of a fair amount of Venus's atmosphere, the planet could start cooling down to a comfortable temperature. There'd still be a lot to do to make it habitable, depending on the life-form it's meant for."

Abby shook her head. "I haven't been able to find that out yet. I'm not sure if it's a vocabulary problem or what. But I don't think the planet-shaper only tampers with planets where success is guaranteed. Apparently if it's anywhere close to the profile, the planet-shaper does its work, but the builders may or may not wind up using the planet."

Rudy glanced at Matt and shook his head sadly. "Maybe whoever built that ship isn't all that different from us."

Shirley Tandler-Gomez dialed nine-one-one and waited. "If the lasers on the shuttlecraft aren't powerful enough to damage the big ship, maybe they would be stronger if every single one of them went on at the same time, all pointing at the same spot on the ship."

"There it is," said Bobby Joe.

Matt looked back at the screen and saw the planet-shaper just coming out from behind Venus. Following it, in the atmosphere below, was the chain of fireballs, more visible now than they had been earlier. In addition, a smaller series of explosions burst in vacuum above the altitude of the planet-shaper.

In the wake of the high-altitude explosions was a dark cloud forming about five times higher than the atmospheric envelope. Within a couple of minutes, Abby had learned from the captain that the cloud was likely to be a solid-smoke material to be left in orbit as a sun-screen to reduce the amount of sunlight reaching the planet. When and if the planet was colonized, a huge array of orbiting shades and mirrors would give the planet an artificially shorter day.

As they watched, a magnified image of the planet-shaper appeared on an adjacent screen. The image swelled farther and farther until it nearly filled the screen. Roughly two-thirds of the glossy surface of the ship reflected stars; the other third reflected the lemon-yellow clouds of Venus.

The image continued to grow until Matt suddenly thought he saw a dark patch on the side of one of the cloverleaf masses. Whoever was controlling the display apparently saw the same thing, because the image shifted until the dark spot was centered in the screen, and the magnification continued.

"What's that?" Rudy said.

"I don't know yet," Matt said. "But it could be good news."

The image kept growing as all the humans watched. Soon it filled half the screen and still kept growing.

"All right!" Bobby Joe yelled. Several of the Archies chattered, either in response to the loud noise, or because they were encouraged also.

As the dark patch grew, Matt realized he was grinning. The ship had a hole in its hull where the city had struck it. The dark patch they were seeing was part of the interior of the planet-shaper. The ship was still functioning, but it wasn't invincible.

18

DEMOLITION EXPERT TO THE STARS

"WE MAY HAVE a chance after all," Matt said under his breath. Part of being a good soldier is trying to find any possible route to success. Another part is knowing when to cut your losses and quit. Privately he had been desperately worried that the planet-shaper had no weakness they could capitalize on.

The dark patch on the side of the planet-shaper said the ship was vulnerable. Goliath was bleeding.

"Are you thinking what I'm thinking?" Rudy asked.

"Maybe."

"If that's an opening in the hull, the ship might be especially vulnerable to a second attack at the same point."

"And the lasers would be worth trying now?"

"Exactly."

Matt turned to Abby. "We've got to get the captain to risk at least a couple of the shuttlecraft. She can see the damage as well as we can. Surely now that we've got a chance to stop this thing here and now she'll be willing to send them out. We've told her we're willing to destroy this ship unless she cooperates, and she may believe that or she may not. Try working on her guilt, if they feel any. They essentially killed the race in the city we threw at the planet-shaper. This has got to be put to a stop."

Abby nodded. "I'll do my best."

As Abby moved closer to the Archie captain, Richard appeared at Matt's side. Richard's forehead glistened with sweat.

Matt said, "You look like you've got something to say."

Richard nodded. "If the Archies send out a few shuttlecraft, they may be able to do enough damage with the lasers. Or they might not. So far the lasers by themselves don't seem too effective against mirrors." Richard swallowed.

"And?"

"And I think one of the shuttlecraft would have a much better chance going in there if it had an additional weapon: high explosives. And obviously that would require an expert to use them."

Matt looked at Richard long enough for the man to back down if he wanted to before Matt finally said, "Am I to understand you're volunteering for the mission?"

"Yes, sir."

Matt nodded. "You're a good man, Richard. I'll have Abby find out if it's possible."

Richard blinked a couple of times and swallowed. Matt was glad to see the man looked as nervous as Matt felt. That was a good sign of sanity. Anyone not nervous about that prospect was either an idiot or unqualified, or both.

Matt reached Abby's side as she talked to the Archie captain. At the first opportunity he had her ask if a human would fit into an Archie shuttlecraft along with the Archie crew. She raised her eyebrows but asked the question.

"Yes," Abby said when she got the response. Softly, her face paler than normal, she said to Matt, "Are we talking about you?"

"No. Richard."

Abby took a deep breath and blinked.

"Now tell the captain we want that human to carry explosives like the ones that damaged this ship. The supplies we brought with us are the closest ones."

As Abby spoke with the captain and her own voice occasionally came from the computer translator, Matt thought he could see what was going on in the captain's mind. The captain wouldn't like the idea of sending a human out there in a shuttlecraft, and she wouldn't like the idea of taking offensive actions that could possibly tell the planet-shaper that it should consider the Archie ship a threat and then act on that threat. What the captain *would* probably like was the idea of getting the explosives off the ship itself.

After several exchanges, the captain finally agreed. Abby said, "I'm surprised. When I started trying to use guilt, it seemed to me the response was even better than when we threatened them."

Matt heard the words, but his thoughts were on Richard. He felt the chill associated with sending a man out to die, almost as if he were pulling the trigger himself. He didn't spend any time trying to rationalize the situation by telling himself Richard had volunteered or that it was a necessary thing to do. Instead he said silently, "God grant you luck, Richard."

To Abby, Matt said, "Can you equip Richard with a small vocabulary? Hand signs or whatever works. Just so he can say things like 'forward,' 'backward,' 'stop,' and whatever else he can fit into a half-dozen gestures the Archies can understand."

Abby nodded. "What are his chances out there?"

"I don't know. Not very good. Just don't let that thought contaminate your actions."

Abby hesitated. Matt knew she was aware of the stakes, but sending someone into battle to die was never easy. He said, "When I used to play handball, I found that if I got a big lead on my opponent, I'd let up. Sometimes I'd win by a big margin anyway. Sometimes I'd win by a small margin. And sometimes I'd lose to an inferior player. There's no room for that kind of luxury in war."

"Yes, sir," she said finally.

"I think I know exactly how you feel." He walked away from her then, partly because the conversation was over, partly because he wanted to wipe a speck of dirt from his eye in private.

A hoarse voice spoke to one of the nine-one-one operators. "If the spiders could use that bubble stuff and some silvery stuff to make some gigantic mirrors, we could focus the sunlight and toast that ship to a cinder."

Richard tightened his grip on the monorail strut as the car sped past a part of the ship he hadn't seen before. He hadn't traveled this fast since before Manhattan had been lifted. The wind assaulted his eyes, which already stung due to lack of sleep, and made him squint.

Squinting into the wind made him feel heroic somehow, like an admiral in the prime seafaring years squinting into the salt spray, hoping for his first glimpse of land in more than a month.

The Archie sitting next to him spoiled the illusion and brought back the tremble Richard could conceal most of the time. At least the Archie wouldn't know that meant Richard was scared. What did Archies do when they were scared? Did they even get scared?

Matt must have understood back there, understood that Richard wasn't the unshakable rock that he wished he could be. At least Bobby Joe hadn't seen the break in his facade. Richard didn't need any more smart remarks from Bobby Joe.

What he wanted was acceptance, friendship, respect. The cool, aloof professional attitude seemed to get Richard respect, but it stood in the way of friendship. Richard could see that, but he didn't know what to do differently.

The monorail car flashed past a series of large coils that stretched from the floor to the ceiling high overhead. Richard was sure the monorail was going much faster than he'd seen the cars move before. He tapped his foot against the knapsack full of the tools of his trade to make sure it was still with him.

"What are you looking at?" he said suddenly to the Archie sitting next to him. The Archie's eye-stalk had swung toward Richard instead of the path ahead. This Archie wore clothing with narrow stripes of blue and red that made Richard's vision vibrate.

The Archie chattered briefly in reply, saying something Richard had no hope of translating. Suddenly he felt his interactions with humans were just as filled with confusion as this recent exchange, just as alien as the Archie next to him, its body resting on a seat designed to support the two segments, its legs folded up around it. When Richard said nothing more, the Archie's eye-stalk swung ahead, making Richard wonder briefly if the Archie's ears were also on its eye-stalk, making it a weird biological analogue of the multifunction sticks in cars that controlled turn signals and headlights.

He kept thinking about the situation, deliberately *not* thinking about what would happen when the monorail car pulled to a stop. He was a typical human being. Why then couldn't he just figure out how to feel comfortable with other humans? Surely they all must be basically like him, have the same desires, the same reactions to similar situations. Why couldn't he, whenever necessary, say *How would I react in this situation?* and then know what someone else would be thinking?

But he knew things did not work that simply. If it had, he'd still be married. He tried very hard to put himself in the other person's shoes, but all too often other people's responses, even Shirley's, were 180 degrees away from what he guessed they might be, even when he felt he was in possession of all the relevant information.

So here he was, doing what he feared most, trying to pretend he wasn't scared. But that was still better than having people think he was a coward.

The monorail car started to slow down. Ahead a door slid open at the base of a huge cylinder that reached all the way to the high ceiling. Within seconds it was obvious that the monorail wouldn't be able to stop before it reached the cylinder; and, sure enough, it went right through the doorway and came to a stop inside, resting under a ceiling no more than five meters high. The Archie stayed seated, so Richard did, too.

The door closed behind the monorail car and the car suddenly began rising. A half-minute later, the gravity faded, then resumed as the car pulled to a stop at a new level. A doorway ahead of the car opened, and the Archie touched a control near the base of the pedestal that supported the chair he sat on.

The monorail car moved silently forward and through the doorway, which closed behind it, and came to a stop on what was apparently a flight deck. Eight black shuttlecraft formed a semicircle most of the way around the stopped monorail car, each of the shuttlecraft sunk maybe halfway into depressions in the deck surface. Overhead was another ceiling screen showing an expanse of stars even brighter than the nights when Richard had been on the farm. Four Archies were busily working on one of the shuttlecraft, using devices on the ends of hoses and cables that stretched from openings in the far wall. A large poster or display screen on another wall showed a panorama of an alien planet, one with a thick layer of clouds. It took Richard a moment of orientation to realize the clouds were in use as a projection screen, but he couldn't tell if the strange characters and small scenes displayed there were advertising or entertainment or road maps or almost anything else.

Richard surveyed a nearby shuttle. Doors were cut into the sides of the craft so that the bottom lips of the hatches were even with the deck floor. The outlines of numerous doorways showed on the walls of the round room, as though spare parts and equipment lay just beyond. The stench of something uncomfortably like burning machine oil hung in the air.

The Archie got out of the monorail car and moved toward one of the shuttlecraft, fortunately not the one being worked on. The Archie extended one rear leg toward Richard and made a curiously humanlike *come here* gesture with one small digit, no doubt having learned that during Abby's short training session. Richard put on his backpack, then gave the Archie a *thumbs up* gesture that it should now recognize as *okay*.

Though most Archies seemed graceful, this one Archie waddled as it walked, and Richard suppressed a nervous grin. God knows he himself was no picture of grace. He wanted to be, to always be cool and restrained and smooth, but his body always betrayed him, making him have to repeat a word in an otherwise perfectly phrased sentence, or making him stumble when he had been proud of how expertly he'd just done his job. When he was defusing a bomb, or wiring a detonator, or any of a variety of near-death experiences required by the job, with the sweat rolling off his forehead, somehow his brain sent the message to the rest of his body: *don't screw up right now.* And his body obeyed. When his life depended on his performance, he was good. He was very good. But when it only *seemed* that his life depended on his performance, he felt like Charlie Chaplin doing one of those deliberately clumsy routines.

The Archie waddled through the open hatch into a shuttlecraft, and Richard suddenly realized just how big the ship was, at least on the outside. The shuttlecraft was almost a city block long, probably half that wide. It must have been sunk eighty percent of its height into the deck.

Richard followed the Archie into a narrow passageway that forced the Archie's body higher because it had to pull in all its elbows. The passageway turned right, went a couple of meters, and then angled downward into the very center of the shuttle-craft.

The amount of light from behind abruptly diminished, and Richard's ears popped as the pressure changed. The hatch had slid closed without a sound, and the craft was presumably pressurizing itself slightly over ambient pressure.

The downward slope of the passageway was easy for the Archie, difficult for Richard. He almost slid down the final meter of the passage as he tried to grip small overhead finger-holds and fit his toes into the small crevices on the sloping floor.

A smell of raw fish and moldy cheese grew stronger now, and Richard felt uneasy in the small space. For the first time, he wondered what Archies ate. The Archie had traveled all the way into the center of the shuttlecraft, and it sat on a bench similar to the one in the monorail car. Richard had expected an acceleration couch of some sort, but now that he thought about it, probably the shuttle possessed the same acceleration-canceling system Bobby Joe had talked about the main ship having.

With the Archie in place in the egg-shaped central space, there wasn't actually all that much room left over for a human companion. Richard squeezed into the compartment, fitting his body behind the Archie's, and he tried to find a posture that wouldn't cut off his circulation.

The rounded shell of the cabin was vaguely like an airliner cockpit except for having a narrower variation in the style of the controls. What seemed to be a thousand small circles of light formed longitude and latitude grid lines where they were visible from the Archie's eye-stalk. Just below each circle of light was a depression sized so that an Archie could push a finger into it. Circling the base of the pedestal supporting the Archie body were two rows of about eight knobs each.

The Archie busied itself at the controls, using at least four of its legs to push briefly on a control here or a control there. Sometimes the light just above the control changed hue, sometimes a blinking light changed to a steady light. Directly in front of the Archie, a silvery ball rose out of the floor, as though levitated by a magnetic field.

The Archie's eye-stalk swiveled toward Richard briefly, then swung back toward the front. If it was afraid, Richard couldn't tell. It poked yet another control, and an octagonal screen lit overhead. Centered in the screen was the Archie captain, and next to her was Abby.

The Archie chattered briefly and the captain responded. Abby said, "I can see you, Richard. Can you see us?"

"Yes. Can you hear me?"

Abby nodded. "Loud and clear."

The Archies chattered some more, and Abby said, "They're going to launch another three shuttlecraft. When they get close enough to the planet-shaper, the other three ships are going to fire on it and take evasive action. The pilot of your ship is going to plot a trajectory that lets you drift closer, like a stray asteroid or something, in hopes that it won't show up as a threat. They think the planet-shaper's hull is strong enough that it won't even bother to react to the three ships firing on it, but they don't know."

"Sounds fine to me." Richard kept his expression casual as he detected a metallic taste. Did this attempt really make any sense?

Moments later Abby asked, "Are you ready?"

Richard nodded. "Sure thing."

"Good luck then."

Bobby Joe suddenly stepped into view. His bald head reflected diffuse spots of light from the bridge. "Richard?" He hesitated. "Good luck to you."

Richard swallowed hard. "Thanks." Bobby Joe's opinion hadn't seemed important to him, but suddenly Richard felt appreciated, and the abrupt feeling made him flush.

The Archie captain chattered briefly.

The Archie pilot gripped the silvery ball with two hands.

Suddenly Richard was suspended in space. The entire top half of the shuttlecraft had disappeared, or more accurately, it had turned transparent. The screen above still showed Abby and the captain on the bridge, and the rows of lighted controls still showed, but it was as if the rest of the shuttlecraft had suddenly turned to glass. Richard sucked in his breath.

Below him, the depression in the deck was clearly visible. It resembled a large empty swimming pool, but with several dark scars apparently caused by a shuttlecraft arrival.

The Archie pilot gripped the silver ball in two hands and pulled it up fast. Richard felt no acceleration, but his stomach suddenly dropped. The huge Archie mother-ship fell away from the shuttle as though some enormous chain on the other side had yanked it away. Richard's perceptions were momentarily trashed, and it took him several seconds to decide what must have been true: the shuttle had just risen very high and very fast. The apparent lack of acceleration made acceptance difficult, but intellectually he knew the shuttle had in fact been the one to move.

The star field was almost complete now, above and below the shuttlecraft, and Richard felt as though he were suspended in space without a suit but able to breathe. Within no more than a second, the dark outline of the Archies' ship had dwindled to a dark pinpoint against the surprisingly close disk of Venus with its turbulent yellow clouds. Except for the lack of acceleration, the experience was something like ejecting from a jet fighter.

Richard and the Archie pilot sat in sunshine sent from a sun that looked even larger than normal but didn't seem very bright, no doubt thanks to some fancy filtering.

The Archie pilot punched a control, and grid lines formed outside the shuttlecraft, as though a giant globe with latitude and longitude lines was centered on the shuttlecraft. The pilot gripped the silvery ball and turned it. Stars whirled and the ship spun in space to a new orientation. When a vector through the nose of the ship came near a dotted-line vector that had been stationary with respect to the fixed stars, the vector line snapped into alignment, just like a drawing program snapping a stylus to designated grid lines.

Richard finally realized one more reason his perceptions had been tricked into thinking briefly that the large Archie ship, now a small dark octagon against the clouds of Venus, had been the one to move. The shuttlecraft was almost perfectly silent. When Richard listened closely, he could hear his own breathing and a faint rush of air, like ventilation air turbulence. Besides that, all he could hear was a *tick-tick-tick* sound that reminded him of a furnace heating up, the metal clicking occasionally as it expanded or contracted.

Three orange dots appeared to the sides of the shuttlecraft, and a red four-leaf clover appeared at the end of the vector pointing the direction the shuttlecraft was traveling. The three other shuttlecraft moved swiftly into a triangular formation, speeding away as they moved into their attack trajectory, well away from the flight path of the shuttlecraft Richard rode in.

Richard swallowed hard as the four-leaf clover expanded, occulting more and more stars as it grew closer. It was no longer the red symbol but instead he could see the actual shiny surface of the ship. The other three shuttlecraft appeared to be approaching the planet-shaper from something more than ninety degrees away from his own course. He wondered how close they'd get before they used their lasers, curious about why he'd seen no shots yet, but then he realized that he wouldn't ever see them, unless they reflected off the planet-shaper's surface toward the shuttlecraft he rode in. In the dirty air over Manhattan, the faint glow had been visible to some watchers; here in vacuum there would be no particles to reflect the light or to be vaporized by the energy surge.

The planet-shaper grew larger and larger until it eclipsed half of the starry sky, its curved mirror surface making it even more threatening than a solid color would have seemed. They were close enough to see the star field shift over the ship's surface as their aspect angle changed.

Richard glanced up at the screen over his head. Matt had joined Abby and the Archie captain. All three were silent. That was just as well; Richard didn't feel like talking right now.

They were close enough now to see the dark hole where the city had hit the ship. It was a dark cavity in a shiny tooth. They moved closer.

One of the shuttlecraft vanished in about a second, like a time-lapse photo of a mothball vaporizing. The planet-shaper was fighting back after all. Richard prayed the shuttlecraft had been destroyed because it had fired at the planet-shaper, rather than just because it was close.

The Archie captain chattered briefly.

"We've lost two of the shuttlecraft," Abby said quietly.

The dark patch loomed, bounded by distorted star fields. Richard forced himself not to wipe his forehead.

Larger. Larger. The dark patch occupied a third of the forward view.

"We've lost the third shuttle," Abby said.

They came closer and closer to the huge hole in the side of the hull. The hole must have been ten blocks wide.

The hole stretched to span all the way from top to bottom, and Richard was suddenly afraid they wouldn't be able to stop fast enough to avoid crashing into something in the interior.

"Are you all right?" Abby asked suddenly.

"Yeah. Why?" Richard looked down at the surface of the shuttlecraft and suddenly he knew why.

"The sensors here say your shuttle was hit."

"Apparently they're right. But we're still okay." Below him part of the clear ship had taken on the misty translucence of a bathroom window. The planet-shaper must have decided to fire on them anyway, but it had just been too late. Richard took a deep breath.

They were inside the hole now. Everything was dark except for some starlight filtering through the hole behind them. Abruptly the interior lit up.

Richard squinted against the sudden light. At first he was afraid some internal lights had come on within the planet-shaper, but he couldn't see any individual light sources. The light must have been coming from the shuttlecraft.

But no, that wasn't right either. He could clearly see shadows scattered around the distant interior walls. If the light came from where he was, it would fill the shadows visible from there. Finally he understood what must have happened. The Archie pilot had turned on image intensification. Whatever process that resulted in the shuttlecraft seeming transparent had been boosted, turning starlight and dim internal illumination into bright light.

Thank God the Archies' eyes responded to intensity somewhere near the same range as humans. Otherwise, he might be helplessly looking around in the dark. Or at the other end of the range, he might be immersed in a more terrifying kind of darkness: blindness.

The interior of the ship looked sculpted or grown, rather

than fabricated. Richard had entered the guts of a starship; he was in the intestines of some enormous beast.

He looked back toward the hole they had come through. The edges of the hole were not the curled-in metal of an artillery hit. Instead the hull of the ship just ended cleanly as though a bullet had torn through a stretched piece of flesh, taking the damaged tissue with it.

Bits and pieces of rock and sheets of building material and bodies from the destroyed city drifted around the periphery of the cavity. Apparently most of the destroyed mass had eventually drifted out of the hole as the planet-shaper braked during its approach to Venus. What remained were only the pieces trapped by ribs or walls in the interior.

Ahead was a large hole in the side of what reminded Richard of the interior of a heart, with several huge arteries leading off in several directions, curving enough that he couldn't see where they led. On that scale, the shuttlecraft was no larger than a blood cell. Apparently the impact of the city hitting the ship caused this opening also.

The Archie pilot aimed its eye-stalk toward Richard and chattered. Richard had no idea what it was saying, but moments later Abby said, "He's asking you which way you want to go."

"Can you see what I see?"

"Yes," Abby and Matt said simultaneously.

"You have any guess?"

Seconds later Matt said, "No. Take your pick."

Arbitrarily Richard pointed at the tube on top.

The pilot moved the silvery ball and the shuttlecraft moved expertly into the tube and began to move forward, staying in the center of the tube. Richard glanced up at the screen and was gratified to see it still showed a clear view. He had been afraid that the transmission would be interrupted by going deeper into the planet-shaper.

Richard opened his knapsack and dug through what he had left. Ninety percent of the contents was plastic explosive. He had brought two timed detonators, but at the moment he planned to use only one. He might change his mind, depending on what he found, but for now he readied what he had for one big charge. He set the timer for four minutes and left it on hold. It was only as he finished that he realized what had been nagging at his subconscious. He'd been concentrating too hard on the wrong problem. The shuttlecraft had no airlock, and he had no pressure suit.

Richard swallowed hard. "Slight problem here. I'm probably going to have to go EVA without a suit when the time comes. Can you find out how fast the pilot can get air back in the shuttle and how long an Archie can go without air?"

Abby and Matt exchanged nervous glances, And Abby spoke to the captain. It took her several tries, apparently because of some confusion over time units. Finally Abby said, "An Archie can apparently do without air for about five or ten minutes. That's the good news. The bad news is that the shuttlecraft is designed for the Archies, and therefore it takes over a minute to pressurize. They figured that was a comfortable safety margin."

"I think I'll be okay," Richard said, more calmly than he actually felt. "I've done some demolition jobs in shallow water, where we snorkeled instead of using scuba gear. I think I can hold my breath that long, and even if I miss by a few seconds I'll know that air is coming back. It's not like if the pressurization is too slow that I wind up sucking water. Plus, if I'm quick, I should be able to get the explosive planted before all the air is gone."

For several seconds after Richard finished talking, all he could think about was how much of a macho idiot he had been for volunteering. Why couldn't they have had something with more punch, like a nuclear warhead? He was so small in comparison to the planet-shaper, he felt as if he was trying to explode a planet with a flare gun. If only they could find something that looked like a control center.

Richard watched the walls of the tunnel as they moved deeper into the ship. The walls were ribbed like an old radiator hose. The Archie pilot had tried its laser on the wall in several spots. Each slash formed and lasted a couple of seconds before it began to smooth over and heal. Ten seconds after a burn, the tunnel looked as good as before the cut.

"Let's save the lasers for later," Richard said. Abby relayed the instruction, and the Archie removed a finger from a control. Richard noticed that each of the Archie's joints was ringed with a fine circle of silver fur.

A junction appeared ahead, and when they reached it, the Archie pilot halted the shuttle so it hovered in the center of the five-way intersection until Richard told it to go straight through. They could get lost forever in this maze if they took too many turns.

The tunnel began to shrink gradually. At first it had been maybe twenty times the diameter of the shuttlecraft, and soon it was down to about ten times the diameter. They came around a gentle curve and found the entire tunnel blocked with what looked like a gray membrane.

"Ask if we can cut through this," Richard said.

Seconds later a bright red spot formed on the wall in front of them. The wall around the spot darkened and Richard began to have hope that they actually could cut through the wall when suddenly the entire wall dilated open.

"Holy crap," Richard murmured.

Beyond where the wall had been was a huge spherical room, many times wider than the tunnel. Other tunnels led from the chamber to every direction, so many tunnels that their mouths, some closed, some open, took up half the area of the chamber wall. The shuttlecraft floated through the dilated doorway.

Suspended near the center of the volume was a gray and red mottled sphere smaller than the shuttlecraft. A dozen filaments connected it to anchor spots on the walls. As they came closer, Richard could see that it wasn't a sphere, but rather was made up of flat shapes, octagons interspersed with squares. The object pulsated slowly, as though it were a deformed heart.

"That's our target," Richard said. Abby talked to the captain, who chattered to the pilot in case Richard's pointing finger wasn't enough of a command. Richard looked behind the shuttlecraft as they moved farther into the huge chamber, watching to make sure he could identify which tunnel they had come through.

They moved closer. The heart contracted every few seconds and glistened in the amplified light, which, in the chamber, had taken on a noticeable purple tinge.

"Have him try the laser on it," said Richard.

Seconds later the pilot put his finger on the laser control again, and a molten spot formed on the surface of the sphere. After fifteen seconds the spot looked no different. They were close enough now that Richard could see crevices at several points on the surface.

"That thing must be carrying off the heat somehow," Richard said. "Or else it's just really tough. Everything in here must be industrial strength. Have him stop."

The laser switched off, and the molten spot returned to its former mottled appearance within a second.

"Have the pilot ready to cut the lines holding that thing in the center as soon as I'm finished and the hatch is closed again." Richard took his knapsack, edged around the Archie pilot, and started crawling up the passageway. "Can you still hear me?"

"Yes," called Abby.

"And now?" Richard called from just around the corner into the middle section of the corridor. He could no longer see the Archie pilot. Apparently the ship's hull hadn't actually turned transparent, but rather the center of the ship was the focus of an elaborate viewscreen.

"Yes."

Richard turned the final bend and found himself at the hatch. He found a couple of adequate handholds. "And now?" he yelled.

"Yes," came Abby's voice faintly.

"Have him position the shuttle so the hatch is near one of the crevices. When I give the signal, have him open the hatch. Tell him to close it again after twenty seconds."

"Will do."

Richard's forehead dripped sweat as he waited the half-minute for the pilot to position the ship.

"He's all set," Abby said.

Richard took several deep breaths, both to calm himself and to oxygenate his lungs. Dear God, please let me live through this. Finally he yelled, "Go!"

The hatch slid suddenly aside and air began to gust out. Directly ahead of him Richard could see the ugly mottled surface with a crevice right in the middle of the stretch he could see.

His ears popped and he tried to swallow fast enough to keep up. The scene began to turn red. The instant the air flow finally stabilized enough that he didn't feel in as much danger of being blown out of the ship, Richard reached into his knapsack and hit the combination on the detonator timer. He made sure he saw it flash once before he hoisted the knapsack by a strap, swung it back and forth twice to gauge the gravity, and hurled the whole thing into the crevice.

His vision lasted long enough to see the knapsack lodge itself in the crevice, and he shut his eyes. Already his lungs felt red hot and his head felt flushed. He pulled back into the corridor and made sure no part of his body would block the hatch as it closed.

Time played tricks on him. By the time the hatch slid closed, he was convinced that five minutes had gone by. He had been expelling the air from his lungs as slowly as possible despite the fact that the air seemed to want to force itself out through his mouth and nostrils.

His ears ached horribly, and he could hear nothing. Please, God, let the air be filling up the shuttle again.

His head rang. His eyes kept tightly closed, partly because of the pain, partly because he worried about damage to them in the low pressure.

Finally he could not wait any longer. His lungs were on fire. He opened his mouth and sucked in as much air as he could, which was nothing. It wasn't like breathing in water, but it was no less frightening. He heard no sound as his lungs expanded, and felt no resistance of air trying to squeeze through his throat. There was just nothing there.

The black before his eyes filled with even more sparkles.

A throbbing in Richard's ears was the first sign that he was in fact still alive. He realized he was breathing again.

His chest was on fire, his eyes stung, and his ears rang. He realized with shame that his shorts were wet.

He heard a hiss of air. He could hear!

He opened his eyes. The shuttle corridor was still tinged in red. He pulled himself along the floor to the point where the corridor dipped down into the control area where the pilot's eye-stalk pointed at him.

"I'm okay," he said shakily. Either his ears were still recovering, or his voice had popped up an octave.

Dimly from somewhere he heard two or three human voices exclaim, "All right!"

Richard started down the sloping corridor on his hands and knees. He was halfway down the corridor when he lost his grip, and he tumbled the rest of the way, banging into the pilot as he jolted to a stop. "Sorry about that." *You damn klutz,* he told himself.

Amazingly the four minutes hadn't elapsed. The pilot had the shuttlecraft hovering near one wall of the chamber. The laser must have been trained on one of the cords between the sphere and the chamber wall, because a spot glowed brightly near the center of one strand.

Richard looked at his watch. Just as he looked back up, one of the other tunnel covers dilated open and eight shuttlecraft drifted into the chamber. At first Richard thought they were Archie shuttlecraft, but he would have been told if eight more shuttles were inside.

One of them must have fired on his shuttlecraft, because abruptly another segment of the hull turned from transparent to frosted translucence.

"What the hell's going on? Those shuttles look like Archie shuttles," Richard said just as the explosive in the crevice detonated.

19

PLAN NINE

FROZEN IN PLACE, Matt watched the screen as Richard's words flooded the bridge, and the alarm in his voice spread through Matt's body. The approaching shuttlecraft did look like the ones the Archies themselves had employed. These were black and boxy, too, though they sported two bright circles on the front surface. The pair of spots suggested headlights, but Matt felt sure they were weapons. Apart from the bright circles, the shuttlecraft looked virtually identical to the Archies' vehicles. As Richard had said, what the hell *was* going on?

The adjacent screen showed a view of what had happened to the ruddy sphere in the center of the enormous chamber. The explosives scattered small fragments and reddish globs into space, filling half the chamber with clutter as though someone had exploded a bowl of red gelatin. Bits and pieces flew into the few tunnels that were open, while the rest of the spray hit the side of the chamber or closed tunnel mouths. Most of the material stuck where it landed, but some of it bounced back into space and drifted.

Half of the sphere was gone. One side of it was nothing more than a huge irregular crater. The half-sphere drifted back and forth as its tethers started to damp the motion. The tethers themselves must also have been the source of nutrients used to rebuild the sphere, because they had all become fatter than before. In spots where the contrast was high, Matt could see that the tethers were acting like engorged blood vessels, carrying fluid inward to the surface of the sphere. The damaged area of the sphere began to grow smoother.

At the same time, the eight newly arrived ships spread apart as if to attack from several positions.

On the screen, Richard shouted, "Get us out of here!" Abby instantly translated through the Archie captain, but Matt was sure the Archie pilot acted even before getting the translation of what Richard had said. Even as the shuttle began to move, the attacking craft opened fire. An instantaneous spurt of red light came from one of the craft, and in line with the flare of red, the hull lost some of its transparency. Spots started forming all over the side facing the enemy, blotches where the clear view suddenly turned to frosty translucence, as though dirty raindrops were falling on clean glass.

"No, not that one. *That* one!" Richard pointed at the tunnel next to the one the pilot was heading for.

Matt held his breath. The only sound on the bridge was coming from Richard's transmission.

More frosted splatters formed on the hull, coming faster and faster. The shuttlecraft didn't make it to either tunnel. When it was no more than a couple of seconds away from the relative safety of even the wrong tunnel, a huge cracking sound came over the speaker.

Only a slow-motion replay made the sickening events clear, but the hull of the shuttle split open. Even before the air had time to rush out, weapon beams crashed through to the inside, and a flame started playing on the interior of the shuttle, like a scientist's butane torch blasting through the open end of a short test tube. Mercifully, the transmission from that point onward lasted significantly less than a second, not even time enough for Richard to scream.

The screen displaying the last image of the interior of the shuttlecraft froze, and the screen showing a better view of the attacking ships froze at the same time.

Matt closed his eyes against the pain. He felt Abby sag against him, and he blindly put one arm around her. From somewhere in the room came sobbing sounds. Bobby Joe shouted, "Damn it!"

Matt forced his eyes open again. The screen they had been watching was black. One of the other screens showed the planet-shaper still in orbit over Venus, still throwing a series of huge sparks down into the atmosphere as though nothing of consequence was happening inside its breached hull.

To the blank screen, Matt said softly, "I'm sorry, Richard. You did everything you possibly could do."

Abby wiped tears away as Matt looked back at her. He gave her a few seconds to recover and then said, "Tell the captain we want to know why it is that the planet-shaper has what look like Archie shuttlecraft protecting its interior." As Matt spoke, he was aware that the captain's eye-stalk was trained on him.

Abby nodded and took a couple of breaths, then began to speak to the translation computer. After her question was complete, the bridge seemed quieter than it had ever been.

After a delay long enough that Matt thought the captain was refusing to reply, she chattered at the computer. Matt heard the response directly from the computer in Abby's voice. "Archies built the planet-shaper."

A flurry of conversation and amazed reactions erupted. Julie moved closer with her minivid.

Matt clenched his fist. "So this whole thing has been some goddamn charade? They're just pretending to try to stop it?"

David Suth stared at the huge Sony screen at the south end of Times Square as The Mayor Channel relayed video from the bridge. The crowd around him had shuddered with the destruction of the craft carrying Richard, and now David felt the outrage of betrayal. The crowd went wild, and the shouting masked the sounds piped down from the bridge for almost a minute. For another fifteen seconds, all David could hear was the sound of people telling each other to hush.

A young voice on the phone said, "Them spiders should use that same stuff that's in the dome. Make a big wall between the ship and the Earth. Or put a gigantic bubble around the Earth so they can't get at it. Or take some of that black stuff that's underground and make it so they can't see the Earth. Maybe they'll just leave."

Almost everyone on the bridge was in motion, either moving from one place to another or simply shifting from one foot to the other. Matt was so angry at the loss of Richard and at the revelation that the Archies had built the planet-shaper that he deliberately forced himself to wait a moment and get a grip on his temper before trying to find out what was going on.

Without being asked more questions, the captain began chattering again. Abby rephrased some of the sentences spat out by the translating computer and said, "The planet-shaper is a real threat. And she says the Archies have honestly been trying to defeat it." More chattering. As the Archie captain spoke, her eye-stalk drooped.

Abby said, "She says she'll give us more information, but that the planet-shaper was built by a . . . a subspecies or one of the Archie races—by Archies anyway. It was built a long time ago, and they now see it as a horrible mistake. They really are building a huge destroyer that should be capable of eliminating the planet-shaper, but it won't be finished in time to help any of the worlds the planet-shaper will visit soon. In the meantime, they've been trying to save parts of the populations. I think the reason they didn't tell us this before is that they are ashamed."

"God almighty!" Matt yelled to no one. He took a deep breath and to Abby he said, "Why can't they just stop the planet-shaper? Turn it off?"

Shortly Abby said, "It's completely automated. There aren't any Archies on board controlling it. They designed it to be autonomous and set it in motion. They figured there would be a chance that some other race might try to shut it off or subvert its goal, so they tried to make it indestructible. Apparently there are safeguards to keep it from destroying worlds occupied by Archies."

"Unbelievable. This is just unbelievable." Matt looked back at the screen showing the planet-shaper continuing to seed Venus's atmosphere. "Is there anything else important we should know?"

Moments later Abby said, "She says no. I really don't have any way to know how straight she's being with us, but my gut says she's telling us the truth."

"I just don't understand how a race that built something like the planet-shaper can now be so ineffectual, so unequipped to live with the consequences."

"We're not dealing with the inventors of the planet-shaper. What we're dealing with is accountants in space."

Matt raised his eyebrows.

"I mean, the captain is no more representative of their race than I am. The Archies on this ship *simply* aren't warriors. They were picked for their ability to cut cities loose and provide life support for them. A crew meant for fighting the planet-shaper would have had completely different selection criteria.

"This is still all too new, but if I'm understanding things right, the Archies are a much older race than we are. Maybe because of that age, they've been growing more and more specialized. For whatever reason, we're generalists compared to them, and the captain has realized that. In fact, I think that's the main reason they're willing to follow our orders; we're the only ones around who are adept at stepping outside the boundaries of their normal job descriptions."

Matt nodded, finally understanding.

"There's something I don't understand," said Rudy. "If Archies and humans can live in the same environment, why would the planet-shaper do anything to Earth?"

Matt nodded for Abby to go ahead and ask.

Abby finished asking the question and listening. "She says one of the planet-shaper's tasks is to eliminate all local life, whether on the ground, in the oceans, or in the air. It seeds the planet with vegetation that supports their own metabolism. Apparently the planet-shaper scorches the surface, then freezes it, then starts the seeding process. If necessary, the planet-shaper performs additional jobs. Venus is too hot, so the planet-shaper is going to leave a huge sun-screen in orbit."

"That must be what it's doing now," Bobby Joe said.

Matt looked at the screen Bobby Joe watched. A series of small explosions trailed the planet-shaper as the ship moved along its orbit. Behind the explosions, what looked like a dark cloud stretched into a wider and wider band, forming a very wide but thin ring around the equator, high above Venus's natural cloud cover.

"I wonder if that stuff is something like solid smoke material," said Bobby Joe.

"If it is, would it stay in a stable orbit?" asked Rudy.

"I don't know. Maybe it'll stay up until they don't need it anymore. Look, you can see a huge portion of the surface already—that patch in the upper right. If they're getting rid of the cloud clover and blocking some of the sunlight from reaching the planet in the first place, I'd bet Venus is going to cool down pretty fast—at least on the time scale we're talking about. I don't imagine anyone's going to arrive here to live in the next few years."

"Does that mean it's almost finished with Venus already?" asked Matt.

"Yes," was the answer from the captain.

"What about scarecrows?" asked Bobby Joe. "If the planet-shaper is programmed to avoid worlds populated by Archies, can we do something quick to Earth to trick the planet-shaper into thinking it's occupied by Archies?"

A moment later Abby reported the captain's response. She was utterly convinced nothing could be done. The criterion was unclear, but evidently a world had to be supporting millions of Archies for the planet-shaper to decide to pass it by. Apparently when the Archies started to settle a new world, they typically had an enormous number of colonists ready to go all at the same time.

"Look," Rudy said. He pointed at the screen showing the planet-shaper. Where there had been an ellipse around Venus, the display now showed a straight line toward Earth. The planet-shaper was moving off rapidly.

"Follow it," Matt said quickly to Abby. "Maintain this distance."

Abby relayed the instructions to the Archie captain, who followed them without argument this time.

"How long do we have before arrival at Earth?" Matt asked.

Abby's face was pale when she passed back the answer. "About three hours."

Matt took a deep breath. "Can the shuttlecraft keep up with us? Can they accelerate as rapidly as this ship?"

The answer was yes.

"I want all remaining shuttlecraft launched. Have them stay close to this ship, but ready to move."

This time the captain seemed uneasy about obeying. She didn't want to lose any more shuttles, she said.

Matt looked at the Archie captain as he spoke to Abby. "We've got to settle this for once and for all. We cannot waste time like this. Remind her this small party of humans did extensive damage to this ship. There are millions more of us watching every move that's made now. And if any request we make in the next few hours is denied, the penalty will be higher than whatever the request would have cost. The Archies started this, and they damn well better be ready to stop it."

Matt went on. "Tell her the Earth and the people on it are far more important than we are, and we will go to any length necessary to guarantee the Archies meet our demands. The Archies caused this situation, and they're damn well going to risk anything we ask them to risk to set things right."

When Matt finished and Abby began to talk to the captain, Bobby Joe said, "Maybe we *can* try convincing them with images. Manhattan is sure to have some stock footage of atomic bomb testing. We could be ready to display it here it in a couple of minutes to show them what we're capable of."

"Good suggestion. But what if she says, 'Great. Let's use it on the planet-shaper'?"

Bobby Joe said, "Never mind."

Abby spoke to her computer, which chattered as Matt kept staring at the captain. For a solid ten seconds after the computer became silent, the Archie stared back, as though trying to arrive at a painful decision.

Matt suddenly said to Abby, "Tell her this ship is useless for its intended mission now since we can't follow the planet-shaper until the drive is fixed. This is their only chance to do something genuinely useful since this ship left port. They owe us that much. And remind her that we're their only hope. We're the generalists, right? We're the ones best equipped to make the decisions right now."

Abby gave the captain the additional direction.

The captain's eye-stalk twitched as she looked at Matt. Suddenly she gave what Matt felt was a thumbs-up sign and he said to himself, *That had better not be the finger.* The captain chattered to her crew and to Abby.

"She got the message," Abby said.

After some more chattering, Abby added, "I'm pretty sure I'm understanding things right. This crew really is essentially a civil service team. They've been trained to save cities, not to wage war, and that's why they've resisted. As you pointed out, their mission cannot proceed for now, and since they're finally convinced that we're military experts, they're willing to follow orders."

Matt nodded, feeling he was anything but an expert in fighting a space battle. He was careful not to show his lack of confidence.

Within minutes the displays showed about a dozen shuttlecraft moving into space near the Archie's ship. The shuttlecraft paralleled the ship's course.

"Good," Matt said. "Now tell her that if nothing else we try works, our last resort will be to ram the planet-shaper."

Abby swung back to relay the message, did a double-take, and then turned again to the computer.

A minute later Abby said, "She says, 'You are right. This is our fault. We are prepared to die, but what about the cities?' "

"Tell her we'll have to decide that later."

When the exchange was complete, Rudy said softly, "Are you dead serious about that possibility?"

Matt shook his head. He spoke loud enough that he was sure his voice would carry to Julie's minivid and to the audience below. "One, I don't even know if that would be effective. Two, I'd have to have permission from the mayor. Three, mainly I wanted the Archie captain to know that we consider it an alternative. I have to assume that if there's any weapon or idea they've been holding back, they'll be honest about it now. And, frankly, I'm not sure how we would force them to do it. If they're all going to die, it's not like we have a lot of leverage."

Matt picked up the walkie-talkie and said, "I need to talk to the mayor."

Dorine answered the call instantly. "Mayor here."

"It's reality-check time," came Matt Sheehan's voice. "If I'm doing things you don't approve of, you need to speak up."

"I know how to manage a city, not fight a war. It may seem

like the same thing sometimes, but it's not. If I see anything that I can't live with, I'll get on the horn, but I'm not about to undermine your authority at this point. You've got my blessing."

"Thank you, mayor. About the possibility of ramming. As much as we want to save the Earth, I don't know that we could justify killing the only remnants of dozens of other civilizations. They're victims as much as we are. I wish we had time to contact more of the other cities. It could be one of them has a weapon that would do that job, but they've been unable to use it because it would destroy their own city. But we've got hours, not days or months."

Dorine swallowed hard. "Do what you have to if there's a way to save Earth. I trust your judgment."

"Thanks."

Matt put down the walkie-talkie and took a deep breath.

Rudy raised his eyebrows. "So, what next?"

"I don't know." Matt turned to Abby. "While we're thinking, tell the captain to take four of the shuttlecraft, move them to a safe distance from the planet-shaper, and turn their weapons into the hole we made earlier. Have them keep them on until we tell them to stop."

Abby nodded.

"All right," Matt said. "We've gotten a lot of suggestions from Manhattan. Some of them may not be feasible, some may be ineffective. We've got to pick something that seems to have the best chances."

Rudy looked at a list he'd been maintaining. "A lot of them fall into general categories. Using weapons against the planet-shaper. Trying to trick it into bypassing Earth. Using the bubble material as a barrier."

Bobby Joe looked at the screen. Matt followed his gaze and saw four of the shuttlecraft had moved close to one another at a distance from the planet-shaper.

"Abby, get them to show us a closeup of that hole if you can."

Moments later another screen showed just that. It was impossible to tell if any significant damage was being done. All they could see was a pulsating red glare reflecting from surfaces near where the lasers were striking.

Bobby Joe said, "The planet-shaper's weapons seem more effective than the shuttlecraft lasers. They're probably *intended* as weapons rather than cutting tools. I wonder if there's a way we can turn the planet-shaper's own weapons against itself."

"Right," Rudy said. "Huge mirrors." He said it with a sarcastic tone, but as soon as he fell silent, he and Bobby Joe looked at each other with widening eyes.

"Maybe it *is* possible," Rudy said. "The bubble material they use to form domes over cities. If the Archies can form some corner reflectors, maybe we could bounce back whatever they're projecting."

"Explain," said Matt.

"A corner reflector is three mirrors intersecting at right angles. Anything hitting one of the mirrors is bounced right back where it came from."

"Right," said Bobby Joe. "And even if we don't destroy the planet-shaper, we could sap its energy, and that might provide protection for our shuttlecraft to get closer."

"How do we get the silver surface?" asked Matt.

"We might not need it," Bobby Joe said. "It could be that whatever beam they're using would be reflected from the bubble material itself. Or it could be the Archies have some metal they can eject. Have one of the shuttlecraft use its laser to boil the stuff and then ram the bubble material against it. If we're lucky, it'll be like dropping liquid solder on glass—it'll form a thin flat coating. It won't be anything near an optical-grade mirror, but it might be enough to reflect a significant fraction of whatever hits it."

Matt said, "Go for it. Have Abby relay whatever instructions you think best. I'll be considering what to try next."

"Next?" said Bobby Joe.

"Yes, next. We can't wait around until we find out if this works. We don't have time. We have to get another plan moving, and another, and another. If we're incredibly lucky, one of them will work. If a miracle happens and two of them work, then maybe we're guilty of overkill. But I don't think that's very likely."

Bobby Joe and Rudy got busy feeding Abby directions for the Archie captain, and Matt took Rudy's list and started examining it.

Within a couple of minutes it was apparent that the Archies did have some nonessential equipment that they could sacrifice for the raw materials. The captain ordered some of the crew to eject it so the shuttlecraft could move it where they needed it. Fortunately, both the planet-shaper and the Archies' ship had finished the initial acceleration phase and were headed toward Earth at a constant velocity, so loose materials would fly side by side.

As soon as Bobby Joe was free, Matt said, "I guess when we have one tool, suddenly every job seems to call for the same tool. This bubble material—we could use a similar technique for making a huge mirror. The lasers on the shuttlecraft. How much heat do they generate compared to the same area of plain sunlight?"

"I don't know. I might be able to make an estimate. Why?"

"Because if we could make a curved mirror that focused the sunlight over a few square kilometers, or even a hundred square kilometers, would that be more effective than the lasers?"

"Even on Earth you can light a cigarette with a parabolic mirror that's probably no wider than your hand. Maybe it would be effective. Like I said, the reflectivity won't be as high as a good mirror, but we could more than make up for that in area. We'd want a parabolic mirror with a very long focal length so it could focus everything that hits it into a point, say, a hundred kilometers away from it. Let me give it a try. The Archies may not be trained as fighters, but the shuttle pilots manipulate the bubble material pretty well."

"Have at it."

A sparkling on one of the screens caught Matt's attention. One of the Archie shuttlecraft had already ejected some bubble material. As Matt watched, the ship slowly formed three planes, making the corner of a cube. Apparently the bubble material in its flimsy state stuck to itself. Finally one of the shuttlecraft flashed the bright light that triggered the bubble material to solidify, and the surfaces took on the appearance of rigid glass.

The shuttlecraft trained its laser on a shiny unidentifiable object. The laser seemed to be pulsing on and off. The object began to glow a dull red as it slowly collapsed into a molten sphere that spun at a leisurely rate.

A minute later, the Archie shuttle gripped the clear box corner and accelerated toward the molten metal. The globe of metal hit directly at the junction of the three planes and seemed to explode. When the view was clear again, at least half of each of the three bubble planes was no longer clear, but instead was shiny and metallic in appearance. They had deposited at least a crude mirror surface.

"Yes!" shouted Bobby Joe.

Another shuttle was in the process of constructing a second corner reflector. Farther away, two shuttles were apparently starting to stretch a huge sheet of bubble material into a gigantic flat plane. The process took ten or fifteen minutes that felt like hours. When the shuttles finished, one of them accelerated slowly against the center of the plane and the perimeter of the bubble plane fell slowly behind as though someone had thrown a rock at a sheet. The curvature didn't look right, though. It was more cone-shaped than parabolic.

The shuttle backed away from the bubble material, which was now drifting slowly off course. The ship maneuvered around and came at the bubble material from the opposite side and started accelerating against the center. The bubble material began a slow transformation from convex to concave, and at just the moment that it finally seemed to Matt to be in a parabolic shape, the other shuttle set off the flash that cured the bubble material and locked it into shape. The curved sheet was so large that it was taller than the planet-shaper.

Several shuttlecraft had been heating metal to coat the surface. A trio of shuttles got behind the curved surface and pushed it through space toward the molten globs. The reflective spots formed as molten metal collided with the bubble material were enormous, probably because the metal spread into a very thin layer. As the shuttles were finishing the parabolic mirror, Matt gave commands for two other shuttles.

The first shuttle to complete fabricating its corner reflector began accelerating toward the planet-shaper, keeping itself hidden behind the reflector. It got within what Matt figured was a range likely to cause the planet-shaper to decide an intruder was present. At the same time, the second shuttle with a corner reflector started toward the planet-shaper also.

Sparks flew from the closest reflector. Seconds later two things were obvious. One, the planet-shaper's weapon had vaporized some of the mirror finish on the corner reflector, and two, a significant amount of energy had been reflected back to the planet-shaper. A dull spot showed on the planet-shaper's surface where the hull was no longer shiny.

The planet-shaper fired at the second corner reflector. Again, material vaporized from the reflector surface, and another dull spot formed on the planet-shaper's hull.

"The large reflector is just about ready," Rudy said.

Matt looked at the screen Rudy was watching. A huge mirror a little like the ones in flashlights hung in space, blocking a quarter of the sky and reflecting a distorted star field. "Good. Have the captain warn the shuttles to stay out of the path, and get that thing pointed at the planet-shaper."

Abby passed on the instructions. Guided by shuttlecraft at its edges, the mirror began to turn slowly.

One of the corner reflectors took another hit, and then the other one, too.

"I've got an idea," Matt said. He turned to Abby. "Ask the captain if they know where the sensors are. How does that thing see?"

As Abby phrased the question, Matt turned to Rudy and Bobby Joe. "If we can put its eyes out, that might be almost as good as destroying it. What if we take molten metal like the Archies used to coat the mirrors and just throw that at the sensors?"

"Could work," Bobby Joe said. "Slick."

"It has sensors at the farthest point out on each of the cloverleaves," Abby reported seconds later.

Matt explained what he wanted them to try, and Abby gave the instructions.

"Oh, no," Rudy said.

Matt looked up at the screen. Seconds earlier it had shown an Archie shuttlecraft and a corner reflector. The bubble material was still there, but it was nearly clear again. The planet-shaper must have used enough energy to vaporize most of the reflecting layer, and the shuttlecraft hiding behind it. A bigger dull gray area covered a section of the planet-shaper hull, so it had paid a price for the damage.

"Have them build two more corner reflectors," said Matt, "And then just toss them at the planet-shaper without using a shuttle to guide them. If we're lucky, the planet-shaper will damage itself even more."

Minutes later on another screen, an Archie shuttlecraft launched a large mass of metal. As the mass moved closer to the planet-shaper, the shuttlecraft trained its laser on it, heating it to incandescence. Twice the shuttle shifted position, apparently to keep the mass on track for its target.

The second corner reflector flared. The shuttlecraft that had been behind it was now retreating, undamaged.

Abby said, "The captain says the large mirror is almost set to focus light on the planet-shaper."

Matt watched the screen as the enormous mirror began to slow to a halt. In an adjacent screen two more shuttles were building corner reflectors.

"All right!" Bobby Joe shouted.

The screen displaying the planet-shaper showed a brilliant spot of light reflecting from the surface. The spot drifted across the surface of the hull. At first, Matt thought the line trailing behind it was an artifact of bright light on his retinae, but seconds later he was sure he was wrong. The intense heat had actually damaged the surface of the ship. Thank God.

The thanks were premature, because suddenly the huge mirror began to turn again as the surface material began exploding off the front of the clear backing. Obviously the planet-shaper was firing on the mirror. Within seconds, its reflective layer had been decimated. And the planet-shaper kept firing at the bubble material as the blasts forced it farther and farther away.

About the same time, the molten glob of metal launched by a lone shuttlecraft came closer and closer until it hit the outer edge of one of the cloverleaves. It splattered against the surface, flattening out and clinging. A huge irregular blotch marred what had been a shiny mirror surface.

"Yes!" Bobby Joe shouted. "Even if we don't destroy this thing completely, it's going to know it was in one hell of a fight."

Matt glanced at the overhead screen. The Earth had grown to a large blue-white ball. They needed far more than just to give the planet-shaper a good fight.

The shuttlecraft near the huge reflector started to refinish the reflective layer, but it had been engaged in the task no more than a few seconds when the shuttlecraft suddenly began to disintegrate.

"Oh, God," Abby said softly.

Another molten glob of metal was speeding toward a different cloverleaf, but the planet-shaper was learning. It blasted the mass to loose atoms before it reached the surface of the ship. Matt was amazed and gratified to see that the mass still managed to pepper the planet-shaper's hull. Dispersed or not, it had still been traveling at an enormous velocity.

Abruptly, the loose corner reflectors and the remains of the parabolic mirror shot out ahead of the planet-shaper and the Archies' ship. Both ships had started to decelerate as they neared Earth.

The Earth grew rapidly on the wall screen as the Archies' ship followed the planet-shaper into a high Earth orbit. At the same time Matt felt more tired than ever before and he managed to continue functioning anyway.

From a safer range, another shuttlecraft continued to direct its weapon into the exposed portion of the planet-shaper's interior.

Without warning, the planet-shaper began to shoot a series of flares into the Earth's atmosphere, starting over the tan and white shape of Africa. Without stopping its deadly hail, the planet-shaper suddenly turned its weapons on the shuttlecraft.

"God damn," Bobby Joe said as he stared at the screen showing the shuttlecraft disintegrating. "It can't get much worse than—"

"Don't say it!" Matt snapped.

The hail of flares continued shooting down toward Africa as

suddenly the bridge shuddered. The Archie captain began chattering to her crew.

Matt swung back to Abby. "What's happening?"

Seconds later Abby said. "We've been hit. Apparently the planet-shaper has finally decided that this ship is where all these shuttlecraft are coming from. The captain is pulling back, out of range."

The bridge shuddered again.

Matt felt a metallic taste in his mouth as he waited for information.

A tinkling bell started to sound. The captain chattered some more. Her eye-stalk trembled.

Seconds later Abby turned to Matt and gave him the captain's assessment. "The second blast hit part of the propulsion system. They can repair it, but probably not in time to get far enough away. The ship is limited to very low power."

Bobby Joe said softly, "So now all that thing has to do is move in for the kill, and then finish destroying the Earth at its leisure."

20

ENCLOSURE

"Oh, God," said Abby. "Now we can't even try to ram them."

On the overhead screen, the planet-shaper was approaching. The chimes continued to ring on the bridge. The Archie captain looked busy, and several screens changed to what were probably status displays, columns of strange pictographs that each blinked at a different rate. Matt thought the captain's gaze was accusatory, but he was probably putting human terms on the Archie. The chimes suddenly stopped, but Matt knew disaster was still imminent.

Matt turned to Rudy. "Is there enough bubble material to enclose this ship? We're screwed unless we come up with something fast."

Rudy's eyes widened. "I don't know, but I've got an idea. I only see one chance, and it's a long shot, but I think it's our best option. Can I have Abby give orders?"

"Quiet, everyone!" Matt said loudly. He was completely out of ideas, and he trusted Rudy's judgment as much as his own. "Go for it," he said to Rudy.

Rudy said, "Abby, tell the captain to take every remaining shuttlecraft and have them start forming very large bubble sheets. Have them try to enclose the planet-shaper."

"But it can shoot through—" Bobby Joe started.

"Quiet!" Matt shouted. "Do it, Abby." Sweat felt cold along his spine, and he wished he knew more about what Rudy had in mind, but time was down to nothing. The only good thing at the moment was that to pursue the Archies' ship, the planet-shaper had temporarily stopped seeding Earth's atmosphere. As the planet-shaper turned, Matt realized it was doing so more slowly than he'd seen it turn before. Possibly the collective damage done by Richard and the other shuttlecraft was finally making it harder for the robot ship to function.

Abby gave the instructions to the captain. The captain aimed her eye-stalk at Matt for just a second, then began relaying orders. As soon as the first orders went out, Rudy had additional instructions to relay.

The planet-shaper grew slowly in the overhead screen as it all too obviously began its approach for a final killing blow. Obeying their orders despite the changed threat, six or seven remaining shuttlecraft began to surround the planet-shaper, each preparing to eject bubble material.

Matt and Rudy fixed their gaze on the screen. Rudy said softly, "If they're successful in getting a bubble around the planet-shaper, tell the captain to change course immediately to keep us as far from it as possible."

"Won't it follow us?"

"I don't think so."

"We won't have time to try anything else." Matt took his gaze from the screen and looked at Rudy.

Rudy met his gaze with the same calm he'd shown in a drawn-out battle in Brazil. "I know. I don't think there's anything else we *can* try that offers better odds."

The shuttlecraft had all matched course with the planet-shaper, but they maintained a cautious distance. Once they were all in position, they each accelerated toward the planet-shaper. As soon as they were all dropping toward the surface of the silvery vessel, they began to eject bubble segments.

The bubble segments grew and grew until they each individually seemed to dwarf the planet-shaper as it loomed in the viewscreen. A minute later the shuttlecraft and their bubble sections had cut their approach distance by half.

The Archies' ship shuddered again. Matt looked at Rudy and they exchanged worried glances as a new set of chimes started and then stopped.

Matt had begun to think the planet-shaper being so close to the Archies' ship had made it focus all of its attention on the ship, but at almost the same time each shuttlecraft let its bubble material loose, the planet-shaper fired on one of the shuttlecraft, disintegrating it. The huge ship fired on one of the other shuttles as it accelerated away, but the shuttlecraft had increased its range enough that it was only damaged rather then obliterated.

Another one of the shuttlecraft winked out of existence.

The bubble layers came closer at an agonizingly slow speed until they finally began to overlap and start to adhere to adjacent sections as though six clear sheets of flypaper were surrounding a large bug. The planet-shaper suddenly accelerated away from the center of the converging bubble sections, but it was too late. The process seemed to speed up then, as the sheets of bubble material sealed together. Seconds later, the flashbulb lights in four of the surviving shuttlecraft exploded light on the bubble surrounding the planet-shaper, and the bubble material transformed into a crystal-clear, hard shell like the one over Manhattan, but completely enclosing the planet-shaper.

"Now!" said Rudy.

Abby instantly gave the command to the captain. The aspect angle of the planet-shaper began to change slowly as the Archies' ship started to limp aside from the path it had been on. Matt found his fists were clenched, and he tried to relax them.

Within seconds it was obvious that the planet-shaper had not changed course to pursue them, but instead was continuing on its original course at the same speed.

"Yes!" cried Bobby Joe. He watched the screen a moment longer, as though to convince himself the planet-shaper really was not following them, and then he turned to Rudy. "How did you—oh," he said, a wide grin suddenly forming. "I understand."

"You want to tell the rest of us?" Matt said.

Rudy took his gaze off the screen and looked at Matt. "The planet-shaper's propulsion system is temporarily disabled. As long as it's inside the bubble, we're safe if we don't get too close. We know some of their weapons can act through the bubble material, even though they apparently can't destroy the bubble material itself. But I'm worried that there's still a chance it can break through that stuff, either now or later. We've bought some time, but we still need to destroy it."

"I know just the thing," said Bobby Joe. "If it can't use its interstellar propulsion system because it's too close to the sun, and it can't use the normal propulsion system because it's in the bubble, all we need to do is somehow stop it relative to the sun. Then we just sit back and watch it fall." Bobby Joe pointed to the display where the sun was visible. The cosmic disposal waited nearby if only they could use it.

Matt said, "All right. The planet-shaper can't speed up or slow down on its own. Can it turn inside the enclosure?"

Rudy nodded. "It should be able to."

"Okay. Abby, have the captain tell one of the shuttlecraft to fly in a slow circle just out of range of the planet-shaper's weapons. Have it deliberately keep edging into the area covered by the sensors we took out."

Abby passed on the instructions, and moments later Matt saw one of the shuttlecraft come slightly closer to the planet-shaper. Seconds later the planet-shaper slowly started to turn inside the enormous bubble as it tried to track the shuttle that kept flying toward its blind spot.

"All right," Matt said. "Tell her to have the shuttle keep moving until the dead sensor is directly in the middle of the shadow side of the bubble."

About the same time the shuttlecraft stopped orbiting the planet-shaper and began to hover, and the planet-shaper stopped rotating, Rudy said, "I think I see what you're doing. Great idea."

"And what is that?" Bobby Joe asked.

"Just a second. Okay, Abby, now have a couple of the shuttlecraft move off to a great distance and then approach the planet-shaper through its shadow."

"Oh," Bobby Joe said. "A push. I like it."

Within a few minutes two Archie shuttlecraft approached the dark side of the bubble around the planet-shaper.

"All right," Matt said. "Now have those two shuttlecraft position themselves next to the bubble and start accelerating as fast as they can. Have them retreat if the planet-shaper starts to turn. We can't risk waiting around for this thing to fall into the sun on its own good time; I want to give it a strong push."

Abby looked relieved as she passed on the instructions. The Archie captain was not objecting in the slightest.

The shuttlecraft pushed against the dark side of the planet-shaper's bubble until that side of the bubble rested against the surface of the planet-shaper. Further effects of the push weren't evident for several seconds, no doubt because of the planet-shaper's large mass, but the bubble-enclosed destroyer finally began moving slowly sunward.

The giant screen plotted a course vector from the planet-shaper. The course just missed the sun. The Archie captain chattered to her crew. One of the shuttlecraft repositioned itself against the bubble, and the vector slowly rotated until it intersected the center of the sun. The planet-shaper began to dwindle to a point and slowly became a speck against the sun.

Matt finally turned to Rudy and said, "Okay. Now why?"

"Why no thrust? Plain old Newtonian physics. I don't know what propulsion method the planet-shaper uses, but unless it operates on principles that are unknown to us, it relies on equal and opposite reactions. And recent events seem to confirm that."

Julie moved closer with her minivid to capture Rudy's explanation, and Matt saw her relieved smile.

"When you fire a pistol, you feel the kick. When you fire a rocket, the rocket moves one way because the exhaust gas is being pushed out the opposite direction. You're trading off high velocity for something small, like the bullet, for low velocity of something more massive, like the gun and your arm."

"That still doesn't answer my question," Matt said, but he already had an intuitive feel for what Rudy was explaining.

"I'm getting there. The equal-but-opposite-reaction holds true for an open system. If you stand on a frictionless flatcar and fire a bullet down the tracks, you and the flatcar will start moving the opposite direction. But if you have a closed system, things change. Suppose you're in a boxcar and you fire a bullet at a target mounted on the wall. The instant you fire the bullet, the car starts to move backward, but as soon as the bullet embeds itself in the target, that equal-but-opposite energy cancels out the reverse momentum, and the car stops."

"It's like trying to run on ice," said Bobby Joe. "If you can't push the ground out behind you, you can't go forward."

"Exactly," said Rudy. "As the planet-shaper tries to accelerate, the body of the planet-shaper pushes against one side of the bubble, and the thrust force or reaction mass presses equally on the other side of the bubble. The planet-shaper now has no more propulsion than a rock."

"You're a genius," Matt said. He was finally letting himself hope that they had really defeated the other ship.

"Nope. I just got to thinking about some of the ideas that people sent up from Manhattan. We never would have succeeded without the people down there suggesting protecting the Earth with a bubble. I just twisted the idea a little."

The group watched in silence as the planet-shaper moved faster and faster toward the sun. When the shuttlecraft had pushed it past the orbit of Venus, moving faster by the second, the shuttle began to slow down. The bubble-enclosed planet-shaper sped faster and faster by itself, slipping steadily downward into the sun's gravity well. One of the large wall screens filled with a heavily magnified image of the planet-shaper inside its bubble, becoming smaller and smaller against the huge mottled disk of the sun.

Next to Matt, Abby said softly, "Please, God. Don't let it get loose. Don't."

Bobby Joe and Rudy bet each other on the range at which the destruction would be visible, both feeling that no material built by humans or Archies could last long enough to disappear inside the sun before vaporizing.

"As far as I know," Matt said, his voice shaking slightly, "Richard will be the first person buried in the sun. Maybe we should have a moment of silence to reflect on his efforts and for those of the Archie pilots who died today."

Abby told the Archie captain what they were doing. The Archies may well have had no similar custom, but they, too, were silent until the humans began speaking again.

"Look!" Bobby Joe said to Rudy.

The bubble surrounding the planet-shaper was glowing brighter and brighter. Just seconds later the bubble vaporized and the planet-shaper exploded like a firecracker tossed into a blast furnace. The largest pieces exploded in a short series of additional explosions as the incredible heat churned metal into mist.

A couple of the Archies leaped high in the air and clasped all eight pairs of hands together before falling slowly back to the floor. Bobby Joe and Rudy screamed and yelled, but Matt paid little attention. The instant after the planet-shaper exploded, he looked at Abby, who looked at him at exactly the same time.

Matt moved closer to Abby. His knees felt weak. He reached out toward her and she moved closer.

"Thank God it's over," she said.

As the Archies chattered loudly and Bobby Joe screamed, Matt and Abby wrapped their arms around each other and hugged tightly. Abby was trembling. A moment later Matt pulled back far enough to see her eyes and said, "Maybe it's just beginning." He kissed her on the lips, and she responded with the same enthusiasm that he felt.

A long moment later, Abby suddenly pulled back, frowned, and glanced at Julie, who, despite having Rudy's arm around her, still held her minivid aimed at the center of the bridge.

Abby brushed a lock of hair away from her eye. She started to talk but had to clear her throat and try again. "Aren't you, ah, aren't you worried that your wife might see this when we get back?" She wiped a tear from the same eye.

Matt frowned for a second until he understood. He smiled. "I don't give a damn what she thinks."

"But I thought—"

"Two days before I reached New York, she said we were through. At the time, it seemed like bad news." Matt grinned even more broadly.

Abby choked. Matt couldn't tell if she was laughing or crying, but the way she kissed him, he decided it didn't matter.

Matt held her tightly for he didn't know how long until finally Julie and Rudy approached.

"Can we interrupt? The mayor's on the line." Julie grinned as she handed Matt a walkie-talkie.

"Yes, ma'am," Matt said into the mouthpiece. He tried as hard as he could to get rid of the stupid grin he felt on his own lips, but he couldn't.

Dorine Underwood's voice was ragged, from either emotion or transmission distortion. "Thank you, Matt. I'll have a lot more to say later, but you did good. You did very, very good."

The line was quiet for a moment. "We're all very grateful. You should see the streets down here. I haven't *ever* seen anything like this."

"Thank *you,* Mayor. We're amazed, too. When you talk to people, let them know that it was their ideas that made it possible. We were so scared up here, we couldn't have done one percent of this on our own."

"Bull. But that's a generous thing to say. Lord, this is a proud day."

Abby touched Matt's arm again, and he said good-bye to the mayor. The bridge finally started to calm down as the Archie captain pointed her eye-stalk at Matt. She chattered into the translating computer. Two of her legs twitched.

Seconds later the translating computer said, "You possess our thanks. We are very-very-very happy to stop. We are ready to help. We possess no experience in placing cities where they came from, but we are ready. What first should we do?"

Abby put her arm around Matt's waist and squeezed.

As Matt looked at the captain, Bobby Joe raised his hand. Wearing his most serious expression, Bobby Joe said, "Just a suggestion, but I think it would be interesting to buzz Brooklyn."